RING ROAD

There's no place like home

IAN SANSOM

D0167183

HARPER PERENNIAL

Harper Perennial
An imprint of HarperCollins*Publishers*
77–85 Fulham Palace Road
Hammersmith
London W6 8JB

www.harpercollins.co.uk/harperperennial

This edition published by Harper Perennial 2005
1

First published by Fourth Estate 2004

ISBN 0 00 715654 5

Set in Sabon

Printed and bound in Great Britain by
Clays Ltd, St Ives plc

Ian Sansom lives in Northern Ireland. He is the author of *The Truth About Babies.*

From the reviews of *Ring Road*:

'It reminded me most of Jerome K. Jerome . . . Mellow, intelligent and very funny, a perfect antidote for melancholy'
Michael Moorcock, *Guardian*

'Calls to mind two other outstanding novels; *Tristram Shandy* . . . and Joseph Heller's *Catch-22* . . . One of those rare books that, once picked up, proves very difficult to put down'
Irish Independent

'In all his rambling, digressive warmth, Sansom insists throughout that, contrary to fashionable opinion, human life is as eccentric and various in the small and overlooked corners as it is in the big city'
Daily Telegraph

'Wonderfully comic'
Daily Mail

'Quirky, perky . . . Here is no ordinary talent'
Spectator

'Daring . . . Funny . . . Fearless'
Times Literary Supplement

'A dissection of small-town life . . . recognisable to any reader who has ever lived in one, in England, Scotland, Wales or Northern Ireland'
Independent

'Wonderfully vivid, easy, natural, funny, and moving'
Oliver Sacks

'Delightful. I have read it with much pleasure'
Joyce Carol Oates

'What a delight! I had no intention of stopping everything to read it – but then I did . . . I have never been to Northern Ireland but now I feel at home there'   Charles Simic

'Cross Jonathan Franzen with Henry Fielding, and what you have is a twenty-first-century lament for times past dressed in eighteenth-century clothing, complete with chapter summaries, footnotes, and an index. Read this book with someone close at hand because you'll want to keep quoting the funny bits'
Library Journal

'Rich and inventive and inclines you toward generosity . . . A humane, big-hearted and sometimes devastatingly funny book, not to be underestimated'   Geoff Nicholson, *LA Weekly*

'A work of tender and bonhomous refraction'
Claire Messud, *Newsday*

'Fluent, flawless, richly observed . . . reminiscent of Roddy Doyle at his very best'   *Jockey Slut*

'A poetic elegy for a community'   *Irish Times*

'Sharply drawn . . . gloriously funny' (BMI *Voyager* magazine)

'Fabulous . . . It made me cry on the Belfast to Bangor train'
County Down Spectator

For my family

Contents

Preface

*Containing the customary avowals, apologies,
concealments of artistry, confidences, explanations and
precepts, and a note on the tipping of winks*

I worked on a farm once, when I was first married, in County
Antrim, and one of the men I worked with had been in London
doing the roads, during the early Seventies, at the beginning
of the Troubles, and he claimed that things were so bad in
those days that he would post ham in an envelope back home
to his family in Belfast. I was never sure if he was having me
on or not – it's always difficult to tune in to another nation's
sense of humour, and I was an Englishman abroad – but I
always thought it was a nice idea, and I like to think of this
book as similar in some way, as the equivalent of some ham
in an envelope, posted in reverse, from me here to you elsewhere, wherever you are. It's probably like ham in other ways
too, some people would say.

When I published my first book, *The Truth about Babies*
(Granta, 2002), my wife said she'd only read the next one if
I managed to make no mention of vomit, diarrhoea, urine,
sperm and other bodily fluids, and I've done my best, although
she may wish to skip pp.5–6, p.103, p.207, and p.306. The
index is designed for those with similar aversions or incli-
nations.

When I sent my mum a copy of the baby book she said, 'That's nice, dear,' which is pretty much what she's said to me since I first brought drawings home from school, and which still seems to me about the right response to anyone claiming to be an artist. These days, reticence is easily underrated. But then so is enthusiasm. When we were growing up my mum and dad provided for us children, they cooked good food for us to eat, they made sure we brushed our teeth and were polite, and didn't watch too much television, they taught us how to make our own beds, helped us with our homework and pointed out interesting things when we were on long car journeys. Perhaps this last explains the footnotes.

The rest of the mechanics of the book are obvious, I hope, and require no further admissions or explanation. (Apart, perhaps, from the brief chapter summaries and epigraphs, which seem to me a mere practical courtesy but which I'm aware are currently out of fashion, and so may seem avowed and unusual rather than commonsensical or natural, like wearing spats, or clogs, or a smock. But fashions come and go – maybe if you keep the book in a cupboard in a few years' time it'll all be back in again.)

Writers are, of course, wilful and selfish individuals who only get away with writing because other people allow them the privilege, but I know from long experience that listening to writers saying their thank yous is a bit like listening to people pray or talking about sex – it's not necessarily unpleasant and everyone does it sometimes, but you do wonder if maybe they could learn to do it in their own heads and in the privacy of their own homes. So I have left all my acknowledgements until the end. They are an apology as much as an explanation.

Anyway, I do hope you enjoy the book – it's meant for you to enjoy. It would be presumptuous of me to say what it's all about, or even to pretend that I know, although maybe you'll understand if I say that as a child on summer evenings, on Sundays, our parents would often have relatives over for tea – this was before barbecues had arrived and when family lived close by – and my aunts and uncles would come and we would sit around the dining table, which now serves me as a desk, and we would eat sandwiches and salads, and we would talk and play games, and I would fight with my cousins, and I can remember that I was amazed that these people were supposed to be my relatives, people with whom I seemed to have nothing whatsoever in common. It was a long and painful lesson, undiminished even by crab paste and trifle, and I thought it would be good to write a book that somehow reflected those Sunday teatimes, and which would remind me of the many different ways in which people live their lives, which is what makes our lives possible.

It would be self-serving of me to say anything else, except perhaps that the town is not meant to be a replica of any particular place, although I believe it does exist, and that I've never met any of the people, although there are equivalents, and that each chapter can be read on its own as well as in relation to all the others, although I hope, of course, that you'll read them all. There are no themes that I'm aware of and any obscurities are unintentional.

It seems necessary, finally, to apologise to the busy reader for this, a preface, which suggests either an uncertainty or an unnecessary formality on the part of the author, or perhaps both. Writers are traditionally opposed to explanation, since it diminishes the effect of the masterly voice and style, but I have always found it a hardship not to be helpful, which is a failing, I know, but it's still better, I think, even now, with the effects of excess everywhere apparent, to be told too much rather than too little. Arrogance, bullying, puffery, rapacity, self-awe and the tipping of winks can get you a long way in life, and it seems to get a lot of authors further than most, but in the end I believe it's better simply to be honest and to try to be explicit. And if you can't be, you should at least try and pretend.

Thank you, again.

Bangor – Belfast – Donaghadee, 2003

1

The Seventh Son

In which there is scenery and Davey Quinn returns to his home town, with some considerable determination, and is shocked at what he finds

'That's some weather we've been having.' That's what people say where I come from, when they don't know what else to say, which is most of the time.

Once we get going we're OK, but it can take us a while to warm up to a conversation – about five years is the average. In fact, in most instances conversation never quite catches fire, but that doesn't stop us laying down the kindling, stating our good intentions, preparing for something that in all likelihood may never happen. We may never get round to the big blaze, we may never exchange a confidence or share a secret or speak out of turn, not even when fuelled by drink, which tends to leave us speechless and starry-eyed, stupefied rather than garrulous and overflowing, but still every day we will happily talk about the weather, and about our children, and about births and deaths and marriages, and thus recently, of course, about the return of big Davey Quinn, after nearly twenty years away.

Davey is famous in our town because he is the seventh son of a seventh son, which is a rare distinction anywhere but nothing short of a miracle here, where the population has been growing for as long as anyone can remember but where the family size is getting smaller – these days a seventh son seems not so much a hopeless indulgence as a sheer impossibility, or an embarrassment, even among the most devout of the dwindling and ageing congregation at the Church of the Cross and the Passion, where Davey's parents still attend regularly and still give thanks for the fact of his wonderful birth, long after the event.

Davey, needless to say, does not share his parents' enthusiasm and never has done. His is a distinction that he did not earn, and did not ask for, and it has proved to be a heavy burden for which he was quite unprepared. It would probably be fair to say that Davey Quinn has found his position in life more difficult to bear than most: his fame has taken its toll. The famous photographs that appeared in the local paper, the *Impartial Recorder*, can still be found framed in pubs and bars around town, places that like to fill their walls with the faces of local celebrities, as a warning and a witness, perhaps, to the meaninglessness and transitoriness of human life, for who now remembers our champion high-diver, Don Kennedy, who competed at the 1936 Munich Olympics, and who walked around town on his hands every morning and did marathon push-up demonstrations in the old market place (which is now the multi-storey)? Or even Barbara McAlesee, the *Impartial Recorder*'s 'Woman of the Week' as recently as 1979, who knitted scarves and hats from the fur of dead pets, and who appeared on the once popular Sunday night television programme *That's Life*, and who exists now only in a faded newspaper cutting behind the counter at Scarpetti's, alongside an example of her handiwork, a muffler, framed, made from the fur of the late Mrs Scarpetti's terrier, Massimo? Or the McLaughlin brothers, the tap-dancing twins who danced their way out of town and into Broadway success in the chorus of the musical *Hold on to Your Hats* in 1943, which starred Al Jolson and Martha Raye singing 'She Came, She Saw, She Cancanned'?

The most popular and much reproduced photograph of

Davey shows him with his eyes sealed shut, wrapped tight in a blanket and stranded in the arms of his suited and black-spectacled father, with his six brothers in duffel coats and parkas crowding around in front, looking utterly fed-up, standing outside the old cottage hospital – formerly the soap-works – on Union Street, which is where all the Quinn brothers were born, two generations of them, and which is long since demolished, which has made way for an extension to what used to be the Technical College and is now the Institute of Higher and Further Education, and which may some day become a university, if the Principal, Hugh Scullion, has his way, which he usually does.*

*Hugh Scullion, it should be explained, for those from out of town, is a man with a mission and a man with a mission statement (see the *Impartial Recorder*, 4 December 1999, 'Principal's Millennium Message'). Hugh has many, many chins and he wears novelty socks. He has a B.Ed. and an M.A., and twenty years solid in F.E. behind him, but most importantly he has energy and he has opinions, and he has made our Institute what it is today, a county-wide centre of excellence, a 'provider of a full portfolio of Higher and Further Education programmes' according to its prospectus, and where once the Quinns were pushed and squeezed and forced out into the world it is now possible to take a night class in Computing or in Accounting or in various Beauty Therapies, taught by accredited professionals, and with concessionary fees available. Early booking advised. Enrolment throughout the year.

Some of the Institute's courses are, of course, more popular than others: Conversational Italian, for example (Thursdays, 7.30–9, in the Union building), taught by the town's remaining Italian, Francesca, daughter of the Scarpettis, who themselves returned to Italy long ago, while Francesca remained and married a local man, Tommy Kahan, a local police officer and the proud possessor of what is almost certainly the town's only degree in sociology. Francesca herself is now of a certain age but of undiminished charms and her class is always oversubscribed. Philosophy for Beginners, on the other hand (Wednesdays, 7.30–9, in the demountable behind the main Union building), taught by Barry McClean, the local United Reformed Church minister, is consistently cancelled, due to lack of interest: he's under pressure to change the course title in the Institute brochure to something like 'Money, Sex and Power', which should draw in the crowds, and then he could teach them the *Nicomachean Ethics*, Kant's *Critique of Practical Reason* and Nietzsche's *Beyond Good and Evil* just the same. Class numbers would probably fall off in the first couple of weeks, but all fees are paid

From this great seat of learning, then, what was once that little cottage hospital, Davey Quinn made not only our local news, but the national news, and the international – within a week of his birth he had straddled the globe as evidence of God's amusement and of the wonder of fornication. The midwife's slap – Miss Carroll's, as it happens, a lovely, jolly woman, who committed suicide a few years ago, the day after her retirement, a terrible tragedy and a loss which was felt by the whole town, many of whom she had brought to life with her own bare hands, with her renowned firm slap – and Davey's cold cry seemed to carry from earth to heaven, and far across land and sea, as far, they say, as America, where his tiny features could be seen on news-stands from state to state and on the televisions of the nation.

These days parents might grow rich on the proceeds of such an extraordinary birth, but back then we were all innocent and little Davey was not regarded as a commodity – he was, rather, and to all of us, a gift. A commodity can at least be bought and sold – it is a free exchange. But a gift implies obligations: it is therefore difficult to refuse or to return. Poor Davey, the runt of the litter, a little miracle, an excitement in all four corners of the globe, was the fulfilment of a life's ambition for his father, Davey Senior, as he became known, and he was therefore, naturally, a huge disappointment to him and hence to himself. Babies, if only they knew the dismal realms they were about to enter, would probably

---

up front, so by the time the students realised it'd be too late. This raises an ethical dilemma for Barry, but Hugh Scullion has pointed out that the only ethical dilemma he's facing at the moment is whether or not to do away with the teaching of philosophy altogether and to replace it with more courses in subjects that people actually want to study, such as Leisure and Hospitality Management, and Music Technology. Barry is currently seeking advice and consolation in the pre-Socratics. His wife is encouraging him to take more of an interest in gardening. Fortunately, the Institute runs courses and Barry is entitled to a discount.

never heed the call and never leave those remote gold and silver coasts from whence they come and have their lodgings. They would pause, consider the darkness, and sit right back down again on their fat little hunkers and never cross the waters into memory and oblivion. Surely no being rushes to embrace its own apotheosis? Unless, of course, that being be man.

Some years ago Davey left to travel the world and to try to escape his unique privilege and responsibilities, to try to escape photographs of himself in pubs and bars, to find riches and even, perhaps, he told himself then, believing such to be possible, to find himself. He got as far as London, where no one believed him – they thought he was joking – if he told them he was the seventh son of a seventh son, even if they stayed around long enough to hear him tell, which was not often and certainly never when he or they were sober or during the hours of daylight, and so in the end it ceased to matter. The wonderful and the terrible, his colossal, inescapable self, became first hilarious and then irrelevant, and finally unmentionable. He found refuge in work and in friendships, and in all the usual and time-honoured traditions. He drank the cup to the lees and there was a vast blur, and in the crowd he became successfully, magnificently anonymous. Among the millions of other talebearers, he lost himself and disappeared.

I don't know the exact circumstances which brought him to the point of return – there are rumours, of course – but he's back and it's good to have him back, and what people are saying is this.

He woke up, they say, and urinated bright red, which was a shock, I guess. Urine is usually yellow, wherever you're from and wherever you're living; it is one of life's few constants, sometimes perhaps a little darker, sometimes perhaps a little lighter, but always yellow, even for the likes of little Annie Wallace and her family, and the Buckles, and the Hawkinses, and the Delargys, our town's Jehovah's Witnesses, who have long since forsaken the wicked pigmenting tints of tea and coffee and alcohol, and birthdays, yet whose holy and clean-living wee is still distinctly yellow. Davey Quinn's urine that morning was a red-wine kind of a red, a welcome colour in a fine-cut crystal glass over a nice evening meal in a favourite restaurant, but never good on porcelain first thing in the morning, and so it was that Davey decided that it was time to come home. He'd been away long enough. His kidney was ruptured. They'd read him his last rites in the hospital, apparently, but he was out and about and fighting fit six weeks later – Davey is nothing if not a fighter – and the very next day he booked his ticket home.

He made it back via our so-called International Airport, which, it has to be said, is not noticeably International – there are tray bakes on sale in the gift shop, for example, and more copies of the *Impartial Recorder* than there are business books in the newsagent – but it has a reciprocal arrangement with a similar airport in the south of France and there's a flight once a week, to and from, which grants them both their titles.

So Davey made it back safely and in some style, but alas his luggage did not make it. It's always touch and go flying in here, whether you'll arrive with what you left with. Most of us in our time have lost something in transit, even if it's only our nerves or our resolve, usually because of the final descent, which requires a steep bank round and a sudden drop of altitude, when suddenly you see home and your stomach is in your mouth and you realise exactly how tiny it is, how small, your town, and your street, and your little house in your little street, how insignificant in the great scheme of things: it can be a sobering experience for someone just returning from business, or a weekend shopping trip or visiting relatives in a city, full of themselves and the complimentary drinks and the bag of nuts. Cities exist in and of themselves, and require no explanation, they just are. In a city you can kick back and relax, and you need only concern yourself with questions of who you are and what you are, and how you're going to be more, and bigger, and better: if you'd ever attended the Philosophy for Beginners evening classes with Barry McClean at the Institute you would probably have called these empirical questions of essence and existence.* A city, in other words, makes you a utilitarian. But when you look at our town you just straight away think to yourself: why? A small town can make you metaphysical.†

Marie Kincaid, who lives in town and who commutes up to the airport, sees people facing up to this question every day, as they step off planes on to the tarmac and into the drizzle, and wonder exactly how they got here and whether there might possibly be a chance to go back. Marie is a Baggage Reclaim Supervisor: she calls the loading bay her Bermuda Triangle and her life is spent attempting to discover its many mysteries. Despite closed-circuit television and X-rays and searches, there's still a lot of theft and loss of baggage: it's almost as if the luggage knows something that the passengers don't, and when they pass through on the conveyor belt at the point of departure they think, well, actually, I quite like it here, thank you very much, and I think I'll stay. There is luggage belonging to people from our town in all the major cities of the world, living under an assumed name.

Davey had set off with two suitcases, which he'd somehow acquired over the years, graduating first from a grip to a rucksack. They were suitcases which Davey had never in fact used except to store his CDs and cassettes, which he'd sold before returning. He'd found it hard to part with some of them, not so much because he wanted to be able to listen to the music, but because he didn't want to forget what it was once like wanting to listen to music, but then he thought, well, I have

* Philosophy for Beginners, Week 1, 'Ethics'.
† Philosophy for Beginners, Week 2, 'Metaphysics'.

a working radio, what more do I need?* What he needed was the money, so he sold his memories, and he reclaimed the suitcases from under his bed and packed.

In the airport, when everyone else had claimed their luggage and the carousel had shut down and his cases hadn't arrived, Davey went to see Marie at the Baggage Reclaim desk and Marie smiled her widest, most uncompromising and half-humorous smile and said, 'Nothing we can do about it, I'm afraid.'

Marie has had the opportunity to practise this particular smile over a number of years now, and it hardly ever failed to work its magic, even on non-native speakers of English. It was a philosophical smile, a smile that suggested that although the loss of luggage obviously caused her pain, she understood from a wider and longer perspective that it was a small matter and that you, the unfortunate but undoubtedly reasonable passenger, should regard it as a small matter also, for thus and this way, the smile implied, lay the path to enlightenment. Davey interpreted this complex smile correctly and filled in a pink form without protest under Marie's benign gaze. The luggage, said Marie, might be over on the next flight. Or it might not. And then she checked Davey's name and signature on the form, which was when it happened. 'I know you,' she said.

---

* He certainly did not need Prince's *Lovesexy*, he realised, or Deacon Blue's *Raintown*, or the Smiths' *World Won't Listen*, or Simple Minds' *Once Upon a Time*, or Marillion, or the Fatima Mansions, or Lloyd Cole and the Commotions, or Blue Oyster Cult, or the Cult, or John Cougar Mellencamp's *The Lonesome Jubilee*, or Edie Brickell and the New Bohemians' *Shooting Rubber Bands at the Stars*, CDs he could not possibly imagine or remember himself ever having wanted or set out to buy, nor any of the dozens of home-made compilation tapes marked simply 'Various', or 'Happy Daze', or 'Paul and Keith's Rave Spesh', on grubby BASF Chrome Extra II (90), and SONY HF and BHF (90), and red and white TDK D90, and Memorex dBS+, and AGFA F-DXI-90 and featuring almost exclusively the music of James, the Stone Roses, the Wonder Stuff, REM, and the Housemartins, and also, invariably, Primal Scream's 'Loaded', The Farm's 'Groovy Train' and Carter the Unstoppable Sex Machine's 'Sheriff Fatman'.

'You do?'

'Of course. I know you.'

'Right,' said Davey.

'David Quinn?' She wagged a finger at him.

'Yes,' said Davey.

She'd caught him: she had him bang to rights. 'The son of David Quinn?'

'Yes,' he agreed mournfully. He knew what was coming.

'The seventh son of the seventh son?'

What could he say? They were words that he hadn't heard for twenty years and he could live without hearing for another twenty more. But he couldn't deny it, although he'd hoped that perhaps he could have got away with it. He'd thought that if he stayed away long enough he might have become unrecognisable to the past, but it was not to be so; the past has a very long memory.

For most of us, for those of us who return home out of necessity, or in mere shame or pity, rather than in triumph and trailing clouds of glory or with our reputations preceding us, the journey home is always a disappointment. For most of us there's never going to be ticker tape and no free pint, no surprise pick-up at the station or the airport, and the best we can hope for is a mild handshake from our father and a teary hug from mum. Which is never enough.

But Davey had wanted nothing more. He'd have been happy to creep back unannounced and unnoticed – a quick pat on the back, then pick up the car from the Short Stay car park and home for a nice cup of tea. That would have been just fine.

They say that everybody wants secretly to be recognised, but Davey Quinn really had wanted to be left alone and it had suited him, the years of anonymity, it had given him space to breathe and to get to know himself. Living away, he thought he'd finally begun to grow into his face, the jut of his own chin, the set of his own nose, the furrows of his own brow: he felt pretty sure that they all reflected his new, different, more secure sense of himself. He thought that he'd found the perfect disguise.

'You haven't changed a bit,' said Marie, hand on hip.

'Really?'

'You get back a lot?'

'I haven't been back in twenty years,' he said.

'Living in London?'

'Yes,' he agreed.

'You'll see a lot of changes.'

'Uh-huh,' he said. 'Right.'

'I'll see what I can do about the luggage,' said Marie, picking up her walkie-talkie.

'Thanks,' said Davey, turning to walk away.

'Honest to God, you look just the same,' repeated Marie.

'Good,' said Davey.

'And that extra bit of weight suits you.' And then she spoke into the walkie-talkie. 'Maureen?' she said. 'You'll never guess who I've got here.'

There was a crackle.

'David Quinn.'

And then more crackle.

'Yes. Him.'

And then crackle again.

'Maureen says welcome home. And Happy Christmas.'

'Thanks,' said Davey. 'The same to you.'

It was getting late and he caught a cab. The driver was humming along to a tune on the radio, a typical piece of bowel-softening Country and Western, sung in an accent yearning for America but tethered firmly here to home. Davey sat down heavily in the back, dazed, and stared out of the window.

So this was it.

Home.

Marie was totally wrong. There weren't a lot of changes. In fact, everything looked exactly the same: the same rolling

10

hills, the same patches of fields and houses, the same round-abouts, the motorway. It was all just as he remembered it. A landscape doesn't change that much in twenty years.

Or the weather.

It had been fine when they left the airport, but now the rain was sheeting down and about twenty miles along the motorway one of the windscreen wipers popped off – the whole arm, like someone had just reached down and plucked it away, like God Himself was plucking at an eyebrow.

'Jesus!' screamed the driver, having lost all vision through the windscreen in what seemed to be a massive and magic stream of liquid pouring down from the heavens, as if God, or Jesus, were now pissing directly on to the car, as if He were getting ready for an evening out, and they swerved across three lanes and pulled over on to the hard shoulder.

'Did you see that?'

'I did,' said Davey.

'Jesus Christ. Blinded me.'

'You OK?'

'Yeah, thanks. Yeah. I'm fine.'

The car was rocking now, as lorries passed by, and then there was a sudden clap of thunder in the distance.

'You wouldn't be any good at repairs, would you?' asked the driver, turning round.

'No, not really,' said Davey.

'Would you mind having a look, though? It's just, I don't know anything about cars. And this asthma.' The man coughed, in evidence. 'It gets bad in the rain.' He reached for a cigarette, put it in his mouth ready to light it and waited, his hand shaking slightly.

'Right,' said Davey, who did look as though he knew about cars and who felt sorry for the man, who reminded him of his father: it was the shakes, and the cigarette, and the thick-set back of the neck; the profile of most men here over forty, actually. 'I'll just go ahead then, shall I?'

11

'I'd be grateful, if you would.'

Davey got out. The cars on the inside lane were inches from him, flank to flank, and the rain was busy pasting his clothes to him, and the wind was getting up, turning him instantly from safe passenger into a sailor rolling on the forecastle in the high seas.

He checked first round the front. The whole of the wiper's arm had gone – just the metal stump remained – so he then made his way round to the rear and started pulling off the back windscreen wiper, in the hope he might be able to use it as a replacement. He managed to cut his hands on the fittings and the spray from the road was whipping up his back, but in the end, with a twist and a wrench, he managed to get the wiper off. And in so doing he dropped the little plastic lugs that had held it in place – they rolled on to the road – so there he was, big Davey Quinn, not an hour back home, down on his knees, soaked to the skin in the pouring rain, reaching out a bloodied hand into a sea of oncoming traffic.

It was no good. They were out too far and the traffic was too heavy. He gave up. He got back into the back seat, drenched, defeated, and dripping wet and blood.

The driver was smoking. 'Good swim?' he asked, chuckling at his own joke. 'No luck?'

'No.' Davey reached forward and gave the driver the back wiper. 'Sorry about that.'

'You're all right.'

The driver called into his office on the radio. They'd send someone along with a spare. It might take a while, maybe an hour or so.

An hour.

Davey thought about it.

Davey had been thinking about coming home for as long as he'd been away – there was not a day went past when he didn't think about it – but it was a journey in which irresolution might still easily overtake him. He had enough money in his wallet and on his cards to be able to go back to the airport right now and get the next plane out, and maybe wait another twenty years before returning. He was, therefore, a man who could not afford to hesitate.

The time was now or never.

He'd come this far: he was going to have to keep going. He was going to have to maintain his velocity.

He said he'd walk the rest of the way.

'Walk?' said the driver.

'Yeah,' said Davey.

'As in, on your feet?'

'Yeah,' repeated Davey.

'Walking? In this rain?'

'Yes,' said Davey one more time.

'Are you joking?'

'No. It's not far from here, is it?'

'Next exit. He won't be long, though, with the spare.'

'No, I'll push on, I think.'

'Well, it's your decision, pal. What's the hurry?'

'I just . . .' Davey couldn't explain it. 'I need to get back. What do I owe you?'

'Well, I'll have to charge you full fare and extra for the damage to the wiper.'

'Right,' said Davey. He believed him.

'No, I'm having you on!' said the driver. 'Jesus! Where have you been?'

'London,' admitted Davey.

'Well,' said the driver philosophically. 'I'll tell you what. This isn't London. We'll call it quits. OK?'

'OK,' said Davey. 'Cheers.' People at home, he thought: they were the salt of the earth.

'Happy Christmas,' said the man as Davey slipped out. 'And good luck.'

Davey had made it about half a mile and halfway down the slip road in the squall and rain before he realised that he'd left his little rucksack, his only hand luggage, in the car.

The rucksack contained a bottle of whiskey for his parents, a bottle for himself and his wallet, stuffed with cash and cards.

He turned and walked back towards the car, in the face of the traffic spitting up fountains in his face.

The car had gone – there was just a wiper on the hard shoulder to mark where once it had been.

So this was how it was going to have to be. He was going to have to return, as he had left, with nothing and in ruin.

He put one foot in front of the other and set off in the wake of the cars' slipstream.

It's a long walk from the motorway to the outskirts of our town – an hour, maybe two, I'm not sure, it's not a walk I'd care to take myself – but eventually in the distance, on that profound horizon, Davey saw the golf club, the outskirts, with its big stone sleeping lions and its 20-foot forbidding hedges, and there was probably a good half-inch of water in his shoes by this time, and his clothes were like wet canvas as he stood and rested his hand on the head of one of the lions and gazed at the entire grey town down below him.

A lot can change in a small town in twenty years. In twenty years men and women can do a lot of damage. There is no mildness in the hearts of small-town councillors and planners, and you should never underestimate what small-town people are capable of. You can double it and double it again, and keep on going with your calculations until you think you've achieved the unimaginable, and still you'd never come close. Any estimate will never match up to the extraordinary outstretched reality.

The people of my home town have outdone themselves. We have exceeded all expectations. We have gone further than was absolutely necessary. We have confounded probability and ignored all the maths. We have been reckless and we have been greedy, we have eaten ourselves alive, sucked the very marrow from our bones, and spat out the remaining pieces.

Davey was amazed. He was heading straight for the centre of town, past all the old landmarks – Treavy's second-hand cars, Pickering's the monumental masons, McKenzie's broom factory and the old planing mill, where they used to stack the sashes and doors outside under a huge tarpaulin canopy, and J. W. John's, the big coal depot, where the coal would sometimes fall over the wall, and we'd go to collect it and bring it home, or dig pits in the woods and gather kindling and try to make fires.

They're all gone, of course – Treavy's, Pickering's, McKenzie's, John's. There is nothing of them remaining at all. It's been quite a clearance. Even the long steep road Davey was coming in on, shin-deep in mud and puddles, what used to be Moira Avenue, a mazy S-shaped road flanked with trees and the cast-iron railings protecting the town's little light industry, is now a straight flat dual carriageway with housing developments tucked up tight behind vast sheets of panel fencing on either side, a good quarter of a mile of soft verges and For Sale signs.

At the very end of the road, a road Davey no longer recognised but which he now alas knew, every foot-aching inch of it, at a big new junction with four sets of lights where the water had formed in deeper puddles, was the Kincaid furniture factory. Or rather, *was* the Kincaid furniture factory. There's nothing there at all now. Just mud, and sprouting weeds, and a sign, 'COMING SOON: EXCITING NEW DEVELOPMENT OF TWO AND THREE BED HIGH-SPEC TURNKEY FINISH TOWN HOUSES', with a high-spec view, it should be noted, of the health centre car park, Macey's the chemists, and Tommy Tucker's chipper, which have all survived the clearances.

Molested by the remorseless rain, Davey Quinn waited for the little green man to tip him the wink, then he crossed over into the centre proper.

The old fire station is still there, but it has been converted into apartments – 'LUXURY, FULLY FITTED APARTMENTS', apparently, and two of them still for sale. The big tower where

15

you used to see the long red hose hanging down to dry –
what we called God's Condom – is long gone.

Some things, though, remain. Down Bridge Street, past the
bus station and the train station and the Chinese takeaways,
the old Quality Hotel, our landmark, our claim to fame, still
sits on the corner of Main Street and High Street, in all its
glorious six storeys, with its balustraded parapet, its castel-
lations and gables, its mullioned windows and square corner
turrets, and its flat-roofed concrete back-bar extension and
basement disco, the site of so many breathless adolescent
fumbles and embraces, a place where so many relationships
in this town were formed and celebrated, and where so many
of them faltered.

It is completely derelict, of course, the hotel, just a shell
these days, a red, rain-soaked crust held up by rusty scaffolding poles and a big 10-foot sign on one of the crumbling
turrets announcing that it has been 'ACQUIRED FOR MAJOR
REDEVELOPMENT', no one knows exactly what. The peeling
red stucco is stained with pigeon shit. It's a wreck, but at least
it's still there. Like a lot of us, in fact.

Sitting, as if in commentary and judgement upon it and
upon us, directly opposite the hotel and facing our only
remaining free car park, are the new offices of the *Impartial
Recorder*, our local paper, a journal of record, housed in a
three-storey concrete building in the popular brutalist manner,
with its red neon sign announcing both its name and the additional words, 'COMMERCIAL PRINTERS'.

Shaking now, with the cold and the shock, Davey set his
face against the prevailing winds and the haze of rain, and
prepared for the final drag before home, up Main Street. Past
Duncan McGregor's, the tailor and staunch Methodist and
gentleman's outfitter. Past the five bakeries, each offering its
own speciality: the lovely treacle soda bread in the art deco
Adele's; the Wheaten's miniature barnbracks; the ginger scones
in Carlton's Bakery and Tea Rooms; the big cheese-and-onion

pasties in McCann's; the town's best fruit cake in Spencer's. Past the four butchers, including Billy Nibbs's dad, Hugh, 'H. NIBBS, BUTCHER AND POULTERER', with its large stained-glass frontage and its mechanical butcher forever cleaving a calf's head in two, and McCullough's, 'ALSO LICENSED TO SELL GAME', with its hand-painted legend, 'Pleased to Meet You, Meat to Please You'. Past the nameless paint shop that everyone called the Paint Shop; and Orr's the shoe shop, and McMartens', their competitors; past the small bookshop, known as the Red Front because of its pillar box flaky frontage; and Peter Harris Stationery; and Noah's Ark the toy shop; Maxwell's photographers; the entrance to the old Sunrise Dairy; King's Music, run by Ernie King and his son Charlie; Priscilla's Ladies Separates and Luxury Hair Styling; Gemini the Jewellers; Finlay's Auto-Supplies; Carpenter's tobacconists; the Frosty Queen, the ice cream parlour, which featured an all-year-round window display of a plastic snow-woman; and the Bide-A-While tea shop, famous for its cinnamon scones and its sign promising 'Customers Attended in the Latest Rapid Service Manner'.

All of them absent without leave. Gone. Disappeared. Destroyed.

And in their place? Charity shops for old people, and blind people, and poor children, and other poor children, and people with bad hearts, and cancer, and dogs; amusement arcades; chip shops; kebab shops; minicab offices; and a new club called Paradise Lost whose entrance features fibreglass Grecian columns and a crude naked eighteen-foot Adam and Eve, hands joined above the doorway and Eve mid-bite of an apple the size of a watermelon; and deep, deep piles of rubbish in the doorways of shuttered shops. Just what you'd expect. A street of bright plastic and neon shop fascia, holes, gaps, clearances and metal-fenced absences. Main Street had once been called what it was. But now, what could you call it? It hardly deserved a name. The old cast-iron street sign has long since vanished.

17

Virtually drowning now, breathing water and no part of him left dry, Davey managed to accelerate his march and reached the brow of the hill.

The Quinn family bungalow used to be on the edge of town, an outpost, past the People's Park and the old council offices, part of a small estate looking proudly over its own patch of green with swings and a slide and a see-saw, and a small football pitch with its own goalposts, which was marked out twice a year by the council, and looking out back over trees and fields.

It's still there. The family home remains. It hasn't gone anywhere.

But it no longer sits as a promontory and is no longer proud. It has been humbled and made small, bleached and filthied not only by the passing of time and the fading of memory, but by the ring road, which has stretched and uncoiled itself around our town, its street lights like tail fins or trunks uplifted over and above in a triumphal arch, leading to mile upon mile of pavementless houses – good houses, with their own internal garages – and to our shopping mall, Bloom's, the diamond in the ring, our new town centre, the place to be, forever open and forever welcoming, the twenty-four-hour lights from its twenty-four-hour car park effacing the night sky, 'Every Day a Good Day Regardless of the Weather'.

The sky was erased and empty, high above the red-brick new estates, as Davey Quinn pushed open the rusty gate – which used to be red – and went to ring on the door of his family home, the prodigal returning. The varnish on the poker-worked wooden sign by the door has long since peeled away, revealing the natural grain of the wood, made pale by the sun and the wind, and swollen by rain, but the house name is scorched deep enough and black enough, and you can still see it clearly from the road: *Dun Roamin'*.

2
Sandwiches

A short account of Bob Savory – his life, his times,
his knives, his mother, his capacity for self-enriching,
self-reproach and his famous bill of fare

The wind would near have knocked you over. It was gale-
force. Bob Savory lost two trees in his grounds: an oak that
was older even than the house, and a silver birch by the far
pond. Bob *has* grounds and an old house. He has ponds both
near and far. Bob is an old friend and, much more than any
of the rest of us, Bob has made it. Bob has it all. Bob has
trees that are not leylandii. Bob has done what seems so difficult to us, but which seems so natural to him: he has made
money.

Bob is a successful local businessman, possibly the most
successful local businessman around here since the titled
landowners and gentlemen farmers and the great whiskered
industrialists of centuries past, when our town used to make
all its own and look after itself, when you might be able to sit
down in your local after a long day's work and eat local cheese
with your local bread and your local pint in your local tweeds
and your local linens round a roaring fire made from the local
logs and then nip upstairs to get a good old-fashioned seeing-
to and a local disease from a good old local girl, and you'd
probably be dead by the time you were forty.

There were reminders of those good old days everywhere when we were growing up, from the big brick warehouses up on Moira Avenue and the polished red granite-fronted offices on High Street, with their huge carved bearded heads over the ornate archways, right down to the hole-in-the-wall boot scrapers and the cast-iron corner bollards and the old drinking fountains at the bottom of Main Street by the Quality Hotel, served by taps in beautiful shell-shaped niches, and the big stone trough for horses, which were all removed for the car park and road-widening scheme years ago, and which no one has seen since – although some people say they now sit as ornaments in the garden of our ex-mayor and council chairman, Frank Gilbey, a man who presided over twenty years of unrestrained and unrestricted planning and development during the last decades of the twentieth century, a man whose name will live on as the mayor who cut the ribbon on the ring road and opened Bloom's, the mall, and changed for ever the face of our town. Everyone knows the name of Frank Gilbey, a man who owns a chain of hairdressers and lingerie shops throughout the county, and who has a roundabout on the ring road named after him. His name will live on, Councillor Frank Gilbey, while the names of those nineteenth-century giants, the great entrepreneurs and philanthropists of the past, which once were everywhere – Joseph King and Samuel Jelly and James Whisker, written above offices and shops, and given to parks and streets and community halls, and on all our school cups and certificates – are now hidden and obliterated.

Bob Savory's fame and fortune may not last for ever but for the moment he is rich and famous and successful, an intimate even of Frank Gilbey's, a business associate, a partner with Frank, in fact, in a number of prestigious developments, a local son to be proud of, and when people ask him what is the secret of his success – which they do, about once a month, in the *Impartial Recorder*, our local paper, which likes to do its best for local business and for whom Bob is about the closest thing we have to a living, breathing, home-grown celebrity, with all his own hair and an actual jawline – he smiles his big perfect white smile, the result of years of expensive cosmetic dentistry and worth every penny, he says, and he looks straight at the camera and he says just one word: sandwiches.

Sandwiches, sandwiches. White or brown, hot or cold, rolls, baps, tortilla wraps, subs and bagels, croissants, pittas, panini, it really doesn't matter what to Bob, as long as you can eat it with one hand and the filling doesn't drip down on to your shirt. So no hot cheese or scrambled egg, and no loose meat, but just about everything else: Brie, bacon and avocado, turkey and ham, egg and onion, tuna and onion, tuna and anything, all-day breakfasts, double- and triple-deckers, roast beef and horseradish, roast vegetables and mozzarella, chicken and prawn and cold sausage, every imaginable combination of cheese and meat and bread, smothered in every kind of mayo and mustard and sauce known to man, and some unknown, some made to a secret recipe known, they say, only to Bob, and handed down from generation to generation. Bob knows everything there is to know about sandwiches. He is our sandwich king, the prince, the lord, our contemporary Earl of Sandwich. When it comes to sandwiches Bob just seems to know what people like. He has a sixth sense. He has an instinct.*

I can remember when Bob was just getting into the catering

* He also has his own website now, and a cookbook, *Speedy Bap!*, which includes chapters on 'Home-Made Burgers that Don't Fall Apart', 'What Next with Tuna?' and an appendix, 'Mayo or Pickle?', in which Bob comes down firmly on the side of chutney. The book is available locally from all good bookshops, or newsagents, price £9.99. It's been a runaway success county-wide. Bob is in demand all over the place for signings and sandwich-making demonstrations. A new updated edition of the book, *Speedy Bap!!*, which is guaranteed a lot of local press coverage and includes all-new chapters on low-fat cottage cheese and wafer-thin ham, is due out soon, with additional recipes gathered from Bob's visits to various Women's Institutes, Soroptomists, the Waterstone's up in the city, and other local groups and associations.

business, or at least had gone into a restaurant and got himself a job, which is perhaps not quite the same thing, but it was a pretty big deal around here and in retrospect it was clearly the beginning of great things for Bob Savory.

Most of us when we left school had ambitions only to get out of town and maybe go to London, to Soho, to get to see inside a sex shop, visit some record shops, and maybe get a place of our own with a few lifelong friends and be able to stay up all night, drinking and listening to loud music, and meeting girls we hadn't been to school with, girls who maybe worked in the sex shops, or who, like us, were just in browsing and who weren't going to be afraid to explore their sexuality. But when it came to it we were content to end up working at the local garage, or on the sites, or going on to the Tech if we had the grades, and living with our parents until they kicked us out, and marrying the sister of a friend, and losing touch with our ambitions and our record collections, but Bob always had a firm plan and a purpose, right from an early age, and he never changed his mind and he never got distracted.

I remember seeing him the day he'd just bought his first set of knives and the look on his face, when he unwrapped them in the pub, to let us all admire: it was the look of a man who knew where he was going in life. It was the look of a man with a sharp knife in his hand and the future before him like a lamb to the slaughter. Bob's knives were not like the knives our mothers had at home. Bob's were German knives, made from high-carbon steel, with three beautiful silver rivets in the handles, not like they were ordinary rivets just holding the thing together, but like they were meant to be there, like they had been ordained, three perfect eternal rings, and Bob sat with us in the Castle Arms on the red velour, with these six- and ten-inch blades, and he rolled up his sleeves and he raised his hands, like the priest with the host, and he balanced the knives on his middle finger, one by one, and they perched there, like beautiful shiny birds come down to rest. They'd cost him his first month's wages and then some, but he was as proud as you would be if you'd just met the woman of your dreams, and he handled those blades with exactly the same kind of care and attention, gazing at them fondly, and perhaps a little shyly, imagining their future life together. Bob told us you could get all sorts of different knives, knives of every size and for every purpose. He said there was even a knife called a tomato knife, for cutting tomatoes, and of course none of us had ever even heard of such a thing as a tomato knife, and we laughed at him and joked about all the other knives he should get: how about an egg knife, we said, where's your cucumber knife, Bob, and your lettuce knife, and your knife for the cutting of toasted ham and cheese sandwiches, huh, and he rolled up his knives, in this brand-new beautiful thick green roll of material, and tied them up with their new strings, and we never saw them again, and that night we went back to our parents' houses with their plastic-handled cutlery and tried to balance bread knives on our fingers.

We were silly to scoff. These days Bob has his own catering company, Old-Fashioned Foods (Cooked the Traditional Way), and a subsidiary called Sandwich Classics. He has a fleet of vans he runs out of the industrial estate, up by the new fire station, and the motto on the side of the sandwich vans says it all. The signs read 'SANDWICH CLASSICS AND SNACK FOODS FOR THE DISCERNING PALET'.*

* Bob's old friend Terry Wilkinson, 'Wilkie the Gut' to many of us here in town – a man who has enjoyed perhaps a touch too much old-fashioned food (cooked the traditional way) in his time – runs a nice little business, The Gist, up on the industrial estate, specialising in vehicle graphics, and he took care of all the graphics on the vans for Bob. Terry left school with no qualifications and few prospects but he now lives in a five-bedroom house with jacuzzi in the Woodsides development, and frankly a few slips in spelling and the odd wandering apostrophe are hardly going to worry him: as far as Terry is concerned a palette is a palet is a palate; just as long as you get – as Terry himself might say – the gist.

The sandwiches are Bob's big earner. They go the whole of the length and breadth of the county. He's talking about setting up a franchise.

Bob also has a stake, a small but significant financial interest, in the big new Irish-themed restaurant out on the ring road – the Plough and the Stars they call it – which offers delicacies such as Turkey O'Toole, and Flannigan's Fish Sandwich, and Banbridge Cajun Chicken Tagliatelle, 'chunks of tender local chicken dusted with cajun spices and served on a bed of tagliatelle, covered in a creamy white wine sauce (vegetarian option available)'. It's good. Or at least it's profitable. People flock to it in their cars, on their way to or from Bloom's, the shopping mall, and the DIY superstores and the big new private gym, the Works, which is right next door. The central feature in the Plough and the Stars – which was advertised on opening in a full-colour two-page centre spread in the *Impartial Recorder* as 'AN ARCHITECT-DESIGNED, WAREHOUSE-STYLE EATING EXPERIENCE' – is a fibreglass whitewashed cottage with three-foot-high animatronic leprechauns who enter and exit on the quarter-, the half-hour and the hour, singing 'Danny Boy', 'Galway City' and 'The Bard of Armagh'. The words of the songs are on the back of the laminated menus and most customers are happy to join in, as long as their mouths aren't full of 'The Kerryman's Garlic Bread (made with fresh Kerry butter)', or 'Belfast City Trifle' and sometimes even when they are.

Bob lives outside town, far from the Plough and the Stars, beyond the ring road, in a house set in its own landscaped grounds, now minus two trees, with outbuildings, and its own jacuzzi, and a games room with a pool table, and table tennis, a minibar, genuine antique furniture and original art on the walls, and a hallway so vast that in the winter he lights a big fire and has carol singers, a twelve-foot Christmas tree, and he invites us all round with our children to play party games, and he sits on this antique chair he calls a gossip-seat – and who are we to argue? – dressed up like Santa, handing out presents, like the proverbial lord of the manor.

Bob has definitely made it.

But Bob is not a satisfied man. Of course, the secret of Bob, the glory of Bob, is that he's not a satisfied man: if he were a satisfied man he'd be just like the rest of us, living in a semi off the ring road, treeless and jacuzziless, and those with a 'discerning palet' would be cheated of sandwich classics and old-fashioned foods (cooked the traditional way). Bob works seven days a week, fifteen, sixteen hours a day, talks endlessly on his mobile phone and he hasn't taken a holiday in years, not since he paid for a group of us to go on holiday with him to a resort in Spain, which was not a success, which was a disaster, in fact – he paid our fares and our accommodation, but he made it clear that we would have to pay for our own food and drink and entertainment, and I think, to be honest, some of us felt cheated, as if Bob should have gone the whole hog and paid for everything, as if he owed us something, and those of us who didn't feel that probably felt that we owed him something, so in the end everyone was dissatisfied. Generosity can be hard to bear and a generous friend can be a burden. Harry made a joke one night when we were in a club in Marbella that the whole thing was probably tax deductible anyway, so it didn't really count, and Bob left the club, caught a cab straight to the airport and we didn't see him for months afterwards.

Not that Bob is lonely, or that he needs our company. He's had relationships with many women over the years – many many women – and he'd like a family of his own, he says. He'd like a big family – a dozen children he reckons he could cope with – but he's not yet found the right woman. He's getting older, of course, like the rest of us, but the women seem to have stayed around about the same age – early twenties, which is undoubtedly a good age, nothing wrong with it at all, and none of us would wish to deny Bob or his female friends their various pleasures, but you can't help but think that even the young can get stuck in a rut. In fact, the young may even be a rut. At the moment Bob is kind of stuck on waitresses – from the Plough and the Stars mostly. As well as his investment in the business, Bob is employed by the restaurant as something called a Menu Consultant, which seems to mean nothing except that he gets to hang out in the kitchens occasionally, and to meet the waitresses and drive them home – he drives a Porsche at weekends and a BMW during the week – and for the first few weeks everything goes fine, but after a while the young ladies always want to talk, and Bob never has much to say. Bob is a doer rather than a talker or a thinker and at the end of a day he just wants peace and quiet, and a little bit of rest and relaxation. He does not want to sit and talk about the state of the world or the state of play between man and woman. He is not a man who enjoys contemplating his own navel: he would rather be contemplating someone else's. So pretty soon he finds himself driving someone else home from the restaurant and the waitresses find themselves waiting tables elsewhere. As a consequence, the Plough and the Stars enjoys a rather high staff turnover, and the loyal front-of-house manager, Alison, says one day they're going to run out of young women in the town to employ and they'll have to start importing them. Bob thinks that this would not be such a bad idea.

Now Bob is, of course, a rich man, a millionaire, although, as he points out, being a millionaire these days is nothing special. Virtually everyone is a millionaire these days, according to Bob, or they could be. Bob reckons he needs at least another £2 million to be really comfortable. He's got it all worked out. With an extra £2 million, maybe a little more, he could afford to live the rest of his life on about £120,000 per annum. Which would be quite sufficient, as long as you've cleared all your major debts. And Bob has cleared nearly all his debts. Except for one.

His mother.

Bob is an only child and his dad, Sammy, Sam Savory, a wiry man with a thick head of hair and as thin as a whippet and as strong as an Irish wolfhound, died a few years ago. He was a sheet-metal worker. He worked hard all his life and then he got cancer and was dead within six months of retiring. Mesothelioma – a cancer caused only by exposure to asbestos. It was not a good death. It was an industrial death. Bob paid, of course, for private nursing, but it couldn't save Sam, and Bob's mum Maureen was ashamed: she felt her husband should somehow have known he was working with asbestos and should have been aware of the dangers, even before anyone knew there were dangers. She blamed him and so did Bob. They felt that it reflected badly on the family. It's difficult sometimes to feel sympathy for the dead and the dying. Sometimes, when someone dies, even someone close to you – especially someone close to you – you just think, how dare you? And in Bob's case, and for his mum, there was also the corollary: how dare you and how dare you die of such a stupid man-made disease, something which was so easily avoidable? If only you'd worn gloves and a mask and some protective clothing you would have been OK. None of this would have happened. None of us would have had to be so upset. It was your own fault. They didn't even claim for compensation.*

* Unlike a lot of people here in town. Martin Phillips, the solicitor on Sunnyside Terrace, has dealt with more than his fair share of vibration white finger, and asbestos exposure, and occupational asthma, and allergic rhinitis over the past few years – dealing with wheezy old and middle-aged men who spent their lives working on the roads, or on the sites, or on the railways, or out in the fields, or in the factories and the steelworks up in the city, which covers just about everyone here, actually, and all of whom are now seeking recompense for lives diminished and cut short, recompense which usually covers about two weeks in Florida with the grandchildren, a new sunlounger for the patio and a slightly better coffin. For further details and information on claiming for industrial diseases contact your local Citizens Advice Bureau or ring Industrial Diseases Compensation Ltd on 0800 454532.

27

And now Bob's mother Maureen has Alzheimer's. Bob can't believe it. Sometimes he'll shout and rage at her, when no one else is there: he can't believe she's really ill. A part of him thinks she's putting it on. Silly woman, he calls her. Silly bitch. Stupid cow. Challenging her. Words he remembers saying to her only once before, when he was a child, after they'd had some argument or other and his mother had said to him, 'You're not too old for me to give you a good hiding, you know,' and he smirked at her and so she did, she smacked him, right across the backside, and he felt the full force of her wedding ring and he never said the words again. Until now. When Maureen deteriorated one of the nurses recommended a book to Bob, to help him cope, but Bob doesn't read books. He does not admire book learning: what Bob admires is expertise. So he buys in twenty-four-hour care. It's the least he can do.

At night when he gets home from work, he lets the nurse take a few hours to herself, and he sits down with his mother in front of the wide-screen TV, in his TV room. He's had the place fitted out with a DVD player and a complete home cinema system – which he'd had to order specially from America. He'd gone to considerable trouble, had got in Harry Lamb the Odd Job Man to help him fix the screen to the joists in the ceiling – but he didn't enjoy watching the home cinema with his mother. It didn't feel natural. He only watched it now with the waitresses. With his mum he preferred to watch TV, like they used to when Bob was a child. They watch anything, Bob and his mum. Films. Football. News. Documentaries. It doesn't matter. It's all the same. It's not the content. It's the act of watching that counts. It is a huge comfort to them both.

Before they go to bed at night, during the adverts, Bob always makes them something to eat. He tends to get hungry around about ten, the same every night, before the news, but it always seems to surprise him, his own hunger. He never seems prepared for it. Sometimes he roams around the kitchen in the semi-darkness, opening cupboards, ransacking for food. Bob is a rich man, but he can find no food in his own house which he would want to eat. What he could really manage would be one of his mum's roast dinners. He could eat a tray of those roast potatoes. A whole tray. They were always so good. The beef dripping – that was the secret. He knows how to do it, of course – you have to get the beef dripping nice and hot in a saucepan, and then you bash the parboiled potatoes around in there for a bit, and season them with salt and pepper, and then slide them on the tray into the oven, and one hour later, perfect roast potatoes. But he could never be bothered to do it himself. It just wouldn't be the same.

The rare roast beef, though. He could definitely eat some of his mum's rare roast beef. And maybe some carrots. And a nice gravy.*

He goes from cupboard to cupboard – chocolates, biscuits, crisps, nuts, crackers. None of it is any good. It's all manufactured. It's all rubbish. He knows it's rubbish. Sometimes the rubbish in his cupboards makes him so angry that he throws it all away, just chucks it in the bin. And then he buys more. He buys more rubbish. This is what happens when you're a rich man in our town. You don't necessarily buy better. You just buy more. Because there isn't anything else to buy. You want something more fancy, you have to leave: you have to go to London, or somewhere else where they do funny spaghetti and truffle oils, and novelty cheeses.

Bob's mother used to make lasagne. And she used to make a salmon soufflé, on special occasions, using a whole tin of salmon – that was good too. And sausage rolls. Macaroni

* Bob's 'Sunday Roastie Wedgie' – cold roast beef, horseradish, English mustard and roasted vegetables in a granary bap – includes just about everything but the gravy (see *Speedy Bap!*, p.44). He did try experimenting with a cold gravy mayonnaise at one time but the combination of beef stock and whisked eggs was too cloying on the palate. It's a simple lesson, but one worth repeating: gravy is best served hot.

cheese. Pies and pastries. And cakes. The smell of baking. The smell of fresh bread. The food then seemed so different. It was all so good. Bob's favourite meal, of all the meals his mother used to make . . . after all these years, he still has no doubt what was his favourite, and every night, between the adverts, he ends up trying to re-create it.

When he used to come home from school he would be just so tired sometimes, and he'd be so hungry, before his dad got home from the works, and so he and his mum would sit down together, his mum drinking her coffee with two sugars and smoking, and him eating the sandwich that she'd made him: white bread and margarine and Cheddar cheese, or sometimes a slice of ham, if they had it in the house, which was not often.

'How was school?' she'd ask.

'Fine,' he'd say. 'I don't want to talk about it.'

'OK,' she'd say and that would be fine. They didn't have to talk: they were mother and son.

They would just sit there, the two of them, looking out of the window, eating cheese sandwiches and waiting for his dad to come home.

So when Frank Gilbey rolled up at Bob's late one night, just before Christmas, Bob ushered him in, asked him to sit down in the big kitchen equipped with every piece of gadgetry imaginable, and about half a mile of granite work surface and a foundry's worth of stainless steel, put the kettle on and put a simple cheese sandwich down in front of him.

'So?' said Bob.

'There's a problem,' said Frank.

30

3

Jesus, Mary and Joseph

Introducing the Donellys, God, The Dog With The
Kindliest Expression, some memories of cinemas long
gone and many other attempted poignancies

There hasn't been snow here for Christmas since 1975, which
seems like yesterday to some of us, but which is already ancient
history to others – around about the time of the Punic Wars,
in fact, to many of the children at Central School, for whom
modern history begins at the end of the twentieth century and
the advent of wide-screen TV and mobile phone text
messaging. Gerry Malone, who teaches history at Central –
who taught most of us in town our history, in fact – has to
be careful not to assume that the students know too much.
He cannot assume, for example, that they know anything
about the Punic Wars, or that Hitler was a Nazi even, or that
mobile phone text messaging was not a means of communication available to Lord Nelson at the Battle of Trafalgar.
Gerry likes to quote Santayana to his students – 'Those who
cannot remember the past are condemned to repeat it' – but
he knows that actually it's the opposite that's true. Those who
can remember the past are condemned to repeat it – again
and again and again. It is the history teacher's burden.

People have been feverishly praying for snow at Christmas
in our town for nearly thirty years, but God seems to have

better things to do with His time than to attend to our prayers, although exactly what it is He's been getting up to recently it's difficult to see: since writing the Bible, He seems to have been on some kind of extended sabbatical. World peace, for example, does not seem to be too high on His list of priorities and, unless you count the weekly healing services at the People's Fellowship, His work, at least around our town, seems to have come to an abrupt end.

Gerry also likes to quote Nietzsche to his students and he always writes up the name on the whiteboard first – the middle 'z' always tends to throw them. 'Nietzsche,' he explains, 'rhymes with teacher.' And then, 'God,' he tells his class, to audible gasps, 'God, according to Nietzsche' – and here he always pauses, with an omniscient smile – 'Is Dead.'

Well. I don't know. Maybe Gerry's being too harsh. Maybe someone just needs to text Him, to remind Him that we're all still here. W T F R U?*

The sleet and the cold have certainly not slowed up the Donellys, who are old friends and neighbours of the Quinns, and who live up by the ring road and who, like the rest of the town, have been busy making their Christmas preparations.

It's going to be a very special Christmas for the Donellys this year, snow or no snow – their first Christmas without any of the children, a kind of rite of passage and a relief in

---

* Bobbie Dylan at the People's Fellowship has been encouraging Francie McGinn to do some discussions with Can Teen, the young people's group, on the question of whether texting can be Christian – a question that has troubled thinkers, in one way or another, as Barry McClean would be able to tell you, for many years. Plato addresses a similar problem, for example, in his *Phaedrus*, in the story of wise King Thamus of Egypt and the inventions of the god Theuth. Francie, however, has not read widely outside the Bible and devotional literature, so he is not familiar with what Barry in Philosophy for Beginners (Lecture 6: 'Epistemology') calls the 'obvious connection between *Phaedrus*, commodity fetishism, and our symbolic lives and psychic habits'. Francie simply calls his discussions 'FDFX?' (Fully Devoted Followers of Christ), and is encouraging more prayerful texting.

many ways, a return to a prelapsarian state, a time long before Mr Donelly's pot belly and his cardies, and the advent of Mrs Donelly's flat-soled shoes. This Christmas, if they wanted, Mr and Mrs Donelly could walk around all day naked, barefoot and freed from toil, the pain of childbirth but a distant memory, and freed also from the prying eyes of their offspring, so they could eat turkey sandwiches from morning till night, *au naturel*, on sliced white bread, with lots of salt and with butter, as God intended them to be.*

The Donellys' youngest son, Mark, their baby, lives in America now, where he works for a firm of hypodermic needle incinerator manufacturers. He is married to Molly, has two lovely children, Nathan (five) and Ruth (three), and can't afford the fare home. Jackie, meanwhile, the Donellys' daughter, is in north London, a nurse, no boyfriend at the moment and knocking on a bit, but not without her suitors, so Mr and Mrs Donelly aren't too worried. She is working shifts this Christmas and can't get back either. Michael – Mickey – still lives in town, obviously, but this year he and Brona are going to her parents' for Christmas: her parents live in Huddersfield. When Mickey told his parents that he and Brona and the children wouldn't be around for Christmas Mr and Mrs Donelly both said fine, that's great, although they didn't really mean it. Mr and Mrs Donelly get to see their grandchildren all year round, so it's really only fair to let the other lot have a go, but Christmas is Christmas.

'It's supposed to be a family time,' said Mrs Donelly to Mr Donelly. Mr Donelly pointed out that Brona's family in Huddersfield were family: they were Brona's family.

'But they're in Huddersfield,' insisted Mrs Donelly. 'It's not the same.'

The Donellys' eldest boy, Tim, is travelling the world. He's thirty-one and should know better but he's working in a bar

---

* See Bob Savory's *Speedy Bap!*, chapter 12, 'Sandwiches à la Turque'.

in Sydney at the moment, apparently, Sydney, Australia, if you can imagine that, and the Donellys are expecting a call on Christmas Day. Tim's said he's planning a barbie on the beach and a game of mixed volleyball with some workmates for Christmas Day, and Mr Donelly really cannot imagine what that might be like, although Mrs Donelly watches a number of Australian soaps on TV and he's sat through them with her a couple of times, and he certainly likes the look of the lifestyle over there. It looks a bit more free and easy. More to do outside. No sleet. If he were forty years younger he might even have considered emigrating. But it's too late for that now.

Mr Donelly had offered to help his wife with the Christmas shopping this year – the first time ever – and she took him at his word and she gave him a list, and so he was down to Johnny 'The Boxer' Mathers, our last greengrocer, the only one remaining, by ten o'clock on Christmas Eve morning, looking for cheap nuts and tangerines, and then he was on to M & S up in Bloom's after that, cursing Mrs Donelly's handwriting all the way. After forty years of marriage she still can't seem to shape her vowels properly – they're too rounded, like the handwriting of a little girl, and you can't tell the difference between an 'a' and an 'o'. Oranges look like *aronges* and apples look like *opples*. Mind you, his is no better: he'd have made a good doctor, according to Mrs Donelly, who used to work as a receptionist at the Health Centre down by the People's Park, so she should know. Mr Donelly was not a doctor, though: he'd been a warehouseman, up at Bloom's, until he'd retired. He used to be a compositor, years ago, but the bottom fell out of the market.

It'll be a quiet Christmas for them without the children, but they're still planning to have a few people round on Boxing Day – the Quinns, with Davey, their celebrated returnee, Mrs Skingle and her son Steve, the scaffolder, who earns a packet, according to Mr Donelly, and Mrs Donelly's cousin Barbara, who is all alone – so Mr Donelly has stocked up, as instructed, on twenty-four Cocktail Pizza Squares ('A fun selection of eight tomato & cheese, eight ham & cheese, and eight mushroom & cheese'), twelve Vol-au-Vents ('Four creamy chicken & mushroom, four ham & cheese, and four succulent prawn'), some mini quiche (Traditional, Mediterranean and Vegetarian), some 'small succulent' pork cocktail sausages, 'fully cooked and ready to serve', needless to say, twelve Chicken Tikka Bites ('Lightly grilled pieces of chicken in a traditional Indian-style marinade of spices, coriander and garlic'), some hand-cooked crisps, and six Chocolate Tartlets ('Chocolate pastry tarts filled with white or milk chocolate mousse, decorated with chocolate curls'). A veritable feast. Mrs Donelly used to do the Boxing Day buffet herself when the children were younger, but she doesn't have the time these days and since it's going to be just the two of them she's even skimping on their usual Christmas dinner: instead of the big bird, the roast potatoes and the mound of sprouts, Mr Donelly has picked up a Small Turkey Breast Joint ('For 2–3, Butter Roasted'), a pack of baby new potatoes ('hand-picked'), some mangetout (from Kenya), and a miniature 'Luxury' Christmas pudding ('packed with plump, sun-ripened vine fruits'). It's the Christmas of the future: their first Christmas alone.

After the shopping Mr Donelly managed to squeeze in a quick pint at the Castle Arms, laden down with his shopping bags, much to the amusement of Little Mickey Matchett and Harry Lamb the Odd Job Man, and Big Dessie, who were all in gearing up for Christmas themselves, and who have never actually been into a supermarket unless accompanied by their wives, and only then to push the trolley.

'All set, then?' Mr Donelly asked Big Dessie, proud of his labours.

'I don't know,' answered Dessie, mid-pint. 'That's all the wife's department.'

Billy and Harry nodded in agreement with Dessie. It was hard to believe a big man like Joey Donelly doing the shopping for his wife on Christmas Eve. Times certainly were changing.

Mr Donelly spent the afternoon at home on a chair, putting up decorations: he wouldn't have bothered if it was down to himself, but Mrs Donelly had insisted. He didn't put up as many as usual, though: it hardly seemed worth it without the children there, and he'd never liked those paper lanterns Mrs Donelly's mother had given them when they were first married and which had remained their central festive decorative feature, their theme, as it were, for over thirty years. They were pink, originally, the lanterns, but they'd browned slightly with age, like raw meat left too long out of the fridge. He put them back in the cardboard box in the loft. He was trying to keep everything a bit more low-key.

Christmas Day itself shouldn't be too bad. It'd probably be pretty much the same as usual. Mrs Donelly would go to church and Mr Donelly would prefer to skip it. They'd have their lunch and maybe watch Morecambe and Wise on UK Gold. They used to play cards in the old days, and Monopoly, but they haven't bothered with any of that for years, not since the children were little, although Mrs Donelly still liked to play a few hands of patience, for old times' sake.

Boxing Day'll be the big day – it used to be a really big deal, years ago. They used to have everyone round, the parents and the grandparents, when they were alive, and brothers and sisters and aunts and uncles and cousins, dead now a lot of them, or just too old, and yet at one time all of them living and breathing and in the here and now, and all piling their plates up high, and roaring their way through the afternoon and long and late into the evening, everyone laughing at everything, slowly filling up, up and away on the bottled beer and Mrs Donelly's hand-made party food. Eaten, drunken, but not forgotten, the ghosts of Christmas past.

In fact, in the old days the Donelly household was full not

just at Christmas but all year round, with family and friends and family of friends popping in, drinking tea and talking, but now the children had grown up and moved out and moved on, and the party was over and the house was quiet, and Mr and Mrs Donelly had been busy these past few years trying to remake their lives. They had discovered to their surprise that remaking their lives was not something they could do very quickly or easily, and it was not something they could do within their own four walls, so the small home that had once housed at least six and was never empty was now too big and housed only two who were hardly ever there. When you want space, it seems, you can't have it, and when you've got it you don't need it.

This was an irony not lost on Mrs Donelly, who was a religious woman and who could therefore appreciate irony and paradox. It always helped, she had found, in church as in life, if you could take a joke: Jesus, for example, as far as Mrs Donelly could tell, had spent most of His time on earth telling people jokes and winding them up. There was nothing wrong, she'd decided, with the teachings of the Catholic Church – after a period of doubt in her late forties, which had coincided with her going on to HRT – just as long as you took them with a pinch of salt. And as the mother of four, having grown accustomed to constant demands and frustrations and irritations, Mrs Donelly's pinch of salt was maybe a little larger than most – more like a palm of salt, in fact. She had found that if you ignored a problem for long enough it usually went away – usually, but not always.

Mrs Donelly did sometimes stay in just to enjoy the peace and quiet in the house: she'd been known to wash her hair and have a bath and draw the curtains and put on her towelling dressing gown at two o'clock on a midweek afternoon, and lie on the sofa in the front room watching television, eating Rich Tea biscuits like there was no tomorrow. But that was an exception: she usually preferred to keep active.

There was all her council work, for starters, which took up most evenings and quite some time during the day.

Mrs Donelly was never going to be the best councillor the town had ever seen, but she cares about our town and she is honest, and these are rare qualities, particularly among our elected representatives. If she were really honest, Mrs Donelly would have to admit that she had become a councillor partly because of the prestige – in her own mind, if not others'. She sometimes found herself saying out loud, as she sat in her little old Austin Allegro outside the town hall, waiting to go in to chair a committee, 'Well, who'd have thought it?'

And who would have thought it? Mrs Donelly had left Central at fifteen without even completing her leaving certificate. She didn't have a certificate to her name, actually, apart from something awarded for attendance at the Happy Feet Tap and Ballet School, which she attended for a brief period when her family were flush and she was fourteen, and which is still going – under the guidance of the mighty Dot McLaughlin, sister of the famous tap-dancing McLaughlin twins, and ninety-five this year and still a size eight – up at the top of High Street, over what's now the Poundstretcher and which was once Storey's, 'Gifts, Novelties, Travel Goods, Jewellery and Coal', a shop which reverberated for years to the sound of Dot McLaughlin calling out 'Heel, Toe, Heel, Toe' and Miss Buchanan banging out a polonaise on the piano.

Mrs Donelly's achievements may not have been certificated, but they were many: she had prepared three meals a day for a family of six for over twenty years, and continued to do the same for herself and Mr Donelly to the present and into the foreseeable future. She knew how to darn socks. She could sew, and had made curtains and bedspreads, and at one time had even made the clothes for the children. She paid the bills and balanced the budget. She had taken up and given up smoking, and she had seen every film made starring Paul Newman. When she was eight years old she'd read out a poem

on the BBC, with Uncle Mac, on *Children's Hour*. She was a
good wife and mother – a good person and adventurous in
her way. (A few years ago she had even bought, but never
worn, some revealing underwear from a catalogue from one
of Frank Gilbey's lingerie shops, a catalogue which some of
the younger girls had been passing around at the Health Centre.
The garments remained in her bedside drawer, however. She
was worried Mr Donelly might take a heart attack.) Above
all, to her greatest satisfaction, she had become a councillor,
elected in 1999, standing as an Independent, with a large –
1026 – majority, so even now, in her retirement, she was busy.

On Mondays there were council meetings, and she liked to
get her shopping done and clean the house, and then things
really picked up on a Tuesday with more meetings and Aqua-
Aerobics and a visit to her mother – Veronica, ninety and
double incontinent, but her mind still as sharp as a razor – in
the sheltered accommodation off Gilbey's roundabout on the
ring road. Wednesdays there weren't usually any meetings so
she might change her books at the library and meet her friend
Greta for coffee in Scarpetti's. Thursdays she had her Italian
conversation class with Francesca Scarpetti at the Institute, a
class Mrs Donelly had been attending now on and off for
about five years, with no discernible improvement in her accent
or any increase in vocabulary, and despite the fact that, like
most of the class, she had never been and had no intention of
ever going to Italy. People attended the class mostly to meet
old friends and to listen to Francesca speaking Italian: it
sounded so romantic, even when she was only asking the price
of a pizza. When she opened her mouth and those sweet words
came out, for a moment time seemed to stop, and you'd forget
about your troubles and about our small town, and you could
imagine you were somewhere else, somewhere bigger and
better, with someone else, and possibly not even yourself. At
the end of each course the class would all drive up to the city
and go to an Italian restaurant, where Francesca insisted they

order in Italian, and they would sit around drinking red wine and laughing, and they might as well have been in some piazza in Rome, or in a villa overlooking fields of sunflowers. The course was well worth the money, just for that one night. It was worth it just to be able to speak Italian to the waiters, unembarrassed, with no husbands around, to have the waiters lean forward, smiling at your accent, and have them nod and say *si, si, signorina*, and *va bene*, and *desidera?*

On Fridays she had to miss council meetings because she took Emma and Amber for the day, her son Mickey's two girls, aged just three and eighteen months, while his wife Brona went to the Institute, where she is training to be a beautician. Brona was always very well turned-out, and the children were too, and Mrs Donelly was proud to push the little ones round town, although she did not really approve of Brona's spending so much on the children's clothes – hers had always made do with second-hand and hand-me-downs – and she also wished that Brona would lay off a little on the tanning. Brona visited Lorraine's Bridal Salon and Tan Shop once every six weeks for what Lorraine called the 'St. Tropez', the kind of tan usually only available on the Riviera in high season, but available in our town all year round. The St. Tropez is a full body treatment that involves exfoliation, body moisturisation, application of the cream and body buffing. It costs £45 for a half-body and £80 for the whole, and Mickey had been so appalled after the first time, when Brona had returned looking like someone had picked her up by the legs and dipped her in chocolate that he'd agreed to pay the extra for the full monty. The colour can be customised and Lorraine had got it about right after the first few treatments. Brona has explained to Mrs Donelly several times that the effect of the St. Tropez was more realistic – and thus more expensive – because it contained a special green pigment, which avoided the orange tinge of some cheaper, inferior tanning applications, and Mrs Donelly did not have the heart to disagree, or to tell Brona otherwise.

On Saturdays Mrs Donelly always made it to the club with Mr Donelly for a few drinks and sometimes a meal, and on Sunday nights she liked to go to the cinema with her old friend Pat, just like they had done when they were teenagers, growing up in town together, before the children had got in the way and they'd missed about twenty-five years of films between them. Fortunately it wasn't too difficult to pick it up again.

In the old days, of course, they'd have gone to one of the three cinemas in the centre of town, the Salamanca, the Tontine, or the Troxy, and then they'd have visited a coffee bar afterwards, maybe the old ABC Espresso Bar on Bridge Street, which boasted the town's first Gaggia espresso machine and offered not only coffee but also Ferrarelle mineral water and Hill's Gingerette and West Indian Lime Juice. In the ABC they'd have then removed their coats to show off their tight-fitting pink cashmere jumpers to boys with quiffs wearing skinny ties, who would be listening to Frank Sinatra and Frankie Lymon and the Teenagers on the jukebox. Now they wore mostly pastels and leisurewear, and went to the multiplex on the ring road – the Salamanca, the Tontine and the Troxy all having been demolished and replaced with a Supa Valu supermarket (the Salamanca), a car park which has recently, controversially, become Pay and Display (the Tontine), despite a campaign in the *Impartial Recorder*, and forty starter homes in a development called the Troxies (the Troxy).*

It was the destruction of the cinemas, those sacred places, that really made Mrs Donelly sit up and take notice, and

* Victor Russell, a supercilious man with a Hitler moustache, who was the owner-manager of the Troxy and who wore a white tuxedo every day of his working life, was convicted in 1989 of arson and fraud: he'd torched the Troxy, trying to cash in on a £25,000 insurance policy. He died in disgrace, in prison up in the city, his moustache intact but his tuxedo long since gone. His wife, Doreen, and daughter, Olivia, now live abroad, near Nîmes, in France, where Olivia is a dealer in art deco antiques. Doreen tells her story in a moving interview with Minnie Mitchell in the *Impartial Recorder*, 22 August 2001.

begin to take an interest in local politics. She was too late to save the cinemas and too late, probably, to save the town. By the time she was elected, the ring road had already been built and Bloom's was under construction. Too late, Mrs Donelly realised that the town she loved was being torn apart and destroyed, and that behind its destruction was the man she had once loved: Frank Gilbey.

Mrs Donelly and Frank Gilbey had been a courting couple, years ago. They were the couple that everyone talked about and everyone wanted to be. They used to go to the big dances at the Quality Hotel and Morelli's, the dance hall at the top of High Street, which burnt down the year that man walked on the moon and which is now Roy's Discount Designer Clothing Warehouse. Even in those days there was something special about Frank: he had a bigger quiff than the other boys and his drainpipe trousers were tighter.

From a distance – a short distance, naturally, in our town – Mrs Donelly had watched Frank Gilbey's inexorable rise, with his lovely wife, her old friend Irene, alongside him, and there were times, of course, when she wished it could have been her: the foreign cruises, the trips to America, their famous weekend city breaks, the beautiful clothes. She'd been into the church, once, when Frank's and Irene's daughter Lorraine had married the bad Scotsman, and the flowers! The flowers alone must have cost nearly £1000. The town had never seen the like. Mrs Donelly sat at the back and imagined herself as the mother of the bride, dressed smartly, though not in the coral pink chosen by Irene, she thought. The two-inch heels were a mistake, also, for the larger lady.

It would never have worked, though, Mrs Donelly and Frank. They were incompatible, not least because she was a Catholic and back then it still mattered. Frank was a Protestant, which is probably what she liked about him: his was definitely a Protestant quiff and Protestant trousers.

Mrs Donelly saw a lot of him still, around town, although

less so as the years went by and their paths diverged – hers into her little job at the Health Centre, and the children and holidays in a caravan by the sea, and his into property management and his homes in several counties and abroad.

She didn't exactly become a councillor because Frank Gilbey was a councillor, but it did give her pleasure to feel herself his equal and adversary, and she enjoyed seeing him at meetings and in committees.

Frank Gilbey, of course, had other reasons for becoming involved in local politics: sentiment was not an issue for Big Frank Gilbey. Frank always described the town hall to Mrs Gilbey as 'the best club in town' and certainly it was more exclusive than the golf club, although it consisted largely of the same people. The difference was that in the golf club all you got to do was play golf: in the council you got to wield power. Sometimes Mrs Donelly and Frank got to sit on the same committees and wield power together, which was more fun than playing eighteen holes and a long way from necking in the back of the Troxy.

These days, at the multiplex Pat and Mrs Donelly would buy their tickets from a machine, Pat would buy a tub of salted popcorn and never eat it all, and they'd sit close to the screen and watch the film, and then they would drive home again to their husbands, who preferred TV, or the pub. Some of the actors had changed on the big screen since the old days, and there was a lot more of what Mrs Donelly called 'sexy talk', which covered talk about both sex and violence, but the stories were pretty much the same as they had been back in the 1950s and 1960s.*

* She missed musicals, though – musicals seemed to have gone out of fashion. *Hello, Dolly!* she'd enjoyed, back in the old days, with Barbra Streisand, and *Sweet Charity* even, with Shirley MacLaine, although that was a bit weird. And Liza Minnelli, *Cabaret*, of course. They were classics. But you couldn't get to see a good musical in our town these days for love nor money, unless you counted Colette Bradley's amateur youth theatre productions of *Fiddler*

Mrs Donelly wondered sometimes if being in the cinema was a bit like what it was going to be like being dead – watching other people's lives unfold and everything always working out for the best. She hoped so.

It was in the cinema that she'd first discovered the lump, a few months ago. She knew what it was straightaway. She was reaching across to get a handful of Pat's popcorn and it was the angle of the reach that did it – her right arm stretching across to the left, hand outstretched. She wished she hadn't now. She'd rather not have known. She wished she'd never reached for the popcorn. She'd never really approved of Pat's popcorn anyway: she thought cinema popcorn was a waste of money. For years she'd been trying to persuade Pat to make her own at home and take it to the pictures in some Tupperware hidden in her handbag. But Pat said the popcorn was all part of the fun: Pat did not believe in stinting, even though she was a Protestant. Unlike Mrs Donelly, Pat was not the kind of person who set out on an adventure with a wrap of sandwiches. Pat was the kind of person who believed that on life's journey you could always find a little place that would happily do some sandwiches for you. Mrs Donelly, having been on holiday several times to the Isle of Man with four children, knew this not to be the case, but she didn't say anything.

Mrs Donelly had not told Pat about the lump. She was starting the chemo the week after Christmas. They'd decided not to tell anyone. They weren't going to tell the children for a bit. They didn't want to spoil Christmas.

While Mrs Donelly was at her emergency council committee meeting, Mr Donelly was out in the Christmas Eve sleet, walking

---

on the Roof and *Oliver!* at the Good Templar Hall, which are OK but which are lacking in a certain something – lavish sets, for example, and costumes, lighting, full orchestras, Topol, Ron Moody; pretty much everything, in fact, that makes a good musical a good musical.

the dog. He walks with her for about two hours every day, come rain or shine. After raising four children, Mr Donelly does not view a dog as a burden: on the contrary, he says, a dog, after children, is a pleasure. It's a breeze. The worst a dog can do is bite and shit, and not usually at the same time, and a dog never asks you for money, and also you don't have to wipe a dog's arse, although the council would've liked you to: any attempt to get dog owners to poop-scoop in the People's Park or to keep a dog on a leash was viewed with scorn by Mr Donelly. He regarded councillors as meddlers, on the whole, apart from his wife, of course, who was simply well-meaning. The whole point of having a dog, according to Mr Donelly, was that you could let it run around and shit anywhere: in a town where even the slightest misdemeanour could find you on the inside pages of the *Impartial Recorder*, dogs represented the wild side, the acceptable face of the animal in man, the beast inside, your only opportunity to act like a lord of misrule and to demonstrate to the rest of the world exactly what you thought of it: rubbish. Allowing your dog to cock its leg on a few council flowers was a means of self-expression for Mr Donelly, and clearly better than running amok around town mooning at police officers, breaking windows, fighting, scratching cars, stealing lawnmowers and bicycles, and weeing in shop doorways, which is what most of the town seemed to prefer to do these days to let off steam. Why the council couldn't have focused more of their attention on that, rather than persecuting innocent dog owners, he did not know.*

Mr Donelly had several times explained to his friend Davey Quinn – Davey Senior – his theory of the therapeutic effects of dog owning and he had even gone so far as to suggest giving pets to hardened criminals in prisons, in order to assist them in their rehabilitation. Davey Senior hadn't owned a pet

---

* For a full account of the ongoing dog-fouling controversy, see the *Impartial Recorder*, 'Letters to the Editor', 1982–Present.

since he was a child growing up on the Georgetown Road, when he'd won a goldfish at the town fair, and on his return from the fair his brother Dennis – son number six to Davey's number seven – had promptly flushed the fish down the outside toilet. When Davey Senior had protested, Dennis had fought with him and forced his head into the toilet bowl, to allow little Davey to try to save the poor fish, a fish which Davey had decided to call Lucky. Even now, fifty years later, when he drove past the sewage plant up past the ring road Davey found himself wondering about the fate of that fish: he wondered if maybe it had made it out into open seas.*
Davey's brother Dennis had eventually ended up in prison and he remained altogether a bad lot, and Davey had therefore a rather pessimistic view about the relationship between man and beasts: he believed that Mr Donelly's rehabilitation scheme was probably unworkable. But a pet was still an unequivocal good, according to Mr Donelly, and a doddle.

* This, of course, seems unlikely, but it's not impossible: there are happy endings, even for fish and the proverbial tin soldier. On 19 May 1991 the *Impartial Recorder* ran a story about Monica Hawkins (née Williams), from the Longfields Estate, who went on holiday to the Isle of Man in 1971, aged twenty-one. While swimming in the sea she lost a solid-silver locket which had been a gift to her from her mother, and which contained a small gold tooth, her father's only mortal remains after he'd been cremated at what was then the town's newly opened crematorium on Prospect Road. Twenty years later, at a car boot sale in the car park at the Church of the Cross and the Passion, not half a mile from the crematorium on Prospect Road, Mrs Hawkins, by that time twice married and twice widowed, happened to be going through a pile of costume jewellery in an old Quality Street tin when something caught her eye – a locket just like the one she'd lost all those years ago. And on opening the locket she found . . . yes, the gold tooth. The stallholder could offer no explanation of how she had acquired the locket – she bought bags of stuff from men in pubs – and after Mrs Hawkins's death her daughter Joanne bequeathed the tooth to P. W. Grieve, the dentist who as a young man had made the gold tooth for Mr Williams in the first place, back in the 1960s, and who now has the tooth proudly on display in his waiting room, along with a bible open at the passage, 'The law of thy mouth is better unto me than thousands of gold and silver' (Psalms 119:72).

'She's easier to keep than your mother,' he liked to joke, sometimes, to his children.

She's called Rusty, the dog – Mrs Donelly is Mary – and she's sixteen and her eyesight's gone, more or less, so Mr Donelly lets her watch TV with him in the evenings, with the Ceefax subtitles on, and he gives her a hot-water bottle in winter. She's part of the family, part Airedale and part Irish Terrier, which is a cute combination, and a few years ago she won a rosette in our town dog show, in the category The Dog With The Kindliest Expression, and rightly so. Her expression is, in fact, much kinder than a lot of the people in our town, so she may not just be The Dog With The Kindliest Expression, she may, in fact, be in possession of our town's Kindliest Expression, full stop – quite an achievement for a mongrel. Mrs Donelly wonders sometimes if Mr Donelly loves that dog more than he loves his own children. It's possible.

When he arrived back home from their customary walk – down to Bridge Street and Main Street, past the Quality Hotel, then up High Street and into the People's Park – Mr Donelly settled the dog into its basket in the corner of the garage, a basket tucked in underneath all the jars and the tins and the tools and the wood offcuts of a lifetime, which might come in handy one day, squeezed in tight between a workbench that used to be the Donelly kitchen table, and Mr Donelly's little Honda 50 with its grey and white trim and its seat bound with masking tape. Mr Donelly hasn't been out on the Honda for nearly two years, since he'd taken a tumble on Gilbey's roundabout. 'The Nicest Things,' they used to say, 'Happen on a Honda,' which may have been true thirty or forty years ago, but now there was so much traffic, even on the ring road, you were lucky if you made it unscathed up to the DIY stores or the Plough and the Stars, and then made it back home again safely.

'I'm not identifying your body when you fall off that thing again and end up dead in hospital, all squashed,' said Mrs

Donelly. 'It's time to hang up your helmet, mister.' You didn't argue with Mrs Donelly.

The helmet hung on a nail over the dog basket.

Saying goodnight to the dog and locking up the garage, Mr Donelly made his way towards the house, his childless, empty house. He squeezed past the wheelie bin with its stick-on number – another ridiculous council regulation, as if anyone would want to steal it – and past the pile of flagstones that he'd borrowed, or requisitioned, in an act of defiance, from the council when they'd been doing the road-widening scheme at the bottom of Main Street, and he peered in at his kitchen window. The kitchen was spotless, as always, the way Mrs Donelly liked to leave it, almost as if no one lived there. The blue washing-up bowl was upended on the drainer, next to the sink, a residue of water and suds on the stainless steel the only sign of recent human activity.

He then went round to the front of the house, to put the car up on the drive. The headlights lit up the windows – new windows, bay windows, which were uPVC and which he'd put in himself when they bought the place from the council. He hasn't yet made good around the brickwork, but the windows look OK: they fit the hole. There's a carriage lamp, and a few shrubs in pots but apart from that the place looks pretty much the same as when they'd moved in as a young family thirty years ago. He can still remember the day as if it were yesterday: their first house after all the flats. He remembered Mrs Donelly marching up and down the stairs with Tim and Jackie – they were babies then – laughing and singing. Their own staircase: that was something.

He locked up the car and went to look through the front window, at his own front room, where hardly anything had changed in all that time: there were the same old ornaments on the windowsill and on the mantelpiece over the gas fire: a small mahogany elephant; a crystal vase; a miniature teapot; a Smurf; the 'May Our Lady Watch Over Your Marriage' imitation-mahogany-veneer plaque with a very attractive-looking BVM in gilt relief on the wall; the same three-piece suite, too big for the room; the same imitation Christmas tree.

He noticed a curtain twitch next door: the new neighbours. For a moment he thought it was old Mrs Nesbit but Mrs Nesbit no longer lived next door – she'd gone first to live with her daughter and then on to the big sheltered accommodation in the sky. They hadn't really got to know the new lot: they kept themselves to themselves. They'd let the garden go.

He decided not to go into the house. Mrs Donelly wouldn't be back from her meeting for another half an hour or so. He didn't want to be in an empty house on Christmas Eve.

So he walked on, down to the end of the road, and turned left.

The Church of the Cross and the Passion is a big, ugly, modern building with an untended patch of scrubland out back and a social club with a car park with a wire fence and empty kegs piled up outside. It would have had a nice view of the People's Park, if you could see out of any of the windows, but the stained glass gets in the way.

Inside the church Mr Donelly sat down at a pew near the altar rail, where the crib was all set up, and there they were, the Holy Family, in that celebrated post-partum pose.

Mr Donelly has lived all his life in our town. He was taught at the Assumption junior school – a tiny little Victorian building down Cromac Street, off High Street, with outside toilets and two demountables, a building which has only added graffiti since Mr Donelly attended. He was taught at the school that Jesus was born in a stable at the inn, and that oxen and asses dropped to their knees in worship, and that there were Three Wise Men, and shepherds – the traditional Christmas story with all the trimmings. His teacher at the Assumption was a nun called Sister Hughes and he loved her, as all the children loved her – a dear old lady telling wonderful stories to boys and girls who didn't yet know the difference between fantasy and belief. Sister Hughes was a good person, a woman who knitted at break times and lunchtimes, making ecumenical woolly hats, mostly, for our town's famous ecumenical charity, the Mission to Seamen, a charity founded by a Presbyterian minister, the Reverend Thomas MacGeagh, and a Catholic priest, Father Thomas Barre, known locally as the Two Toms, who in 1912, after the sinking of the *Titanic*, had decided to found a charity which would minister to seamen of many denominations and faiths and of none, and which would demonstrate to them God's care and love at a time when He Himself seemed to be absent from the high seas.* Our town is thirty miles from the sea, far enough for us to think of ourselves as landlocked, but close enough for seagulls to make it into the dump for scavenging, and for most of us to enjoy at least one day trip in the summer. Sister Hughes had died mid-hat, when Mr Donelly was eight years old, and he was terribly upset. You

---

* The Woolly Hat for Seamen Scheme has long since been abandoned: the Mission now seeks instead to provide every sailor of every nation with a small, waterproof, shockproof CD player and an evangelistic CD containing hymns, sermons and prayers. The original knitting patterns and accompanying pamphlets can, however, be consulted in the Mission to Seamen Special Collection at the library – contact Divisional Librarian Philomena Rocks for details. A typical 1952 pattern and outline reads thus:

WOOLLY HAT FOR SEAMEN

Ladies, keep up the good work! Not only do these colourful hats provide much needed protection from the harsh sea winds, but also a cover for many a bible smuggled on board ship bound for pagan lands. Every one of us can share in God's ministry to the needy simply by picking up our knitting needles! So don't hesitate, ladies, get knitting today, to advance the kingdom of God!
Pattern for Hat:
3 balls 20g d.k. wool.
Using No. 10 needles cast on 132 sts.
1st and every K.2 P.2.
Continue until work measures 2½ inches.
Change to size 8 needles and continue to double rib until work measures 9½ inches.

might ask, what is death to an eight-year-old – what can he possibly understand about it? Well, death is presumably exactly the same for an eight-year-old as it is for the rest of us, nothing more and nothing less: it's a complete shock.

One of the other big shocks in Mr Donelly's life was later to be told at secondary school that it wasn't a stable at all and it may not even have been an inn, and that there is, in fact, no record of any oxen and asses dropping to their knees, and that the Three Wise Men were astrologers, and that the whole Nativity thing was put about by St Francis to lure ignorant and simple people into the Church. Mr Donelly had attended St Gall's secondary school – a stone's throw from his parents' house on the Georgetown Road, a slum area, really, now demolished and the rubble used for infill on the ring road. His teacher of religious instruction at the school was a former priest, a bitter man called Conroy, who was married with a child and who had a mind like a cat's, and who treated the boys like idiots. If Mr Donelly had ever wanted to date the beginnings of his confusion about the person of God and the mediating role of the priesthood then he could have identified Mr Conroy's classes: first lesson on a Monday and last lesson on Fridays, back in the 1950s. Mr Conroy's classes had begun the long slow withdrawing of Mr Donelly's own personal sea of faith, which seemed to have left him washed up here and now, staring at the crib, looking hard at the figures of Jesus, Mary and Joseph.

Shape top:
1st row *K.3 tog. K.9 repeat from * to end (110 sts).
2nd and every alt. row Purl.
3rd row *K.3 tog. K.7 repeat from * to end (88 sts).
5th row *K.3 tog. K.5 repeat from * to end (66 sts).
7th row *K.3 tog. K.3 repeat from * to end (44 sts).
9th row *K.3 tog. K.1 repeat from * to end (22 sts).
11th row *K.2 tog to end (11 sts).
Thread wool through sts, draw up and fasten. Sew seam.

51

He looked hard at Joseph. Mr Donelly had always felt sorry for Joseph. He could identify with Joseph. Joseph was a minor player in the gospel story – he hardly got a look in at Christmas. Joseph's beard and gown were all chipped, showing the white plaster underneath – he looked unkempt and uncared for. He had blank eyes and a doleful countenance. Mr Donelly tried to imagine what it would be like being Joseph – he must have had a pretty difficult time of it, when you think about it, human nature being what it is, probably having to put up with a lot of snide remarks and ribbing about Mary and the Spirit of God down a back alley. Mr Donelly read a book once, years ago, one of the only books he'd ever read, which had rather put him off – *The Holy Blood and the Holy Grail*, or *Chariots of the Gods*, or *The Coming of the Cosmic Christ*, one of those books which he'd picked up at a church jumble sale – which claimed that Jesus was fathered by a Roman legionary called Pipus, or Titus, or Bob, or something. Mr Donelly didn't want to believe it then and he doesn't want to believe it now, and he hopes for Joseph's sake that he never had to hear such ugly rumours and instinctively he leans forward over the crib – checking over his shoulder to make sure no one is watching – and he covers Joseph's ears, pinching his plaster head between forefinger and thumb. Joseph's head is tiny.

Then Mr Donelly gazes up at the altar over the top of Joseph's head and he imagines all the relics tucked away in there. He imagines all the visitors starting to turn up at the inn and pestering poor old Joseph – nutters, most of them, no doubt, and all of them looking for souvenirs.

He looks at the Baby Jesus in the manger – the centrepiece, as it were, the Nativity's cut-crystal vase on the sideboard. Jesus's face has been touched up so many times with pink paint that his features are flaking and unrecognisable. And then he looks at Mary, who's in good condition, hardly a mark on her, although her robes are a little faded, and Mr Donelly suddenly remembers all the other stories he was taught by Sister Hughes at school, about rosemary acquiring its fragrance after Mary supposedly hung out the Christ Child's clothes on a rosemary bush and all the stuff about the Holy Babe being rocked in His cradle by angels while Mary got on with her needlework. It was all just folklore, of course, but still, staring at the pathetic figurines and remembering the stories, shaking with cold in the vast dry spaces of the church, Mr Donelly can understand why it's all lasted, the whole Nativity thing, why it's outdone all the pagan myths and all the other competing mumbo-jumbo. It's because of the newborn Babe, and because of the poverty of the Holy Family and the slaughter of the Innocents, and all the supposed business in the stable, and the figure of Mary. It is the perfect image of warmth and shelter from what we know to be the cruelty and hatred and sheer indifference of the world, the same now as it was then. If nothing else, the Nativity was a nice idea.*

Mr Donelly is not a man much given to self-reflection and he hasn't allowed himself to worry too much about the future. But right now he wishes his children were here with him for Christmas. He wonders how many more Christmases they'll all have together. He sits there for a long time, and for the first time in a long time, like all the children of our town at Christmas, Mr Donelly found himself praying.

Mrs Donelly had long ago given up on prayer and she had just two wishes now before she died: she would have liked to have seen her daughter Jackie married; and she'd have liked to prevent Frank Gilbey from destroying any more of the town. The first of these wishes had yet to be fulfilled. But in the second she might just have succeeded.

* An unorthodox view of the Virgin Birth which Mr Donelly happens to share with Barry McClean, the Gnostics, David Hume, Friedrich Schleiermacher, certain twentieth-century German theologians and the former Bishop of Durham, David Jenkins.

As chairman of the Planning Committee it was Mrs Donelly's responsibility to examine all planning applications and she had taken great pleasure this evening in being able to turn down an application by Frank Gilbey for a change of use for the Quality Hotel, one of his companies' recent acquisitions. In her opinion, and in the opinion of her committee, and even in the opinion of the town centre manager, the weak-jawed and usually pusillanimous Alan Burnside, a man with pure clear jelly for a spine and cream-thickened porridge for brains, the town did not need more luxury apartment blocks. What it needed was a meeting place and town centre space accessible to the public, where the public would want to gather as a community. What it needed, in other words, was what it had with the old Quality Hotel.

Frank had already heard rumours from friends on the committee that this was going to be the decision, so he wasn't shocked, and he'd already spoken to his partners, to Bob Savory and to the people who needed to know, and he had instructed his solicitor, Martin Phillips, to begin preparing the appeal, but on Christmas Eve, as Mr Donelly knelt up from his prayers and Mrs Donelly got into her Austin Allegro and looked up into the sky, and thanked her lucky stars, it felt to her, for a moment, like victory, if not a miracle.

It would have been nice if I could tell you now that there'd been some snow, just to finish things off, but I cannot tell a lie, and God and the weather are not always answerable to our needs and desires, and I'm afraid sometimes sleet is as good as it gets. There was sleet.

4

The Dump

*Describing an auspicious occasion – a party in a pub
– which demonstrates the wholesomeness of life
amidst the usual waste and humiliation*

You wouldn't have thought so, but the range of temperatures
here in town can be pretty extreme. It can get all the way up
to the seventies on occasion in July and even on a winter's
afternoon, when the sun's out, you sometimes see young men
sitting outside pubs in their shirtsleeves. In February, on a
good day, on a bright day, outside the Castle Arms it's like a
playground: little groups, little huddles, jackets off, joking and
having fun. In our town such an opportunity is not to be
missed: the sun here always tends to go to our heads.

But, alas, the unseasonably warm weather has not been
good for my old friend Billy Nibbs: in the heat, the smell
coming out of the skips and those big metal bins can be pretty
stiff. In the summer you can actually smell the dump from the
car park outside the Plough and the Stars, which is two round-
abouts downwind, where all attempts at landscaping have
failed to solve the problem. A few scented-leaf pelagoniums
on the windowsills and some sweet william outside in huge
terracotta-plastic planters are no match for the stench of the
accumulated waste of our town. Goodness knows what people
are putting in there: Billy spends half his time redirecting

gardeners with grass cuttings to the GREEN WASTE ONLY bins, and the other half directing householders with stinking black plastic bags away from the NO FOOD WASTE bins. People do seem to be ashamed about their rubbish, or confused. There's been talk of recycling – one of the town's councillors, Mrs Donelly, no less, who has a cousin in Canada, is very keen; she says that's what they do over there – but whether this will solve the problem of people's shame or increase it, it's difficult to say. No one wants to be reminded of their own waste: to have to separate it all out would simply be embarrassing. We'd rather future generations sort it all out for us – and Billy, of course.

It may just be the sweat and the bins, then, that make Billy smell so, but it may also be the ham. Billy Nibbs is addicted to ham. Absolutely addicted; there's no other way to describe it. He lives by himself and has never been that interested in cooking, and after a few years he found he'd got into a routine. Every night on the way home from work he buys his bacon for his breakfast from Tom Hines, our one remaining butcher, and every morning he eats it straight from the frying pan, mopping up the juices with a slice of bread, dispensing neatly with the need for a knife, or a plate and, indeed, for any washing up whatsoever, since the frying pan will always do for the next day, and the next; and then for lunch he has a ham sandwich with mustard, and for dinner he usually eats at his mum's, or at Scarpetti's, the Italian late-night café in Market Street, which is no longer owned and run by Italians, Mr Scarpetti and his family having eventually returned to their native land like most incomers within a short time of having arrived here, once they realise that our town is, in fact, like every other small town on the face of the earth and no better than what they've left behind, unless, of course, it's a civil war or state torture, and even then it can be a tough decision to decide to stay. We have no actual culture to speak of and no cuisine, unless you count the tray bakes and the microwave morning sandwiches from the Brown and Yellow Cake Shop. We can boast no local beer even, let alone a wine, and we have no town square, our festivals extend only to the traditional half-hearted summer parade and fireworks – Frank Gilbey's attempts to organise a jazz festival a few years ago having ended in disaster – and we are not known for the warmest of welcomes.* But Mr Hemon, who now owns Scarpetti's – and who is Bosnian – has stuck it out for eight years and it looks as though he's going to stay, and he does a fair imitation of Billy's mum's sausage, chips and beans. In honour of his predecessors Mr Hemon offers espresso coffee – two heaps of instant instead of one – and keeps a bowl of Parmesan on each table, along with the usual condiments, and believe me, if you've never sprinkled grated hard Italian cheese on one of Scarpetti's legendary big breakfasts with two fried slices, then you really haven't lived, in our town.[†]

---

[*] We were renowned at one time, of course, for our annual Bicycle Polo tournament, held out on the fields that people called the Bleaches, which were used many years ago for bleaching linen, but which have long since been buried under the Frank Gilbey roundabout on the ring road. The tournament had been founded by Field Marshal Sir John Hillock in 1933. Like Tolstoy, the Field Marshal took to cycling in old age and became an enthusiastic advocate of the sport. His bicycle polo team, the Rovers, sponsored by Raleigh, had achieved some small national fame, and the tournament had brought crowds to the town every May Day until 1947, when tragedy struck: a young man, Elvin Thomas, just twenty-one years old, who had survived Tobruk, died from a punctured lung sustained from an injury caused by a loose spoke during the tournament finals. The Field Marshal disbanded the team and bicycle polo has never been played again in town.

The highlight of Frank Gilbey's inaugural and one-and-only week-long jazz festival, meanwhile, a few years ago, was a performance on the Saturday night by Chris Barber and his band, the keepers of the flame of British trad jazz. No one at all had turned up to hear them play and they went home without even opening their instrument cases. Frank had had to bail out the festival from his own pocket.

[†] Tiberio Scarpetti and his family lasted here for nearly ten years, which is not a bad innings, actually, for incomers, but unfortunately they were ten years too late for the worldwide craze for espresso bars, which had orginally sent the older Scarpetti brothers out into the world to make their fortunes

I think maybe it is all the pork that gives Billy that funny smell, because he smells the same all year round, so it can't just be the heat. As you get older there's no doubt food can play havoc with your system: Davey Quinn, I know, for example, hasn't eaten a Chinese takeaway for years, after a night out in south London which started in a pub, went on to a club, and ended up with a couple of tin-foil tubs of hot and spicy Cantonese which wouldn't usually have bothered him, certainly not while in his teens or twenties, but which left him in his early thirties unable to breathe and writhing around, choking up whole sweet-and-sour pork balls, and he ended up in casualty having his stomach pumped, and he can only remember that the stuff they pumped in looked black and the stuff they pumped out was yellow, and he stank for weeks afterwards. He has never again touched chicken in a

---

– Domenico to Australia, Bartolo to Los Angeles – and twenty years too early for the coffee shop revival, which meant that in the end Tiberio, the youngest of three brothers, who had a lot to prove but who had drawn the historical and geographical short straw, returned to his home town of Termoli in Italy with nothing except his Gaggia machine and a lot of unsold stock of fizzy mineral water and canned ravioli. Tiberio had worked like a dog for years, turning what was once Thomas Bell's dank, dark little hardware shop, 'Whistle and Bells: All Your Hardware Requirements', on Market Street into our own local little Italy, all black-and-white tiled floors, indoor plants and mirrored walls, with a state-of-the-art red Formica counter. He held out for a long time against offering chips with everything and all-day frys, but in the end he gave in and lost heart. He'd kept a bowl on the counter for tips and when a decade had passed without a single person ever placing so much as a penny in the bowl he knew it was time to pack up and leave: this was not a place Tiberio intended to grow old. His daughter Francesca remains, of course, married to Tommy Kahan, but Tiberio has never been back to visit, has never even been tempted; he has sworn never to return. The sign above the door of the café still says Scarpetti's, but apart from the Parmesan and the Nescafé espressos there remains no other indication that this was ever the town's Italian quarter: Pukka Pies™ have long since replaced the ravioli. Mr Hemon's only improvement on Tiberio's original decor has been to put up tourist board posters on the walls showing scenic sights in Bosnia, but all meals come with chips.

black-bean sauce: the food of all our youths denied for ever to him. I myself – like most of us – have had to give up kebabs.

Davey waited a while after his return to town before calling in to see Billy Nibbs, and he hardly recognised him when he finally caught up with him – he had to do a double take. Billy these days looks exactly like his father, Hugh – right down to the thick black beard and the shiny steel-toe capped boots. Hugh ran one of the four butchers that used to exist on Main Street – not a single one remaining now, leaving only Tom Hines on High Street, who is not and never was the best, whose sausages are thin and greasy, whose chops and mince are too fatty, whose joints are overpriced and who has abandoned all pretence of providing dripping, black pudding, or the cheaper offal, the standard fare of the traditional family butcher, and who has opted instead to sell his butcher's soul for the likes of hot and spicy Cantonese ribs, ready-stuffed chickens and pre-wrapped bacon from a wholesaler based in Swindon. Hugh was much the better butcher and famously bearded, a man who'd hung on to his facial hair right through the Seventies, when beards were still popular and even admired, when even Tom Hines had worn one, to hide his many opulent chins, and right on into the Eighties and through the Nineties, when beards became more scarce and rather frowned upon, certainly by people buying meat, perhaps because there was always the suspicion of some flecks, some tiny filaments stuck somewhere in there, although Hugh was scrupulous about washing the beard every night with Johnson & Johnson baby shampoo, to retain its softness and to try to be rid of that distinctive high, minty, slightly gamey smell of freshly butchered meat.

Hugh's dying wish, that he'd had written into his Last Will and Testament, was a surprise for his wife, Jean, who'd begged him for years to update his image: 'I INSTRUCT,' ran the rubric, 'on the event of my predeceasing my wife, that my beard be shaved.' It was not the strangest request or instruction that the family solicitor, Martin Phillips, had had to incorporate into a will – you'd be surprised what secrets you can hide from your family and what you might want eventually to reveal. Even us little people can keep big secrets. In his cups and among friends, when he'd loosened up after a few holes and a few gin and tonics in the golf club, Martin Phillips would sometimes boast of being the keeper of the keys to the skeleton closets of the town, but he never revealed his secrets and he never told tales.* No one would have believed him anyway.

When Hugh died, Martin Phillips carried out his instructions to the letter – he brought in Tommy Morris, the barber on Kilmore Avenue, our last proper barber, who refuses not only women but who won't cut children's hair either, not until they're sixteen and old enough to decide themselves exactly how short they want to have it, and who usually charges

---

* Actually, there was one that he let slip, when he was on a camping holiday with the children in the south of France, many years ago, and he'd got into conversation one evening with an expat at a bar near the campsite, and somewhere into the second shared bottle of the local red he confessed that he was a solicitor and started complaining to the stranger that the worst thing about his job was always being asked to pad people's insurance claims and become party to petty frauds, and he happened to mention to the expat the name of a client, Trevor Downs, from up there on the Longfields Estate, whom Martin believed to be faking his own whiplash injuries. Some time later the expat happened to mention this story on the telephone to his brother, who happened to be a minicab driver in Glasgow, who then happened to mention it in turn to someone in the back of his cab who turned out to be Trevor Downs's wife, Tara, in Glasgow on a shopping spree funded by her husband's considerable personal injury income. It may be a small world, but it's also a messy one, thank goodness: in the retelling of the story the name Trevor had been translated into Terry and the Downs had disappeared, which is the only thing that kept Martin Phillips from being sued and out of hospital. These days compensation claim racketeering is so widespread and so common, even in our town, where everyone seems to have slipped and fallen, that Martin no longer even bothers to mention it, even when abroad.

£2.50 for a wet shave with a cut-throat razor, although on this occasion he waived his fee – so when she visited her husband for the viewing, Jean was able to kiss Hugh's smooth cheek for the first time in thirty years and her tears glistened upon his face. At the crematorium Billy had read a poem. There was not a dry eye in the house.

Billy had always been a keen reader, *Marvel* comics mostly when we were young, but in his teens he had moved up to literature and it wasn't long before he started writing the stuff himself. I can still remember clearly the first poem he ever showed me. We must have been about fifteen. It began:

> The sun doesn't shine
> way down in the blue.
> In the deep sea of liquid
> dark memories come on cue.

I'm no literary critic, but I didn't think it was too bad and I told him, and he was encouraged, and so I feel now, on the publication of his first book, that I have in some small way been instrumental in the bringing to public attention of a new voice.

The launch party was just recently, in the Castle Arms.

Billy was there, of course. And his mum Jean was there. Davey Quinn was there. Bob Savory was there. Davey is effectively working for Bob now, in the kitchens at the Plough and the Stars, and it seems to be going OK. He's only working as a kitchen porter, part-time, but it's a start, it's something to help him get back on his feet. Davey must have worked at two dozen different jobs during the twenty years he was away, and in a dozen different places, so he was used to starting over. He did a lot of bar work at first, way back when, and then he was in Berlin for a while, when there was a lot of work on the sites after the Wall came down, and then he was in Holland on the tulip farms, and then he had a go on the campsites in France, and then it was back to England and the usual casual jobs, the temporary, the unsuitable and the strictly cash-in-hand: he was variously a care assistant, a windscreen fitter, a supermarket shelf stacker, a warehouseman and a bouncer. He drove a bus, he did security, he did landscaping and he did ventilation installation. He preferred jobs where he didn't have to think: he lasted only two weeks in tele-sales and he did his best to avoid computers. He worked for six months for Otis Elevators, which was a great job and was pretty much the summation of his career: full of ups and downs and going nowhere. It was a rootless existence and he wouldn't have had it any other way.

Things haven't been easy for Davey since he returned. He's been staying with his parents, and it's never good for a grown man to be thrown back upon the mercy of his parents. Mr and Mrs Quinn are good people but it's hard not to judge your children when they're under the same roof as you and you have to see them every day, and they're old enough to make their own mistakes but should know better, and Mr Quinn, Davey Senior, has had to bite his tongue on many occasions, from the breakfast table to lunchtime, dinner and beyond, and he is not a man used to having to withhold his opinions. He has been trying to persuade Davey to join him in the business, a painting and decorating business, a business started by Davey Senior's own father, Old Davey, way back in the 1920s, and a business which provides a good living for Davey Senior and no fewer than three of Davey's brothers, Daniel, Gerry and Craig. But Davey is holding out. One of the good things about leaving town all those years ago was that he didn't have to join the family business and now he's back he has no intention of doing so.

It's been a difficult couple of months, then, but Davey has picked up with a lot of old friends and a lot of them were at the book launch. Sammy the plumber was there. Francie McGinn was there. Francie's wife, Cherith, was hosting the

Ladies' Bible Night so she couldn't make it, but Bobbie Dylan was there, chatting to Francie, and it was nice to see them both looking so happy. Bob was between waitresses, so he was there too. All the old crowd. There was also a photographer from the *Impartial Recorder* – actually, *the* photographer, Joe Finnegan. Joe calls himself a 'lensman' and he likes to say – to himself, if no one else – 'I don't take sides: I take photos.' He'd turned to photography late in life, after the failure of his picture-framing business, a lovely quaint little place on Market Street, two doors down from Scarpetti's, where Joe never seemed to do much actual picture framing but instead spent most of his time chatting to old friends, and so, of course, he couldn't compete with the real professionals, with the much bigger and glitzier chain store, Picz 'N' Framz, when it opened up at Bloom's, which has its own car park and a trained staff, and a wide range of ready-framed prints and posters, in many sizes, ready to hang. Also, to be honest, Joe liked a drink.

So Joe was snapping away, half cut, with his Leica, which is not a hobby camera, but with which he somehow still managed to produce the standard hazy amateur mugshots for the paper: a grinning Billy with his arm draped round Frank Gilbey, our ex-mayor; a grinning Billy with his arm draped round Frank's daughter Lorraine, shying away; Billy with his mum; and Billy with all of us. It made a full-page spread in the *Impartial Recorder*. My favourite photograph of the evening is one of Billy cheek to cheek with our old English teacher, Miss McCormack, who'd made it to the launch even though she's moved up-country now to live with her sister, Eileen, and to look after their elderly father, the big Scotsman Dougal, in his declining years, even though she is strictly teetotal and claims not to have visited a pub since her sister's engagement party over forty years ago, a party that famously ended with Dougal McCormack, a fervent Methodist, knocking out his prospective son-in-law when the young man had indulged in rough talk and ribaldry. The young man seems consequently to have thought twice about marrying into the family, for the two sisters became spinsters and were frozen in time. Miss McCormack looks exactly the same now as she did twenty years ago when she was teaching us, which may be proof, as she had always insisted, that literature is one of the higher virtues and is good for you, like classical music, and art, and Guinness, of which there was, of course, plenty at the party – draught and bottled – as well as sparkling white wine. It was a good evening. Everyone who was anyone was there.

The only problem was: there were no books.

There were plenty of sandwiches: egg, cheese and ham, laid on by Margaret, who runs the bar at the Castle Arms. (Bob Savory, needless to say, was not impressed with the spread and since he has made it a rule never to eat the competition he was stuck on cocktail sausages and crisps all night, which is hardly enough to sustain a man through a heavy evening's drinking, and by eight o'clock he was drunk and bitter and complaining about the mere look of the sandwiches, about how presentation was everything in catering and how that was something that people round here had never really understood, how a chiffonade of parsley and a squeeze of lemon could make all the difference, and how we all got the food we deserved, which was certainly not Quality Food for the Discerning Palet, and if Billy had only asked, he said, he'd have done him a deal, and we could right now be eating chicken tikka with crisp lettuce and mayo on granary, or fresh buffalo mozzarella with roasted vegetables in a tortilla wrap, although to be honest most of us preferred plain ham and cheese with a pint, but we didn't like to say so.)

Billy had put £100 behind the bar for drinks and Margaret, who'd known Billy since he was born, and who had always bought her meat from Billy's dad, Hugh, twice a week all her adult life, had silently added another £50 of her own, to keep the evening flowing. She'd always had a special place in her heart for Hugh, a strong man whose big forearms and black beard had reminded her of her husband, a merchant seaman who'd gone missing overboard in mountainous seas in the Atlantic, aged just twenty-seven. Margaret had never remarried, had never had children and she ran the best bar in town: there was hardly an adult male who hadn't enjoyed his first under-age drink under her watchful gaze, and who in later years hadn't felt the lash of her tongue and the threat to drink up and go home or have you no home to go to? Margaret was, everyone agreed, one of the old school. She'd had a cancer scare a couple of years ago, and regulars at the Castle Arms had raised over £1000 and sent her on a Christmas Caribbean cruise, which she had to pretend she'd enjoyed, but which she'd hated. The sea reminded her of her husband and she'd spent most days sitting in the boat's main bar – Bogart's – telling people all about her own little pub back home. The ship's bartenders, of course, grew to love her and showed her everything they knew about mixing cocktails, for which there had never been a big demand in the Castle Arms, but when she came back there was a brief fashion for Gimlets and Gibsons and Singapore Gin Slings, and for a time Margaret stocked almost as much angostura bitters as she did good Irish whiskey. Frank Gilbey liked to boast to his friends at the golf club that Margaret made a better dry martini than he had tasted anywhere in the world – and he had tasted a few.

Margaret belonged in our town. She belonged behind the bar.

Billy's was the first book written by someone any one of us actually knew, the first book written by someone from our town, in fact, in living memory, although we do, of course, have the usual roster of nineteenth-century hymn writers and minor poets, whose work for the most part expresses repressed sexual longings and deep theological confusion, and quite often the two at the same time.

Fill thou our life, Lord, full in every part,
That with our being we proclaim Thee,
And the wonders of Thine Art.

Come quickly, O Lord Jesus,
That the world may know Thy Name,
Fill our ears, Lord, and our eyes, Lord,
That our hearts may know no shame.

Fill the valleys and the mountains,
Inspire us with Thy sweet breath,
Till all Israel's sons proclaim Thee,
King of Glory, raised from death.
                          (Nathan Hatchmore Perkins
                               McAuley, 1844–1901)

These were not words that any self-respecting teenage boy could sing in a school assembly without blushing or laughter. Nathan Hatchmore Perkins McAuley – a minister, apparently, who had lived in the old manse on Moira Avenue, which had gone with the ring road and which was now the site of eighteen starter homes – was inadvertently responsible for more detentions than any other single individual in the whole history of Central School.

One former pupil at Central, Tom Boal – stage name, Big Tom Tyrone, even though he wasn't actually from Tyrone – had obviously enjoyed and remembered the Reverend Mr McAuley's deep apprehendings and had somehow ended up on the folk circuit in Greenwich Village in the 1960s, singing about longings of his own. Turning to Country, he had recorded several albums in Nashville in the 1970s and he toured occasionally and had returned one year to town, for his mother's funeral, and had come in to school as a special favour to an old friend, our history teacher, the notorious motorbike-riding and leather-jacket-wearing Gerry Malone, a man who'd been known to do tapes of the Grateful Dead and the Band for favoured boys in the sixth form. Mr Malone introduced Big Tom Tyrone as a contemporary of Bob Dylan and Joan Baez, people we all thought were dead, or hippies, or myths, like the Greeks and the Romans, and certainly it was a surprise for us to meet someone so obviously old and yet so utterly unlike our parents: he might as well have been Odysseus, or Elvis Presley. None of us who were there will ever forget Big Tom Tyrone's long, thinning hair and his cowboy boots and his acoustic version of Nathan Hatchmore Perkins McAuley's 'Fill thou our life, Lord', which he turned into a sleazy twelve-bar blues with a bottleneck middle section whose effect of longing and moaning came about the closest that most of us had ever heard to the sound of a woman in the act of lovemaking. The school's headmaster, a Brylcreemed man, a Mr Crawford, the predecessor of the current incumbent, Mr Swallow, was furious and ended assembly early. Girls hung around after the assembly for autographs – some of the better-looking girls too – and Big Tom Tyrone happily signed, in exchange for a kiss, and he must have been in his fifties at the time, I suppose, the age of our own fathers. We couldn't believe it. Billy and Bob and me had decided by that lunch break that we would form a band. We lasted about six months before we split, suffering from the usual musical differences and the lack of a drummer, and it was then that Billy turned seriously to poetry.

Billy's book was being published by a firm who had advertised in the *Impartial Recorder*, which Billy had foolishly taken to be a recommendation. The *Impartial Recorder* also carries advertisements for psychics, money trees, life coaches, 'The Truth about Israel – the Key to World History' booklets, and 'Hard-To-Believe-But-It's-True-We're-Giving-It-Away-Today-And-Today-Only-Its-An-Unbelievable-And-Unrepeatable-Bargain-But-All-Stock-Must-Go!!!' furniture stores, cut-price supermarkets and wood flooring specialists. Billy had submitted his work by post, enclosing a small fee, and he had received a letter in reply just a week later, much different from the replies he usually received from publishers: it described his work as 'original', 'extraordinary' and it went on to use the kind of adjectives which Billy had secretly known for many years might properly be applied to his work, but at which he had blushed on reading and rereading. As well as its obvious literary merits the book, he was told, in the opinion of the publishers, could be a major commercial success. The publishers believed that they could guarantee reviews in national newspapers, magazines and literary journals, and prominent displays in all the major bookshops. Because of the extra distribution and publicity costs that this would involve, they wondered if they could possibly ask Billy to contribute about £1000? Out of this sum Billy would receive two free copies and he had an option to buy another 500 at a greatly reduced rate. The publishers said the initial print run was going to be about 1000: an enormous number for a first book by an unknown author.

Billy had inherited some money from the sale of the butcher's shop and its fittings after Hugh's death, so he gladly paid up, sat back and waited, and he believed for a long time that he was actually going to see the book.*

* It exists still only in typescript, the book. The only two poems of Billy's ever to have seen the light of day were published in the first edition of the magazine *The Enthusiast* (PO Box 239, Bangor, BT20 5YB, www.the enthusiast.co.uk). The first of these poems, 'To the Reader', seems to be some kind of uncompromising envoi:

> Listen: you don't like it, then leave.
> My aim has only ever been to be popular
> with the less sophisticated type of audience,
> especially in the suburbs and provinces.

The second poem, 'I'm Nobody, Who Are You?', runs to over a hundred lines and considerations of space obviously preclude us from reprinting it here, but readers who have attended Robert McCrudden's popular Creative Writing class (Poetry) I or II at the Institute, or similar, might be able to detect throughout this longer work the influences of Arthur Rimbaud, George

But after the humiliation of the bookless book launch, days turned to weeks and then to months, and there were still no books received, and Billy's letters and telephone calls went unanswered, and in the end Billy decided he was going to have to go and see his publishers personally. He wore a suit and tie, as for a business meeting, asked for a day's leave from the dump and took the train.

Herbert, C. P. Cavafy, Geoffrey Chaucer, Hart Crane, Bertolt Brecht, John Berryman, Emily Dickinson, the Gawain Poet, William Blake, A. E. Housman, Francis Ponge, Marianne Moore, Thomas Hardy, Robert Frost, or Pam Ayres.

5

Fellowship

A Good Friday Carvery and Gospel Night (Featuring the Preaching of the Word by Francie McGinn, Country Gospel Music by Bobbie Dylan and All-You-Can-Eat Barbecued Meats)

The sun finally came out on Friday, breaking through after what seemed like months of gloom, what seemed like years of low grey cloud and drizzle, what seemed, in fact, to some of us here like the new Dark Ages, the return of the famous 'black springs' of the 1950s when there wasn't a green vegetable till August and the only thing you could buy in the market throughout the summer was potatoes. When the cloud lifted, Francie McGinn turned his face to the big blurred halo in the sky and thanked the Lord.

'Altostratus,' he said.

Francie has always been interested in the weather and he had gone into the ministry, the two things being somehow connected in his mind, something to do with storms and rainbows and the supernumerary. Francie would not have been your obvious choice as a minister, what with his lack of any obvious social skills, his terror of public speaking and his terrible psoriasis, which always tended to flare up when Francie had to address a congregation, but God does seem to have a sense of humour and so, when He called Francie, in His infinite wisdom He did not call him to a nice quiet life working in an office, as a filing clerk perhaps, or an assistant administrative officer in the local council – recently relocated, of course, from its fine old five-storey stucco building overlooking the People's Park, with a girdled and globe-breasted Queen Victoria standing guard outside on a plinth, to a new purpose-built place on the ring road. No, God works in mysterious ways and He seems curiously uninterested in the workings and decisions of local councils, so when He called Francie – a sweet, shy, nervous man – He called him not to a life of pleasant quietness but to a life which involved a lot of standing up in front of large and not always sympathetic crowds speaking to them enthusiastically about Jesus. It was a calling which required certain skills of exposition and expostulation, and a certain amount of necessary hand-waving, which Francie, who had always been a little stiff in his manner, had never quite mastered. His sermons were examples of free association, in which he grappled with, and was often floored by, complex passages of Scripture and the use of the microphone. Just watching him up there at the front of his congregation was enough to break your heart. It was enough to bring you to tears, or to your knees.

As if both to identify and to defy his own native lack of ability, Francie had had an alphabet painted around what in other churches would have been called a nave, but which in Francie's church, the People's Fellowship – a place on South Street, which used to be the old Johnson Hosiery Factory, round the back of the Quality Hotel – was just a blank back wall lit by halogen spots and uplighters. The alphabet read, in thick black letters three and four feet tall:

ALL unsaved people are sinners. You must BELIEVE and CONFESS your sins to God. Christ DIED to save sinners. The Lord knows EVERY secret thing. We are saved through FAITH in Christ. GOOD Works alone will not save. Punishment and HELL await sinners. IMAGINE the darkness that will fall from on high when all men will be JUDGED by the Lord. You shall KNOW and LOVE the Lord, who in His MERCY is willing to save sinners. NOTHING can separate us from the love of God, and the Lord Jesus Christ is the ONLY way of salvation. The Lord will PARDON backsliders, but you must REPENT of your wrongdoing in order to be SAVED. There is joy in TESTIFYING to the Lord. WHOSOEVER WILL may be saved.

The sign painter, Colin Crawford, who was a friend of a friend of a member of the congregation, and who had learnt his trade years ago in the Tech's once renowned sign-writing classes, seems to have run into problems with some of the more difficult consonants – what good things does God do that begin with the letters Q and Z? – but the effect was impressive nonetheless.* When Francie stood up to preach, sweating into the microphone, at the front of that hall, you had the impression of a performing flea caught up in the pages of a vast Bible.

From an early age, certainly from when I first knew him, Francie had described himself as a Bible-believing Christian. The Bible, to Francie, was a bit like God is to most other Christians: something to be relied upon and worshipped, but

---

* There are no sign-writing classes any more, of course – people like Wilkie the Gut, with his vinyls and self-adhesives, have put paid to them (see note, p.23) – and Colin himself has been reduced to mere painting and decorating in order to supplement his income. It's been a comedown, for a craftsman. It took Colin about fifteen years to master the various skills of sign-writing, and these days he's lucky if he gets to do the occasional bit of rag-rolling and marbling, or a *Teletubby* mural for a rich kid's bedroom. He works out of a little shed in his back garden and over the door he's painted the famous inscription from the entrance to hell in Dante's *Inferno*, in a nice, simple, chiselled-edge Gothic: 'Abandon all hope, ye who enter'.

72

which nonetheless remains utterly inscrutable and not necessarily something you'd ever be able to understand.*

Francie was naturally a quiet and modest man, but he was ambitious for Jesus, and was always coming up with exciting new schemes for promoting God's Word in and around town. He would sometimes take a full-page advertisement in the local paper announcing forthcoming events and in the summer he held evening meetings in the car park in the centre of town, out in front of the Quality Hotel, near the new faux bandstand, with its brick podium and tarpaulin-effect sheet-steel covering, where every night he erected a large sign announcing an 'Open Air Gospel Meeting', just in case anyone was in doubt as to exactly what a group of twenty or thirty adults wearing Bermuda shorts and big grins and sunhats were doing, shaking their tambourines and playing guitars and handing out tracts to amused skateboarders and passers-by. Everyone knew it had to be something to do with Jesus – where we live, there's no other excuse or explanation for such behaviour. This is not Miami Beach, or Brighton. In the winter Francie tried Fish-and-Chip Biblical Quiz Nights and Line Dancing, Ladies' Pool Nights and Indoor Carpet Bowls for the over-sixties, and there were, of course, all the usual weekly Parenting Classes and Toddlers' Groups and Bible Studies, but the highlight of every year was undoubtedly his Good Friday

* Barry McClean, the United Reformed Church minister who teaches Philosophy for Beginners at the Institute and who does not actually believe in God *as such*, would have called Francie's a 'believer's faith'. '*Credo quia absurdum*', as he likes to tell the ever dwindling numbers in his classes, 'To believe because it is absurd. The believer's ultimate reassurance. The final abandonment of reason.' Barry's own studies in philosophy and religion have alas brought him no reassurance of any kind, and the exercise of his reason had led him only to several obvious and depressing conclusions: that two contradictory statements can be true; that there is no rational order of things; and that the mind is incapable of knowing truth. As a consequence, Barry's sermons – or 'talks', as he likes to call them – are rather lacking in conviction. And his evening classes can be confusing.

Carvery and Gospel Night, an evening which included the Preaching of the Word, Country Gospel Music by Bobbie Dylan and all-you-could-eat barbecued meats, provided by Tom Hines, who is a brother of a member of the congregation, all for a very reasonable £5 per head.

A couple of years back Francie's wife, Cherith, was on a detox diet, which meant she couldn't eat dairy products, bread, pasta, oranges and half a dozen other foodstuffs, including red meat, and in order to display solidarity with his wife Francie was doing the diet too, so they were both going to have to miss out on the Good Friday Carvery, something they usually looked forward to: the closest they usually got to meat was supermarket mince, which is at best an approximation. It was for her liver, Cherith said, the detox diet, but to be honest she could probably have done to lose some weight, as could their teenage daughter, Bethany, who had not been tempted by the diet, and who had also secretly started smoking cigarettes and going out with boys who were non-Christians, and who wore black eyeliner to church, and who, during her father's sermons, sometimes sat sending text messages of a sexual nature to her friends.

That Easter, the year of the diet, Francie and Cherith were also having a new kitchen put into their house on the estate – nothing too expensive, nothing too flash, but, as all the elders of the church agreed, it did need updating – and whether it was the stress of the kitchen, or the lack of protein and carbohydrates and the smell of the barbecued meats, or perhaps the manifold charms of Bobbie Dylan herself that did for Francie I do not know.

Bobbie Dylan was christened Roberta and was not a fan of Bob Dylan until she heard the *Saved* album, and then it was but a short leap into the whole world – the admittedly small but pleasantly cosy world – of Christian rock, a world which the leather-trousered Roberta now bestrode like the proverbial colossus.

Roberta had been converted at the age of twenty. There is probably no good or bad age to become a born-again Christian, but twenty is perhaps one of the worst. It meant that Roberta had enjoyed a few years of tasting the fruits of this world and now, as she emerged into her mid-thirties, she could still taste the many, the complex flavours on her tongue: the terrible sweetness of all those things that as a born-again Christian she knew it was right to deny herself. She tried not to think about it too much and it was not something she liked to admit, but sometimes she had a hankering after the world and its ways. Sometimes, for instance, at night, in her one-bedroom flat on Kilmore Avenue – with its lovely en suite, tiled and decorated by her own fair hand, with a nice fish motif and a power shower – she would drink several glasses of Chardonnay while watching American television programmes in which strong women with beautiful hair and clavicles and good upper-body strength boasted to each other of their sexual conquests, and their ability to please and to dominate men. Just watching them Roberta would feel ashamed and excited. Watching *ER* had the same effect, and also Sebastian Faulks's novel *Birdsong*.

Not that the world of Christian rock didn't have its excitements. Roberta had toured extensively throughout Ireland, Scotland, England and Wales, and had been to many Christian rock festivals throughout Europe – in Germany, for example, and in Holland. She had released no fewer than five CDs of her own original material and although she hadn't yet had a breakthrough in America, where the competition was pretty fierce in its own Christian way, she was already big in Korea, where Christians seemed to appreciate her work, which was influenced by the many traditions of Christian and sacred music: gospel, soul, country and mid-period Bob Dylan.

Like Bob Dylan, and like many another rock musician, Roberta had been tempted at times by rock'n'roll's inevitable accompaniments and attractions. There were times when she feared that sitting in recording studios late at night with unshaven men drinking beer would prove her undoing.

But when it came to Francie's Good Friday Carvery and Gospel Night Roberta's mind was set firmly on her music and her ministry. She had showered and washed her hair, and laid out her best clothes: a pair of black leather trousers, a white long-sleeved blouse and a pair of black boots with a slight heel. She had straightened her hair with straightening irons, put on a little lipstick – a sheer glossy rose – and applied some kohl and some mascara round her dark-brown eyes. The look was a combination of rock chick and bride of Christ which she hoped was pleasing both in the eyes of God and of man.

As for Francie, he was wearing his usual minister's outfit: a brown car coat with pockets large enough to accommodate a Good News bible, a range of tracts and a Scripture Union diary; a pair of grey sta-prest casual trousers, the pockets jangling, full of keys and small change for emergencies (Francie does not possess or carry credit or charge cards, and encourages his congregation to cut up their own); a blue bobbled V-neck pullover thinning around the elbows; a check shirt with blue and red biros tucked in the breast pocket; and a good plain pair of Clark's shoes from Irvine's ('Clark's, Norvic and Bective Brands for Ladies, Kiltie Shoes for Children, Savile Row for Gentlemen'), the laces securely double knotted. He looked, in fact, like most of us do here, both the men and the women: the unmistakable look of people who are not in full charge of their own wardrobes, people who get dressed once a year by Father Christmas and who do not feel any further need to add to or to accessorise their festive knitwear, or to worry about some small thing like a wrong-sized shirt collar or polyester pants. Francie had gone straight from being dressed by his mother to being dressed by his wife, both of whom were more interested in questions of value for money than any considerations of style or current fashions, but fortunately clothes had never been important to Francie. Apart from a couple of troublesome years in his teens when he had rebelled against hand-me-down duffel coats and had insisted on a red harrington and dealer boots, he did not dress to impress. It was not necessary. Francie was not setting out to attract the attentions of the opposite sex. He had never kissed another woman apart from his wife and, indeed, he could probably count every kiss he had bestowed upon her, in every place and everywhere, although, actually, recently the kisses had become rather scarce.

Not that Francie's and Cherith's was a loveless marriage. On the contrary. Their lives were fulfilled in many ways. They enjoyed the fellowship of the congregation and they both regarded it as a privilege to be able to minister together: this was their role and their mission in life, and they desired little else, although sometimes, if he were honest, Francie would have to admit to entertaining improper thoughts. Sometimes, for example, he wondered if he'd have been better off as a Catholic priest. He liked the idea of a sacramental role, something that involved a little less Doing – fewer committees and less street evangelism – and a bit more good old-fashioned Being. Sometimes he thought he wouldn't at all have minded a Roman collar, or wearing a soutane. And sometimes he imagined female members of his congregation modelling swimwear.

On that Good Friday, though, such thoughts were far from Francie's mind. On that fateful night Francie was worrying about the kitchen.

He and Cherith had argued before coming out – after they'd eaten their microwaveable quiche and a salad consisting of a small hard tomato, two sticks of celery, a pyramid of sweetcorn and half an iceberg lettuce, the barbecued meats at the Carvery being strictly prohibited to them. They had argued again – for it was not the first time – about what an appropriate work surface for the new kitchen might be. A laminate was cheapest, of course, which is what Jesus would have wanted, but Cherith had been trying to persuade Francie that a good hard solid wood or even a granite surface would wear better, and so in the long run it would please Jesus and the elders of the fellowship just as much. Francie quoted Scripture – 'Blessed are you poor, for yours is the kingdom of God', Luke 6:20 – and Cherith rejoindered with some verses of her own – 'In the house of the righteous there is much treasure', Proverbs 15:6 – which was something they only ever did when they were really annoyed with one another. In the end they had left the house having to agree to disagree.

Cherith, of course, did all the cooking and food preparation, and most of the washing up, as was appropriate for a minister's wife, so she spent a lot of time in the kitchen. But Francie was the expert. He had started out life with his father as a kitchen fitter – McGinn's, which still has its small showroom up there on Union Street, near the old Kincaid furniture factory. McGinn's specialise, and always have specialised, in kosher kitchens, but unfortunately for Mr McGinn there aren't that many Jews in our town – only two, in fact, as far as Mr McGinn is aware, although there may be others who don't keep kosher, and one can only pray for their souls and for God's forgiveness. There are not even that many Jews further afield – the only synagogue in the county, a fine example of Victorian optimism, was knocked down twenty years ago, to be replaced by a garage, a Chinese takeaway and a joke shop, Joyland, offering 'Jokes, Magic, Tricks', which is now itself derelict, good clean fun these days being about as unfashionable as religious orthodoxy. This meant that Mr McGinn had to travel far and wide for business, which was not convenient, but it was worth it. He'd gone into kosher kitchens because kosher kitchens meant two sinks. 'And two sinks,' he would say, with the kind of mad and unassailable logic that Francie himself had inherited, 'are always better than one.'

Francie had met Cherith shortly after he'd given up the kitchen fitting, when God had called him away from installing kosher sinks with his father to the full-time saving of souls. It was not an easy calling. Francie had been brought up a good Catholic and he was the youngest of ten children, his parents having married when they were nineteen and his mother having been pregnant every year throughout her twenties. By the time she was thirty she looked fifty and Francie's dad had finally put his foot down, told her it was time to shut up shop, pull down the shutters and put a stop to all the shenanigans: the house was never quiet, he said, and all the children were having to compete for attention. Some of Francie's brothers competed for attention by drinking and staying out late at night with unsuitable girls, and his sisters were mostly given to tantrums, smoking, and bleaching their hair. Francie competed for attention by becoming very devout. He was a conspicuously good boy and when he grew up, he said, he wanted to be a priest. This made his mother happy.

He gave up his priestly ambitions, however, when he was just sixteen and he attended a rally organised by the Assemblies of God. At the rally there was singing and dancing, and a full band with a drummer and percussionist and a six-piece horn section, most of whom were black and many of whom swayed as they played their wonderful, loud, joyful music. This was not the kind of colour or spectacle that Francie had ever seen at the Church of the Cross and the Passion, where it was regarded as pretty racy of Father Baird to persist in smoking his pipe on a Sunday and to claim to prefer the Mass in Latin, and where there had been much argument one year about the choir singing a modern setting of the Psalms. Attending the rally therefore had approximately the same effect on Francie as seeing stars in the daytime sky, or the feel of a woman stroking your thigh, a favourite fantasy of Francie's ever since his piano lessons with a certain Miss Buchanan, lessons which required Miss Buchanan to squeeze up unnaturally close to her pupils on a small piano stool.* It was a kind of ecstasy. From the Assemblies of God Francie soon moved on to the house church movement and by the time he was twenty-two he had left kitchen fitting to attend a bible college – a large old crumbling house in Hampshire with Portakabins in the grounds – where he had undertaken numerous feats of healing, many of them involving people with one leg mysteriously slightly shorter than the other, marathon sessions of speaking in tongues and the laying on of hands, and the studying of the Bible without the inconvenience of learning Greek and Hebrew. It was great fun. It was better than kitchen fitting. Francie preferred the Church to his family. He was no longer one out of ten. He was one in a million: he had been chosen by God. And by the time he returned home to set up a church of his own he was ready to choose a wife.†

He met Cherith while evangelising on the street. She was with a group of friends going to a nightclub – Scruples, in the basement of the Quality Hotel's back-bar extension, a

---

* Miss Buchanan did this with everyone, in fact, male and female, as many of us in town could testify – it was nothing to do with Francie McGinn. It was a piano stool, after all. Miss Buchanan had never married and was good friends with – was a companion to, indeed – Miss Carroll, the town's midwife, who was Miss Buchanan's senior by twenty years. As Miss Carroll's retirement approached, however, Miss Buchanan decided to marry Thomas Odgers, the auctioneer, whose daughter by his first wife was one of her pupils. Odgers, an old-fashioned man with wild ginger hair and mutton-chop whiskers, was rumoured to be seeking a son and heir. As is well known, Miss Carroll committed suicide shortly after her retirement and Mrs Odgers (née Buchanan) bore no children. On her husband's insistence she gave up teaching the piano.

† God had told Francie to choose a wife while Francie was at the bible college in Hampshire, by drawing Francie's attention to a number of possible helpmeets among his fellow female bible students and tormenting him with 1 Corinthians 7 and constant thoughts of his filthy imaginings, and acts of self-arousal in his dormitory and the communal washrooms. Wisely, Francie had never allowed his own daughter, Bethany, to attend so much as a Youth Fellowship weekend away.

club which is long gone but which many of us still remember fondly. Francie had spoken to the girls about Jesus, and Cherith said she was a Christian already.

'But have you asked Jesus into your heart?' asked Francie.

It was not an obvious chat-up line, but Cherith liked the way he looked her straight in the eye when he spoke, and she liked his honest and open smile, and to be honest Francie rather liked her long blonde hair and her small firm breasts.

At the time he was twenty-two and Cherith was just sixteen. Two years passed in chaste and secret engagement, with Cherith attending Francie's church, first in the Central School hall and then in the community centre on Windsor Road, and on the day of Cherith's eighteenth birthday Francie presented himself at her parents' in his best and only suit and tie, and asked for her hand in marriage. Cherith's mother Barbara thought it was wonderfully romantic, while Cherith's father Ron said – in private, to Barbara – that he'd rather his daughter married a drug dealer or a criminal than some weird religious cradle-snatching nut who was running a church which didn't have its own premises. But when he discovered that Francie was an heir to the McGinn kosher kitchen empire he relented, welcomed Francie into the bosom of the family, and he and Barbara toasted their good fortune with a bottle of sparkling white wine.

Cherith and Francie were married in the People's Fellowship, which had finally moved to its own premises in the old Johnson's Hosiery Factory, where the paint was still wet and the plaster still drying, and where a new blue plastic banner hung across the main entrance over the words 'STOCKINGS, NYLONS, TIGHTS AND FLESHINGS' carved deep into the granite. The new banner read, in white on blue, with stylised orange flames licking around the edges of the words: 'GEARED TO THE TIMES, ANCHORED TO THE ROCK'. At the wedding Francie preached a sermon which focused on some of the more lurid and explicit passages from the Song of Solomon, and the Worship Band played their sweet spiritual music. Bethany was born nine months later.

Bethany was their first and last child – Francie and Cherith both felt that there were so many needy people in the world and that the Lord had called them to minister to them, and so Francie had gone and had the op. Sometimes Cherith felt that they should have gone on and had a big family, but Francie had had enough of big families and he was not the best with children: he was a serious man, with weighty matters always on his mind, and his eyes fixed firmly on the glory of God. Cherith admired her husband and thought he was a good person, but she did sometimes wish that he would lighten up a bit.

As for Francie, he often wondered how he had ended up a minister, since he was clearly such a bad person. He frequently found himself tormented by his impure thoughts, but this was not something he felt he could discuss with Cherith, who was a good person and who always wore long skirts below the knee, who never lost her temper, and who was placid in all matters personal and physical. The closest they had ever come to a frank discussion of their sexual needs and preferences had been a couple of years before when Cherith had asked Francie what he would like for a birthday present and Francie had asked for a video of the singer Shania Twain. This seemed tantamount to requesting under-the-counter hard-core pornography to Cherith, who bought the video nonetheless and who had convinced herself that her husband obviously needed to keep up with popular culture and music in order to be able to communicate effectively to the church's young people. Late at night, when he was supposed to be preparing a sermon, Francie would sometimes sit in the dark, with the curtains drawn, and watch the singer perform. And he would wish he were performing with her.

That night, the night of the Good Friday Carvery, Bobbie Dylan sang about Jesus coming into people's hearts and filling them with joy, and about love overflowing, and as she stood there at the microphone, the lights shining upon her, her backing band chugging away in the background, the smell and the smoke of Tom Hines's barbecued meats hanging in the air, it seemed to Francie that Bobbie was the incarnation of everything he had ever dreamed of: a sanctified version of a rock goddess.

Before his Preaching of the Word Francie went to the Disabled toilet – which was doubling as Bobbie's changing room – to congratulate and thank Bobbie for her performance.

The two of them were deep in an embrace when Cherith walked in. There had been a long queue for the Ladies, as usual, and Cherith thought she could get away with using the Disabled.

The Carvery went ahead as planned. Francie preached the Word. And Cherith went home and packed.

6

Massive

In which Paul McKee, a hindered character, works from home, eats biscuits and attempts to unleash his enormous talent

There's been a lot more weather recently – masses of the stuff – but the rain held off for long enough last week for Irvine's Footwear, 'Always One Step Ahead', to be able to put in their new shopfront. There was nothing wrong with the old shopfront, actually, but as Mr Irvine explained to Big Dessie Brown's daughter Yvette, a cub reporter on the *Impartial Recorder* conducting her first big interview for the paper – which was a success, which was praised by everyone, even the editor, Colin Rimmer, and which Big Dessie now has proudly magneted to the fridge – 'Bigger windows showing more shoes means more choice means more customers.' Irvine's old hand-painted fascia has gone, then, with the stained-glass fanlight and the cracked plastered niches: IRVINE'S is now spelt in red plastic on white, and there are the obligatory pull-down metal shutters. It took two men just two days to rip out the old and bring in the new, and Mr Irvine is delighted with the results. Mr Irvine is getting on a bit now but he still likes to think of himself as a go-ahead kind of guy: he had the town's first electric cash register, years ago, and he accepts all the major credit cards today, still something of a rarity among our few remaining small businesses and sole traders.

Mr Irvine is a man who understands selling and who understands shoes: he has always had a feel for feet and Irvine's has always been a popular shop, particularly among the wider-footed men and the narrower-footed women of our town. For a long time it was the best shoe shop around: now, of course, it's the only one, if you don't count the chain stores in Bloom's, which we don't. Irvine's is the only shop between here and the great beyond where you can still buy all lengths of shoelaces and ladies' brogues.

Next door to Irvine's is the old Brown and Yellow Cake Shop, which has retained its original wide windows, its little recessed entrance and its barley-sugar columns, and where, as well as the old brown and yellow cakes, they do baguettes and ready-to-bake garlic bread to take away, and hot and cold snacks, including a very popular bacon and egg morning sandwich – 'Start the Day,' says the handwritten fluorescent orange star-burst sign pinned to the front of the microwave, 'the Right Way', the right way in the Brown and Yellow Cake Shop being to load up your system with sugar and saturated fats and carbohydrates, and maybe a polystyrene cup or two of tea or instant coffee. The Lennons, Sean and Mary, who own the shop, like to keep their staff costs to a minimum, so they employ only two shop girls, Deidre, who is seventy-three and deaf, and Siobhan, who is seventeen and pretty typical. This leads inevitably to long queues, but in our town a long queue is not necessarily a disincentive to shop: indeed, it may be a recommendation. There are a lot of people around here who are more than happy to join the back of a long queue, and who feel a genuine sadness when they arrive somewhere and there's no queue to latch on to: queuing in our town is a vital sign. If you're queuing you're still alive: you have something to be thankful for, you're looking forward to the future, even if it's only a nice tray bake for elevenses or a fresh floury bap with some soup for lunch. The Brown and Yellow Cake Shop is busy, then, as always, full with people on their way to work starting the day in the right way and celebrating their existence. Mr Irvine is buying a celebratory cream horn for later: he does love a cream horn and that new shopfront is certainly something to celebrate.

Next along is Nelson's Insurance, which always looks shut, and then Lorraine's Bridal Salon and Tan Shop, which is shut and has been shut for some time because Lorraine has been in hospital again recovering from a mystery illness – they say it's the slimmer's disease and she certainly is thin, which should be an asset in her line of business, where every customer is watching weight and could do to lose some, but Lorraine is getting so thin now that people notice and comment, and not always favourably. It's not good to be too fat or too thin in our town: about a maximum 38-inch waist and a 44-inch chest for a man and nothing below a size 10 for a lady. It's not good to fall outside the average: it's not good to stand out. We have noticeably few tall women in town, for example, and all our hairstyles lean towards the same, men and women. Even our ethnic minorities are not really large enough to be minorities: they are still individuals, which is just about OK. If you stray too far off the mean, or there's too many of you, it's best to move away: that's what cities are for, after all. If you want to be different that's fine, but we'd rather you did it somewhere we didn't have to see you every day.

Lorraine's problem is the opposite, in fact, of her noticeably roly-poly father, Frank Gilbey, a man who stands out, but who can carry his weight, due to his age and his charm and his general assumption of seniority. If anyone in our town had ever used the word chutzpah – and the Kahans and the Wisemans may have done, but in private, so as not to shock, behind closed doors, tucked up in their kosher kitchens, provided by McGinn's, our kosher kitchen specialists – they'd have used it about Frank Gilbey.

Frank these days is a man under pressure – his appeal against the council's refusal to allow him change of use for the Quality Hotel had become bogged down in the usual paperwork and bureaucracy, which Frank has no time for and which his solicitor, Martin Phillips, should have seen coming, and he's facing a few cash flow problems as well, although nothing he can't handle, he tells himself – but when he's at his best, when he's on form, you might say Frank is the kind of man who puts the 'pah' into chutzpah. Frank is a man whose influence and whose tentacles stretch far and wide in our town. In fact, there just aren't enough local pies into which Frank can put his little fat fingers, so his grasp has reached as far as a share in a racehorse in Newmarket and a number of investment properties in southern Spain.*

Frank had set up Lorraine in the Bridal Salon and Tan Shop after her disastrous and painfully short marriage to the bad Scotsman, who said he was an actuary but who was also an alcoholic. It was a difficult time for Lorraine, who turned to sunbeds and to binge eating as a comfort, and for Frank, who was then still mayor, and for Frank's wife, the town's first lady, Irene. It was just lucky that Frank was such good friends with Sir George Sanderson, the proprietor of the *Impartial Recorder*, or the paper might have had a field day.

On the opposite side of Main Street, the dark side, the opposite to the bridal side – what we call the Post Office side – an unnamed shop owned by an out-of-towner who may or may not be foreign and who employs sixteen-year-olds to run the place and who doesn't seem to have invested too much in his staff training, sells cheap toilet rolls, king-size cigarette papers, novelty items and out-of-date foodstuffs. Next to them is what used to be Swine's, the newsagent and sweetshop, which after fifty years of selling sweets from jars by the quarter

* For a full account of Frank's business interests, see the *Impartial Recorder*, 20 June 2003.

has recently thrown in the towel and caved in to the inevitable tide of videos and instant microwave burgers. It was always a mystery to us as children how a man as miserable and as thoroughly unpleasant as the late Mr Ron Swine could preside over a place so magical and so beautiful and so full of delights. All those jars of liquorice and lemon drops and cherry flakes and dinosaur jellies seemed like treasures to us, locked up and kept in a palace by an evil giant, who begrudged handing over even the slightest of penny chew or gobstopper.

The evil giant's daughter, Eva, now runs the shop and she is a lovely sweet woman who waited until after her father's death to change her name by deed poll, and she is patiently explaining to an old man who wants to buy a quarter of butterballs that *Wine*'s don't do them any more. Eva had wanted to change her surname to something romantic and evocative, something like Monroe, or Hayworth, perhaps, but when it came to filling in the form she could hear the voice of her dead father nagging her about the cost of changing the shopfront, so she'd gone for the cheapest option and bought a pot of all-weather black gloss and gone out under cover of the night to erase the offensive initial. Of course, people from out of town sometimes get confused and locals have been known to set out to irritate and annoy Eva by going into the shop and asking for a bottle of Chardonnay or some cans of super-lager. Eva just shrugs it off: it's a small price to pay for her freedom from the tyranny of some ancestor's idea of a joke, or their job as a pig man. She suggests to the old man in search of butterballs that he try the Pick 'N' Mix up in Bleakley's, the big department store in Bloom's, the mall. The town's only other old-fashioned sweetshop, and Wine's only town centre competitor, Hi, Sweetie!, on Central Avenue, closed last year, on the site that is now Sensations.*

Next to Wine's, where Main Street is slowly collapsing into

* See note, p.183.

the Quality Hotel, is the Select Launderette – motto, 'Dirty Collars Are Not Becoming to You, They Should Be Coming to Us' – which is full, today being Wednesday, half-price-for-pensioners day. Betty and Martha, who run the shop and who would, in fact, qualify for Wednesday's generous discount themselves, if they'd ever admitted to their ages, or looked them, are just about run off their feet. Betty is known to Martha and to the regulars as Iron Betty, and Martha as Martha the Wash. The pair of them talk all day and listen to local radio, they have eighteen grandchildren between them, have recently both given up smoking and they have no intention of retiring, although they have started to shut up shop for an hour at lunchtime, so they can sit and nap in the room out back. They have worked together for thirty years, eight hours a day, and have never spoken a cross word.

Just off Main Street, in South Street, builders are busy repointing brickwork, a postman delivers parcels, a dog squats at the side of the road and then trots on, and the man on the corner with a garden prunes his roses.

Paul McKee watches them all from his bedroom window: Paul is unemployed.

Paul is not from around here. He married Little Mickey Matchett's daughter Joanne just over six months ago. It was a registry office job – presided over by Ernie King's son Alex, who took over from Mrs Galt as registrar a few years ago now, and who has finally got the hang of it, the right kind of smile and the right signature* – and it was close family only, and Paul had to hire a suit and he's so skinny he couldn't get one to fit. He looked pathetic, like a matchstick man, said Joanne's mum, and not a groom. Joanne wore blue and did without a bridesmaid, but she had her little nephew Liam as a ring bearer. The reception was in the upstairs room at the

* See pp.273–274.

Castle Arms, a venue which was not without its charms, as long as you overlooked the York Multigym and the punch-bags, and the other boxing paraphernalia, including a three-quarter-size ring, which were used by the Castle Ward Amateur Boxing Club on Tuesdays and Thursdays. As long as you kept all the windows open the smell of the sweat wasn't too bad.

Paul and Joanne had met in Paradise Lost, where Paul was DJ-ing on Friday and Saturday nights: it was a handbag kind of a crowd, but Paul enjoyed doing it. The money was good and sometimes you do have to prostitute your art: his set list included the Jackson Five and James Brown for emergencies. Neither Paul nor Joanne believed in love at first sight, but it seemed to have happened to them, without the assistance even of mind-altering substances – which Joanne does not agree with – and they counted themselves lucky. Unfortunately, Paul lost the gig at Paradise Lost when he and Joanne went to Ibiza for their one-week honeymoon and he's had trouble picking up anything since. He has big plans, though – he's just in a period of transition at the moment. Joanne jokes at work that he's a kept man, while Paul tells people that he is working from home, which he is, and he does, as much as anybody can: to be honest, he finds that there are too many distractions and too many biscuits for working at home to be a great success. Still, he's working on a few things. He's been trying to get a job in the music business, as a sound engineer or something, through a few contacts at the Institute. His tutor there was Wally Lee, a man with the occasional goatee and thinning hair swept back into a ponytail, a man in his fifties who wears stone-washed denim jeans and retro Adidas trainers, who sports a dangly earring, who wears sunglasses all year round and who has been known to wear leather trousers – in our town! – and who has no idea how he ended up here, who puts it down to amphetamines, who plays jazz at the Castle Arms on a Sunday lunchtime while people huddle over tiny wobbly tables and eat roast pork with boiled vegetables and mashed potatoes, and suffer Death by Chocolate, a man who has come a long way, who worked at one time as a keyboard technician on tours by Jean Michel Jarre and Chick Corea. Wally is an alcoholic, a dope fiend, and an incoherent and incompetent teacher, but he had inspired Paul, which can be a dangerous thing to do to young people in our town and which can lead to all sorts of trouble. Under Wally's influence, Paul became determined that he was going to do something, that he was going to make something of his life.

But first this morning he has to get up and make Joanne a cup of tea. It feels like a punishment, this, for Paul, a man who like many unemployed young men in our town only really comes alive around about midday, and who only begins to feel good when he has a beer in his hand after about six o'clock in the evening. He had a job as a fork-lift driver for about six months, but the hours were killing him – 7 till 6, five days a week, for a measly £200, through the books, which was the equivalent of just one night on the decks, cash in hand. Still, he put himself through it and he puts himself through this, the morning tea-making routine. Joanne has always said that she can get up and make her own tea – she's only twenty-two years old, after all, and a feminist – but the one good thing Paul's mum ever said about his dad was that he always used to make the tea in the mornings and so it seemed to Paul like the right and proper thing to do, a man's job, an adult responsibility and no excuses. He listened to a lot of gangsta rap at home and tea making is not a big part of the whole gangsta rap worldview, but sometimes in life you have to make compromises. After tea in bed Paul actually gets up again, to set out the breakfast things: cereals, milk, toast, marg and jam, which is a one-up on his own absent father and more like the behaviour of a saint, frankly, than a DJ, let alone an Eminem in the making. While he's sorting out the Shreddies, Joanne has a shower and gets dressed, and gets herself ready for work. Joanne has a job as a trainee catering supervisor at the hospital up in the city, which is long hours and shift work, but pretty good pay. When she's on days she departs from the house at 7.30, leaving Paul ten hours before her return.

When Joanne goes, Paul's day can really begin: he goes back to bed for an hour, exhausted already from all the effort of tea making and breakfast. Then, around 9, he gets dressed and goes out to buy a newspaper.

Eva's rush hours are 7 to 9.30 in the mornings and 4 to 6 in the evenings, weekdays, and 9 till 12 on Saturdays. She shuts on Sundays, despite demand, because she is a committed Christian and has recently started to attend the People's Fellowship, down round the back of the Quality Hotel. She likes the music and, like a lot of the older women in the congregation, she finds that she feels a motherly instinct towards Francie McGinn, particularly since his problems with his wife. She's less keen on the speaking in tongues and the hand waving, but before taking up with the People's Fellowship she'd been going to the Methodist for almost thirty-five years, during which time no one had said a kind word to her, she knew all the hymns back to front and upside-down, and she had grown tired of wearing long skirts and a hat – a knitted cloche that had belonged to her mother – so she was glad of the opportunity to wear jeans and a sweatshirt to services, and she figured that no church was going to be perfect.

Eva doesn't know Paul, but she doesn't like the look of him – he seems to have this effect on many people. His eyes *are* close together, and his hair *is* shaved short, and he does wear gold chains and a sovereign ring, and sportswear, and a baseball cap pulled low, and she knows that this doesn't necessarily make him a bad person, because she is a Christian and she tries to think the best of people, whatever they look like, but still she likes to keep an eye on him every morning when he comes in to choose which paper to buy – most people already know before they enter the shop, but Paul enjoys the privilege of being both unemployed and having had the benefits of a liberal education, having done the two-year course at the Institute in Music Technology with supplementary modules in Media Studies, so he likes to think he's pretty media savvy. He takes a while choosing – suspiciously, in Eva's eyes, who is unaware of his sophistication. Paul always considers, at least for a moment, the *Financial Times*, but he knows that that's to come, a treat for later in life, when he's big, somehow, and eventually he picks the *Daily Mail*. That's enough of a stretch.

He goes home the back way with his paper, along the lane between the houses, picking his way between the dog turds and the empty plastic cider bottles, and through the yard and in the back door, and goes into the kitchen. He spends a lot of time in the kitchen these days, smoking, making his plans, sitting at the breakfast bar staring out of the window, making cups of tea. One of the reasons why Joanne wants them to own their own place is so that they can have a nice big kitchen with fitted units and enough room for a table. Paul doesn't mind the kitchen, actually – although there is a smell. Frank Gilbey, the landlord, claims he's getting on to it. Joanne's mother thinks it's a disgrace: she thinks they should get on to the council. She does not agree with the standard of kitchens in private rented accommodation. She does not much agree with Joanne and Paul these days, in fact, and their life choices: she had hoped that her daughter might have had more sense than to marry an out-of-work DJ. Paul is not exactly the son-in-law she had imagined for Joanne, a bubbly, hard-working girl, with lots going for her and a good social life. Paul is pigeon-chested, a loner, has multiple body piercings and has been in trouble with the police several times, although fortunately Joanne's mother does not know exactly how many times, or for how long.

Paul was first in trouble when he was fourteen, when he

was part of a scam involving bogus charity bags organised by his Uncle Michael. His Uncle Michael had seen the scam featured on an American daytime television talk show and he was so impressed that he decided to import it – Michael liked to think of himself as an entrepreneur. He bought a thousand heavy-duty black bin bags, got a mate to print up a few leaflets on his computer, dropped off the bags with the leaflets at homes all around the city, then just went back a few days later to collect the goodies, which he resold at markets and car boot sales throughout the county. It was like taking the proverbial candy from a baby.

CLOTHING APPEAL

Dear householder(s), please donate whatever clothing, bedlinen, blankets, shoes and other household and electrical items that you may find no further use for. All suitable items will be sorted and shipped directly to African and Eastern European Countries to improve the local welfare. Please leave the bag provided in plain view outside your door on the day nominated below. Collection will begin at 9 a.m. sharp. Thank you.

That was Exhibit A. Michael, Paul's uncle – or the criminal mastermind, as he was described in court – got six months' suspended for that. Paul was lucky: he only had to see a social worker.

Joanne's mum didn't know about the charity bag fiasco. Or about Paul's disorderly behaviour and obstructing police when he was seventeen (six months' suspended), his driving without due care and attention (£250), his driving without a licence, without insurance and without an MOT certificate (£275), or even his driving while disqualified (four months' detention and £150) and his unlawfully damaging a police car (£175). She only knew about his causing criminal damage to property (£200 for smashing a window at Paradise Lost, plus £75 compensation), which had recently been prominently featured in the *Impartial Recorder*. Paul wasn't proud of it himself, but he couldn't see what she got so upset about. It was a minor offence and they had it coming to them, sacking him just because he was going on honeymoon, and anyway he was drunk, which is hardly a sin.

One day soon, though, Paul is going to prove them all wrong – he's going to be a big success – but in the meantime he drinks his cup of tea and goes through to the front room, or at least he gets down on his hands and knees and crawls into the front room. On the far side of the room is the window, and he crawls over and crouches below the sill and peeps out.

It is odd behaviour, but there's a reason for it: the woman living opposite is watching Paul, waiting to catch him out. She's spying on him. He's sure of it.

You see, Paul, like a lot of people in our town, is paranoid. It's not clear whether it's the drugs or being unemployed, or what it is that's done it to him. He has taken a lot of drugs in his time, but it could just be the effect of being married. Marriage affects a lot of us that way – it can make you want to duck for cover. Marriage can mess with your head in much the same way as a class A drug: it's a kind of neurotoxin, marriage. The first few weeks Paul had coped with it fine, but as time passed and he realised he was actually going to be living with Joanne every day, and in perpetuity, he started to feel a little jittery and restless. He began to get depressed. He became withdrawn and uncommunicative. He came to resemble the rest of us.

Paul missed the DJ-ing. He dreamed of another life. He used to tell himself that he was going to be massive: that was the word he used in his head, all the time, when he was practising his music.

'Massive,' he would say to himself, 'I am going to be massive.'

It had started out as a challenge, but had turned into a comfort and then a kind of mockery: he knew that he was never going to be massive. He wasn't able to stick with it. He wasn't able to stick with anything. That's what his teachers and his social worker had said.

He didn't even know if he was going to be able to stick it with Joanne. It had seemed like a good idea at first, getting married, then coming to town, getting a little house, so they could be near Joanne's family. It seemed like the kind of life that Paul had always wanted. Joanne was all right, he loved Joanne, but he found it hard getting on with her family. He tried to get on with them, but he didn't share their interests and they didn't share his: they had never heard of drum'n'bass, or ragga, or big beat, and jungle to them is a place with trees. Joanne's family's interests were restricted pretty much to Joanne's family, and Paul was never going to be a part of that. He hadn't realised that when you got married to someone you were marrying into their family: it had never occurred to him. He didn't know that was how families worked. No one had told him.*

He tried working on his decks during the day, but he found himself quickly getting bored and then he realised he was frittering his time away, hanging around the job centre and the shops, always restless, and like a caged animal at home. Which is when the woman across the road started getting on his nerves. He became convinced that she was watching him. She watched him every day, nine to five, settling into her armchair first thing in the morning, her small table next to her with her tea things and a pile of magazines and library books. An hour for lunch and then back in the afternoon. Paul knew what she was doing: he'd seen her.

Paul did not want to give her the satisfaction of seeing him unemployed. It was none of her business. He'd bought some

* He should have attended the 'How to Be a Family' seminar series at the Oasis, based largely on Cherith's reading of Robin Skinner and John Cleese, and *Freud for Beginners*, and her admiration for *The Forsyte Saga* in the BBC adaptation, and *Roseanne*, and *Butterflies* with Wendy Craig.

net curtains and put them up in the front room and the bedroom. Joanne had complained that they made the rooms too dark. He said that they needed their privacy, that he didn't want the neighbours to see what they were up to. One Sunday he got Joanne to go outside and check if it was possible to see him behind the curtains.

'Just a shadow,' said Joanne. He decided then he'd have to keep down during the day, so that nobody would be able to see him. They wouldn't even be able to see his shadow.

He peeps out of the window and sees her there, reading, sipping tea. An inquisitive old lady with nothing better to do than to look out of her window all day. Paul felt bad enough without people checking up on him all the time. He knew by the way people looked at him. He knew Joanne's family thought he was a shirker. He thought Joanne probably thought he was a shirker too.

'But I didn't marry you for your money,' she says sometimes, joking. It didn't exactly make him feel any better. She never really said what she'd married him for, actually, and he had no real idea either.

Paul lies down on his stomach in the front room and turns on the telly. He does his best to be quiet during the daytime. If he listens to the radio or watches television he turns the volume right down, and he uses headphones on his decks, so no one can hear him. Not that there's anyone else around to hear him. The fella next door is at work, of course, and the people on the other side. He watches TV and smokes a cigarette. He's given up smoking dope: it's too expensive and Joanne didn't like the smell, and it made him tired.

It was difficult to say what had given Paul the most pleasure in his life, what had made him happy. He thought about this a lot at the moment, believing it might unlock the secret of what he should do next. They were mostly little things that had made him happy. Silly things. There was the time he'd won at the county Rabbit and Cavy Club event, for example – a silly wee thing, looking back on it, but it had meant a lot to him then. He'd won it with his black-and-tan buck, Bucky. They'd won the Junior Any Colour Tan class and Paul had imagined himself as a respected professional breeder, sweeping the board at rabbit shows worldwide. London: 'And the Winner of the All-English Fancy Challenge is . . . Paul McKee!' Paris: 'And the winner of the European Fancy Grand Challenge is . . . Paul McKee!' Singapore: 'And the winner of the Asian and Pan-Pacific Best in Show Award is . . . Paul McKee!' He'd have liked to have moved on to French lops: he liked their big long ears that dropped down the sides of their faces.

But it had all gone wrong: Bucky had come to a bad end. Paul used to keep Bucky on the landing of the flat, and there were some older boys on the same floor who'd got into drugs and Paul's mum had had to speak to them a few times, and then one night, when he was eating his tea in the kitchen by himself – sausage and chips that his mum had left in the oven for him when he got home from school, while she went out to work – he looked outside and he saw two of the boys, smiling and laughing, they were totally off their heads, and they took Bucky from his hutch and threw him over the balcony. They were on the fifth floor. Paul was about eleven, and he ran outside and the boys just laughed at him. That seemed inexplicable at the time. Paul had cried for hours and when his mum came back from work, exhausted, she just said to him, 'Well, life's hard,' which was irrefutable.

At lunchtime he eats two packets of crisps, an apple and some crackers, and at 12.30 he goes upstairs. He peeps out of the window. There's nothing happening. The postman has done his rounds, the builders have knocked off, the man on the corner with the garden has gone in. Even the old woman is probably on her lunch break.

He decides to lie down on the bed and have a think. He thinks maybe he'll have a nap.

Paul doesn't sleep well at night, now that he's started

sleeping during the day. He doesn't like sleeping during the day, but it has become a habit. He always dribbles and wakes up with a headache.

So he lay there, dozing, and trying to keep himself awake, trying not to think of all the things he could have done that day, like working and having weekends off, like normal people. He tried again to think about what he was going to do with his life. What he really wants to do is something spectacular – but who doesn't? He wants to create his own thing, be his own person. When he was at the Institute he cut some dub plates of his own and they played it, only in the studio there, but still, to have your music played, to be somebody. That was a buzz. Being married, on the other hand, is not a buzz, on the whole, he has found. Or being in our town. These things are ruts and a rut is pretty much the opposite of a buzz.

The only person Paul has talked to about his plans is his best friend from the Institute, Scunty, who is pretty much as his name suggests, and who has a mohawk haircut and a pierced lip, and who is into computers and who works in the Big Banana, the independent record shop up at the top of High Street, and who has promised that he will design some flyers for Paul – all Paul has to do is decide what he needs the flyers for.

What Paul has in mind at the moment is some *thing* – he can't be more specific – some kind of thing, some kind of thing like the things he's read about in books. He's read about the rave scene in the 1980s and the 1990s, but he was hardly even born then, so it's all academic to him. He'd studied it at the Institute, where for two years he learnt the theory and practice of music technology, all about channels and monitors and gates and compressors, and attended seminars and lectures with titles like 'Smashed Hits', in which tutors like Wally Lee – sad, unmarried, middle-aged men not originally from our town with creative facial hair and skaters' T-shirts – would examine issues of musical freedom of expression, beginning with Elvis Presley and ending with Puff Daddy, and Paul would sit there trans-fixed, listening to people talk about Frankie Knuckles and Marshall Jefferson, men who took an art form, shook it up and made it into something new. That's what he wanted to do. He wanted to make something happen. He wrote a long essay once about acid house and another one about the invention of breakbeat. They were good essays. He got nearly 60 per cent for those – they were his highest marks.

He dozes off to this ambient mix of memories and am-bitions in his head, and he doesn't wake up until four o'clock, the whole afternoon wasted and almost time to make the tea.

He checks to see if she's still there, the old woman oppo-site. She is. He feels exhausted after the sleep. Sometimes he's sure he can actually feel himself getting older, actually phys-ically older by the day – his life draining away. He used to exercise, but he couldn't really be bothered with that either these days. (After Bucky, he'd started going to the gym, straight from school. He trained for a while at the All Saints boxing club, up there in the city. There were loads of big names who'd started out there: Micky McCann; the Monaghans, the boxing dynasty; Mickey Hillen; Tom McCorry. He told himself that he was going to be a great boxer. He was going to be like Barry McGuigan. He was going to be a Great White Hope. But he couldn't stick that either. He didn't like getting hit. Or having to get the buses. In the winter he'd rather go home and watch the telly.)

He goes downstairs and while he gets the tea ready he switches on the radio.

It's the local station, Hitz!FM, a phone-in, and there's a woman on from town complaining about the high prices charged by vets. She's had to pay £150 for her dog to have a hysterectomy, she says. The DJ on the radio, he's called Julian Johns, he thinks he's hilarious. He thinks he's some kind of a shock-jock. He says that if the woman were to go into a private hospital to have a hysterectomy it would cost her – what? – about £3500, what with the anaesthetist's fees and everything. So what on earth is she complaining about? She's getting a bargain. Paul laughs for the first time that day. It was ridiculous to compare a human with a dog.

The programme ended and Paul got some peas out of the freezer compartment, and another programme came on, a panel discussion about the protection of the county's historic architecture, and they had on a local councillor, a woman, Mrs Donelly, talking about the need to preserve our heritage, the usual stuff, and then suddenly she mentioned the derelict Quality Hotel, which was just round the corner from where Paul was standing peeling potatoes. Mrs Donelly says she can remember when they used to have big show bands at the hotel in the old days, and dances, and people came from miles around to enjoy themselves. 'We had,' she says, 'the time of our lives.'

This rings a bell with Paul. He has been looking for somewhere to have the time of his life all his life. He's been thinking about a venue for ages: whatever it is he's going to do he's going to need somewhere to do it, and he knows it needs to be somewhere big. Which rules out most places in our town, unless it's the People's Park, but he doubts the council will grant permission, since they even stopped the circus coming a few years ago, because of all the horse shit and the damage to the flower beds and the grass.

Potatoes peeled, he crawls into the lounge to watch TV and wait for Joanne to come home.

It's a lovely sunny evening.

He thinks, maybe when Joanne gets home they'll go for a walk, down to the Quality Hotel, just to have a look.

7
Plumbing

*An introduction to the Oasis, further miseries and
tragedy, and a warm bath for Billy Nibbs*

It's been raining, again, midsummer, and for a plumber rain
is just another reminder that there will always be leaks and
that we shall never be dry, that this life is a vale of tears, that
we evolved from the slime, from the earth's boiling soup, the
bouillon of all existence, and that we shall eventually return
to the same.

A rainy day is not a good day for a plumber.

But then again there are really no good days in plumbing,
which is something that people who are not themselves
plumbers tend to forget. People tend to call plumbers when
things have gone badly wrong and plumbers do not therefore
tend to see human nature at its best, or the world through
rose-tinted glasses. There are only so many toilets you can
put your hands into before you begin to doubt the idea of
human perfectibility, and there is no sunshine and no soap
strong enough to cleanse a man of such doubts once he has
begun to entertain them, so in middle age the wise plumber
starts to specialise in kitchen and bathroom refits – work
which pays better and which, if you do it right, is guaranteed to put a smile on people's faces. A new shower unit can
do wonderful things for a person's self-esteem. However much

trouble you might have with your shower heater unit, or your wall brackets, or your curling sealant round the shower base, it is as nothing compared with the horror of a cracked cistern and the sight of a downstairs ceiling sagging like a huge pendulous breast, and a householder standing underneath it, like an idiot, with a bucket and a stick.

Sammy had never exactly been a happy plumber, but he had accepted misery as an occupational hazard. He was a silent man whose misery and whose silence we had always tolerated and even admired, but which had deepened into a terrible depression a few years ago when his four-year-old son Josh got sick on New Year's Eve. Sammy's wife, Sharon, who was a woman who did not share her husband's gloom, but who loved him nonetheless, had arranged to go out with a few friends for a girls' night out, to see out the old year and see in the new, and Sammy, who had never really enjoyed New Year's Eve and who always preferred to stay in and watch TV, had been more than happy to babysit.

Josh had complained before he went to bed of a slight headache, which Sammy had thought nothing of, and which he had put down to all the videos, but then the little fella had woken during the night with diarrhoea and vomiting, which Sammy put down to the fizzy drinks and sweets. Sammy was, of course, more equipped than most fathers to be able to deal with the mess, which he quickly cleared up, and afterwards he had treated himself to a couple of beers, to congratulate himself on his calm and his efficiency, and to welcome in the New Year. Over the next couple of hours, though, Josh's sickness had developed into a fever and then unconsciousness, and by the time Sammy had got the boy to the hospital early next morning, after he'd tried to wake him from his sleep and failed, he was in a coma. He never recovered.

Little Josh made the front page of the *Impartial Recorder* for three weeks running: first his coma, then his death and finally his funeral. There were full-colour photos – photographs of the grieving parents, of Sammy and Sharon, and a photo of Josh the paper had got hold of from his playgroup, down there on Russell Street. Joe Finnegan, the 'lensman', had refused an instruction from Colin Rimmer, the paper's editor, to use a telephoto and focus on the parents' tears, but the stuff Joe shot from a distance outside the hospital and of the funeral cortège was bad enough. It was not an auspicious moment in the newspaper's history and not a story that anyone in town could feel proud of: there were letters of complaint. Colin Rimmer replied, refusing the charge of prurience in his column, 'Rimmer's Around', invoking the Watergate scandal, the death of Princess Diana and other examples of the freedom of the press, where the public had a right to know. Even Bob Savory, a long-standing friend and supporter of Colin's, felt that on this occasion he had gone too far. But the damage had been done.

After the funeral, Sammy did not leave the house for about a month: he was too ashamed and often at night, for a long time afterwards, Josh would come to Sammy in his dreams, and he'd be sick again, and Sammy would carefully clean him up and put him to bed, and Josh would say again to Sammy the last words that Sammy had heard him speak – 'Poo and pee myself, Daddy' – and then Sammy would wipe the boy's fevered brow and he'd fall off to sleep, and everything would be OK.

But then Sammy would wake up from the dream and be sure there was a smell in the room, only to find that he had soiled the sheets himself. It was a terrible judgement that his body was wreaking upon him and he was completely unable to cope, was totally overwhelmed, in fact, and, naturally, he had started to drink.

He found himself unable or unwilling to comfort or be comforted by Sharon, who said she didn't blame him, but she did, really, and he knew she did, but he couldn't talk to her about it and she couldn't talk to him about it, and he had also spurned the comfort of his family and friends, preferring instead to spend time in the pub. He avoided the Castle Arms, though – anywhere he was likely to meet any of us, or any of his friends – and started drinking in the Armada Bar, which is a Spanish-styled place up by the station with flaking bull-fight murals and a plastic imitation vine, a bar 30 feet long and only 5 feet wide, a bar shaped like a ship, with no tables, with stools only, where you can buy wine by the carafe and single cigarettes, and where there is only country on the jukebox, and which is the bar where people tend to go in our town when things have gone wrong in their lives, and which usually makes things about a thousand times worse.

Colin Rimmer, the editor of the *Impartial Recorder*, which had caused Sammy and Sharon so much grief after the death of Josh, made the mistake of calling in to the Armada one night for a drink and to catch up with local gossip, and when Sammy saw him he got up, dragged Colin from his stool and punched him hard in the face, just once, catching him off balance and knocking him down on to the floor and wiping the lopsided grin from his face.

Sammy was about to start in on Colin proper when Niall the barman got a hold of him. 'You're barred,' he said.

'Thanks,' said Colin, getting up painfully from the floor.

'Not him,' said Niall. 'You, you lowlife. Now get out.'

Sammy didn't pay for another drink all evening.

And so, within a year of Josh's death, Sammy had lost his wife, his house, his business, and he was busy drinking in the park from seven in the morning and in the Armada till late at night, seven days a week, returning to his bedsit down at the bottom of Kilmore Avenue only to sleep and to dream. He stank and, to be honest, he felt that it was all that he deserved.

It is as much a surprise to Sammy, then, as to anyone else, that within two years of the death of his son he has remarried and started up again in business, although this time not as a plumber.

Sammy and his new wife and business partner, Cherith, now run a small shop, a studio and offices opposite the car park, next to the Quality Hotel. And last week was the grand opening.

We were all there, a lot of us, to celebrate a new beginning for Sammy and for Cherith, and to wish them well.

Like Sammy, Cherith has been previously married also, of course – to Francie McGinn, the minister at the People's Fellowship. It remains a popular little church – and Francie remains a popular minister, still, despite everything. He decided right from the start to stay on and brazen it out, and God and his congregation seem to have forgiven him.

Cherith, though, had not. She had not given Francie a second chance: it can be much more difficult to forgive the pious than to forgive the average sinner, and actually Cherith was secretly delighted at not having to be a minister's wife any more. She went on another diet that actually worked, took some exercise, and took to wearing cropped tops and bumster trousers, and after the divorce came through she started going out more at night, to pubs and clubs, and she had started to drink and meet young men in Paradise Lost who wore after-shave and owned fuel-injected cars, but that was too depressing, and after a while she started to stay in more, but she kept on drinking, and she was getting through about a bottle of Chardonnay a night, plus a couple of lager chasers to clear her head, and two or three large glasses of Amaretto during *ER*, after a bath, and maybe a drop of Bailey's Irish Cream on the cereals in the morning – she was a sweet-toothed drinker – and in the end she kind of washed up at Alcoholics Anonymous, where she met Sammy, and the two of them clung to each other like two ships without a port.

The business was Cherith's idea, after she and Sammy had sobered up and had got themselves back on their feet, and they'd got married at sunrise on a beach in Thailand, and they had enjoyed aromatherapy and saunas and therapeutic massage in their luxurious honeymoon hotel. We've never had anything quite like that in our town and Cherith was quick to see the gap in the market, and thus was born their business, the Oasis – not quite as luxurious, perhaps, as the place in Thailand, and lacking the same sunny aspect, but with good intentions nonetheless.

It's open now, just a week old – you can go in yourself and have a look. In Oasis, the Shop, Sammy and Cherith offer a range of books on subjects such as shamanism, life coaching and reiki healing, and a wide range of loofahs, seaweed scrubs and scented candles. From Oasis, the Office, they plan their dolphin retreat adventures, and classes in warrior yoga and belly-dancing, but it's the Oasis Aqua-Studio, which overlooks the car park in front of the Quality Hotel, that really is the centrepiece.

Cherith and Sammy have invested in a spa pool from America, called the 'Oasis', which is top-of-the-range, and in which and through which they now offer aqua-massage, water dancing and Dynamic Movement Therapies. Sammy plumbed the whole thing in himself – it was a big job, the pool is a monster – and they had to have the floors reinforced and fulfil all kinds of safety regulations, and it took about a month to get it up and running properly. But finally it was done and the room fixed up with dimmer lights, and decorated in tasteful soothing aqua colours, and it sits there, the spa pool, in the middle of the room, with a view to the car park out front and to the People's Fellowship out back, like a beached vessel stuck in the middle of town, or a tiny liquid sea, and when you switch it on and you turn down the lights, it has the pleasant sound of a bubbling brook, the sound of water running away from you in the dark.

Billy Nibbs got to try it the night before the big opening last week – he was the first customer. Sammy and Cherith had invited him specially – Billy is Sammy's oldest friend and he is certainly someone who looks like he needs some time in a brand-new top-of-the-range relaxing spa pool.

Like most of us here in town Billy is in the habit of looking gift horses in the mouth and he'd taken some persuading, but in the end he had agreed to come and give it a go, and he slipped off his clothes and slipped into the warm water, and as he lay there looking up at the ceiling, bubbles all around him, he thought about the recent past; and Sammy, who had been stocking the shelves downstairs with books about Emotional Intelligence and Wisdom Traditions, appeared at the door and gave him an embarrassed little wave.

'How is it?' asked Sammy.

'It's good,' said Billy, getting up to get out.

'You're supposed to stay in and relax,' said Sammy.

'Right.' Billy had never been in a spa pool before. In fact, lately he'd hardly ever been in the bath.

'It'll do you good.'

'OK.'

Billy closed his eyes and tried to relax. He was at a pretty low ebb.

After the bookless book launch he'd gone to meet his publisher, and the train was two hours delayed, and there was no buffet car, and the windows did not open, and the trolley service was suspended, all of which had made Billy feel very Philip Larkiny, and he had consoled himself by stroking his thick black beard and trying to imagine his book, the book he was about to see and claim for his own.

He imagined it produced in beautiful dark-blue thick board covers, the embossed imprint of his publisher running along the spine. He also imagined a cheap paperback edition, distributed worldwide, with a beautiful cover designed by a famous artist, an artist who probably also happened to be a personal friend. He felt sure he'd have got on with Damien Hirst. He imagined launch parties in several European cities and big limos at airports, a ticker-tape parade in New York, the Nobel Prize even – well, he was maybe getting ahead of himself there.

He found that thinking about all this cheered him and

aroused him – made him forget about the lack of ventilation on the train and the shortage of hot and cold snacks and beverages – and he snuggled deeper into his seat, his eyes closed, tucking his hands between his legs, and he could almost feel himself fingering his book, he could feel its coolness, the weight of its white wove pages between his fingers, the fulfilment of so many years' ambition and desire.

Thinking about it left him feeling deeply satisfied and exhausted, and he fell into a deep sleep, and when the train arrived at its final destination he awoke refreshed, bought himself a street map and hurried off to his publisher's offices, his anticipation turning finally to excitement.

He'd had to walk for what seemed like a very long time down residential streets, past blocks of flats and houses being refurbished at ridiculous expense, having all their original features painstakingly replaced, and all the fine modern fittings removed and thrown into skips – in which he had, of course, a professional interest, and over which and into which he cast a professional eye – and in the end there was nothing to indicate that number 47 on the Dublin Road, a large three-storey terrace which remained unrenovated, was a business premises at all, except that taped under the doorbell, on a scrap of stained white paper, was the name, written in biro, the name that he had imagined a thousand times running down his spine, and on his title page: Byrne & Co.

Billy rang the bell. There was no answer. There was another piece of paper stuck below the bell. It said, 'Bell not working. Please knock. Loudly.'

Billy did as was suggested and eventually he heard movement from within the house.

An elderly man opened the door, dressed in green jumbo cords and a T-shirt featuring a cartoon drawing of a man with wild staring eyes and chattering teeth and the words 'Caffeine High!'. The man wearing the T-shirt wore tartan carpet slippers and was completely bald, except for the hair growing from his nose, and his ears, and up around his throat, and the back of his hands. A pair of glasses dangled from a rainbow-coloured cord hung round his neck. There was the unmistakable smell of gin and cigarettes.

'You are?' asked the man.

'Billy Nibbs.'

'And this affects me how?'

'You're publishing my book.'

'Ah!' said the man.

'And I haven't received any copies of the book yet, and I . . .'

'Goodbye!' said the man, slamming the door and bolting it behind him.

'Hang on!' shouted Billy.

'Go away!' said the man, retreating off into the hallway.

Billy shouted through the letter box, but his calls went unanswered. All the curtains in the house were drawn – there was no way in, or round.

Billy stood on the doorstep for a long time before he went away and started the long walk back to the station, past the skips and the houses, and he only realised gradually – could only allow himself to realise slowly, to save himself the pain – exactly what had happened to him.

He felt sick. He felt like an idiot. He felt like crying. He felt as though someone had cleaved away the innermost parts of himself and left him hanging like an empty carcass. There was no publisher. There was going to be no book.

The journey home was different from the journey down, although it was just the same train, going backwards, and the same scenery in reverse. The weather outside had taken a turn for the worse and Billy found himself staring out of the window, watching his too too solid and semi-permeable flesh fast disappearing in the rain. He looked at his reflection and what he saw suddenly did not look like a writer. All the great writers look like writers. Evelyn Waugh in his tweeds. George

Orwell in all that prole gear. Beckett in his roll-neck. They're always done up – the men in particular – as if they know what they're about, like applicants keen to make a good impression. With his beard and his earring and his novelty tie Billy Nibbs did not look like a writer. He looked like an eccentric council employee, a man who tended to skips and bins and bottle banks, and who read books in his spare time, and who wrote bad long poems.

When he arrived back in town Billy headed straight for the Armada Bar. He recognised most of the people in there, but no one spoke to him, and he did not speak to them. The Armada was not a bar where conversation was expected, or encouraged, or condoned.

By the time he left the Armada he was feeling a lot worse. He had that feeling, that feeling like it's three or four in the morning and you've been drinking since about six and you've been at a party and you're walking home and it begins to rain and you've no coat and there are no buses and you can't afford a taxi and you think about the countless ways you've let yourself down at the party and the good time all the other people were having and you sit down at the side of the road and hold your head in your hands and there's a bunch of young blokes you hadn't noticed before in a bus shelter on the other side of the road, and they all have shaven heads and are wearing sports-casual clothing and baseball caps, and they are all staring at you. It was that kind of feeling.

That's what literary failure feels like. It feels like you're about to get a kicking.

When he finally made it in safely through his front door he made a cup of tea and sat down and stared at the reproduction of Van Gogh's *Sunflowers* which hangs heavily in a snap-frame above his flimsy blue Formica-topped fold-out kitchen table. The picture is one of Billy's favourites. He also has a reproduction Matisse in the hallway – one of those blue blobby women – a stained Escher in the bathroom and a

111

blurry Monet thing above his bed. In our town, this virtually constitutes a gallery. But the flat is not a gallery – it's a bedsit down on Kilmore Avenue, with its own separate kitchen and bathroom. 'This is Luxury You Can Afford,' said the landlord when Billy came to view the property fifteen years ago.

The landlord was Frank Gilbey. Frank liked to call personally to collect the rent once a month and Billy could understand that. There is no real satisfaction in a standing order. If you're a landlord you must want to see that look of fear and anger and frustration in the eyes of your tenants as they hand over their hard-earned cash to you to keep your children in private schools and your good self in fine clothes and cigars and vintage sports cars. In fifteen years, Frank Gilbey had never once asked Billy Nibbs how he was, or who, and he ignored every one of Billy's requests for maintenance or repairs or rent rebates. The place was gradually deteriorating, but it didn't matter to Frank Gilbey, because he was just sitting on the property, waiting to sell it on for redevelopment when the time was right. In the meantime he could afford to let the place just fall apart.

Which, arguably, Billy was too: he had no book, no woman, no prospects and nothing to show for it, his thirty-odd years on this earth. At this moment he felt something of an affinity for Van Gogh, the difference being, of course, that Van Gogh was a genius and Billy could still see the colours in his sunflowers, in a poor reproduction, over one hundred years after he'd painted them, even in the dark and under the influence, while Billy's cup of tea looked a pathetic grey already, like the walls in the flat and his own miserable insides.

Billy stared at his walls and finished his grey tea, thinking about Van Gogh.

(Van Gogh chopped off his own ear, didn't he? But it wasn't his whole ear. It was his lobe. The *lobule*. It couldn't have been the whole thing, because you lose your hearing: it sort of funnels the noise in, doesn't it, the fleshy bit? Billy couldn't remember how. Sometimes he wishes he'd listened in science at school, then he might be able to remember useful stuff like that, like how birds sleep and why penguins' feet don't freeze, and how mirrors work, and why the moon is round. Or even basic stuff, like the names of clouds and birds and body parts.)

Billy rinsed his mug in the sink and made his way unsteadily to his bedroom-cum-sitting room, pausing only to kiss a lovely blobby blue Matisse breast along the way.

There were books and papers piled high on the floor, which in the dark looked a little like artful piles of bricks, or stacked tyres, and there were clothes spilling out imaginatively from the wardrobe, whose numerous constituent MDF body parts had long since parted company from each other, peeling apart as if possessed by demons or by the thing in *The Thing* or the alien in *Alien*. The duvet was very limp. On the desk there were bits and pieces of poems, and some congealed scrambled egg and bacon on a cracked plate.

Looking at the mess that was his life, Billy wondered for a moment if perhaps he could wrap the whole thing in cellophane, or set it in plaster and sell it wholesale to some collector in New York, or to Charles Saatchi – £10,000 would do him for a year. Or £5000. Or actually, Billy would probably settle for some free cinema tickets and some extra points on his Sainsbury's reward card, and a few celebrities at the gala exhibition opening. He'd take whatever second-rate champagne swillers were currently on offer. Oh yes. Bring 'em all in. Kill the fatted calf. Come and feed your faces on canapés, ye Mighty. And as they all gathered to admire his handiwork, all the critics and the publishers and the editors, Billy would rise to address them and he would say . . . He would say . . . Do you know what he would say?

He opened his eyes. He was still there, lying in the spa pool. And looking out of the window, he saw the offices of the *Impartial Recorder*, its big red neon lettering staring at him, lighting up the night sky.

And suddenly he no longer felt self-pity or frustration. He no longer felt like a poet. The pool had entirely cleansed him of those feelings. It felt like a tide had gone out on his emotions, washing away all the murk. Now he only felt clear, pure white anger – anger towards his publisher and towards Frank Gilbey, and towards all the other people who had treated him wrong in his life. Suddenly he knew what he wanted to say. Suddenly the way seemed clear.

Sammy came in to find Billy getting dressed – he'd finished stocking the shelves downstairs with little books of calm. 'Did you enjoy that?' he asked.

'I did, actually,' said Billy. 'I feel much better.'

8

The Steam Master

Containing several shocks and surprises for the Quinns, both father and son

It's been blue skies for nearly a week now, and temperatures hot enough for young men to strip down to T-shirts and tattoos, and women to lie out in the People's Park in bikini tops, sipping Bacardi Breezers and listening to the radio. It's positively Mediterranean, though with more techno, maybe, and not as much garlic. Davey Quinn Senior has been house painting and he's as brown as a berry: Mrs Quinn says he looks like a black man. He's so brown, in fact, that his tattoos have virtually disappeared: they look like shadows, or large areas of skin cancer possibly.

Despite being up the ladder and out in the sun ten hours a day, Davey Quinn Senior has not been applying sun cream, much to Mrs Quinn's disapproval: his old bald head is peeling so badly it looks like a hot chestnut and he leaves flakes behind him in bed. Davey Senior does not really believe in sun cream, although unknown to Mrs Quinn he has been using a lot of Deep Heat recently: he's been suffering pains in his hands and in his knees and in his hips again.

Davey Quinn Senior is sixty-three years old now and built like a boxer: hands like mangles, a chest like a barrel, arms like joints of meat and a back almost as broad as it is stiff.

His knees are thick and swollen, and almost entirely without cartilage. When he bends down to pick up a paint pot these days there is a grinding of his joints, like a machine without oil. He drinks about triple the recommended units per week, takes three sugars in his tea and six in a flask, but he doesn't eat like he used to. He sleeps for no more than five hours a night, often waking at 4 a.m. with back pain and a terrible need to piss. He had trouble with his prostate a few years ago – he pronounces it 'prostrate', deliberately, to annoy Mrs Quinn, successfully – and he has cut down on the beer and now drinks mostly wine and spirits. He'd never drunk wine until he was in his mid-fifties – most of the men he knew still didn't, but Davey was not a stick-in-the-mud in his drinking habits and he liked to keep up to date. There was even a time, during the early 1970s, when he drank martinis, but that was just a phase, everyone was doing it – even in the Castle Arms and the Hercules Bar there were grown men drinking sweet drinks from small glasses, with olives and slices of lemon. Davey Senior fancied himself now as something of a connoisseur, if not a wine buff exactly. Mrs Quinn would occasionally take a glass of chardonnay, or a rosé, but Mr Quinn preferred the red wine – you couldn't beat a nice New World Shiraz, in his opinion. He gave up smoking five years ago – having first down-shifted to low-tar – after his friend Jacky had been diagnosed with lung cancer. Davey Senior had found it hard giving up: it took him two years to stop completely, but he'd been determined. He didn't want the same to happen to him as had happened to Jacky. Jacky had died and he was only fifty-six years old, and in Davey's terms this meant Jacky was a young man, a baby almost: Davey, at the time, was fifty-seven. Jacky had been in the year below him at St Gall's. It was a shock and a sadness to see him go – of course, you always wonder who's going to be the first among you to go, and when they go you can't help feeling that somehow it was the right thing, that it was never really meant to be you, that you were always the one destined to hang around for a little longer than the others, even if it was only to apply a few more coats of paint to your crumbling walls and to enjoy a little extra elbow room at the bar. It's a terrible truth and one you can't live with for ever, but when an old friend dies, you draw a little strength from their passing.

Davey Senior had learnt his lesson from Jacky and had tried an acupuncturist for the smoking, a Chinese fella, Doctor Ye, recommended to him by Little Mickey Matchett, whom Davey used to play football with and who's had terrible trouble with his cartilage – the old footballer's disease – and who now swears by what he calls the 'foreign medicine'.

Doctor Ye is known to most people in town as 'the other Chinaman' – Mr Wong and his family from the takeaway being the first, the most important and the most popular.* Doctor Ye's parents arrived here from China in the 1950s. They were actually from the same town in China as the Wongs, and when they heard over there how well the Wongs were doing and how much they liked it here – something, one

---

* The Wongs have been here for over fifty years now and they have made their contribution to society – the original Mr Wong, Huaning, or Hugh, as we called him, became chairman of the Old Green Road Allotment Holders' Association, where he grew prize-winning chard and begonias, and his daughter Zhu, or Sue, is now headmistress at the Assumption primary school, where she insists on phonics and observing saint's days. Through providing generations of us here with spring rolls and egg-fried rice the Wongs helped provide their family back in China with enough money for Flying Pigeon bicycles and Snowflake refrigerators, and more recently, enough for a car, a DVD player and Manchester United replica kits. Mr Wong got to visit his sister in Beijing before he died a few years ago, the first time he'd ever been back, and he was glad he made the trip although 'it looks like Birmingham,' he told the *Impartial Recorder*. There was standing room only for his funeral at the Church of the Cross and the Passion, and Hugh's son Rao, or Ray, now runs the takeaway but it looks as though he'll be the last in the line. Ray's own children, Jonathan and Sally, are keen to break with tradition: Jonathan is still at school but he works weekends and evenings at Becky Badger's Animal Surgery and Pet Centre, and would like to become a vet; Sally is studying for a degree in Art History up in the city and would like to be a TV presenter or, failing that, a lecturer.

117

suspects, had been lost in the translation – they thought they'd give it a try, and they managed to steal a passage and get out, and for years they ran a little upholstery business from home, a house on the Brunswick Road, full of bare naked chairs and vast blankets of fabric, and they kept themselves to themselves, quietly assimilating and getting on with the endless task of mending and making good. They got to like milk in their tea, and toast, and they got into pub and club refurbishments, big business here in the 1980s. The children were privately educated, at Barneville House, the old boarding school beyond the ring road, and they all made it to university. The eldest son, Stevie, Doctor Ye, now operates out of his own house on Cromac Street, where he eats macrobiotic, as much as is possible here, and has a little pagoda built from breeze blocks and rendered and painted in Dulux Weathershield 'Golden Sunrise' in the front garden, and a nice water feature – installed at enormous expense, but which was tax deductible – and he spends his days in his converted front room burning herbs and sticking long thin needles into the fat white fish-bellied bodies of the people of our town.

Not a lot had changed, according to Stevie's dad, Mr Ye. He did chairs: Stevie does people.

The acupuncture hadn't actually worked on Davey Senior's smoking – he'd managed it in the end with gum – but while he was seeing Doctor Ye, Davey had mentioned the trouble he was having with his shoulder and Stevie had popped in a couple of extras, for free, and – bam! – it was like electric currents racing through Davey's body.

'It felt like being rewired,' he told everyone down at the Castle Arms, including Georgie Hannigan, who is an electrician and who rather doubted it – he's been electrocuted a couple of times himself and he knows it's not something to boast about. Davey Senior had briefly become an acupuncture bore: talking about yin and yang, and energy channels and meridians, but he found that people's eyes soon glazed over

118

when he started talking about it and, without either the interest or the ability to pursue the subject further, he soon got bored with it himself. The needles became just a pleasant memory.

He was thinking about acupuncture now, though, for the first time in a long while, and about private medical insurance, as he lay on the floor, the sharp point of a paintbrush, or something, possibly a body part, digging in his back. He had no idea what had happened to him.

There'd been a touch of drizzle first thing in the morning and he'd moved inside on a job, and one minute, just a moment ago, he'd been up the ladder, quite high, cutting in, using one of those so-called 'heritage' colours that everyone was so keen on these days – and which all looked like bird shit if you asked him – in one of the big old houses on Fitzroy Avenue, with the thirteen-foot ceilings and the ornate plaster covings, and the next thing he knew he was lying on the floor, looking up at a freshly painted ceiling.

Davey Senior did not panic. The worst thing you can do in a situation like that is to panic. For the self-employed, falling off ladders is something you come to expect now and again, like a letter from the taxman asking you to come in for an interview. As he lay there, Davey Senior remembered the many who had fallen before him, or at least the ones who'd admitted to it: Jacky, who'd lost two fingers when he was working in the steel plant and took a tumble from a gangway; Scotty, the big Scotsman, who was a glazier and who had the scars to show for it; and of course Davey's old friend Dessie, Big Dessie Brown, a friend from way back. Dessie had had it the worst of all of them, of course, had suffered the biggest fall, but then look what had happened to him. Dessie was the living proof, in our town, that there were sometimes silver linings.

Dessie had been a roofer and had broken his back when he fell off one of the new builds doing the slates on one of the first estates built outside the ring road. The injury nearly finished him off – he walked bent double, like a cripple, with a stick –

119

but he always referred to the fall as his 'lucky break'. He said that when he was lying there looking up at the sky, unable to move or to speak, it was like a revelation, a visitation of the Blessed Virgin Mary, and that what She was saying to him was clear and unambiguous, and it had changed his life for ever and in an instant. It might be better, the BVM seemed to be suggesting to Big Dessie, to pay someone else to climb roofs for you. From that moment on Dessie had never looked back. He never climbed another roof, and now he lived in a six-bedroom house with a swimming pool, tennis courts and views across open fields. He ran a full team right across the county – sparks, joiners, plumbers, plasterers, painters and decorators, the full works – and he paid no heed to niceties like tax and National Insurance, which the Blessed Virgin didn't seem to have been too bothered about Herself, and he drove a specially modified Rolls-Royce Silver Shadow, with a disabled badge, and he'd always stand Davey Senior a pint if he saw him down the pub, and they would reminisce about old goals and fixtures. Those were the days. He used to pay for his drink from a big roll of cash he carried around done up with an elastic band.*

Davey Senior was thinking about that big wad of cash and he was looking for his own silver lining all the way to the hospital, where the doctors told him the worst: he'd cracked two ribs and three vertebrae. He was going to be off work for some time.

Well, Davey Senior was a man who could not afford to be off work for some time. His three sons in the business, Daniel,

---

* Wallets, in our town, are still considered effeminate, a foreign practice, something you see people using on holiday in the Canary Islands, or the Balearics, or in America. Most men still prefer the jingle of loose coins in their pockets and the risk of losing the odd fiver in the wash – just to remind themselves of what it was like to be young and single. In our town it's the ladies who tend to carry the cards in their purses – most men here cannot handle plastic. An elastic band or a metal money clip is about as far as most of us will go in the direction of organising our personal finances.

Gerry and Craig, could keep things ticking over – they were good boys – but at the end of the day they were going to be a man down, and with all the contracts coming in they couldn't afford to be. They had a school to do, the new Collegiate School up on the ring road; and houses; and shops; business premises. Davey was running a big small business and he was going to need someone he could trust to take care of some of the smaller jobs, a body, someone who knew the business, who could work unsupervised, and someone he could rely upon to uphold the standards of the Quinn name. Above all, he needed someone whom he didn't need to pay.

Davey Senior had not been to church in thirty years, and he no more believed in the Blessed Virgin Mary than he did in the tooth fairy and Father Christmas, but as he lay in bed in the hospital, considering his dilemma, eating his hospital food, he had an idea.

On his first day back home, out of hospital, the first day of his convalescence, he asked Mrs Quinn to cook up a nice meal to celebrate his return: a good plain meat pie, maybe, with mashed potato and gravy, followed by a treacle pudding. If the way to a man's heart is through his stomach, then Davey was determined to cut a swath, using all the complex carbo-hydrates at his disposal.

Since his own return home Davey's son, young Davey, the seventh son of the seventh son, has tried to avoid eating with his parents. He just couldn't face the same meals he remem-bered from his childhood: he was amazed, in fact, that they were still eating the identical stuff, twenty years on, with only the occasional added variation of a microwave lasagne and a token bottle of olive oil in the kitchen cupboard to register the fact that this was not still 1976, that this was post-*Ready, Steady, Cook*, this was a new millennium and not the culinary Stone Age. It was pies still, mostly, in the Quinn household, and puddings for pudding, and Mr and Mrs Quinn were even using the same plates that Davey remembered, and the same crackle-plastic-handled cutlery, and the English hunting-scene place mats. His parents' house depressed him in general and unutterably, but the kitchen – the kitchen depressed him more than anything, and in every detail, from the fake marble finish on its lonely brown breakfast bar, to its varnished tongue-and-groove on the walls, and its faded venetian blind perpetually at half-mast, even though no direct sunlight penetrated through the leylandii which now shaded and protected the bungalow on all sides.

No good things had ever happened in the Quinn family kitchen, as far as Davey could remember, it was just too small for anything except cooking and washing up, which of course is what a kitchen is for, except for the middle classes who, even in our town, tend to use their kitchens for the same varied purposes the Quinn family had always used the pub: in order to drink, and to argue, and to meet their friends. If the kitchen is the heart of the house, like people say, if that was really true, then the Quinn house had a serious coronary problem. The Quinn kitchen was not a place where family meals were shared, or problems discussed, where children did their homework while Mummy made muffins, or even where crockery was thrown, or cafetière coffee drunk late into the night while thrashing out personal or global political problems. It was simply a place, a narrow space, where for years the Quinns had eaten Findus Crispy Pancakes and Angel Delight, in rotation, all seven brothers taking turns on one of the two stools, only one of which – the TV stool – afforded a clear view of the television in the adjacent front room.

In fact, the only interesting thing that had ever happened to Davey in that kitchen was that when his father or mother spoke to him at mealtimes, now as then, Davey always seemed to know exactly what they were about to say. His parents had induced in him from a young age a permanent sense of déjà vu, but this was not, alas, Davey realised early on, because he was an alien abductee or because in another life he'd been a Cherokee Indian and was blessed with the gift of second sight or the Third Eye – it was simply because his family repeated themselves. Endlessly.*

Over the past few years Davey had grown accustomed to eating by himself, often in silence, or with his friends, when and where he wanted, usually in cheap curry houses or pizza places, and he only ate food he liked, with people he liked. In all his years away he had managed to develop for himself just one home-cooked speciality, chicken-celery soup, which when eaten with a slice, or preferably two, or even three, of wholemeal bread, Davey had found usefully combined both protein and roughage, and also those all-important vitamins and minerals that go to make up that all-important balanced diet that you always read so much about in the papers and on the side of cereal packets. There is a knack to soup-making – it's all about balancing smoothness and acidity – and Davey Quinn believed that with his chicken and celery soup he had mastered the art. This is his secret recipe:

CHICKEN-CELERY SOUP
1 can chicken soup
1 can celery soup
Combine soups. Heat. Serves 4–6.

* In summary, Quinn family conversation consists of little more than a dozen repeated phrases, like the language of a primitive tribespeople, the No-Hopi, perhaps, of the Back of Beyond. These phrases are: 'I don't know what the world's coming to', 'No', 'I said no', 'Oh, dear', 'Well', 'Sorry, what did you say?', 'Fine', 'What time will you be back?', 'What do you want it for?', 'What do you want to do that for?', 'Because it's too expensive', 'Would you like a cup of tea?', 'Would you like another cup of tea?' and 'I don't know what that's all about at all'. There are some variations according to time, place and the person speaking, but not many. Non-verbal communication between family members lacks the same subtlety and tends towards a single expressive raising of the eyebrow, although Mr Quinn does make occasional use of tutting and Mrs Quinn of desultory head-shaking.

There was a microwave in the kitchen of the shared house in west London where Davey had eventually ended up before returning home, and his cooking had increasingly come to rely upon and revolve around the microwave's limited capacities: so Mondays, for example, was usually baked potatoes with cheese and baked beans; Tuesdays was baked potatoes with anchovies; Wednesdays, chicken-celery soup; Thursdays, baked potato with pesto. Fridays, Saturdays, Sundays varied according to whereabouts, although it was often a meal out with friends, or a meal in with his housemates. (He also used to patronise an excellent kebab shop, called The Sultan's Delight, on the Uxbridge Road, more than once a week, where the proprietor, Dimitri, had lost his left-hand forefinger in an accident with hot oil and where privileged regulars, among whom Davey was proud to count himself, got to call him One-Finger and were given a few more slices of meat and some extra chilli sauce, if Dimitri was in the mood.)

The Tuesday-night baked potatoes with anchovies – Davey's other claim to culinary innovation, apart from the chicken-celery soup – he liked to call his Mystery Potatoes. All you had to do was put the potato in the microwave for ten minutes, then scoop out the flesh from inside and mix it up with chopped anchovy fillets and then scoop it all back in and do the potato for about another five. And then . . . Surprise!

The first time one of his housemates, Jane, had tried a Mystery Potato, she had cut into it, releasing that lovely strong, slightly constipated anchovy smell, and revealing the lovely dark mush inside, and had refused to eat it, had hurried to the bathroom, in fact, and had not returned for some time. No one else apart from Davey seemed to like it.

The crust on Mrs Quinn's meat pie, meanwhile, had been cooked to the point of explosion, the mincemeat inside dried stiff with Oxo, and the mashed potato was sober and cold. The carrots were chopped into chunks, the gravy was Bisto, and the New World Shiraz was fresh in from the shed and in contrast to the accompanying hot, strong cup of tea. Davey Senior kept on quietly refilling Davey's wineglass and his mug with tea, and he waited until Davey had cleared his plate before he popped the question.

Would Davey, he wondered, consider taking on some jobs while he recovered from his fall – would Davey, in other words, reconsider his long-standing opposition to working in the family business, and come and work for Quinn and Sons?

Davey, of course, refused point-blank: it was a conversation they'd had enough times not to need a rehearsal, or even a pause for thought. Also, he had his work at the Plough and the Stars, as a kitchen porter, so it was out of the question.

'But a kitchen porter,' began Davey Senior.

'What?'

'Compared to the family business . . .'

Mrs Quinn saw how things were going. She felt her husband should have known better and she tried to move the conversation along, but Davey Senior persisted and positions became entrenched.

And then the treacle pudding arrived.

It was not the pudding itself that mattered. The pudding was much like any other: dry and suety, and too much of it, in a sticky pool of treacle. The point of a pudding is not to be unique and special: the point of a pudding is to be like other puddings.* Also, there is no such thing as the single-serve pudding: no one is going to bother to steam a pudding just for themselves. A single man does not make himself puddings: a pudding requires a family or at the very least some guests. Without others a pudding simply does not exist. A pudding is proof that there is such a thing as society. Davey,

---

* Those who have attended Barry McClean's 'Philosophy for Beginners' will perhaps recognise in Mrs Quinn's pudding a reflection or shadow of the problem of Plato's theory of forms and of various theories of identity through time, including Quine's 'no entity without identity' and Frege's *Foundations of Arithmetic*.

who was struggling back at home, who had spent so many years alone and away from his family and from this town, and not all of them happy, away from puddings and pies, and whose idea of a dessert was a bar of Dairy Milk from the twenty-four-hour garage, or something not quite defrosted in an Indian restaurant, now found himself completely defenceless in the face of his mother's sugar and suet, this little mound of family values, and the sight of it and the taste of it, and another large helping, and a glass or two of the brandy his father had been given for Christmas last year by a satisfied customer, warmed and softened his cold, cold heart.

It was a feeling and a warmth which had more or less worn off by nine o'clock the next morning, however, when arriving at a house in his dad's van, with 'Davey Quinn and Sons' painted on the sides, to announce himself to the owners.

It was a couple, the job – a Mr and Mrs Wilson, and just one room. The Wilsons are new to town and their house is one of the old houses, up near the golf course, one of the few remaining houses we have with the original sash windows, which Mr and Mrs Wilson are determined to retain and maintain, and which afford pleasant views of the all-new, strictly-uPVC development, Woodsides, whose name is something of a misnomer, since they had to cut down the wood to build the houses.

Mr Wilson enjoys his elevated aspect and mature landscaped gardens to front and rear, and is a senior manager with Solly Wiseman's industrial and contract cleaning firm, CleenEezy, which has its offices on the industrial estate, up there off the ring road, near to Bloom's. The couple have a baby on the way – just weeks away, in fact – so they don't have the time to do the decorating themselves, as Mr Wilson is at pains to explain to Davey, implying that he would have been more than capable of doing it himself, actually, and probably better, under normal circumstances. In our town, even if your wife is about to have a child and you work in middle management and you can afford to have people in to do work for you, you still have to pretend that you would and could do it yourself, if it weren't for mitigating circumstances. You have to do a lot of face-saving in our town: as a people, we are not natural employers. All our middle classes here clean for their cleaners and we have turned the necessity of DIY into a virtue.

Mr Wilson was busy and on his way to work, wearing one of those shirts with the cutaway collar and the bone inserts – shirts which he loves and he has one for every day of the week, plus some in reserve – and a big fat tie in blue and yellow chevrons. He probably has some of the best ties in town: he orders them from London, from the pages of the *Sunday Times* magazine. Mrs Wilson is wearing black, has not a dyed-blonde hair out of place and is on maternity leave.

The Wilsons are undoubtedly the future of our town and not its past: they are proud of their leather sofa and their wide-screen TV, and quite right, since there is really nothing like relaxing on your own leather sofa at the end of a hard day, a glass of Czech-style beer in hand and satellite sport on the telly. Mr Wilson was thinking about it already, in fact, as he made his excuses and left for work.

They'd done most of the major work now, Mrs Wilson was explaining to Davey, touching her bump. Now they just wanted to get started on the decorating: her mother was going to be staying for a few weeks after the baby was born and so they wanted to begin with the spare room. Quinn and Sons had been recommended to them, 'by word of mouth,' she said, with a barely suppressed smile of satisfaction and knowing, 'word of mouth' appearing to her to be almost as good as a lifetime guarantee, a shibboleth, or access to the secrets of some cabalistic organisation or cult. Which is pretty much what it's like, actually, which is the reality of living in a small town. You need the inside information in order to survive: you have to have the knowledge. Cities are full of amateurs – you can get by on a lot of bluffing in a city – but a small town is full of adepts.

Davey hauled his stuff in from the van and was shown

upstairs to a large room whose walls were covered with a thick embossed paper and a built-in wardrobe. Mrs Wilson didn't think the room had been touched since the house was built – Edwardian, she said. 1928, reckoned Davey – you get an eye for these things. Davey Senior could date decorative effects to within a year – flocks, swags, Anaglypta, floral wall-papers, dados, rag-rolling – and it was an eye for detail, and for other people's mistakes, that Davey had inherited. This particular room, he guessed, had been gussied up in some haste, in about 1989 by the look of it, with a voile at the window and curtains with tie-backs on a long pine pole, but the wallpaper was old, and original, and painted thick: it was probably the wallpaper that had gone up when the house was built, said Davey, unable to hide what he was surprised to hear sounded like regret in his voice.

'But that's not a problem?' asked Mrs Wilson hopefully, hesitating by the door.

'No,' said Davey, 'it's not a problem', and did his best to radiate confidence, which seemed to work: Mrs Wilson could, of course, have no idea that Davey had spent no more time painting and decorating in the past twenty years than he had flossing his teeth. But he looked the part. He had borrowed his dad's old bib and braces.

'I'll just have to . . .' he began, by which time Mrs Wilson was away downstairs. Despite his height, at six foot two, Davey had become instantly reduced, like his father and his grandfather before him, to being just another little man in a big house. Nothing changes.

He manhandled all the furniture into the centre of the room – a large antique chest of drawers, inherited, Davey guessed, two large lamps, a couple of bedside tables, the double bed – and he covered them all with a dust sheet. Or almost with a dust sheet. The dust sheet he'd brought in from the van wasn't quite big enough.

First he dismantled the built-in wardrobe – a pathetic effort, made of plywood nailed to some 2" x 2", with badly fitting louver doors.

'What are the only essential tools for painting and decorating?' his father had asked him when he was young. Paintbrushes, Davey had guessed, wrongly. A scraper and scoring knife? No. A papering table? Nope.

'The only essential tools for painting and decorating – like all jobs – don't forget this – are a large screwdriver and an even larger hammer.'

The wardrobe had been fitted straight on top of the paper, so Davey just hammered away to his heart's content, and once he had a nice square room he could begin.

Undoubtedly Davey Senior's favourite bit of kit, when it came to stripping, his best investment, was an industrial wallpaper steamer, the Earlex SteamMaster®, a beautiful machine, imported from America, of course, a work of art almost, like a big fat metal toaster, enclosed in a metal cage so strong you could stand on it, with a two-gallon water tank, lightweight steam pan, and over two hours of stripping time. Davey Senior loved that machine and now his son was growing to love it too. For the professional painter and decorator, the SteamMaster® was just about the best thing to have happened since lead-free paint. When Davey used to help his dad, of course, when he was young, it was still just the three Ss – Score and Soak and Strip – and the only gear you needed to prep a room was a bucket of water, some Fairy Liquid and a stripping knife, or if it was really tough a bottle of vinegar. Those days were long gone.

The water in the SteamMaster® took thirty-five minutes to heat and when the light went out the machine was ready and Davey held the steam plate up against the wall, held it with his left hand up in the far right-hand corner, just like his father had taught him as a child, and started stripping with his right. You had to keep the plate moving, otherwise it blew the top layer of plaster. As Davey held the steam plate to the paper, the adhesive dissolved beneath.

Davey worked for two hours without stopping, steaming and scraping, the paper coming away all gluey in his hands. As he peeled back paper and scraped down to the plaster, it felt like stripping the skin from a fish, like taking a clean edge to life and scraping it back to its beginnings, to guts and bones. He'd forgotten how much he enjoyed it. The wallpaper stuck to his skin in tiny wet scraps and patches, so that eventually his hands and face were covered. He'd gone all crinkly. He felt like an old man.

Davey's grandfather, Old Davey, had established the business in 1924. Davey never knew him, and knew of him only through photos and old family stories – a bull-necked man with eyes brown like mahogany, a man who liked his pints, apparently, but who worked hard, and not a bad man – self-taught, a good singer, second tenor in the town's male-voice choir, the son of a farmer from up-country, a man who had fought in two world wars and made his own way in life.

His grandfather represented to Davey his whole idea of history – there was no history further back, nothing before him, the man whose wife had borne the seven sons. It was his grandfather who had determined Davey's name, and his life, and when Davey left town twenty years ago it wasn't really his father he was escaping, or himself, it was this man he'd never met and his influence, reaching out to him across the years.

Just to the right of the window, as he was tugging at the paper, thinking about his grandfather, Davey saw what looked at first like some cracks in the plaster.

But it wasn't cracks. It was writing on the wall.

You always sign the wall: that was another thing his father had taught him when he was young. That was what you did, if you were a good tradesman and proud of your profession. Paper or paint, it didn't matter, you always signed and dated the wall. So that others knew you'd been there; proof of a job well done.

The writing was a neat copperplate, in pencil, perfectly

straight, each letter the size of a finger or a thumb, and in three scrapes Davey had the whole thing clear:

David Quinn, 20 August 1929

His grandfather. Old Davey. The first Davey Quinn. He'd been here first. He'd done the room.

The hair stood up on the back of Davey's neck, a sensation he had experienced only once before, when Angela Brown had grabbed him, pulled him towards her and kissed him, unexpectedly, his first real kiss, by the monument in the People's Park.

His grandfather's hands – he couldn't get the thought out of his head – had covered these same walls, the same space, hanging the paper, pasting this paper, the paper that lay in shreds all around him.

And, just the same as Angela Brown's kiss, Davey had no idea what this meant, but he knew that it meant something and that it had consequences, and he found he had to steady himself; and as he looked outside he saw that it had grown misty, that a thick fog had come rolling in, and then he realised that he had not ventilated the room and that it was not fog rolling in at all, it was condensation, and that the room he was in was now a very wet room indeed. He bent down and touched the dust sheets on the floor and the sodden carpet beneath, and as he glanced at the soaking dust sheet on the bed, he felt dizzy and he felt droplets on his head, and he looked up and saw that the steam from the mighty Steam-Master® had softened the lath-and-plaster ceiling, which was now hanging down, just inches above his head, and as he reached up, instinctively, and touched it the whole thing came tumbling down upon him.

And when he came round what he saw was the pregnant Mrs Wilson standing over him and the writing on the wall.

131

9

Closure

*In which the rot sets in and Frank Gilbey
wears L.L. Bean*

Monday night there was a red sky at sunset, the glow spreading right across towards the east. It was unusual – people remarked upon it as they were going into the school, many of them for the last time. Even the weather, they said, looked valedictory. Actually, they didn't say it looked valedictory.

'It looks bad,' they said, 'a red sky.'

The school is closing. Central School. Our school. The place you went if you weren't smart or you weren't Catholic or your parents weren't rich. They've been talking about it for a long time now, ever since the opening of the new Collegiate School out on the ring road and the changes in the post-primary selection procedures, but now it's finally happening. The inspectors arrived at the end of last year. Their report – just two weeks in preparation and less than one hundred pages in length, a report like all reports, feeble and thin and white, and punching well above its weight and far below the belt – recommended immediate closure. There were, of course, the well-attended public meetings in response and a community delegation to the Secretary of State to put the case against closure. The High Court granted leave to move for judicial review. But still the school is closing. The falling attendance cannot be reversed and the failing standards cannot easily be remedied, despite all the valiant efforts of Mr Swallow and his staff.

The rot set in with the stories being leaked to the *Impartial Recorder* about the building of a new school better to serve the community on the ring road: current provision, according to unnamed sources, was 'inadequate', and 'radical proposals' were being considered. From that moment Central was fighting a losing battle. No one wants to send their child to a school that's about to close, or that's rumoured to be about to close. No one wants to be associated with the inadequate, not even round here. We may *be* inadequate, but we don't care to know it, thank you. Mr Swallow had meetings at the time with the editor of the *Impartial Recorder*, Colin Rimmer, a former pupil himself at Central, a man who as a boy played rugby for the school, who was a tight-head prop, but who was otherwise undistinguished and who hated most of his classmates almost as much as they hated him, a man who suffers from our common small-town delusion of grandeur, who seems to think he's running a national paper and whose weekly column he calls 'Rimmer's Around', in which he mocks and satirises all that most of us here hold dear, including truth and beauty and scouting and people who write letters of complaint about dog fouling. Colin Rimmer told Mr Swallow, in no uncertain terms, to let him get on with running his paper and he'd let him get on with running his school. When Mr Swallow appealed to his better nature as a former pupil, Colin just laughed and then he wrote about the meeting in his column, suggesting Mr Swallow had lived up to his name and done it with his pride. It was first blood in the school's long slow death from a thousand cuts.

Mr Swallow has already lost most of his teachers – a massive haemorrhage: all the younger ones and anyone with remaining ambitions – but he doesn't blame them, he has encouraged them to leave, in fact, and has offered them every assistance. They're not rats, he has had to explain to his deputy, a bitter woman with a pudding-bowl haircut and lemon-sucking lips called Miss Raine, who is what people in our town would call a 'career' teacher, which is a euphemism, which means a woman aged over thirty who has not found a man and who is never likely to, a woman who wore stout shoes and pink acrylic and elastic-waisted skirts, and who believed that every teacher should be proud to stand on the prow while the ship went down. These people are not rats, he'd had to explain to her, they're just human. We're all human, he had to remind Miss Raine, and there's nothing we can do about it.

By Easter the school will be closed, the school that Mr Swallow has presided over for thirteen years: long enough to see the first of the sons and daughters of former pupils returning to years 1 and 2, pupils who, like all the others, must now be reschooled, who must make the trek out to the new school with its squeaky-clean anti-climb- and anti-graffiti-painted walls separated from the rest of the town by four lanes of traffic and a few quick-growing conifers. Miss Raine will be going into teacher training, where she belongs. But Mr Swallow is doing the honourable thing. He's going down with the school. He'll be taking early retirement, to lick his wounds and to mend his broken heart. A school can break your heart, if you let it. A school is capable of exciting every human emotion and fulfilling none. A school will take everything you've got and show you no mercy. It knows no sympathy, cares nothing for your cares and grants no favours. Central was Mr Swallow's first headship and it will be his last, and he knows that he has failed himself and the children, which is a terrible knowledge. He doesn't say anything about it, because he is not a man given to self-pity and he does not have the time, but his wife knows how he feels, he doesn't have to tell her, and once the school has closed she wants them to move away from town and make a new start. She has a sister in Australia whom she hasn't seen for twenty years and she's suggesting a three-month trip away, with a stopover in Singapore going out and Los Angeles on the way back, and spend the money and worry about it later. She's had enough of responsibility. She's had enough of a grumpy husband with hair going greyer every day, made a scapegoat and a laughing stock by people who didn't know the meaning of hard work and dedication. The man she married, the man who was appointed head, was a young man with big ideas, and enough skills and enthusiasm to fire people up and make the place work, even a place like Central. But he had been betrayed by the times and it had aged them both, and she doesn't want to be around in the aftermath: there is already speculation in the *Impartial Recorder* that the site will be sold off for redevelopment as another multi-storey car park, in an attempt to regenerate the town centre, which is a bit like trying to revive a failing marriage by taking other lovers. What the town centre needs no one can give it back. What the town centre needs is its past. It needs its heart. What it needs is its school.

It was the big farewell concert last week. Former pupils were invited to return and the school band was re-formed specially for the occasion.* There were speeches and an auction, with proceeds going to the very education authority

---

* They struggled, the band, with an ambitious – some might say over-ambitious – programme including the William Tell Overture, 'El Capitan', 'Trumpets Wild', 'Colonel Bogey', 'Amparito Roca', 'Hootenanny', 'I'm Getting Sentimental Over You', 'Bridge over Troubled Water' and an arrangement of themes from TV soaps. It was quite a racket, from a band who in their heyday were twice runners-up in the highly competitive annual regional schools brass and woodwind competition. Alan Netteswell – known as 'Wobble Tit' to band members – was conducting once again, though rather half-heartedly. Alan was our town's peripatetic brass teacher for twenty-five years and he used to sweat buckets, thrashing the brass players into shape on Mondays after school, and Wednesdays from 7 till 9, but peripatetic music teachers were among the first to go in the local authority job cuts back in the 1990s, along with playing fields and sports, and Alan now works as a night supervisor at our local secure unit for young offenders, along with the school's former groundsman and the part-time rugby coach. Alan hasn't picked up his trumpet for years.

which had forced the place to close, an auction at which Mr Swallow himself was expected to wield the gavel. It was the final humiliation and it stuck in the throat. A headmaster selling off his own school's tables and chairs: the *Impartial Recorder* published the picture on its front cover. Even Joe Finnegan, the lensman, felt uncomfortable with that one. Mr McGee's pickled snake fetched £50. Blackboards were going for £40. Music stands were £5 apiece, trophies and shields and school uniforms were sold in sets and boxes, and the piano went to Dot McLaughlin's Happy Feet dance studio for £150. A set of four Duralex glasses cost Billy Nibbs £1.

A lot of people managed to make it for the ceremony, and this in a town where it can sometimes be difficult to gather enough people together for a party, even if you're offering free drink and nibbles: it just depends what's on the telly. We are people who are averse to gatherings of any kind, suspicious of the motives of anyone who organises or enthuses outside the traditional 11-till-1 slot on a Sunday morning, and distrustful equally of politicians, amateur theatricals, joggers and people shaking tins for charity. Even the Freemasons have never really got a hold in our town – you could wait a long time here for a funny handshake. This is a town where people who play bowls are viewed as radicals. Young people are allowed out until they're twenty-one and then they're expected to knuckle down, draw the curtains by 6 p.m. and watch television until retirement, when some tea dancing or perhaps a long-awaited cruise will be permitted.

But last week there were cars parked the length and the breadth of High Street and some people, they say, came from as far afield as London, people who are known to have second homes and who are on to their second husbands or wives, and who'd heard the news on the grapevine, or on the telephone from their ageing parents, and had decided to make one last journey to lay memories to rest, and perhaps to marvel at the sight of older and fatter and less successful friends and their clearly unsuitable spouses. Cards of commiseration and best wishes were read out from former pupils who couldn't make it, those who have escaped entirely – the lucky citizens of America and Australia, and some of the former Soviet republics. It seems people are prepared to go a long way to get away, and then they spend half their time wishing they were back.

There were couples there that night in the school who had come to visit the sites of earlier conquests and romances, and the changing rooms and the bike sheds, it is said, echoed to the sounds of passions past and present. There were also people who wished simply to walk down dark corridors, and to stand at the front of empty classrooms, and to remember how much they hated *The Canterbury Tales* and the periodic table. People were lining up in front of blackboards to do impressions of Miss McCormack and Gerry Malone, and there was much sitting on radiators and reckless smoking, and the staff room, of course, was packed all night, as was the headmaster's office. Many people lay down on the bed in the nurse's room, and there was the general unscrewing of room numbers and coat pegs – there was even an attempt to remove a water fountain from outside the science block.

Frank Gilbey cut through the crowds that night and of course everyone was pleased to see him, teachers and former pupils alike, although he had been an unremarkable student nearly half a century ago: he was in the 'listeners' group in the choir, which meant he wasn't allowed to sing; he was never chosen for any teams; and he was in neither the top nor the bottom streams in any of his subjects. You would hardly have noticed Frank at school, in fact. Not like now.

Frank, these days, is unmissable. He is quite a character. That's how Frank describes himself to himself when he looks in the mirror – 'quite a character'. He has the maturity now, the strength to carry it off, his character, to shoulder the weight of his own personality. Frank's character these days weighs about eighteen stone, give or take a few pounds, is balding and sixty, and it wears a vicuna overcoat, a tailored shirt and jacket, smart slacks and the proverbial tasselled loafers. Frank's character has grown in direct proportion to his wealth, which is now substantial and which in a town like ours goes a long, long way.

Frank actually refers to himself, disarmingly and in company, as 'Big' Frank Gilbey, for obvious reasons. He looks a bit like the Incredible Hulk grown old – although he isn't green, obviously, he's more a grey-brown-salmon sort of colour, a colour somewhere between pink pebbles and concrete. He was a handsome youth, Big Frank Gilbey, pretty, almost, pale and fine-featured, features which have, of course, coarsened and grown thick with time, and which these days look like they have been painted on with wide, heavy brush strokes. He has the look of a self-portrait in oils, a look that can only be achieved through years of heavy smoking, fried food and wilful self-neglect. He has what one might almost call an upholstered face, a face, in fact, like the sourdough bread in the *River Café Cook Book (One)*, a book which Frank bought Mrs Gilbey after one of their weekend city breaks to London, after they had enjoyed a classic meal of *zuppa di cannellini con pasta, risotto al tartufo bianco,* and *torta di polenta con pere e miele* (Mrs Gilbey had kept the menu), overlooking the River Thames, and 'Well,' Frank had said, as he often did when he was enjoying himself, so as not to forget, 'this is the life' and Mrs Gilbey had agreed, although she couldn't really see the point of London, to be honest.

Frank likes London, but he *loves* New York. New York is Frank's kind of city. He was telling people, at the school closure, who were asking him how he was and what he was up to, about his recent trip to New York with Mrs Gilbey, for one of their city breaks, for which they are renowned, and which are considered the height of sophistication in our town. A city break, for us, is the equivalent of a Grand Tour, available only to couples on double incomes, the rich retired, or the independently wealthy, of whom we have few.

'New York,' Frank was telling anyone who asked, after he'd told them all about his theories about 9/11, 'is my kind of city' and everybody knew what that meant.

Frank loves everything about New York, but then he loves America in general – the attitude, the clothes, the rock'n'roll music, the large portions. He had a plate of nachos once – this is funny – just as a starter, on holiday in Florida, and the plate was so big, and it was piled so high, he got Mrs Gilbey to take a photo of him trying to eat it, and it's there, in another book of the photos that they never look at, but which Mrs Gilbey continues to buy and to fill and to label, year on year, cheap photograph albums documenting the life and the good times of Mr Frank and Mrs Irene Gilbey (née Nicholson), and their lovely daughter, Lorraine. Frank's little pink head is peeking over a small mountain of tortilla chips topped with bright yellow melted cheese, his little red eyes sparkling in the flash.

Frank has been to America many times – New York, and LA, and Toronto, which doesn't really count, but Mrs Gilbey had insisted, because she thought she might prefer it, because it was supposed to be cleaner and more like Europe, but it wasn't and she didn't. It's Florida they've been to mostly, doing fly-drive holidays with Lorraine. Sometimes Frank wishes he had been born American, but he's done his best to make himself over. As a young man he loved Elvis, and he'd stuck with him right through the Las Vegas years, sporting a quiff and sideburns until about 1987, when Elvis was decent in his grave and Frank's property business had started to grow, and he'd moved on to the town council and he needed a new image, and he started to model himself more on Marlon Brando in *The Godfather*. Mrs Gilbey told him once, on one of their city breaks, to Edinburgh, where they stayed in a nice four-star hotel with a pool, that as he grew older he reminded her a little bit of Gene Hackman – she didn't say in which film, but Gene Hackman was pretty close to Marlon Brando, and about as close as Frank was ever going to get, and he really thought that was one of the nicest things his wife had ever said to him. Frank drinks vodkatinis in the golf club, and at home at the weekends he eats pastrami sandwiches, 'on rye', as he likes to say to Mrs Gilbey, although you can't actually get rye bread in our town, but the Brown and Yellow Cake Shop does a nice wheaten, which is a close approximation, at least in terms of density, and Mrs Gilbey always tries to have one for him in the house, in case he takes the fancy. Pastrami you can get, of course, fresh off the shelves at the supermarket up in Bloom's, but Mrs Gilbey is not a fan. She says pastrami is just Spam with a fancy name.* Frank and Mrs Gilbey maintain separate space in the fridge: she has her low-fat ready-meals and her cottage cheese and her Philadelphia Light, and the medicine she has to take for her diverticulitis, and Frank has his pastrami and his salami and his stinky cheeses. They share a taste only for gassy lager and Australian chardonnay, which they keep next to the milk and help themselves to. And as in the fridge, so in bed: Mr and Mrs Gilbey have slept singly for about twenty years, coming together only occasionally when they have shared enough of the lager and the chardonnay for them to forget and for it not to matter. Mrs Gilbey tells Frank it's because of his snoring, but actually, right from when Lorraine was little, she'd wanted her privacy at night – she couldn't

---

* Spam has fallen out of fashion in town, of course, along with other tinned meats, and has been replaced largely as a sandwich filling by wafer-thin ham (see Bob Savory, *Bap Express!*, pp.94–101), which is hardly an improvement, but while on holiday in Hawaii some years ago Frank and Mrs Gilbey were astonished to discover that Spam is still highly regarded there. They even visited a restaurant that was entirely devoted to the cooking of Spam and it took a long time for Mrs Gilbey to wash the taste and the memory of the house speciality – Hot 'N'Spicy Spam and Rice – from her mouth.

stand him going on about all his deals and his plans and the intrigues – and she really can't stand to see him naked any more. She'd never truly enjoyed that side of the marriage.

At the school closure Frank was not dressed, as he was usually, like a mafia don. He was dressed more like somebody out of an L.L. Bean catalogue – button-down shirt, a V-neck jumper, chinos and a braided leather belt. Frank recommends L.L. Bean to all his friends at the golf club and L.L. Bean is now quite big around here, among those who drive company cars and are in the know, making Frank responsible for what the town looks like in several senses. With his property companies and all his power, and his hairdressers, lingerie shops and his elegance, Frank has determined both our architecture, our women's hairstyles and underwear, and our gentlemen's attire. Frank also uses words like 'movie' and 'ass' and 'gas' when the English equivalents would do, but this has not caught on. On the whole people here still prefer to use English.

Frank's casual clothes that night, though, were a disguise, because he was at the school strictly on business. Like most of the people who were there, Frank was looking for closure. He wanted to keep an eye on Bob Savory, who had kindly agreed to undertake some business on his behalf.

Bob was trying to strike a deal with Davey Quinn. Bob and Davey go way back – to football, mostly, but also to school, and before that, even, to BB. The aim and purpose of the BB, the Boys' Brigade, an aim and purpose which Bob and Davey had learnt and recited as children, was 'The Advancement of Christ's Kingdom Among Boys and the Promotion of Habits of Obedience, Reverence, Discipline, Self-Respect and All that Tends Towards True Christian Manliness'. In practice, the promotion of the habits of True Christian Manliness involved playing Kim's Game, marching around a large hall in a blue uniform on a Tuesday night and learning how to cook pineapple upside-down cake. In our town, this is what we mean when we talk about Advancing Christ's Kingdom.

Bob Savory did not himself believe in God, even at an early age. God did not figure large in the mind or the life of even the high-stepping, blue-shirted, five-year-old BB Bob Savory. Bob was an infant atheist: the world, as far as Bob could see, was a given and he saw no need to seek a cause. Bob himself was all the cause he needed: he was self-sufficient from an early age, going so far, as his mother had once liked to boast to her friends, as wiping his own bottom before the age of two, quite an achievement in our town, where until recently most of our mothers stayed at home tending to the personal needs of their infants, and where potty training was therefore quite often long postponed, especially for the boys, who never quite caught up with the girls in the long race to maturity. As he grew older, though, the precocious and bottom-wiping Bob became the determined, the driven and the self-starting Bob, the Bob of local sandwich legend, the Bob who did not suffer fools gladly, who always got what he wanted, and who saw the need to believe in God as a sign of weakness to which some of his more feeble-minded friends, colleagues and employees were inevitably prone, just as some of them were prone to support Manchester United, or to commit acts of petty crime, stealing jars of mayonnaise, say, or remnants of ham-on-the-bone. Religion, Bob believed, was a kind of disease, a bug or a parasite that resided in the minds of the weak, the sad, the lonely, the merely salaried and the hopelessly unsuccessful. God was, to Bob, just a common nonsense, like the common cold and depression, and a strong will was enough to keep them all at bay. Even when his father was dying – indeed, particularly when his father was dying – Bob did not for a moment tolerate the idea of a God. He was appalled by his mother's incredulity, which had become worse with her Alzheimer's, a disease which Bob believed, like God, was a kind of weakness that people were either prone to or not.

Bob was not prone. Bob was mentally fit and healthy, and he intended to stay that way. He read the *Financial Times* from cover to cover every day, and inspirational business books, which he bought by the dozen, and he avoided all weakness in his life – he did not smoke and never had, and he hardly drank, except in occasional lonely bouts of self-punishment. No one had ever seen Bob drunk: then again, no one had ever seen Bob smile. Bob did not indulge and did not imbibe. He firmly believed – and he believed that he had been proved right, on the clear evidence of his success – that at a business lunch, say, the refusal of even a social glass of wine marked a man out as an individual of peculiar strength of character.

'You set the trend, Bobbie,' his mother had told him when he was young, when boys at school had teased him because his blazer was of a cheap nylon and he received free school dinners. And Bob has set the trend. These days we're all of us eating out of the palm of Bob's hands. These days, at £2.99 for a triangle pack of deep-filled BLT, Bob is making us all pay. In the world of the sandwich Bob is like God Almighty, and in the world of the Irish-themed restaurant he is – as he had occasionally been heard to announce to the staff at the Plough and the Stars – Jesus H. Christ.

The closest thing to a weakness – if you could call it a weakness – in Bob's life was sex. Bob enjoyed sex in much the same way that other people enjoyed smoking or drinking, which is to say often, carelessly and at some personal expense.*

*Like Francie McGinn, and like Davey Quinn, and like many of us here in town of a certain age, Bob's first experience of sex, or the first whiff of it, was at the home of Gary Carville. Gary is known around town these days as a good cheap electrician – which he is – but when he was younger he was known primarily because his parents had been blessed with three lovely daughters, and Gary was the only boy, the youngest, and so he and his dad Ronnie, outnumbered two to one, had always welcomed other boys and men into the house with great enthusiasm, and so for many of us Gary's

Things had begun to go wrong for Bob recently, though, regarding sex, and he could pinpoint exactly when it had happened, when the problems had started, during a moment of passion with one of his waitresses, a girl called Christine, who had large thighs and was only filling in during the summer holidays, before going back to university to study Accountancy. Bob liked Christine – he joked with her that maybe when she was qualified she would like to come back to work as his accountant, an idea that appealed to Bob, who was excited by the idea of being able to combine his two favourite pursuits – sex and money. His own accountant, Finlay Maguire, had a moustache and played rugby at weekends, and Bob was many things, but he was not – as was sometimes rumoured around town, because of his age, and because he's still unmarried, and because he wears clothes that fit – he was not a man who kicked with the proverbial other foot. Except that on that fateful night, during his close embrace with Christine, Bob had found himself thinking about Finlay Maguire, and it came as a moment of terrible shock to Bob and not something he could easily explain to himself. No one in town would have believed it, if they'd known, and certainly none of us would have suspected. Davey Quinn, for

---

was the first place we got to taste whiskey and Coke, and to view the naked female form on the pages of glossy magazines. A night of under-age drinking in the Castle Arms would often end with the suggestion to go to Gary's, which meant food, videos, access to a cupboard in the kitchen by the back door filled with an apparently inexhaustible supply of alcohol, and possibly the sight of Gary's sisters' underwear hanging to dry in the bathroom, which to most of us meant much more than the unimaginables pictured in Gary's stash of magazines. Even in those days Bob had managed to go much further than the rest of us and had taken the opportunity to get to know one of Gary's sisters – the lovely red-haired Patricia – with whom he claimed, and we had no reason to doubt him, that he had spent many interesting afternoons on her candlewick bedspread. When Ronnie discovered what was going on we were all barred, alas, from the Carville house, and it felt like God expelling us east of Eden.

example, had no idea, even though he and Bob went back a long way, which is why Bob was allowed to – but was dreading to – ask Davey what he was about to ask him.

'Davey, listen,' he said.

Bob often told people to listen, even though such an instruction was not usually necessary in the context of a conversation, but Bob always felt the reminder was a help.

'I've a wee favour I need you to do for me.'

'Well, big fella,' said Davey, who had taken to addressing all his friends as big fellas, although strictly speaking, at six foot two, he was by far the biggest among most of us fellas. The phrase was a kind of verbal stoop. 'It depends what it is. If it's money you're after' – and he patted his pockets – 'I'm afraid I'm a little short at the moment.'

Money was the big joke between Bob and Davey. Bob had so much of it and Davey none, the disparity was so large that the only way they could make sense of it was to laugh about it.

'No, it's not about money,' said Bob. 'But it is something I'd like to pay you for.'

Now, Davey did not much like the way this conversation was going. You don't pay a friend for a favour, even Bob Savory should have known that. But that was the whole trouble with Bob these days – he no longer seemed to be able to tell the difference between favours and business. In any small town there is a point at which favours and business inevitably begin to merge and this point is often on the golf course, or in the golf club bar, which is also the place where right and wrong frequently decide to give up their differences over a gin and tonic, and agree to find a more congenial and common way forward. Also – and you often notice this on the golf course as well – the rich have a kind of Tourette's syndrome when it comes to money. They can't help but talk about it. They no longer have control over it. The money begins to control them, like their spoilt and unruly children, invading every conversation.

'I'll come to the point,' said Bob, while Davey finished the dregs of an instant coffee. 'You know the Quality Hotel?'

Davey did indeed know the Quality Hotel. Like everyone else in town, the hotel held fond memories for him, in Davey's case memories of being sick in the toilets, from drinking too many Jack Daniel's and Coke, and of head-butting a reveller on the steps of the concrete basement disco. 'Yeah.'

'Well, we need to get rid of it.'

'Right,' said Davey vaguely. 'Do we?'

'We do.'

'We?'

'You.'

'Uh-huh. You're losing me here, Bob.'

'Listen, Davey.' Davey was listening. 'I've heard that there are small fires in there sometimes.'

'Oh, really?'

'Yeah. You know, you get dossers down there, sometimes, sleeping in some of the old rooms?'

'Right.'

'Well, I don't know how it happens exactly, but I suppose sometimes one of them might have been smoking and their cigarette end might not have been disposed of properly.'

'Right.'

'And whoosh!'

'Whoosh.'

'Yes. Might happen again. Any time. A big fire.'

'Yeah, I suppose.'

'Good. Well, let's shake on it.'

Davey was absent-mindedly extending his hand before he caught himself on.

He noticed Frank Gilbey loitering by the headmaster's office, listening in to their conversation.

'Hold on, mate. Do you mean . . .' He glanced at Frank Gilbey. 'You mean you want me to . . . ?'

Bob raised an eyebrow.

146

'No,' said Davey. 'No, no, no. Come on. I'm not getting involved in anything like that.'

'OK,' said Bob in businesslike fashion, wrapping up the conversation. 'That's fine. We need never speak of it again.'

'Fine. Do you want another coffee?'

'No thanks.'

'OK.'

'It'll be like that other thing we never need speak of.'

'What?'

'I think' – and Bob smiled at this point, relishing the sentence – 'we both know what I'm talking about.'

What Bob was talking about was the reason for Davey's departure all those years ago, the reason he left town and never returned. The reason why Davey Quinn had left and which he'd thought he'd put behind him.

10

Print

*In which Billy Nibbs and Colin Rimmer become
instant and rewarding companions, and go in
search of drama and catharsis*

In summer, at night, it can sometimes be hard to get to sleep
here. Not because of the sound of the cicadas, or the late-
night café culture and the revelling and the parties, or the
heat even, but because of the sheets. We still prefer man-made
fibres, most of us, for most purposes, both in bed and out,
even though they make you sweat like a pig and leave you
all sticky. They don't take as much ironing, that's the thing,
that's why we like them. And they do keep their colour.

When he can't sleep in the summer because of the sheets
and because the window in his bedroom doesn't open – the
frame's been painted over too many times – Billy Nibbs lies
awake sweating the ham out of his system and thinking about
his heroes. Billy's heroes have always been, in no particular
rank or order, Che Guevara, James Stewart, Bono, Xena
Warrior Princess, Nelson Mandela, George Orwell and the
two journalists who broke the Watergate scandal whose names
he'd long ago forgotten. Billy was a thoroughgoing cynic with
a propensity to idolise the worthy dead; he was a typical
pessimist, with the pessimist's secret bedtime hope that this
is in fact a wonderful life and that ours is a wonderful world,

whose great wonder and whose secret have only been temporarily mislaid and are just waiting to be discovered, probably by Billy himself, when he's half awake and not really looking. Which is why he liked working at the dump and why now he was working for Colin Rimmer on the *Impartial Recorder*.

The *Impartial Recorder* was a newspaper which insisted on the simple goodness and simple rightness of life, insisting upon it in the face of all the local evidence of wrong, all the graffiti, dog dirt, car crime and head-on crashes to the contrary. In the *Impartial Recorder* there were no big ideas, there were no ideologies and no purely evil days. There were only personal triumphs and tragedies, inconveniences rather than scandals, with a nice cup of tea always on the horizon and a boiled sweet in your pocket to keep you going. In the pages of the *Impartial Recorder* there was never any profanity, nor any superfine English, and nothing was incomprehensible. Even amidst the darkness there was always a Soroptomist's meeting going on somewhere, an award being presented over a glass of sherry for sixty years of service to a voluntary organisation, an evening of old-time gospel music in a church hall, a charity trekker who'd lost twenty pounds and raised a thousand, or a civic delegation come to admire the way we do things here.* If a newspaper could be said to

---

* To consult the *Impartial Recorder* archive at the library, contact Philomena Rocks. An entire run of papers, between the years 1965–73 are missing, though, unfortunately, because the then local librarian, Barry Devlin, was during that time under the influence of the Troggs, the Small Faces, the Rolling Stones, marijuana, acid, speed and a lot of Carling Black Label, and he took an executive decision not to bother to keep any local papers, using the library's basement storage area instead as a rehearsal room for his band, the Tigers, who were a kind of cross between the Animals and the Beatles, and whose single, 'Hello There!', reached no. 39 in the UK charts in February 1967. The library archive does, however, boast an almost complete run of the *New Musical Express* covering the period, which is some small consolation: they reveal that the Kinks played here, apparently, at Morelli's in

have a theme tune, the theme tune of the *Impartial Recorder* was Joe Cocker and Jennifer Warnes singing 'Up Where We Belong'.

But this was not necessarily what the paper's editor, Colin Rimmer, felt it should be. He felt the paper's theme tune should be something more like Bob Dylan singing 'Blowin' in the Wind', or the Clash playing 'Police and Thieves'. Colin was a man who'd become the editor of an MOR newspaper which he despised, but which he'd been determined to transform; he'd set out to shake things up, like a young Elvis, or like Dylan going electric.

'Journalism,' he often told his staff, thinking this might impress them, 'is the new rock'n'roll.'

Many of Colin's staff have grown up with Eminem as a staple and it's their grandfathers who listened to rock'n'roll, but Colin was doing his best. He was the kind of editor who made a point of not wearing a tie, who read *Private Eye* and style magazines as well as *The Economist*, and who sometimes wore jeans to important meetings. He wasn't exactly ripping up the rule book, but he was taking a stab at it. He was making an effort.

On his appointment as editor, almost fifteen years ago, when he was still a young man, a young turk even, a tyro returned to town from stints with local papers outside the county and the occasional feature in a national, with a full head of hair and a set of Penguin Modern Classics to rival anyone's in town, his own laptop and a whole load of newfangled ideas about tele-working, QuarkXPress™ and Photo-Shop™,

---

1966, as did Dave Dee, Dozy, Beaky, Mick & Tich, and the Wombles a little later. Barry Devlin has retired now and is divorced, after a high-profile court case in which he was found guilty of threatening his wife Julie with a knife after a marathon seventy-two-hour drinking binge, which began on a ferry to the Isle of Man and which ended up in Casualty, but he still has his popular and appropriately titled Sunday night slot, 'Blues Unlimited', on Hitz!FM.

Colin had set out his stall and made his changes. He'd managed to axe Spencer Bradley's bat-watch column, and he'd decimated Blair Saunders's weekly full-page bird-fanciers page and made it into a monthly. He'd also cut deep into the fat of the bowling and fishing pages, removing some of their vital organs, leaving them weak and incapacitated, but still just about functioning. He'd vetoed cricket and outlawed all mention of school football. He'd even managed to reduce the vast, swollen size of the weekly column written by Lesley Sanderson, the young wife of the newspaper's grand and elderly proprietor, Sir George Sanderson, from 2000 words to 1000. Less, he had managed to convince her, was more. The magic word with Lesley – what had done the trick – was 'minimalist'.

'Yes, of course,' she'd agreed, her discreet diamonds and blonde highlights flashing in the fluorescence of Colin's office, 'like Philippe Starck?'

'Exactly,' he'd said. 'Brevity is the soul of wit.' And of lingerie, he'd thought to himself, but fortunately he'd had the self-discipline and foresight not to say so aloud. He might have had some absolutely bang-up-to-the-minute notions, but even he knew that it was not a good idea for a young editor to become involved with the proprietor's wife.

Apart from his initial changes, though, and despite all his big plans, the *Impartial Recorder* is substantially the same today as it was fifteen, or even fifty, years ago and for most of his readers that's just what was wanted. There was still the one-page 'Udder Bits', the farming round-up page, and the stomach-churning, heavily sponsored 'Forks and Corks' bar and restaurant reviews, the weekly 'Good Book' bible study, and the interminable blurred photographs of weddings, anniversaries, eighteenth-birthday parties and charity events. Colin's controversial editorial page – in which he had lambasted and attacked local businessmen and bureaucrats, farmers, doctors, teachers, social workers, church leaders, the police, celebrities, the nuclear family, gays, dog owners and the bearded – had proved a little too rock'n'roll for our town and had lasted less than six months before the solicitors' letters and letters of complaint had led to Sir George leaning on Colin to give it up, and so his opinions were now restricted, carefully leashed and legally vetted in his short column, 'Rimmer's Around', and his dreams remained unfulfilled. He had imagined the paper as like a just and mighty lion, bestriding truth, protecting the pride and devouring those who sought to challenge it: instead, it was more like an earthworm passing mud. Rock'n'roll the *Impartial Recorder* most definitely was not: a little bit country, maybe, and ever so slightly operatic, but mostly it was like old-time dancing. The *Impartial Recorder* remains a slow-foxtrot kind of a paper.

But Colin did not blame himself for failing to live up to his own expectations. It was not in his nature to do so. He was a journalist, so he blamed other people, particularly the paper's proprietor, Sir George.

Sir George and his lovely wife Lesley live in a big house – *the* big house, really, the Manor – far out from our town, in the country. The town is basically where all the middle-income earners live, those of us who work in shops or offices, schools, factories, those of us who buy second-hand or flat-pack furniture and do DIY at weekends with the wrong tools, while outside town, in the country, is where the people live who work up in the city, or in the vast sugar-beet fields, people who have inherited furniture and tools, or their brothers' wives. They are, quite literally, a breed apart.

Sir George Sanderson is the complete and utter countryman, from the tippy-tip-top of his Burberry cap to the dirty scored soles of his six-hole brogues. He is a gentleman farmer who likes to hunt and ride, who uses Latin abbreviations in conversation and who'd been something in the City – even his wife isn't sure what – and who is now a non-executive board member of several companies, which means many lunches in London, and so he is hardly ever seen around town, and if he is seen it's in his slightly mouldy heirloom three-piece tweeds and a four-wheel drive. The fragrant and ubiquitous Mrs Sanderson, on the other hand, wears chunky hand-knits made by people with learning difficulties, and knee-length wellies, and she rides a mountain bike into town twice a week, in fluorescent lycra, and she keeps dogs and horses, and smokes cheroots and writes a column extolling environmentally friendly farming methods, young artists and the work of Paulo Coelho. She believes in the Glastonbury Festival, and recycling, and in plastic surgery for those who can afford it. Between them, in fact, Sir George and his wife pretty much cover all the bases for Colin Rimmer. He despises everything they stand for.

But Colin had had to learn to rub along with them. They paid the occasional surprise visit to the offices of the *Impartial Recorder*, where they insisted – 'No! Absolutely!' – on drinking the instant coffee along with everyone else and Sir George cracked jokes with the secretaries, and Colin was expected to visit them out in the country every couple of months, to drink Fair-Trade tea with Mrs Sanderson and to empathise with the plight of indigenous peoples, and to take a drop of whiskey with Sir George, and to reassure him that sales were good, that they weren't spending too much on luxuries like tea and coffee, and that advertising revenue was on the increase.

In his long career as a journalist Colin had found that he could rub along with just about anyone if he wanted to – it was whether or not he wanted to that was the question. Colin was a divorcee, a man possessed of few friends, many enemies and a wide circle of acquaintances. He had always believed in cultivating contacts and his contacts now outweighed anything that might properly be said to be a relationship by about a hundred to one.

Billy Nibbs, for example, was a contact.

As a good newspaperman, Colin had taken the precaution of getting to know Billy, in case anything ever turned up at the dump that might be of interest. Colin had no idea what this anything might be, but it might be something: weapons-grade plutonium had turned up before now on municipal dumping grounds, and bodies, and stolen works of art by Old Masters. Not in our town, of course, where it's mostly old fridges, and damp hardboard and hedging, but there was always a first time, and when the first time happened, Colin wanted to be there. Colin popped in to see Billy every few weeks – he worked through his contacts using his Rolodex on a monthly schedule – and Billy would make Colin a cup of tea over the gas stove in his hut and they'd talk.

It had turned out that the two had much in common. They were both great readers and they were both writers, in a way. They certainly both wanted to be writers, and they both harboured huge and entirely unrealistic literary ambitions, which is often the next best thing to being a writer, certainly in our town, where every middle-class housewife would be the next J. K. Rowling, if only she had the time and someone to do the cleaning. Baseless hopes and fantasies of any kind can quickly cement a relationship, particularly between bitter, middle-aged men, as in the mutual admiring of powerboats or younger women – you can usually spot the desperate shared enthusiasm in the glinting hollows of another man's eyes, in the soft sag of the belly against the shirt and in the emerging capillaries around the nose; and of course what usually happens in our town is that you learn to recognise and over-come these desires by taking up golf and gin and tonic, or rediscovering football, and laughing too loudly at other men's jokes. But Billy and Colin were not natural joiners, or golfers, or laughers. They had taken instead the long alternative route to friendship – via books.

Billy himself had abandoned poetry for the moment, had

kissed goodbye to the Muse, crushed by his experience with his publisher, but Colin was still working on his magnum opus, late into the night and early in the mornings, before work. Billy is one of the few people in town who knows about it, but it's not a secret: one day it'll all be out in the open, so I don't think I'm breaking a confidence to reveal that Colin has been writing, has been for a long time, a novel about a character called Derek, a novel which is provisionally titled *Derek* and which is modelled loosely on Kingsley Amis's *Lucky Jim*, a book which came as a revelation to Colin when he first read it in his teens and which has remained for him the absolute, undisputed example of what a good book should be: funny, satirical and the work of an absolute misery.

In Colin's *Derek*, Derek is a brilliant, shabby, but immensely lovable and wise-cracking journalist who runs a local newspaper, and who is spectacularly and hilariously unsuccessful with women.

Colin had come up with the idea for his book and had found the time to write it when his wife, Lisa, had left him, with their children, the twins, shortly after he'd been appointed editor of the *Impartial Recorder*, when he was working eighteen-hour days, seven days a week. Lisa had left Colin for an architect called Stephen, a man who paid her some attention and who liked to climb mountains at weekends, and who'd designed and built his own house, and Lisa had moved up to the city to be with him and to pursue her own career as a teacher of the deaf.

'I can get through to them better than I can get through to you,' was Lisa's parting shot to Colin, after a crockery-cracking row.

In Colin's novel *Derek*, Derek is married to a woman called Louise, who is a teacher of the blind, and they have triplets. In the novel Louise falls in love with a structural engineer called Martin. Martin is killed while paragliding. He turns out to have been a bigamist and a credit card fraudster, and he is not good in bed.*

The book was going OK, but Colin was having problems with the plot. Having spent years peering behind the scenes of everyday small-town life, he found that he had an excess of story: he had become overcome by story, in fact, and was unable to make any sense of it. He'd become befuddled. The book seemed to be going nowhere. It lacked a climax. Also, he had a problem with character. He didn't seem able to write a character who was not himself, which was proving to be a disadvantage for a budding novelist. What he really needed, he knew, was more drama and more catharsis.†

In Billy's little hut at the dump Colin and Billy would talk literature and drama and catharsis, trading names in much the same way boys at school trade sweets or sandwiches. Having swapped and traded D. H. Lawrence against William Gibson over a number of months, and Tolkien, and J. G. Ballard, and John Irving, and many of the other authors beloved worldwide by teenagers and autodidacts, Billy and Colin had finally come together in agreement that *The Catcher*

---

* 'Louise rolled away from under Martin once again, revolted and unsatisfied. The only thing that kept them together, she realised, was his money: without it, as a man, as a lover, as a father to her three beautiful children, Martin was nothing. She couldn't understand why she had ever left Derek, who was sexier (even though he was balding and a little bit fat), funnier (even though he could admittedly be quite moody and uncommunicative), braver (even though he had failed to stand up to the builders that time who had clearly overcharged them), stronger (even though he never took any exercise and had let himself go and could hardly lift the coal bucket), a really very talented journalist (even though he only worked for a local paper) and a great cook (even if he only ever made spaghetti bolognese). He understood her needs as a woman and as a teacher of the blind. She resolved once again to return to him and beg him to have her back. But would he forgive her?'

† Both of which are readily available, actually, for a small fee – concessions available – from Robert McCrudden in Creative Writing (Drama) 1 at the Institute, Thursdays 7.30–9. There is a handout.

in the Rye was probably the greatest work of twentieth-century fiction. Billy had actually made quite a strong case for *Franny and Zooey*, but it was so obviously one of those books that Colin was only pretending to have read that Billy soon abandoned his position. This often happened, Billy allowing Colin the benefit of the doubt, despite Colin's considerable seniority – he was in his mid-forties now, if anyone asked, although he had actually passed the mid-point some years ago. Colin had to admit that he was a little in awe of Billy, even though Billy sported a beard, because Billy did seem to have read everything ever written, all the greats, all the way from Shakespeare through to Nick Hornby – all those years working at the dump had not been wasted – and Billy could also quote chunks of poetry from memory, which Colin found immensely impressive, despite himself. Colin was actually thinking of introducing a poetry-quoting sidekick into his novel, as a kind of foil for Derek. He thought that might jazz things up a bit, maybe give things a bit of momentum.

It was over a strong cup of tea in Billy's hut one day at the dump, during a heated debate about the problem of evil in the work of Philip Pullman, that the subject turned – as it often does in our town – to the question of Frank Gilbey.

Billy Nibbs had many reasons for disliking Frank Gilbey and not just because he was his landlord. Frank had become increasingly identified in Billy's mind with Them, the many enemies with whom Billy was engaged in fighting. These enemies, like the Romans, Angles, Saxons and Jutes of old, seemed to keep on coming, in waves, again and again, except they now consisted mostly of the legions and galleys of the Rude, the Dishonest, the Unhelpful and the Lazy, not to mention the many brute barbarian Consumers whose appetite for consumer goods and for remodelling their homes kept them coming back to the dump, day after day, year in, year out, raping the land and depositing their spoils. For Billy, Frank Gilbey was undoubtedly one of Them: in Billy's *Inferno*, landlords ranked just above the panderers and seducers, and just below those who had given in to unnatural lust.

Colin had other, more complex reasons for disliking Frank Gilbey.

It has to be said that Colin is not someone who makes friends easily and when he did make friends it usually wasn't long before he came to despise them. If someone was his friend, Colin believed, there was probably something wrong with them, or why would they want to be his friend in the first place? Did they not have enough friends already? Colin was not what you would call a positive thinker.

If he'd ever attended one of the personality workshops at the Oasis, run by Sammy and Cherith, Colin would probably have been identified as having a self-esteem problem and he might have tried to do something about it. Of course, for Colin to have been attending one of Sammy's and Cherith's personality workshops in the first place he'd have had to have been a different sort of person – he wouldn't have been Colin. He'd have had to have been the kind of person who attends personality workshops. If he had been more like someone else, though, he might eventually have gone into counselling or psychoanalysis, and if he had done, his counsellor or analyst would probably have made a big deal of the fact that Colin Rimmer had never known his real parents.

Colin himself had never made much of this fact. Very few people in town even knew that he'd been adopted because it seemed to Colin an irrelevance and not something he chose to talk about.

Colin had been brought up by a couple named Felicity and Philip Rimmer, and he had treated them, for better and for worse and in every way, as though they were his parents: indeed, they were to him his real parents. There were no others waiting in the wings to claim him as their own. Philip and Felicity were the real thing; they were not impostors. Felicity – who was called Fee by everyone, including Colin –

had at one time been an actress in rep and was big in amateur dramatics in and around town, and Philip had taught at Barneville House, the private school, out there on the Old Green Road, and they were good, kind, cultured people, the kind of people who hardly exist here any more, who seem all of a sudden to have disappeared and nobody knows where they've gone, the kind of people who subscribe to the *National Geographic* magazine and who attend classical concerts in the city at weekends, who smoke and drink in moderation, who always read the Booker-nominated novels, who are sceptical about television, and who have dinner parties at which they always have an amusing story to tell about themselves and about their amusing week, and who can't have children of their own.

So Colin had grown up among books and music and a piano in the drawing room, and napkins rather than serviettes, and there was a tree house in the back garden, which had trees and a shed with a window, which Fee called the summer house.

Fee had been perfectly straight and up front about things, and when Colin was sixteen she had told him that he was adopted, and she had offered to help him trace his birth mother, but Colin wasn't interested in tracing his birth mother. Indeed, he hated the term *birth mother*: he thought it made him sound like some kind of wild animal, like a feral child, like he'd been suckled by wolves and brought up among native tribespeople. Colin's friends at school didn't have birth mothers, they just had mothers, and everyone knew what a mother was and what she did, and Colin was perfectly happy with Fee as his mother, who fulfilled all his criteria, thank you very much. She was all the mother he needed. He didn't need an extra helping of mother. He couldn't care less about his birth mother. He didn't want to know anything about her. His birth mother remained only a rumour, and Colin was a journalist and was only interested in facts.

159

And the fact was both Fee and Philip had been good parents to him and they were long dead now. They'd been in their late thirties when they'd adopted Colin, and by the time he was twenty they were both gone, Fee riding her Norton 500cc motorbike – a fiftieth birthday present from Philip – and then Philip himself, in grief and guilt, a year later. They'd left a terrible financial mess behind them: unpaid credit card bills and multiple bank accounts, insurance policies which refused to pay out and a house with a leaky roof. Colin had known that things were bad even when he was a child: they'd had to withdraw him from the Barneville House prep school when he was eleven and send him to Central instead, but it was only in death that the full extent of their financial problems became apparent, and Colin had been forced to sell the big leaky house to pay the debts, and all he was left with was a dozen tea chests filled with junk and mementoes, a lot of crinkling paperback books and a quite ridiculous baby grand piano, Fee's pride and joy, which he'd refused to sell and had managed to manoeuvre through the french windows of his terraced house on the Brunswick Road, and which now took pride of place in his back room: you couldn't actually open the door to the room to get in; you had to enter through the french windows, and then slide underneath the piano and squeeze up on to the stool to play. Colin stuck mostly to scales.

It was when they'd died that Colin had moved back to town. He'd worked all over and he could have gone anywhere, could have left the town behind, but he somehow felt he owed it to them, to stick around and let people see that they hadn't been forgotten or their memory abandoned, that he remained as evidence of their having lived rich and fulfilling lives. Also, to be honest, he did feel that if he moved too far away he'd somehow lose contact with some part of himself, his history and his sense of belonging. At least if he remained in town there might still be someone out there who belonged to him, and he to them, though they might pass each other in the street and not know it. So, barring some serious psycho-analysis, Colin wasn't going anywhere: he was here for the duration. He felt like he owned the place, but also that the place owned him; they were co-dependent.

Colin had probably inherited his strong sense of owner-ship from Philip who, as well as being the geography master at Barneville House, was once our town's most famous amateur film maker and archivist. Philip used to show his cine-films at the Quality Hotel – one week's full performances once a year, for over twenty years, in the week between Christmas and New Year, matinées every day at 2.30 – and people would pay to come and see them, and the money would help pay off a few debts. Philip filmed scenes of everyday life – people at work and play, annual local events – and then he used to splice them together into a full hour of viewing, and halfway through the screenings Fee would strap on a tray and walk down the aisle, selling home-made fudge and toffees in paper bags. The shows were an institution, when our town still had institutions: what we have now, of course, is more convenient shopping.

All of Philip's old film was upstairs rotting in the tea chests in Colin's loft. Colin had never gone through them or looked at them: he'd seen the films so many times he didn't need to see them again. He could screen them any time and anywhere without difficulty in his memory, where he was guaranteed the best seat in the house. He was always there in the films somewhere: somewhere on the periphery, part of a larger drama. He could see himself now: there he was with Fee, in short trousers at the start of the 1969 county cycle race, silently calling out to the face behind the camera, waving and smiling; there he was again with Fee, at the first drive-in car wash, up on Moira Avenue, before the ring road. And there he was, pointing at a duchess, and there again, gazing at a snow drift, or looking at a fallen tree at the top of South

Street. Colin's image of himself as a child was of a child observing rather than participating, watching history in the making, rather than making history. Maybe this was why as an adult he despised anyone who tried to make him a spectator, or who denied his right to act as and when and however he felt like it. Colin did not need to pay a psychiatrist to tell him what he already knew.

So perhaps there really was no true mystery as to why Colin so disliked Frank Gilbey. As a good friend and business associate of Sir George Sanderson, Frank had come to presume upon Colin's good nature too many times. He had required Colin to observe and not to act, to behave as though the events he heard reported and witnessed were on some quaint, fading cine-film playing on a blank white wall at the Quality Hotel. Colin had not, for example, reported on Frank's daughter Lorraine being admitted to the psychiatric unit, or to the clinic for her eating disorder, even though his contacts could offer proof and evidence. He did not report or follow up on persistent rumours that Frank was behind the mysterious demolition of at least a dozen houses of listed status around town. Even the road abandonment schemes and the awarding of the contract for the building of the ring road to a colleague and friend of Frank's at the golf club had gone unmentioned. About all this Colin's lips had been sealed, his eyes closed, and his fingers far from his keyboard and the keypad on his mobile phone. He had maintained a dignified silence, had gazed on in childish innocence, and turned his fire instead upon lazy traffic wardens and fly-posters, and utility companies digging up the roads.

Frank Gilbey was one of the main reasons the *Impartial Recorder* had not turned out to be what Colin had hoped.

Over their conversations about literature in Billy's hut at the dump Colin realised that he had found in Billy someone who, like himself, was angry, frustrated and dogged in the pursuit of the truth. Truth can, of course, be a dangerous thing to pursue, since it is evanescent and very possibly non-existent. Nonetheless, here in our town, as elsewhere, truth is a topic much discussed, and not just between Billy and Colin. Regularly, by nine o'clock on a Saturday night all sorts of truths are being discussed and emerging, and a Sunday, in many ways, is a day of recovering from the onslaught of truth on a Saturday night. On a Saturday night, right across our town, marriages were tested, friendships forged and broken, revelations made, calmnesses disturbed, as the effects of wine and beer made themselves felt and truth began to slip out and run amok. Church is actually the place where we go to hide from the truth, where we can pretend that we can manage ourselves and what we know of ourselves, and perhaps appeal to ourselves and to others and to God to assist us. Truth, naked, was more frequently seen and heard in the Castle Arms on a Saturday night than in the People's Fellowship, just three doors down, on a Sunday morning – and this was something of which Colin Rimmer, among others, was well aware.

One morning in the hut Billy mentioned to Colin a rumour that Colin had heard many times before – the hoary old rumour that in Frank Gilbey's back garden were the ornaments which had mysteriously disappeared with the road-widening scheme nearly ten years ago, the big stone trough and the beautiful water fountain from outside the Quality Hotel. It was a silly sort of a rumour and a nothingy sort of a story, but Colin knew it meant something: it was symbolic. If they could get Frank Gilbey for the garden ornaments, that would just be the beginning. Colin said that he would dearly like to know the truth about this rumour, and Billy had said that he reckoned anyone could find out the truth, if they set their mind to it. OK, said Colin. You can be my undercover reporter. Which is how Billy Nibbs ceased to be a poet and finally got into print.

11

The Quality Hotel

At midway, an apparent digression

A hundred years of weather has done its best, has done its work on the Quality Hotel, a building which is no longer in the full flush of its youth, a building which might properly be described as weather-*beaten*, a building sick, defeated and on its last legs: there is penetrating damp, rising damp, dry rot, wet rot, moulds, fungus, spores, weevils and beetles of every kind. It's a building with water in its lungs and a loss of strength in its limbs. It is a poor, poor palsied building, feeble, full of fractures, incontinent and immune-deficient. Life has been hard on the Quality Hotel. It has sustained a lot of knocks. Frankly, it's a miracle the place is still standing. The scaffolding helps.

It was built in 1873. Or, at least, work began in 1873. Like most things in our town the Quality Hotel has been a perpetual work-in-progress, a good idea, a dream and a conception rather than a thing complete and in and of itself, a place in whose beginning was its end, which promised more than it ever delivered and which is now long past its best. The Quality Hotel was never really completed and now it's nearly finished.

It was perhaps fitting that the architect of the Quality Hotel was a man named More O'Ferral, a talented daydreamer and a full-time blusterer, a man whose exaggerated claims for his

164

professional achievements were matched only by his sketchy knowledge of fundamental engineering principles, a man of whom portraits show a weak, nervous, weaselly face hidden behind a vast, impressive and deeply suspicious beard.

After building the Quality Hotel More O'Ferral was appointed the town's first Clerk of Works, a position he held until his death. His portrait hangs to this day in the council chambers, the big bushy beard and the beady eyes overseeing proceedings – the timeless face of the patriarch and of the professionally shifty.

The records show that More O'Ferral was born locally, right here in town, up on Fitzroy Avenue, into a chinless, wealthy family of bankers and merchants. He was a sickly child, of an artistic bent of mind, and when he was sixteen he left home, determined to flee to Paris to pursue an artistic career, but by the time he arrived in London en route, he'd already run out of money, and in one of those compromises masquerading as practical common sense for which our townsmen are well known, he decided to abandon his dreams of painting nudes in Montmartre and drinking absinthe with bohemians at the Moulin Rouge, and he became apprenticed instead to a Clerk of Works in Tower Hamlets. He lied about his skills, his knowledge and his experience: his career as an architect had begun.*

More O'Ferral's largest project before taking on the Quality Hotel had been the building of a Turkish Baths in Bethnal Green in London, a project which, if certain of the burghers of our town had known about it, might have caused some objections and concern about More O'Ferral's involvement with any building project here. But needless to say no one

* I am indebted here and in what follows to Ross Liddell's invaluable three-volume biography, *More O'Ferral: The Early Years* (1967), *More More O'Ferral: The Years of Fame* (1973) and *No More O'Ferral: The Final Years* (1980), published by the Fireside Gleanings Press in association with the Architectural Heritage Society.

from our town had ever been to the Turkish Baths in Bethnal Green in London and More O'Ferral was better known – or at least, had let it be put about by his family and friends – for designing a chapel and a small arcade of shops, neither of which projects had actually been built, but for which the plans existed and were simply going to waste. The Quality Hotel, therefore, when it was built featured, naturally, a large Turkish Baths, a chapel and a small arcade of shops.

These features at the time had been unique in their combination, if not eccentric, and were never quite completed. The Turkish Baths, for example, had been ornately tiled and plumbed, fitted with its own small boiler house and decorated with various curious carved marine and piscine specimens, mainly porpoises, which were easier to shape in sandstone than fish – scales are tricky – but the Baths had a short lifespan of just a few weeks before problems with leaks of steam into the bedrooms shut it down. Guests initially mistook the heat and humidity for passion, but even the most ardent of lovers eventually noticed the aromatic fog and the unusual damp, and the condensation on the mirrors. The carpenter for the chapel, meanwhile, a Mr Fitzsimmons, a renowned local craftsman, had died unexpectedly, chisel in hand – he'd slipped and carved out an artery, bleeding to death on an unfinished altar rail – and so the necessary pews and pulpit somehow never materialised, and the chapel was never consecrated and never found the role for which it was destined, but was furnished instead with occasional chairs, a double-end settee and an ottoman, and became the room where the hotel's lady guests sometimes took their coffee and spoke of suffrage. The tradesmen – the tobacconist, the stationer, the confectioner, the tailor – who had taken the opportunity to open up business in the miniature arcade of shops, with its beautiful high glazed vault connecting the hall and lobby of the hotel with the dining rooms, had soon found that trade was seasonal and had closed.

The owners and founders of the hotel, the McCreas, had done their best to make the most of More O'Ferral's inspirations and follies in their advertising, in handbills and newspaper copy that can now be consulted in the local history archive, upstairs in the library on the Windsor Road, under the watchful gaze of Philomena, or Maureen, or Anne, or one of the legion of our other woolly-jumpered part-time librarians. Schoolchildren are in fact the only people who actually do consult the archives, for the purposes of school projects, but like God and Diet Coke, and helpful lady librarians, it's good to know they're there, in case we ever need them.*

According to the historical evidence, and despite their obvious mistake in employing O'Ferral in the first place, the McCreas had enough sense to see that it was necessary to advertise the peculiar charms of the Quality Hotel as offering distinctively different things to different people. Thus,

---

* According to a recent article in the *Impartial Recorder*, the library, which was opened in 1910 with a £1,000 grant from Carnegie, may in fact soon be facing the threat of closure, unless the council grant a request for £25,000 to provide for new mandatory disabled access and to comply with recent changes in Health and Safety legislation. Unfortunately, as the council finance director, Hugh Harkin, points out in the article, the library's borrowing figures have been decreasing over the long-term, with this year's figures already being down substantially on last year, although this may be because the library is now open for only four days a week, and all its specialist journals, periodicals and pamphlets have been sold or dumped, the reference room has been turned into what is called the Poetry Café and over a quarter of the lending section's shelf space has been removed in order to accommodate twelve on-line computers. Philomena, Maureen and Anne are all looking for work elsewhere. In the article Arlene Kirkpatrick, the divisional librarian, who has been responsible for what she calls the 'Big Make-over' and for 'updating Andrew Carnegie', denies rumours that she will soon be leaving to take up a post in sales with Donovan's, the pub and club management company. (As of writing, Arlene Kirkpatrick has recently resigned from her position as divisional librarian to take up a position in sales with Donovan's, the pub and club management company.) Contact library for opening times.

depending on which publications you read – there's an advertisement in *The Times*, for example, and one also in the *Impartial Recorder*, surely one of the only occasions on which these two journals have been united in common purpose – the Quality Hotel was either a 'First-class Family Hotel' or a set of 'Cheap Billiard Rooms Offering Private Dinners on the Shortest Notice'. Courting couples were wooed with the promise of 'Special Rooms for Wedding Breakfasts', well-to-do and progressive young women were drawn in by the 'Ladies' Coffee and Meeting Room' and others, perhaps, by promises of 'A Porter Up All Night' and 'Every Comfort Requisite'. The hotel was even, apparently, and presumably on the strength of the leaky Turkish Baths, 'A Hydropathic Establishment', and then again and also, presumably on the employment of a local doctor, a suitable place of recuperation for 'The Nervous, Hypochondriacal, Dipsomaniacal, or Strictured'. Each type and variety of advertisement, however, ended with the same boast, which had been dreamed up by John McCrea and to which John's wife Nora had added an important coda: 'Good Cooking and Extreme Cleanliness', each advert concluded, 'Limited Numbers Received'. This hint of exclusivity, Nora felt, represented the very meaning of quality itself. A liberal table and starched sheets meant nothing if meant for everyone.

Nora was a black-haired country girl, the daughter of a local landowner, who had always had ideas above her station. She was the driving force behind the establishment of the Quality Hotel. She it was who had persuaded her husband John and the brothers McCrea, successful tobacco merchants, to put their money into a hotel in the first place. Nora it was who had visited the south of France and Italy, and stayed in beautiful, golden hotels, lit by the Mediterranean sun and dappled by cypresses and bays, so different from the uniform grey of our own town, and Nora it was who'd returned from these trips with an expanded waistline, new shoes, trunks full of trinkets and souvenirs, and a vision to change for ever the face of our solemn little town, with its occasional sycamore and rowan, and not a single fine restaurant or high-class clothing shop. She wasn't the first person who thought she could turn the place around and she would not be the last.

John McCrea had determined that if his wife had to have a hotel here – a place where, let's be honest, no hotel should naturally be – then it needed to blend in and be something that at least looked like a linen mill, say, or a soapworks, but Nora had insisted on the Italian palazzo style, and of course More O'Ferral had ideas of his own, and together the three of them, John, Nora and O'Ferral, had argued and fought over almost each door and window and stone in the building, so that in the end the Quality Hotel gloried in every classical column type, and in huge industrial corner chimney stacks, wrought-iron balconies, a terrace and Italianate gardens. With the final addition, at More O'Ferral's insistence, of dozens of carved stone birds and snakes, in homage to John Ruskin, and Nature, and St Patrick, the place had ended up as a kind of demented vision of Anglo-Hiberno-Pan-European-Colonial-Imperial luxury – six storeys of pink and yellow sandstone, with whimsical wrought-iron palm tree grilles on the windows and an entrance like the steps to a workhouse. Even in its heyday the Quality Hotel had the appearance of a palace designed by the confused and built by the tired and emotional, the whole thing a monument to divided loyalties, strong personalities, and the variable and occasionally questionable skills of our own local tradesmen and builders.*

* There's a saying you still hear around town, not often, but it doesn't mean it no longer holds true: 'Too much pudding will choke the dog'. The Quality Hotel did not choke the dog, but it did kill a horse. This is a true story. Right up until the early 1970s the hotel was a popular morning meeting place for the farmers and the market gardeners and the butchers who used to arrive early for Wednesday and Saturday market, before the market became the multi-storey car park. You could get a good cup of coffee and

Nora had wanted to crown the whole thing with bronze sculpted medallions showing portrait reliefs of herself and John over the entranceway, but More O'Ferral had managed to dissuade her. There were some kinds of ugliness which even he could not tolerate, although he had made an exception for Nora herself, in the flesh, whose face and whose considerable years, he found, belied her youthful and energetic body, and who had become briefly his lover, on the terrace, in the Turkish Baths and the arcade, and, to O'Ferral's eternal shame, in the putative chapel. Nora's reputation among the workmen at the Quality Hotel was legendary – she had adopted 'foreign practices' it was said – although she never stooped lower than a mason and to the bricklayers her charms were only a rumour.

More O'Ferral was just twenty-four years old when he began work on the hotel, a bearded boy, really, but his professional reputation had preceded him. The McCreas had heard much about this brilliant local young man and his achievements, mostly from More O'Ferral's own family, with whom they occasionally dined. Of course, neither of the families

---

a hot buttered roll for sixpence in the hotel's dining room, or from Norton Brogue, who'd set up a coffee stall in competition outside the hotel, offering 'A Matutinal Beverage as an End to a Night's Dissipation'. Saveloys were Norton's unique selling point and innovation, and the sale of coffee and saveloys kept him in business for nearly thirty years, before he left for Australia with his daughter on an assisted passage in the 1950s, where he finally abandoned saveloys, took a job in a bicycle repair shop and became a barbecue aficionado. Tommy Corrigan, who worked at the Sunrise Dairy, was standing outside the hotel at Norton's stall one fine morning in June 1928, drinking his morning cup of coffee and eating his saveloy, chewing the fat with Norton, having been up since 4 a.m. scrubbing out the kegs and measures ready for the day's deliveries, when one of the cast-iron balconies on the front of the hotel fell down and killed his horse, Flinty, who was tethered outside the hotel, drinking from the stone water trough. These days, Tommy would probably have sued the hotel and been able to retire on the proceeds from his dead horse and his own trauma, but back then he just had to get on and pull his own float for six months before he could afford to buy another horse.

could have foreseen the great turbulence that was to befall More O'Ferral's personal life, and which was to affect his work and was to determine, for better or for worse, the design and building of the Quality Hotel, our town's remaining one great landmark and our link with the past.

Shortly after his appointment as architect to the McCreas, More O'Ferral's young wife had died unexpectedly in child-birth. This was the reason his drawings and designs for the Quality Hotel had taken such a dark and unusual turn, people said: it was owing, they said, to his grief. What they didn't know was that it was owing also to his increasing reliance upon opium, which he was using to help him overcome his sense of loss and to rediscover inspiration. He was stuck, frankly, for ideas, and he couldn't think about anything except his wife and Nora's constant interfering and entreaties, and the hotel he was designing, on paper and in his head, was becoming more and more like a monument to his marriage, a phantasmagoric place of remembrance and longing, and when it was built, for all of its fripperies outside, it remained within a dark, crypt-like building, opening out into vast and inexplic-able spaces. Sigmund Freud, if he'd been around in town at the time, would undoubtedly have had something interesting to say about More O'Ferral's state of mind, and he might have warned the McCreas not to employ a man clearly suffering from several kinds of complex. Down the years, visitors to the Quality Hotel often remarked that the black marble columns in the hall and lobby made the place look more like a mausoleum than a hotel and indeed, if it weren't for the domed stairway, one of Nora's suggestions, and the even-tual introduction of electric light, the entire entrance hall would have been lit by only two iron lamps bearing flames by the door, creating the illusion of walking into an under-ground vault. The Quality Hotel, from the moment of its conception, was a monument to money ill spent, to sex and to death.

More O'Ferral himself was dead by the time he was fifty, dead, they say, from the overwork and strain caused by his last project – the designing of a moving covered walkway intended to facilitate easier shopping on our town's busy streets, a project far ahead of its time and doomed to failure, but which eventually found its fulfilment in Bloom's, the mall, more than a hundred years later, with its escalators and its famous motto, 'Every Day a Good Day, Regardless of the Weather'. His visionary project exhausted him. And the ferocious drug habit and an attack of syphilis probably did not help.

Uncovered and exposed, the vision that originally shaped the Quality Hotel has also long since faded and died. People's ideas of what is or what is not an aspect of quality changes, and so over the years More O'Ferral's Turkish Baths were transformed into a palm court, where people could take tea and listen to the music of string quartets, and then eventually the palm court itself became a lounge area where people could take afternoon Nescafé and listen to muzak, or Abba. The dining room, with its vast leaded windows overlooking the Italianate garden, was briefly an art deco ballroom and later a dance hall with a sprung floor. Rooms had been modernised piecemeal over the years, most of them cut in half and then in half again, until the hotel had over 300 tiny rooms with identical orange carpets and more stud walls than originals. The chapel became a library and eventually a games room. The arcade of shops, which at first offered perfumes and tobaccos of every kind and combination, became an arcade filled with slot machines, video games and vending machines. By the 1960s people even from our town had begun holidaying abroad, where they could be guaranteed warm weather and cheap food, and so quality no longer meant what it used to: there was no longer a desire for refinement. There was a desire, indeed, for the opposite. What we desired in our town, as elsewhere, was more and cheaper.

The hotel accommodated itself accordingly. A large neon sign was erected over the carved entrance, stating, simply, 'QUALITY', and then, soon, 'QUALIT', then 'QUA IT', and then finally just 'QU IT'. There was the concrete back-bar and disco extension. During the 1980s there was even a short-lived attempt to turn the hotel into a conference facility, the chapel becoming a room with a slide projector and stackable chairs, but apart from the local council, who used the facilities for some town-planning enquiries, our town did not support a business community which could utilise such state-of-the-art facilities.

After the conference failure came the weekend antiques and collectables fairs, and the record fairs, and the psychics and healers, and briefly, Frank Gilbey's jazz festival, which attracted no more than a couple of dozen punters to turn out and listen to some pot-bellied men play Dixieland in the remains of the lounge, which now resembled the day room of an old people's home.

For all its recent history of inevitable decline, though, there is not a resident in town above the age of consent and below the high tide of senility who doesn't have some fond memory of the Quality Hotel. One of our oldest residents, Mrs Malone, who lives in the Gables – by far the most prestigious of our many old people's homes, which boasts residents' parking, landscaped gardens and views over the People's Park, all of which are, strictly speaking, surplus to requirements, since most of the residents are half blind and none of them any longer owns a car – claims that she can remember being at the Quality Hotel when she heard news of the outbreak of World War One in 1939.

'No, Mother,' Gerry her son would always say. 'The First World War began in 1914.' As a history teacher Gerry was accustomed to correcting.

'I know what I know,' she'd say.

'The *Second* World War began in 1939,' he'd insist.

'Well, we shall have to agree to disagree, Gerard,' she would say and fall into another gentle sleep.

Mrs Malone is shrivelled now, has emphysema, looks like an oven-ready bird and is about the weight of a sparrow, but back in the old days she'd been glamorous in a way that no one these days is glamorous, and no one has been for about fifty years. Photographs of her with the late Mr Malone outside the Quality Hotel, arriving for a Masonic Ladies' Night, show him with hair that looks as though it has been glued into place and a three-piece suit, and her in a borrowed stole and long gloves, staring proudly at the camera – and they were just average people, they were nothing special – and if he was honest Gerry would have to admit that one of the reasons he'd taken up the study of history was to try to understand that look, and to try to recover some of that glamour, and that confidence. Gerry wore a leather jacket and listened to music by the Grateful Dead, but he intended, as he got older, to switch to suits and a fob watch, and maybe a panama hat in the summer. Gerry is now nearly sixty years old, so he's taking his time. The leather jacket, in the meantime, was meant to evoke T. E. Lawrence rather than James Dean, but this was a fine distinction that was lost on the people of our town. Gerry's area of specialisation was the 1930s – that period when his parents were young adults and the Quality Hotel was still, just, a place of wonders.

Gerry's own memories of the Quality Hotel were typical of his generation. What he remembered were the 1960s, the time when the hotel first passed out of family hands, when it was acquired by the famous Mr Brittle, who'd bought it from the McCreas, the descendants of Nora and John, who had tired of the hotel's fading glamour, and the spiralling costs of repairs and maintenance. This was the era of the ice cream parlour and the coffee bar in the lobby, where live bands – skiffle, mostly, and nascent rock'n'roll performed by the likes

174

of Barry Devlin and the Tigers* – could be heard between 6 and 9 only on Wednesday and Friday nights, while residents attempted to eat their warm roast dinners and their pies in the dining room, which had once been the library, surrounded by shelves long since denuded of books, and replaced with swaths of treen and silver-plated silverware.

It was when Mr Brittle sold up and bought some land on the coast of southern Spain – clearly foreseeing the future – that the hotel's final phase of decline began, the era that most of us still remember.

The new owners, the people who bought the hotel from Mr Brittle, were a consortium headed by the shadowy Mr Miller, a man, people said, 'with city money behind him'. They were responsible for the addition of the concrete back-bar and disco extension. The Italianate gardens were used as a dumping ground and the vast windows leading out were removed and bricked up. Another bar appeared in the entrance hall, in order to attract passing trade. In these final refurbishments every penny had been spared and every last improvement carried out in Formica, plywood, and unplaned 2" x 4". The Quality Hotel had finally achieved its apogee.

In these last years only the disco, which at first was 'Jumping Jack's', then 'Scruples', then 'Club 2000', could boast a profit: there were restrictions on numbers, but some nights during the summer, when people would travel in from the city and the country, there were as many as 2000 dancing like John Travolta, and then like Jennifer Warnes and Madonna, and then body-popping, and then round their handbags, and throwing shapes. The disco manager, Cliff – known as 'The Libyan' on account of his dark good looks and the fact that his father came from somewhere far away – doled out a grand in the hand, cash, no questions asked, to big-name DJs from local radio and television who travelled out to play a set, and

* See note, p.149.

175

then travelled back up the new motorway as fast as they could, after a rousing finale of 'Heigh Ho Silver Lining' or 'Lady in Red'.

The hotel, at this point, was to all intents and purposes finished. The consortium of owners took no interest and one day the whole place was simply closed, no fanfare and no announcement. One Friday night there was a disco and the next night, when people arrived wearing their casual trainers and with condoms in their pockets, the doors were closed, locked and bolted, and everyone had to make do with early chips and home.

The place has since been completely stripped, at first by Mr Miller and his backers, who managed to auction off the larger parts of kitchen equipment, and the beds and the sofas. Elderly Mrs Malone, although she didn't know it, sat on a part of the Quality Hotel when she was in the day room in the Gables, developing sores, vacantly watching morning television, and every Thursday she ate a chunky vegetable soup which had been served with a ladle from a kitchen that had once been the boast of the county and had seen the back of *velouté aux fleurs de courgette*. A small revolving leather chair which now sat in the Gables's duty manager's office had once, it was rumoured, seen the behind of More O'Ferral himself.

After the first stripping came the scavengers. In one memorable night someone managed to pick off about 2000 Bangor Blue roof slates, plus several hundred yards of copper piping, some lead flashing, the remaining art deco-style door handles and about a mile and a half of architraves and skirting. After that the real looting began and before long there wasn't much left for the rest of us. Parquet floors were burned for bonfires. Banisters were snapped. Terrazzo floors hacked up and used for missiles. The stud walls were punched and kicked through, and set light to, opening up the hotel's original and vast womb-like spaces, and for a while More O'Ferral's monument to his wife was revealed once again in all its original glory. People said even the guard dogs were spooked by the place and would howl at the ghosts who inhabited the halls and corridors, but pretty soon the contract to patrol the building expired, the dogs departed and the hotel was left to rot in peace.

But still it has its residents, of course, rats mostly – the great-grandsons and great-granddaughters of the original rats who inhabited the ash pile which stood hidden behind the summer house in the Italianate garden – and pigeons, and the occasional alcoholic like Jerry, who sleeps in his clothes on the bandstand in the old Turkish Baths, a position which gives him a commanding view should anyone attempt to come at him unawares. Drug takers had at one time colonised the old library, but a steel door now kept them out.

To be honest, it's hard to feel much nostalgia for the building these days and the Quality Hotel's current owner, Frank Gilbey, was not a man who could feel nostalgia at the best of times. Like Stalin, Frank believed – as he often told Mrs Gilbey and anyone else who would listen – that you couldn't make an omelette without breaking a few eggs. (Although as far as Mrs Gilbey was aware, Frank had never actually made an omelette. He had boiled her an egg once, for breakfast, when she'd been ill after the Scotsman had left Lorraine, and she thought she couldn't find the will or the energy to get up and do things, but the egg had been boiled hard enough to bounce and by lunchtime she was back on her feet. Men, Mrs Gilbey was forced to recognise once again, are useless in a crisis, and not that much good the rest of the time either.)

Frank believed that progress was inevitable and that quality had to be reinvented, time and again. Frank believed that plastic was a natural improvement upon wood and to be preferred in most instances; he believed that uPVC windows were better than sash; that Frank Sinatra on CD was better than Frank on vinyl; and that aerosol cream in a can with a half-life of a hundred years was preferable to the perishable stuff from cows. Frank believed in progress.

Nonetheless, even though he never liked to look back and he always preferred the future, Frank couldn't deny that he'd had his good times at the Quality Hotel in the old days. He'd saved up and taken his parents there once for their wedding anniversary, years ago, the first time they'd ever eaten out. Back then, the Quality Hotel was the only place you could eat out in our town – this was way before Wong's and Scarpetti's. Frank had insisted that his father order the beef Wellington, the most expensive item on the menu. His mother had the scampi. It was the first time that Frank had really realised what money could buy you: attention, power, respect, people taking orders from you at the click of a finger. It was a revelation. Because he could still remember as a child, when his family didn't have two pennies to rub together and he'd been sent to the hotel with his brothers to beg for scraps round by the kitchen door, queuing with their pillowcases like the other children from the tight end of town, waiting to receive any crusts and knobs of bread that the cooks saw fit to throw away, or even the occasional pig's cheek for a Sunday dinner. People would hardly believe it today, but this was within living memory, his own memory. His lifetime. And frankly, after that, no one had the right to deny him anything; after that sort of a start in life Frank Gilbey was entitled. Jerry, who is one of our most notable town tramps, who has a magnificent yellowy beard, actually worked in the kitchens in the Quality Hotel years ago and he had always had a kind word for children like Frank when they came round looking for scraps, and if Jerry was ever out begging Frank always made sure he gave him at least a pound.

Times have changed, for all of us.

Frank could remember taking his little girl Lorraine to eat out at the Quality Hotel, and Lorraine, of course, is no longer his little girl. She's over thirty now and divorced. Frank preferred not to think about that.

And then there were the dances. It was the dances that

everyone remembered, even Frank. He'd been pretty fast in those days, quite a racy kind of a fella, and he'd often take girls out into the Italianate gardens, to see what might develop, and things frequently did develop, and as a thank-you he sometimes gave them a photograph of himself at Blackpool, wearing a Kiss Me Quick hat, as kind of a memento.

But that was all a very long time ago, and the past, as Frank always liked to remind Mrs Gilbey, is history.

12

Unisex

Francie McGinn gets his hair cut and
surveys the wondrous cross

It was a good day to get your hair cut: wet and cold, but with a definite hint of sun high in the sky, an unmistakable gesture of hope in autumn, the kind of day when your body reminds you that despite what you think actually you're not dead yet, and that it might be possible to change your life and turn things around, shake things out and spice things up a bit, with the addition of just a few subtle tints and the trimming of a few split-ends, or maybe even a hair extension or a soft perm. A grey day, but just bright enough to suggest silver linings, a day to run a comb through your hair and to delouse your dog, to wriggle out of your foul-weather gear and slip into something more comfortable.

Francie was missing Cherith, and he was missing her in a way he hadn't expected. (Members of the congregation may wish to turn the page at this point.) He was missing her in bed. Before the split, Francie and Cherith had been married for long enough for there to be no sense of adventure or mystery when they slipped into bed together, synchronised, like two trained circus puppies, at the end of each day. When Francie and Cherith hopped into bed, Francie in blue flannelette to the right and Cherith in pink to the left of him, they usually dropped straight off to sleep, give or take five or ten minutes of reading the Old Testament, which they both found more effective than either a hot milky drink or a modern novel. It may be, in fact, that God designed the names of the descendants of the tribes of Israel as a kind of resting place for a Christian's cares, a calming velvet hand, a charm and spell for tired and troubled souls. The Bible, one might even argue, is a kind of ark, somewhere to sleep while visiting this planet, an *accouchement*, a deathbed and an arbour all in one, the ultimate bed-and-breakfast.

But now with Bobbie Dylan, Francie remembered what it was like, being in a bed with a woman who was not a wife of long standing. Being in bed with Bobbie Dylan required much pillow talk and adjusting of the coverlets. It required a retraining. It was not an easy lay.

As a minister, Francie had to perform all day, every day. The performance was not his only, of course – he was sustained and supported in his work by the grace of God. When he visited people, when he spoke, he was often conscious of being used by the Holy Spirit. But when he was in bed at night with Bobbie, the Holy Spirit seemed to desert him and he was all alone, with a beautiful woman, and, he had to admit it, he was terrified.

This had, of course, led to all sorts of problems, problems which Bobbie had been more than prepared to help Francie overcome. Francie had had no idea that these sorts of things could be managed and handled; with Cherith, relations had always taken their own natural course, one way or another, and that had been enough for both of them. Now here he was, a full-grown man in his own bed, feeling like a little boy.

Bobbie was equally shocked and surprised: it felt to her like teaching your grandmother to suck eggs. She'd never lived with another Christian before, and certainly not a Christian minister. So she was surprised to find that Francie was less than fastidious when it came to certain practical Christian household chores and in matters of personal hygiene. In her book, and probably in the Good Book too, according to Bobbie, the use of products from the Body Shop was virtually a commandment. In this life, frankly, about the closest we're ever going to come to God is the sound of Enya and a running bath, the sight of a set of nice shining taps, and the smell of ylang-ylang and sandalwood aromatherapy oils.

Francie, it must be admitted, did not always pick up his own clothes at night and he had continued to resist Bobbie's attempts to smarten him up. She'd tried to get him out of his sta-prests and his lumberjack shirt, at least to get him into something from Marks, but – and Francie didn't tell Bobbie this – when he was slipping into and out of the clothes in the changing rooms, staring in the full-length mirror at his cheesy white buttocks and his flanks flecked with spots, his wasted upper arms and his protuberant belly, he was terrified at the prospect of further self-transformation. He didn't think he could take any more: on top of everything else, he didn't think he could cope with the sight of himself in chinos.

But he'd agreed to get his hair cut.

For as long as he could remember, probably his whole life since he was about five years old, Francie had gone to get his hair cut every two or three months by Tommy Morris up at the top of Kilmore Avenue. There was never really much of a queue: Tommy had you in and out before you could say straight or tapered, and anyway, whatever you said, it was all basically a variation on a Number 2 on the back and sides and a Number 3 on top. Tommy never spoke to you, he smoked the whole time he was cutting, and he'd lived happily with his companion, Andy, for twenty-five years without anyone seeing fit to question it, mention it, or even consider the possibility that Tommy was not as other men are. After work Tommy drank his Guinness in the Rose and Crown, bet on the horses, and he and Andy were never seen out in public after dark. They were regarded as upstanding citizens and most men in our town wouldn't even consider going anywhere else for a haircut.

So Francie, of course, had never before been into Central Cutz. When he stepped inside it felt like treason. It was a humbling experience.

Central Cutz is named not for its close approximation to some Platonic ideal – a golden mean – of hair cutting, but rather for its convenient town centre location. It's on Central Avenue, of course, a few boarded-up shops down from Inspirationz, which offers quality cards and giftware from around the world, and opposite Sew-Biz, where Mrs Nelson, whose son has married a Romanian, does garment alterations and listens to Classic FM. Central Avenue also boasts a health food shop, Full of Beans, which is full of beans, although Mandy Gamble, the owner, is not: weighing in at around sixteen stone and with some serious personal hygiene problems and prone to depression, Mandy is not a great advert for vegetarianism or Culpeper herbalism. But Central Avenue remains probably the closest thing we have here to a Latin Quarter. On a Saturday night, midsummer, if you were very, very drunk, it might almost seem like the barrio.*

---

* Central Avenue also now boasts our first and probably last sex or 'adult' shop – Sensations – on the site of what used to be Ted Ainley's confectionery and tobacconist, Hi, Sweetie!, and before that, the Temperance Café ('Dinners &c. Can Be Had on the Shortest Notice'). The Sensations window display features pink and silver balloons and streamers, suggesting that the façade might merely conceal a slightly offbeat Clinton Cards. Pastor Boyd Mann of the Bethel Free Baptist Church on Fork Hill has committed himself to standing vigil outside the shop until it's closed down. Boyd sports leaflets and wears an old-fashioned 'The Wages of Sin Is Death (Romans 6:23)' sandwich board, which he picked up from a clearance sale up in the city, at a Baptist church which is now a cappuccino bar, but he has never in fact had the pleasure of confronting any of Sensations' customers with leaflets or sandwich board, since they tend to wait until he's gone for a coffee at Scarpetti's before entering and buying their pink and silver balloons and streamers, or whatever it is that's available inside. Trish Legge, the shop's manager, simply avoids Boyd by using the entrance at the rear. Boyd's wife,

Central Cutz is not a barber's: this is an important distinction to make. Central Cutz is what is still called in our town a Unisex Hair Salon, although it's perhaps not immediately clear from the outside that they do, in fact, cater to men as well as women: only the presence of a pile of *GQ* magazines next to the *Cosmopolitan*s and *People's Friend*s on the little curly-wrought-iron coffee table by the window indicates that indeed they do. The walls inside Central Cutz are painted a rich terracotta and feature stencilled rustic motifs and découpage picked out by recessed spotlights, a quease-making effect that Francie himself had previously only seen demonstrated by tanned, skinny women on house make-over programmes on TV. It is not the interior of a barber's shop.

After settling into a chair and waiting for twenty minutes, reading a magazine featuring an interview with an actress and singer he'd never heard of called Jennifer Lopez, who rather reminded him of Bobbie Dylan – which unnerved him – Francie eventually plucked up the courage to speak to the receptionist and ask if he could go next, but apparently you're supposed to book an appointment for a consultation in Central Cutz, you don't just sit and queue, which he hadn't known, and no one had told him, but he was told there'd been a cancellation and he could have an appointment with a senior stylist, someone called Jackie, or Jacky, or possibly even Jacqui. Francie wasn't sure whether to expect a man or a woman.

Jackie turned out, in fact, to be a man, although a man sporting pencil-thin sideburns, like the go-faster stripes on an old Ford Capri, or the markings on a basketball, tapering to a point and a halt just short of his mouth, and with no hair whatsoever round the back and sides and a sort of short wet-

---

Lizzie, would quite like him to pack up the vigil and come home and help her out with their three young children, Japheth, Shem and Ham, but Boyd is actually quite enjoying himself – the vigil makes a nice change from door-to-door visiting and preaching sermons, and it's a lot more fun than changing nappies.

look bubble perm on top. Francie tried never to judge on first impressions, but he did not like the look of Jackie. Jackie did not look like a barber. He did not look like Tommy Morris.

Jackie guided Francie to a chair, which was the kind of fold-up director's chair you see in films about Hollywood and also in Habitat, and not a barber's chair at all of the kind that Francie was used to, and he asked Francie what he wanted done, and Francie said he wanted a haircut – he'd never really had to instruct Tommy – and Jackie said, in a voice crisp with sarcasm, 'Right! Any preferences at all? You want to give me a clue?' and Francie said that he wasn't really sure, he hadn't thought about it, and Jackie said, in what was quite clearly a patronising tone, 'OK, what I'll do is go round the back and sides, bring it in really nice and short, and then I'll wash your hair and cut on top by hand, does that sound all right?' Francie agreed that that would be OK.

Jackie picked up his scissors and Francie closed his eyes and started to regret having given in to Bobbie Dylan's entreaties. He tried not to think about it. He reflected instead on what had been a long and difficult year, full of ups and downs.

After the split with Cherith, Francie had experienced a long dark night of the soul, and he'd gone before his congregation to try to explain. God had spoken to him, he said, and He wished Francie to lay a fleece before Him, and so that was what Francie was going to do: if the majority of the congregation did not feel they could support him as minister, he would resign from the position.

In the end Francie lost about fifteen members of the congregation – young families, mostly, and he could understand that. A young family does not wish to see on a Sunday morning a reminder of everything they were missing out on as a young family on a Sunday morning – the sight of a man who had shrugged his shoulders and walked away from the difficulties and responsibilities of family life, and walked straight into something a lot more interesting. So the young families had

185

gone. The singles, the spinsters, the elderly couples, the young and the mad had mostly stayed on, and that was enough.

Jackie was pushing Francie forward: having never had his hair washed in a barber's before, Francie wasn't sure what was happening and resisted, and Jackie said, 'Wash your hair, yes?' as he might to a child or a senile old man, and when he leant forward towards the basin Francie thought for a moment he was going to be sick. He let the water wash over him.

After he had rededicated himself to the Lord's work before his diminished congregation, Bobbie had begun to encourage Francie to introduce all sorts of innovations, and within a few months numbers had picked up again to what they were before his split with Cherith. Bobbie herself had settled into a regular slot during the Sunday morning services, and under her guidance and encouragement the People's Fellowship Worship Band – or just the Band, as Bobbie called them – had begun to play a little more up-tempo, a little tighter and a little louder. She felt that the music had been stuck in a 1970s MOR praise and worship mode – too many ballads – and it needed updating. It was her idea to start using pop songs and replacing the words with Christian lyrics. This was a massive success: the Band's sanctified version of Eminem's 'The Real Slim Shady' (chorus: 'Will the real Saviour please stand up? / I repeat, will the real Saviour please stand up?') bringing them to the attention of the *Impartial Recorder*, and then the local commercial radio station, Hitz!FM, where Bobbie was interviewed at length about her vision for the church.*

Bobbie did have her misses, though, as well as her hits.

---

* Bobbie's vision for the church, revealed in the interview, was a vision which resembled in large part and in almost exact detail the television programme *Friends* – a vision of comfortable intimacy, of good taste and good humour, the church as a kind of spiritual coffee shop with sofas. She believed in what she called a more 'seeker-sensitive' church, a church which responded to the needs of the person seeking God, a church which was 'real' and which ministered to each individual's 'inner child'.

She didn't always get it right. She had rechristened the Young People's Group, calling it Can Teen, and that seemed to work, but her Drive-In Services were not a success. The Drive-Ins were something she'd seen when she'd been to Nashville for a Christian country music convention a few years ago, and she thought it would be worth a try here. She had persuaded Francie to hire the main car park in front of the Quality Hotel from the council for a month of Sunday nights, and the council were more than happy, since it prevented boy-racers gathering there, burning rubber, and throwing beer bottles at the police and passers-by. Francie had then managed to borrow a cab and a trailer from T. P. McArdle, a big name in trucking locally, whose wife is a member of the congregation, and they brought down the church's PA, and the electric piano, set it up on the back of one of T. P.'s lorries and held their services. You had to wind down your window to hear and there was an order of service for every car, and it was quite a novelty. The first week they attracted about sixty vehicles in all, ranging from an old Datsun Sunny to a couple of BMWs. The Hegartys, Jerome and his wife, who have five children all under ten, and who are the closest thing we have here in town to actual hippies, came in their VW combi-van and blocked the view. They cooked sausages and beans during the hymn singing and ate them during the sermon, and Francie did find the smell of frying a little off-putting – but then, that's open-air preaching for you. Jesus probably had the same problem with the fish and loaves. By the second week the numbers had dropped right down, and by the third week the boy-racers had started to appear back again at the car park, turning up the volume on their stereos, pumping their horns, and drinking Smirnoff Ice and tequila slammers while Francie was trying to preach the gospel. It would have tried the patience of a saint. The fourth week, fortunately, it rained, the PA shorted and Francie insisted that they call the whole thing off.

But by now Bobbie had the bit between her teeth, and she suggested that Francie needed to update and improve and generally overhaul his entire preaching style. Francie wasn't used to anyone, apart from God, offering him advice on his sermons, but he was more than happy to listen to what Bobbie was saying: he'd never really felt comfortable in the deeper waters of interpretation and explication and exegesis, and now here was Bobbie offering him a lifeline and a way back to the comforts and shallows of a simple faith, which is where he'd begun, after all, and where he felt more comfortable. She suggested he might like to lighten up a bit and try telling a few jokes, and that he maybe take a theme sometimes rather than just a text, and instead of only announcing the times of services in the *Impartial Recorder* along with all the other churches, she encouraged him to advertise. The first of his new-style sermons – 'God, Is that You Talking, Or Was It Just the Cheese?' – was advertised prominently in the *Impartial Recorder*, next to an ad for the Woodflooring Warehouse Super Sale ('BUY! BUY! BUY!') and a Happy Hour at the Armada Bar ('DOUBLE SPIRITS £1'), and was backed up by a feature, with a photo, based on a press release that Bobbie had put together on the Fellowship computer. It made quite an impact. Francie's next sermon, 'Jesus: Bling Bling, or BaDaBaDaBooom?', brought in a few more of the curious and the under-thirties, as did 'Does God Ever Say "Oops"?', on the problem of evil, and 'Cheer Up! Some Day You'll Be Dead', on the Second Coming and the Book of Revelation. But by far the biggest crowds had been for a gospel meeting that Bobbie had persuaded Francie not to announce, as usual, as simply 'A Gospel Meeting', but to advertise instead with posters and flyers asking, 'Is This Really My Life, or Has There Been Some Kind of Mistake?' Six people gave their lives to Christ that night, a record for the People's Fellowship and possibly for the town. There were murmurs within other churches about a revival at the People's Fellowship, something we haven't seen here since 1959, the year of the Great Revival, when the Spirit descended upon the Baptists during a week of meetings held by a travelling evangelist from Stockton-on-Tees called Maynard Rogers, whose name lives on in our town in legend and in the name of the Baptists' coffee bar and meeting rooms on Mountjoy Street, the Maynard Rogers Rooms (which are currently in the process of being converted into a Christian Internet café). Baptists, of course, are known to be both prone and partial to revival, and some of them had started sneaking down to the evening services at the People's Fellowship in search of the Spirit, who seems increasingly fickle these days and who no longer seems to favour the mainline denominations.*

Once Jackie had shampooed and rinsed his hair, Francie said, through gathered phlegm, 'The shampoo smells nice, like almonds.'

And Jackie said, 'Well, what did you expect it to smell like? Cat's pee?'

And Francie said no, he didn't expect it to smell like cat's pee, actually. He wasn't sure what he'd expected it to smell like.

'You know,' said Jackie, 'it's like when I cut some people's hair and they say to me, "Wow, that's really good" and I think, like, well, yeah, what did they expect? I'm a hairdresser, not a butcher, d'you know what I mean? I'm not chopping up meat here, am I?'

---

* Not everyone, however, approves. The People's Fellowship has, in fact, recently come under fierce attack for its methods from Pastor Boyd Mann of the breakaway Bethel Free Baptist Church on Fork Hill. In his pamphlet, *The Spiritual War for the Souls of Men*, Pastor Mann – a former Hell's Angel and motorcycle courier from Newtownstewart – groups the Fellowship together with Mormons, Freemasons, Jehovah's Witnesses, Seventh Day Adventists, Scientology and Satanism, in presenting a threat to orthodox Christian teaching. The pamphlet is available from the Bethel Free Baptist Church, or from Boyd himself outside Sensations on Central Avenue, price £1.

And just as he said that he nicked Francie's ear with the razor. 'Oops, sorry,' he said and Francie felt a tiny trickle of blood on his neck. He closed his eyes again.

The cross had also been Bobbie's idea. She'd been trying to persuade Francie for a long time that it would be good to erect something on the roof of the church, to put the place on the map. The People's Fellowship is, of course, really just the old Johnson Hosiery Factory, done up a bit, and it still looks pretty much like a factory: there's not a lot you can do on a tithing budget to transform a nineteenth-century industrial space into a modern, twenty-first-century place of praise and worship. As things began to pick up, though, and the Spirit definitely began to move, Bobbie felt that the church needed to make a more dramatic statement, that it needed to announce itself more clearly to the town as a holy place, and a happening place. Francie had said they couldn't afford expensive signage or neon, so Bobbie had put on her thinking cap and had just gone ahead and asked Marion, one of the Fellowship's many spinsters, to ask her brother Harry, Harry Lamb the Odd Job Man, if he wouldn't mind knocking something up. Harry was more used to doing fiddly wee jobs around town – installing Slingsby loft ladders and clearing blocked guttering – and he hadn't done a cross before, but he said he'd give it a go.

A large cross is not, in fact, that difficult to make. If the Romans could do it, after all, with their primitive tools, it was hardly going to be much of a problem for Harry with his circular power saw, a rotary electric planer, some galvanised angle brackets and his tradesman's discount at the World of Wood. Harry liked to think, actually, that he could probably improve on the original design, and he put together a few drawings for Bobbie to have a look at, sketching out crosses in all sorts of different shapes and sizes, using different joints and finishes which he thought might look quite impressive. But Bobbie felt that the cross needed to be like a real cross, a cross that a man might actually be crucified on, so in the end Harry had kept it simple and used some 4" x 4" tanalised timber, with a 6-foot crossbeam to accommodate a man's outstretched arms, and a 12-foot upright. Harry was not a believer himself, but he had to admit that putting the cross together had made quite an impact on him. It was a pretty gruesome bit of kit, when you looked at it up close, and hardly something to be scoffed at or mocked. He went for belt and braces to connect the two beams, using a half-lap joint with a metal plate and bolts to secure it, and then the Young People's Group – Can Teen – got to work on it, and had it primed, undercoated and finished with two coats of a pure white weatherproof gloss, guaranteed to last six years, sealing each coat under Francie's guidance with a prayer and a blessing. Harry set the whole thing into a concrete base up on the roof of the People's Fellowship and it looked pretty cool, the young people agreed.

The problem was, though, on a sunny day, the cross whited out against the sky, and in the rain and mist you could hardly see it.

So the Day-Glo paint had been Bobbie Dylan's next idea.

And then the floodlighting.

Jackie was showing Francie the back of his head in a mirror, the haircut complete.

With the Day-Glo paint and the floodlighting you could see the cross from about two miles away, even if you were wearing dark glasses, which of course no one in our town does, unless they're Wally Lee, or one of the mothers of the children at Barneville House, or unless they're actually blind or partially sighted, and even then they might have been able to make out a vague outline, or just felt it there, burning in the night. You could certainly see it, even on a grey day, from Bloom's and the ring road. Which is when the council had got on to it: they wanted the Fellowship to take it down, or to pay £250 for an application for planning permission. And then the *Impartial Recorder* picked up on the story and started a campaign, prompted by Bobbie, 'Save the Sign of Our Salvation', and it looked for a while as though the cross might get to stay, for free and gratis, until someone who was visiting his mother in town, and who hadn't been here for a long time, was momentarily distracted by the sight of what looked like the first sign of the Second Coming, and drove straight over a mini-roundabout on the ring road and into a municipal flower bed, taking out a lot of expensive bedding plants.

So Harry Lamb was instructed to take a chainsaw to the cross, and he carved it up, and that was a sad day for Francie, a day of humiliation, and Harry sold the wood on to a friend who runs a stick and log business out of the industrial estate, and it has been used to light fires throughout town ever since.

Francie was trying to smile at the face looking back at him in the mirror.

'Well?' said Jackie.

'It's nice,' said Francie. His teeth were a bit yellowy.

'You look like a new man,' said Jackie.

'Yes,' agreed Francie.

'You never know, you might get lucky tonight!' said Jackie, his tapering sideburns crinkling up into a smile.

Which was really the moment, if he had to identify a moment, at which Francie realised that he did not belong here and that he had made a terrible mistake.

Francie would not be getting lucky tonight. Just for the record, and for the sake of the congregation, Francie and Bobbie are in fact no longer sleeping in the same bed. They just weren't compatible. Bobbie is always cold at night and Francie too hot, and they'd tried one of those dual-tog partner duvets, thirteen tog on one side, ten tog on the other, which have been on sale up at N'Hance, the furniture and interiors place in Bloom's, but the duvet just didn't do it. Bobbie wanted still more warmth, and she was piling the bed high with jumpers and dressing gowns, and in the end Francie had given up and gone to get some sleep downstairs, where he used to sit awake reading the Bible or watching late-night TV or Bobbie's exercise videos. She had a full range of pop and soap stars doing boxercise, yoga, aerobics and everything in between – they'd had to clear some shelf space to accommodate them all. Some of Francie's devotional works had had to be shifted to under the bed.

Also, at around the same time, Francie had been forced to move some of his clothes into a suitcase – Bobbie had so many clothes there wasn't enough room for them all in just her half of the wardrobe. She kept on buying new clothes all the time; Francie had had no idea this was what women did. As far as he could remember Cherith could get by for years on a couple of sweatshirts and some elasticated skirts, and they'd shared socks (which may have explained the persistent athlete's foot). But Bobbie just kept on buying and buying. She preferred cheap clothes, actually, for no moral or spiritual reason except that if she bought something cheap and only wore it a couple of times it didn't matter so much. She had maybe two dozen pairs of shoes in constant rotation. And the make-up. Cherith had never really bothered with make-up except for special occasions – Christmas, say, or Easter, which usually merited some lipstick and a bit of blusher. But Bobbie had this big box – a large metal box – and because she was used to performing, she would wear a kind of stage make-up all the time, which Francie had to admit he found impressive, except perhaps at breakfast, when he did find it a little grisly, particularly if they were having a fry.

The women in the congregation had all loved Cherith, who was like them, who was shy, who preferred slacks to skirts, and who wore the wrong bra size, just like they did. But now it was the men in the congregation who loved Bobbie. Francie couldn't help but notice that the members of the Band seemed to be swelling week by week, male members of the congregation offering up their hitherto undisclosed talents as percussionists, backing singers, roadies, supporters and general encouragers. Bobbie's position within the People's Fellowship was becoming unassailable.

It was when she suggested that they spend Christmas in Tenerife, though, that Francie had to put his foot down. She'd tempted him with the idea of langoustine pool-side on Christmas Day.

'Sure,' she said, 'isn't God there in Tenerife just the same as he's here?'

'Yes,' Francie had had to agree, but that was hardly the point. He was a minister and he had responsibilities.

Bobbie had granted him that, but she insisted that they needed something to look forward to at Christmas, which is how Francie had ended up agreeing to her idea for the big Christmas Eve concert. She was calling it on the posters 'The People's Fellowship Annual Big Night Out, Featuring Bobbie Dylan and the Band' in big font, and noting, in smaller font, 'Featuring Also the Wise Men, the Virgin and the Little Baby J'.

Francie ran his fingers through his gelled hair and looked up at the sky. God forgive him.

13

Deep Freeze

Containing a revelation

The sky, Mrs Donelly herself might have said, was the colour of the back of a used teaspoon. It was a day already drunk to the dregs and all washed out. A typical day here: nothing much to report and nothing much on the horizon, only clouds, and biscuits.

Mrs Donelly had led a quiet life, a used-teaspoon kind of a life, even by her own estimation. Anything she'd achieved she'd always dismissed, from a good apple pie with custard to the birth of her children to the chairing of a difficult council committee, and she always treated praise with the same ironic raising of a thin, pencilled-in eyebrow, whether it was praise from her children, from her colleagues, her employers, her husband, or even, as she sometimes liked to think, from the good Lord Himself. 'Well,' she would say, 'there you are now.'

She had only ever worked part-time, to fit in around the children. Hers was what she and Mr Donelly both referred to as the 'little job', her job as a receptionist at the Health Centre, even though it was often her little job that had kept the wolf from the door and their heads above water. A few extra pounds a week can make a big difference in the raising of a family. It can mean the difference between, say, one fish finger or two in a sandwich, and the difference between patching a patch and

195

a new pair of trousers. Every penny she'd earned had gone on feeding and clothing and caring for the children, and even when the children had left home and things had taken off and she became a councillor and had to attend evening meetings, Mrs Donelly always tried to put others first. She always made sure that Mr Donelly had something ready for his tea, for example, even if it was only a slice or two of wafer-thin ham, some buttered bread and some shavings of iceberg lettuce: the important thing was that there was something on the plate. Mr Donelly, of course, appreciated her efforts, and felt it was only right and proper. He didn't want her to get too carried away with all the council business and get too big-headed.

Mr Donelly could not abide big-heads. In the Castle Arms, if they were discussing some young footballer, say, who was playing at the height of his powers and earning lots of money and going out on the town with beautiful young women, and Big Dessie and Little Mickey Matchett and Harry Lamb the Odd Job Man were saying fair play to him and how great it was, Mr Donelly would just give a slight tut and a shake of his head, and that was enough of a dampener, enough of a reminder, to him and to them, that there were no heroes any more, that the age of chivalry was over and that the rich or the powerful were no more deserving of respect than anyone else. Like a lot of people here in town, Mr Donelly wasn't exactly a socialist but sometimes he sounded a lot like one: here, where we are, socialism and pessimism are pretty much the same thing.* It doesn't matter how many goals you score,

---

* Our local politicians, for example, fall into two categories, the Happy and Generally Contented, who tend to be conservative in their habits and thinking, and the Sad and Generally Discontented, who tend to lean towards the Left. But there are, of course, exceptions to this rule. Olivia Wallace, our first pioneering female councillor back in the 1940s, believed passionately in social justice and the Soviet Union, and in allotments and modern art. She bought olive oil from the chemist to cook with and she wore her hair cropped short like a man, but she was also unfailingly polite and cheerful

or how much money you make, or whatever you've achieved, everyone is basically the same according to Mr Donelly and, frankly, if you're looking for a hero you're better off with a dog, because people are bad, but dogs can at least be relied upon, as long as they're properly trained. Here in town people tend to take a post-lapsarian, pre-millennial view on most things: these may not be the End Times exactly, but they're certainly closer to the End than when we were all young.

Mr and Mrs Donelly had met long ago, in a Golden Age, when Mr Donelly was an apprentice at the printworks up on Moira Avenue, when men still worked with hot metal, and Mrs Donelly was working in the Carlton Tea Rooms, where the waitresses still dressed as waitresses and the diners wore gloves, and there were pure white tablecloths and a three-tier cake stand on every table. They'd met at church; they used to see each other at Mass. Mrs Donelly had stopped going for a while in her teens, but then she'd been so shocked at what had happened between her and Frank Gilbey that she began attending again. She wanted a new start in life. She'd believed for a while that what she wanted was the fast life that Frank Gilbey had to offer, but then she had realised that the fast life involved all sorts of complications and difficulties for a young woman in our town in the 1950s, so she settled for Mr Donelly instead.

Mr Donelly was not just Frank Gilbey's replacement, but his opposite. Where Frank had been all hard edges and cheekbones and energy and a big quiff, Mr Donelly was soft and friendly, just like a big bear, really, with his hair all muzzed

---

– not even the Soviet tanks rolling into Hungary in 1956 or into Czechoslovakia in 1968 could wipe the smile from her face. Gilbert Payne, on the other hand, at the opposite end of the political spectrum, was mayor back in the 1970s, and he believed in tradition and in the free market and in cricket and thick-cut marmalade, but it seemed to make him miserable – the contradictions were just too great. He committed suicide in 1979, just at the point at which Mrs Thatcher might have cheered him up.

up and wearing his dad's old cast-offs. He was shy, modest and apparently thoughtful. When they were courting he used to bring her presents of pats of butter wrapped in newspaper, and eggs, and the occasional chicken – his parents were from up-country and he had that country way of speaking, and that manner, that Mrs Donelly had liked so much and eventually had fallen in love with.

There had been a downside, of course, to Mr Donelly and his country ways: Frank Gilbey he most definitely was not, thank goodness, but Frank Gilbey he most definitely was not, alas. Mr Donelly was lacking in a certain keenness of spirit and he was not what you'd call adventurous. When it came to holidays, for example, Mr Donelly believed that abroad was probably overrated, and not that much different from here, except somewhere else. He liked plain food, plain speaking and he could sniff out the slightest sliver of garlic in one of Wong's Chinese takeaways or the faintest hint of cant in the *Impartial Recorder*, and he was not what you'd call a conversationalist, and he didn't eat fish, not even on Fridays; there was just something about it he didn't like, the smell of it, largely. But fresh fish doesn't smell, Mrs Donelly had always insisted. It only smells when it's going off. If it's fresh, she'd say, it doesn't smell at all. It does to me, Mr Donelly had always replied.

For their wedding anniversary one year Mrs Donelly had booked them into a little French place up in the city: one of the girls at the Health Centre had recommended it. It was a gourmet night, where you ate whatever the chef prepared, and it was quite expensive, but Mrs Donelly thought they might push the boat out just for once. It wasn't every day, as she'd had to explain to Mr Donelly, justifying the taxi fare and persuading him into his smart jacket, it wasn't every day that you've been married for thirty years. The chef did fish soup as a starter. Followed by salmon. And then wild boar. Wild boar, it turned out, was one of the other things Mr

Donelly did not much like. The evening was not a great success. After that, they stuck to Scarpetti's and the occasional Set Menu B from Wong's, without the garlic.

(Just for the record, though, so that he doesn't sound small-minded, which he is not – he's just sure of his opinions, which is a welcome privilege of middle and old age, after all the embarrassments and uncertainties of youth – Mr Donelly, it should be said, also dislikes politicians, cat lovers, litter louts, whom he calls 'litter louts', men who wear earrings and children who are rude, precocious, or noisy.)

Mr and Mrs Donelly's own children had not been rude, precocious, or noisy. Well, rude, maybe, when they were younger, and noisy, but definitely not precocious. None of them had been a big-head, which was a major achievement, in Mr Donelly's book. Preventing big-headedness: this was an important aim and intention of parenting, according to Mr Donelly. None of Mr Donelly's children thought that they were better than they were. They knew their place. And as it turned out their place was far from here: one of them was in America, one of them was in London and one of them was travelling the world. Mickey lives in town, of course, but he is married to Brona, who clearly has her eyes set elsewhere: once she's done her training as a beautician and the children have to start school, she'd quite like them to move to Huddersfield, to be near her parents, or even to Manchester.

Mrs Donelly had been thinking a lot about her children recently, all of them. She was sorting out her will. She'd been very well organised. She had all the documentation carefully arranged in a manila folder. She'd started sorting things out as soon as she'd known. She was diagnosed in the November of last year and by March she had all her personal effects sorted. She'd started going through her wardrobe, throwing out anything she hadn't worn for a year or more: she certainly wasn't going to be needing it now. She cleared her drawers and began using up old tins in the cupboards – good-intentioned foods, mostly, like kidney beans. They ate a lot of chilli con carne.

She'd started on the baking back in May, after they'd given up on the chemo. She didn't want to leave anything too late, to chance, or to Brona, who'd be happy with a shop-bought cake and a couple of quiches from Marks. She made tarts and pies and cakes and some sausage rolls. She filled her own freezer, and then she had to ask Pat to take one or two items. And Brenda. And Big Anne. She didn't tell any of them she was leaving food with any of the others and she didn't tell them what the food was for. She just said she was getting ready for Christmas early and she'd run out of room in her freezer. They all had grown-up children now, so they all had spare capacity, and they understood. None of them refused. None of them asked questions. In our town, even when the children have all grown up and gone away, the women still plan Christmas like it's a military campaign, so no one was surprised when Mrs Donelly said she was stocking up early, getting a few bits done in advance. Indeed, what happened was that they all started stocking up too, adding to the usual store of crackers and wrapping paper and Christmas napkins bought half-price in the January sales and tucked under the bed, so that by October there were enough trays of mince pies on ice around our town to feed Santa and all his elves for a month.

So the food was prepared and frozen, and Mrs Donelly was ready, pretty much. She knew she was going to be in hospital by about September, so in August she went to see Martin Phillips to deal with a few last things.

Martin Phillips keeps his offices in one of the less salubrious areas of town, down the end of the optimistically named Sunnyside Terrace, which is tucked just within the ring road and which backs on to scrubland, and which is a street where the pubs have no windows and where a lot of the windows have no glass and where the floodlit petrol station on the other side of the ring road serves as the only local amenity and corner shop. Martin Phillips keeps offices there because it's cheaper and it's good for business, because he's closer to his clients.

He lives on the other side of town himself, naturally, and he likes to begin every day with a run round the golf course, and then back for a shower and a bowl of muesli. He's a small, slim man of fifty-five with the body of a twenty-five-year-old – not bad for here, where the reverse is usually the case – and he still has a full head of hair which was last styled in the 1970s. He always wears smart-casual clothes, the same at home as at work: he's aiming for, and achieving, the look of an off-duty pilot, with the assistance of his wife Lynn, who buys most of his clothes, except his novelty socks and boxer shorts, which he likes to choose himself. Lynn takes care of the children, children Martin had never really understood or particularly liked, and who felt exactly the same about him. Two daughters. He'd really have liked a son, and it'd been a great relief to him when the girls reached their teens and had started bringing boyfriends home, and he could talk to them about cars and motorbikes and football, and make manly jokes, often at the expense of his wife and daughters. His daughters' boyfriends always got on well with Martin Phillips. His daughters and his wife, on the other hand, thought he was a creep.

Martin was always in the office first. He made a point of that. It was a responsibility. Also, it meant that he could avoid the school run. Being stuck in the car with the children with nothing to say and having to listen to their music depressed him: it was a bad start to the day. Being in first to the office gave him the psychological advantage. He imagined that his receptionist and his secretary envied him. His business partner, 'Big' Jim McCartney, didn't usually arrive until 10, having dropped off his own children at school. Unlike Martin's children, who attended Barneville House, Jim's attended Central, which suited Martin. He and Jim were equals in the partnership. But he felt – and he felt it was pretty obvious, actually, to anyone who cared to examine the evidence – that he was the de facto senior partner.

Every morning, after opening up and putting on the coffee, Martin switched on his computer, flicked through the post and he was ready for the day. 'Bring it on,' he would say to his secretary, Laura, when she arrived with the first set of briefs and documents. He said this to her every day. And then he always cracked his knuckles. It was driving her crazy.*

On the morning of her trip to see Martin Phillips, Mrs Donelly had taken a long walk into town. The Buzy Bus was far too busy in the mornings for anyone except lazy schoolchildren to tolerate it and, anyway, Mrs Donelly had always resented the spelling. She strode in – and she could still stride, she was happy to report – past landmarks long gone. Past Carpenter's the tobacconist's, where her father used to buy his pipe tobacco for himself and the Gallaghers for her mother, both of them, alas, dead of cancer by the time they were sixty; and past Priscilla's Ladies Separates and Luxury Hair Styling, where Priscilla herself had done her hair for twenty years; past Gemini the Jewellers, where Mr Donelly, after some prompting, had bought her an eternity ring for their thirtieth wedding anniversary; and Carlton's Bakery and Tea Rooms, where she'd had her first proper job; and past good old Hugh Nibbs the butcher; and Noreen Orr's dad's shop, the shoe shop, Orr's, where she'd bought the shoes for her wedding and Mr Orr had given her a discount, which is the kind of thing you never forgot; and then the Quality Hotel, still the town's focal point, tethering High Street to Main Street, its domineering presence still helping to make sense of the mess the town had become.

* The only thing that kept her sane, in fact, was her amateur dramatics. See pp.325–366.

202

Mrs Donelly's appointment was at 9.30. She had fifteen minutes. As far as she could remember she'd never been late for anything. She'd certainly never been late for Frank Gilbey. She always thought of him here, going past the Quality Hotel. Frank had been a man of such charms back then, and she'd been pursuing him for so long, at dance after dance, that when he finally suggested they walk home together she'd agreed, although she'd known, of course, where it was leading – leading towards the garden of the Quality Hotel. The gardens were surrounded by a high wall – the same wall she was passing now, which was covered in billboards advertising Bloom's, 'Every Day a Good Day Regardless of the Weather', and which was now black with age and covered with graffiti, but which had once been whitewashed a pure white white. It had once been possible to penetrate these walls, on payment of a small sum to P. J. Bradley, who was one of the porters, and who ran a number of scams and schemes out of the hotel. It was possible for young lovers to gain access to the gardens, entering through the kitchen delivery entrance round on Tarry Lane. Three knocks, and a couple of shillings, and you were in. Mrs Donelly had never been into the gardens before. She'd heard other girls talk about it in hushed tones in the Carlton Tea Rooms, and at the dances in the hotel and at Morelli's, but she could still remember the first night she entered, thinking it was one of the most beautiful places she'd ever seen.

The gardens were not large, but they had been designed by Nora McCrea herself, set around a large pool, which had later been turned into a swimming pool, and there were palm trees and cobbled walkways, with hidden trysting places set in among the shrubs and specimen trees, with a Grecian-style bathing hut and summer house facing the hotel. At midnight P. J. Bradley locked the doors leading from the ballroom, so the garden was private, and anybody's, for a sum.

Frank and Mrs Donelly had sat down on one of the stone

benches by the summer house. She could recall the cool of the stone, the damp moss through her dress, and trying to remember her posture. Posture was important in those days. They smoked Gallaghers. Frank produced a small hip flask. Mrs Donelly remembered they talked about what they were going to do in the future.

Frank, of course, was going to leave town and travel the world. He'd probably live in New York, he said, or maybe California. He hadn't quite decided. There were opportunities everywhere. He was going to set up his own business. He was working on the details. He certainly wasn't going to make the mistake his father had made, he said, getting trapped into a marriage and children when he was only in his teens. Mrs Donelly could remember him saying that clearly: he was warning her, telling her what she could expect. He was going to make his money first, he said. And he was going to have some fun. Did she want to have fun, he asked. Yes, she remembered replying and it was at that point, as far as she can recollect, that he slipped an arm round her waist. He was going to be like Elvis Presley, and James Dean, he said.

Again, as far as she could recall – it was a long time ago – Frank Gilbey did not ask Mrs Donelly what she was going to do with her life. It was not a question you asked a girl back then and Mrs Donelly hadn't even really considered the question herself. She knew she didn't want to be living here for ever. She thought she'd probably be going somewhere else, but she didn't quite know where somewhere else was exactly. Somewhere else for her was probably not as far away as America, but maybe with someone like Frank, someone from here, it would be OK. They'd have each other to rely on. Although she'd have been sad to leave her family and friends behind, of course, and she had her little job in the tea rooms – maybe she could do something like that in America. She'd really have liked to be a nurse, actually, or a doctor. She asked Frank if he thought they had female doctors in America.

Probably, said Frank. Anything, he said, was possible in America.

As they gazed at the dark pool, reflecting the moonlight, in the middle of the Italianate gardens in the centre of our small town, it was possible to imagine themselves anywhere. It was easy to imagine elsewhere.

Mrs Donelly was imagining travelling on a vast boat, arriving at the Statue of Liberty. She was imagining their many American children, growing up wearing Mickey Mouse ears and drinking milkshakes. Frank was imagining a land of opportunity where he would be able to realise himself. And it was as these fantasies were being played out in their minds and across the water that Frank had managed to undo the catch on Mrs Donelly's brassière, and had begun to discover the unexplored territories of her body, a new, trembling continent revealing itself to him.

Mrs Donelly could remember even now, as she was striding past the hotel's high walls, how cold his hands were and the fumbling roughness, and how America had become confused in her mind ever after with a kind of thrusting insensitivity and restlessness, and an unwelcome determination to overcome and to dominate. She had realised then, in the moonlight of our small town, that there were things of which she was unaware even here, and of which she had no experience, depths and breadths which you did not have to travel to discover. And Frank, after claiming the territory, felt a kind of disappointment that had become familiar to him as the years went by, which helped explain why he would often sit up late at night, when Mrs Gilbey had gone to bed, reading newspapers and watching television and drinking malt whisky and thinking about life. He no longer had to seek America – America had come to him unbidden, on television, in the magazines, on film. So, in a sense, he'd never had to go, there had been no need. He'd been lucky to live in a time when America came to him, generous with its gifts and influence.

But he still felt somehow that he'd missed out. That he'd been robbed.

Mrs Donelly sat in Martin Phillips's waiting room, where everything spoke to her of home: the frayed and worn carpet, the splash of paint over the skirting. She liked this place and its cosy informality, even here on Sunnyside Terrace, where people were too afraid to go at night.

'Hello, Mary,' said Martin Phillips. He always called his clients by their first names: it established a rapport. 'Come in, come in. Sorry to keep you waiting. Now, what can we do you for?'

'Well, Mr Phillips,' said Mrs Donelly, maintaining her dignity and settling herself into a chair, 'I have some important business I wish to conclude.'

She'd had the child, of course. She was too scared to do anything else. Her father had threatened to beat her unless she told him who'd done it to her. But she never did. She never told him. And she'd never told Frank. Or Mr Donelly. It was her secret. Her baby. Her firstborn son.

14

Self-Help

In which the author sets out and fails to disprove that Men are from Mars and Women are from Venus

It's been blue skies for Cherith for a long time now – holiday weather. Whatever the temperature and no matter how damp, it's the Azores overhead for Cherith, a perpetual high-pressure front. She'd lost three and a half stone by cutting out all snack foods, dairy products, tea, coffee, taking up aerobic yoga and doing a couple of hundred sit-ups every morning. She had forsaken each and every kind of ibuprofen and paracetamol, and instead ate a lot of fruit, drank at least two litres of water a day, enjoyed the occasional enema, and her urine was the colour of sparkling mineral water, with just a hint of tint – flavoured sparkling mineral water. She wore no man-made fibres, had her hair done once a month in Fry's – which is the fancy new salon up on Abbey Street, with wall-to-wall MTV, coffee in proper cups and a monthly magazine bill that would pay everybody's wages at Central Cutz and then some, and it's just a pity Noreen Fry couldn't be persuaded to call it something else, so it didn't sound like a chippy – and she wore a crystal to channel positive energies.

She had good chi, her yin was balanced with her yang, her communication channels were open, she practised the seven habits of highly effective people and she could fit into some of her daughter's clothes. She'd been granted custody of Bethany after the divorce from Francie and even Bethany seemed happy – Bethany of the perpetual, seemingly endless teenage sneer, of the secret smoking, she of the hormone furies and the constant 'WTF!' texting. Bethany loved living with Cherith – whom she now called 'Cherry', obviously, rather than 'Mum' – and with Sammy, who doted on her, unlike Francie, who resolutely remained 'Dad', and who'd always been rather preoccupied with God and the problem of salvation, who'd been so wrapped up in the church, in fact, that he was really a live-at-home absent father, more like a vague Holy Spirit, you might say, than the historical Jesus. Francie could hardly have been called a disciplinarian, but he did believe that to spare the rod was to spoil the child, which meant that he would occasionally emerge from contemplation and prayer or the laying on of hands, to object to bad manners, and boyfriends, and certain kinds of unsuitable skirt. But Sammy was more like a friend to Bethany than a stepdad – he was most definitely just 'Sammy' – and these days it was Cherith, if she wanted to, who was wearing the unsuitable skirts and there was no one to disagree with her or prevent her. Sammy was cool about that, as about most things. He even allowed Bethany to smoke in the house, as long as she only did it in her room and at the moment she was hooked on something that her friend Finn had sold her, which he called the Devil's Weed: he said it was a mix of legal herbs and herbal extracts with psychoactive effects similar to those produced by illegal substances. What Sammy didn't tell her was he'd tried it himself and it was Benson and Hedges, as far as he could tell. The trouble with children these days was that they were all smoking Marlboro Lights; anything stronger and they thought they were blowing their minds.*

---

* This should not be taken, of course, as a recommendation for high-tar cigarettes. These days fewer people smoke in our town, as elsewhere, although this is not primarily for health reasons: most of us simply cannot

The business, the Oasis, was going from strength to strength: they were developing new ideas all the time, setting up new courses, introducing new product lines into the shop. Scented things were always very popular – scented stones being the latest variation on the theme, from a company based in Portland, Oregon, calling itself Sweet Honey from the Rock™, who produced lemon-and-verbena pumice stones and cocoa-smelling loofahs, and cinnamon worry beads, among other things. But the main cash crop remained the self-help books and tapes. Cherith herself was addicted. She'd read *Men Are from Mars, Women Are from Venus* from cover to cover at least half a dozen times – it was, in her opinion, the original and still the best – and she'd started to run some new workshops, based on her reading, workshops she called 'The Rough Guide to the Road Less Travelled (Beginners and Advanced)', and 'Emotional Intelligence for Couples (Gays and Lesbians Welcome)'. They'd also organised a successful weekend conference on alternative therapies, which had drawn in practitioners from all over. They'd had a herbalist come over from Germany. He was very fat and had bad eczema, unfortunately, which was a little off-putting, and he advocated a form of naked whole-body massage using a kind of bouquet garni steeped in a chilli oil, which did not prove popular among the Oasis clients and which might, in fact, have been better suited for the purposes of roasting chickens. Doctor Ye, the town's acupuncturist, held twice-weekly clinics, and they'd also brought in a reflexologist, a chiropractor and

---

justify the expense, so we're all eating more crisps and sweets, which are cheaper, but which provide a similar satisfaction and give us something to do with our hands. Bob Savory's chip-flavour hand-cooked crisps, Chip Crisps ('They're not Chips, They're not Crisps, They're Chip-Crisps!') and his mini-sandwich range, Chunky Butts, are currently his best-performing product lines. Judging by the litter on High Street and Main Street, and the average backside, most of us now seem to be eating a fairly substantial snack about once an hour, every hour. But it's better than smoking.

Barbara Boyle, the chiropodist who runs her own little business in Michael Gardens. Barbara was doing the best business of all of them: corns and bunions, it seems, are as much a physical and spiritual challenge to the people of our town as fused spines or bad auras.*

What was strange, though, what disturbed and unsettled Cherith, was that now she was no longer married to a minister, now that she was a bona fide and successful businesswoman in her own right, she somehow felt more pious than she ever had before. She and Sammy ate sensibly, took exercise, never drank intoxicating liquor, never argued, never raised their voices and between them they seemed to have no strong opinions about anything whatsoever, apart from which essential oils to use. They had an accountant and money in the bank, and it seemed unnatural. When she was married to Francie, Cherith had been used to spiritual highs and lows, the battle for souls, the fight between Good and Evil, and cheap biscuits with Nescafé coffee. These days she was more interested in self-realisation and self-preservation through detox diets, natural juices and meditation. She and Sammy seemed to have lulled each other into a kind of wide-eyed, cranberry and echinacea-fuelled sleepwalk.

The death of his son, little Josh, had had an extraordinary

---

* Barbara specialises in athlete's foot and fungal nail infections, actually, ailments so common here in town that they barely merit a mention, even among friends of long standing – most of us never even bother to get them treated, passing them around freely among family members and fellow swimmers at the Leisure Centre. But when they get really bad, when the skin is rubbed raw and the nails are all black and thick and crumbly, or when we can no longer walk, that's when we beat a path to Barbara's door, and she works her magic with her clippers and ointments and creams. Barbara has arguably done more for the well-being of the people of our town than all our councillors and churchmen and do-gooders put together. Young people tend not to think of chiropody as a career – it suffers from something of an image problem – but if you or your young person are interested in going into the caring professions you could do a lot worse than considering your feet. Barbara loves her job, keeps her own hours *and* she drives a Mercedes.

purgative effect on Sammy – a man never given to outbursts or great enthusiasms – leaving him entirely calm and incapable of rancour. He was a walking, talking, living endorsement of the benefits of AA and self-administered self-help literature. Sammy spent hours every week in the spa pool, often lying there silent after the Oasis was closed, gazing out at the car park in front of the Quality Hotel, just floating, entirely lost to the world.

Sammy had given up on himself after Josh had died and he believed others should have given up on him also. And when they hadn't, he couldn't bear it. The condemnation and punishment that he felt were necessary and right and proper he'd had to provide for himself. And just as he had condemned himself and, with the help of drink, punished himself, he had at first believed that it was up to him, and only within his gift, to forgive himself, to repair himself and put himself back together. You can take a man out of plumbing, it seems, but you can't take the plumber out of the man. The trouble was, Sammy could find no way to put things right, or to fix things: no amount of work with a pipe wrench or a blowtorch was going to bring back his little Josh. So when he discovered Alcoholics Anonymous, and the writings of M. Scott Peck, and the love of a good woman, he was amazed and relieved, and he had come to rely entirely upon them. They had helped join him back together.

If Cherith had learnt anything from her reading of *Men Are from Mars, Women Are from Venus*, and she believed she had, then it was this: men and women are not the same. Cherith had known this instinctively, of course, for a long time, long before Oprah, and possibly since consciousness. She had always known that men were somehow inferior. As a child growing up she'd regarded her father – taking a lead from her mother – as a kind of genial buffoon, good for certain obvious manual tasks, such as clearing drains and stripping a turkey carcass, but for little else, and she had always been amazed that the boys at her school were incapable of concentrating for long enough to get more than about three out of ten in spelling, and how messy their handwriting was, and how smelly they were. Her decision to marry Francie had been at least partly based on the assumption that as a minister of religion he might have had slightly higher standards than most other men, which he did, in some ways, although, of course, standards are one thing and maintaining them quite another. No man can keep up with all the odd jobs in life, or all the other demands of morality.

What the book didn't mention, though, what *Men Are from Mars, Women Are from Venus* had missed – and what now seemed to Cherith an important, essential truth, and one which she was coming to understand through her course, 'Emotional Intelligence for Couples (Gays and Lesbians Welcome)' – was that men are not, in fact, all the same. A better title for the book, in Cherith's opinion, might have been *Some Men Are from Mars, Some Women Are from Venus, but Also Vice Versa, and Actually Some of Us Are from Mercury, Jupiter, Saturn and Also, Clearly, Uranus*. When she was living with Francie she had, of course, loved him, and now she loved Sammy, but what she had with the both of them, and the love she felt in each instance, was quite different. With Francie what she'd had was a kind of intimacy. With Sammy what she had was free out-of-hours counselling. Sammy was monosyllabic, basically, which people often mistook for his being a good listener. But Sammy was not a good listener: he was just a bad talker. Amidst all the turmoil of her split with Francie, Cherith had found Sammy's taciturn and reliable manner serene and calming, but now she just found it frustrating. She was finding she was having to practise her yoga breaths more and more, in order to maintain her equilibrium, and she found herself lighting more joss sticks around the home and at work, and doing her 'Om' louder and more furiously. Sometimes she even had to turn the volume on her personal stereo all the way up to twelve, in order to drown herself in 'Fields of Gold' with Eva Cassidy.

Sammy had no idea that he was becoming an annoyance. Having opened up and made himself vulnerable after the death of Josh, he had gradually begun to shut down again and although he had enjoyed his moment of self-discovery and revelation, now he'd found Cherith he felt no need to explore further. He was abstaining. He had plateaued out and come to rest. This, he felt, was as good as it gets. He and Cherith had the business together, they meditated together, they practised tantric sex, unsuccessfully, together, following the instructions in a lavishly illustrated book from the shop; in fact, they were often together entirely, for twenty-four hours a day, in and out of bed, at work and at play. It wasn't so much a decision as just something that had happened. They had both been very vulnerable individuals when they met and they needed all the support they could give each other. After the death of his son, Sammy no longer quite trusted himself and he looked to Cherith to do the trusting for him; after the shock of the split with Francie, Cherith had needed reassurance and a steadying hand. They'd both required someone else to help to keep them sober and they had become, in effect, their own mutual-support network.

But Cherith did not need a mutual-support network any more. She had been sober for more than two years and what she needed now was a husband: she needed a challenge and a little more conversation. When Cherith thought of the word 'husband' – which she tried not to do too often – she didn't think of Sammy, even though they had married in some style, in Thailand, on a beach, at sunrise, with him in a tuxedo and her in a cheong-sam, and prawns and champagne to follow. No, when she thought of her husband she thought of Francie, whom she'd married in her mother's old wedding dress and a cardie, and Francie in a lounge suit, in the People's Fellowship, with a mountain of sausage rolls and a river of Shloer at the reception.

Thinking about it now, what Cherith had admired about Francie, the reason she'd married him, was that he was prepared to make himself into a kind of holy fool: he was willing to take risks and he knew it was OK to make mistakes, because he knew he was a miserable sinner. Francie was not scared of the world and its ways: his only judge was God. Cherith knew him to be essentially a decent person seeking to work out his salvation. Unfortunately, she knew him also to be hypocritical, treacherous, unreliable and a shameless adulterer.

But as for Sammy, well, Cherith wasn't sure that she knew him at all, who he was, what made him tick, or what he wanted. She'd become increasingly concerned about all the time he was spending in the spa pool. He used to disappear in there for a couple of hours on a Wednesday night when she was taking her classes in 'Emotional Intelligence for Couples (Gays and Lesbians Welcome)' and she used to wonder what he was doing while she was talking about the waves and cycles of relationships, and encouraging people to open up to each other and share. When she asked Sammy what he'd been up to, he'd always say, 'Oh, nothing much' and that was it, end of conversation. At least with Francie he'd have claimed to have been praying to bring in the Kingdom of God. She was beginning to feel that she could have done with doing the course in 'Emotional Intelligence for Couples (Gays and Lesbians Welcome)' herself.

To her surprise the course had indeed attracted a middle-aged couple from out of town, two women, Wenda and Clare, who didn't actually say they were lesbians – they didn't wear badges – but who Cherith could only assume were lesbians, because they both wore matching car coats and mannish shoes, and one of them had her nose pierced. Wenda, the pierced one, is fifty and works in the in-store bakery at the supermarket up in Bloom's. She'd been married for over twenty years and raised two children before she had the nerve to give it up and follow her heart. Her heart had led her out of town and into the country and to Clare, who is ten years older and a full foot shorter and wider than Wenda, and who is a woman who seems never to have entertained any doubts about herself or anything else. She had been a civil servant at one time, and then she'd helped found and run our local Credit Union, the first in the county, up there on the Longfields Estate, which has brought to many of us here our own affordable three-piece suites, reasonable loan terms and taught us how to consolidate our debts. In any realm or endeavour Clare is not a woman to be argued with – a former senior clerical officer with a strong social conscience, a demon of efficiency – and the cottage she now shares with Wenda out at the Six Road Ends is both cosy and immaculate, decorated with photos of Wenda's children, old civil rights posters and other things that reminded Clare of the 1970s: rattan furniture, Joan Baez record covers and macramé, mostly. In the 1970s Clare had been at perhaps her most beautiful and most determined. A photograph of her in a silver frame which stands on the telly shows her holding an 'Official Picket' sign outside the Department of Health and Social Security, looking for all the world like our own local Yoko Ono, in a duffel coat and glasses. Wenda and Clare had no real place in Cherith's class: they didn't belong there. They already seemed to know all the answers.

Yet even they had been going through a rough patch recently – even they, who are lesbians, probably, and who you might have thought, therefore, had already ruled out half the problems in any relationship. They'd been arguing, which they had never done before, and so they weren't quite sure how to do it; they'd not established any ground rules. Wenda believed storming out and door-slamming to be acceptable, but Clare did not, while Clare favoured sulking and silences, which offended Wenda. Their arguments stemmed from little things, mostly, and they were having to face up to the complications and strains of any long-term relationship. Clare had been trying to give up smoking, at Wenda's insistence, and Wenda was unhappy at work in the in-store bakery, work which she felt was demeaning for someone who'd read

Jeanette Winterson, and she had been trying to resolve her relationship with her elder daughter, who'd never come to terms with her mother's decision to announce herself as a lesbian. Just the usual.

Another couple on the course, Louise and Stephen, were thirty-somethings with a twelve-year-old son with autism who was destroying their relationship. It wasn't his fault, they knew, but was it theirs? There was also Gertie, who had married a much younger man, Jim, after her husband had died of throat cancer, and now Jim had been diagnosed with multiple sclerosis. Was this bad luck? wondered Gertie. Pete and Joan, meanwhile, were coming to terms with their children leaving home and with the consequent middle-aged dissatisfaction and spread, and they were asking themselves, well, now what?

As they all sat around problem solving and creatively visualising, and using the whiteboard in one of the convector-heated meeting rooms at the Oasis, what they called the Steiner Room, these confused, sad, genuine people reminded Cherith a little of her and Sammy, except with one important difference. You could tell that they loved each other, instantly, the moment they arrived, the moment you set eyes upon them. There was something about it, in the way that Wenda and Clare looked at each other, or the way that Gertie and Jim held hands. It was beautiful to see, people so much in love, and it made Cherith panic. On a Wednesday night, after the class, when they'd shut up shop and returned home, and when she'd kissed Sammy goodnight and switched out the light, she would lie awake in bed and all she would feel was lonely, and the silence seemed to echo between them.

Sammy would also be awake, actually, but he never heard the echo: he was somewhere else. He had never talked to Cherith about this, but the evenings were the time he devoted to thinking about his son, every night when he was in bed, and when he was in the spa pool. This was his special time with him, when he checked out of this sad, dark world and checked into this wonderful, secret, other world, to get an update on how he was, his little boy. Sammy saw his son every day, in the light of the bright imaginings in his head, and it was almost as if he were alive.

It was a trick he'd stumbled upon by accident one night, when he was still drinking. It was Josh's birthday, 14 August – he'd have been five years old – and Sammy had been lying out in the People's Park, sprawled on the grass near the war memorial, full of super-lager and Thunderbird wine, and he missed his son so much, and he wanted to wish him Happy Birthday, and when he closed his eyes he found he could just about see him, looming over him, tall and proud, almost as if he were really there, and he looked just a little older than Sammy remembered him, as if he really were still alive, growing up and growing old. By practising, Sammy found that he was able to imagine his son almost entirely lifelike. He found it best in the spa pool, obviously, because there were no distractions. But in bed at night was the next best thing.

He tried not to do it too much – he knew it was wrong – but he couldn't give it up. He'd tried other things. He tried just praying, but that didn't work. And he tried this Buddhist practice that he'd read about in a book from the shop, a practice called *metta bhavana*, friendliness development, where you meditate on your own positive qualities, then those of others, and you chant, 'May you be happy' and 'May you be well'. It was supposed to release you from the burden of responsibility for others. But he couldn't keep that up. He couldn't release his son. He wanted him there, with him. He wanted to be responsible for him.

He tried to limit himself. He calculated that if Josh were alive, if he'd been at school, and Sammy were still plumbing, Sammy'd maybe have seen him for just a couple of hours every morning, and a couple every evening, but then all weekend pretty much, or at least twelve hours each day, give or take the odd hour for emergency call-outs. So if he added up all the hours – 2 + 2 x 5 + 12 + 12 = 44 – that was how many hours he might have spent with his son every week. If you divided that by seven it gave you just over six, an average of six hours a day, which he then divided in half, to be reasonable, which meant that he could afford to spend three hours a day with his son.

The only unreasonable thing, of course, was that Josh was dead.

But in Sammy's mind, in his imagination, he was alive and well, and growing up fast. He got on really well at primary school – Sammy had taken on extra work so that he could have piano lessons and he played midfield for the school football team. Sammy got to take him to quite a few matches. Josh's favourite food was sausages and beans, and he liked playing with his friends. For his eighth birthday Sammy took him to see the new Harry Potter film, and they went on holiday once a year to Disneyland. He lost a front tooth falling off his bike, but he was OK. He did well in the transfer tests at school and went on to the grammar, where he excelled in both the sciences and the arts. He loved Lego and then he loved his bike. And finally, of course, he loved girls. Sammy vetted his girlfriends. He'd helped him buy his first car. The wedding had been lovely. And then there were the grand-children, three of them, all of them gorgeous, just like their dad. Josh coped well with the strains of being a father and in time he became a grandfather himself.

These dreams and fantasies were by far the sweetest part of Sammy's days, the clearest and the most refreshing, and he saw nothing wrong with them, apart from the obvious.

So this was the problem, the silence that lay between Cherith and Sammy, though Cherith didn't know it, and there was nothing she could have done about it, even if she'd known, nothing she could have done to help Sammy. Because Sammy didn't need her help, or anybody else's. He was fine.

His son was still alive.

15

Line Dancing

*In which Mrs Gilbey puts on her chaps and discovers
pleasure, and Mr Gilbey sucks on a Chupa-Chup*

The warm interior of a car on a cold evening: this is the closest
that most of us in our town are ever going to get, or would
want to get, to regression therapy.* With temperatures low
and the winds high, the fan heater on, the knob turned all the
way round to red and the stereo playing classic rock – if it all
comes together just right, if it's cold enough outside and the
roads are clear enough, this is worth about a month of twice-
weekly counselling sessions to us here in town. This is true
demisting. If Sigmund Freud had owned a nice little hot-hatch
or a supermini with heated seats and he had friends he needed
to get to see on the other side of town, you can't help thinking
that the world would have been saved a whole lot of time and
trouble. A warm car on a cold night can of course cause problems – and you see some of them walking around town every
day. But it can solve a lot of problems too.

Frank was waiting in the car. It was the Jaguar. Frank
admired American cars the most, of course, in terms of the

* Although it is on offer at the Oasis, actually, a new course, along with
'Humming to Heal', 'Rainbow Dancing' and a new series of Reiki master-
classes. Contact Cherith or Sammy at the Oasis for details.

styling, but a Jag was more sensible for his purposes, tootling around town, keeping up appearances. The Jag was his runaround. He also owned an MG GT coupé with a V8 engine – a beautiful little thing with a top speed of 125 mph, and only a couple of thousand of them made. It was not a good car for cold weather, though; not a good car for our climate generally. He had a BMW as well, for Mrs Gilbey, and a Range Rover – and of course you get a lovely ride in a Range Rover. But Frank liked the Jag best, partly because an old friend of his had the dealership up in the city – Buchanan's, Ken Buchanan – and Frank believed in doing business with friends if at all possible, plus Ken organised a nice little owners' club, run by his lovely daughter, Trisha, which offered a free car wash and valet every Saturday morning, and Frank liked to drive up early on the motorway, drop the car in, chat to Trisha, who was always polite and nicely made-up, and who laughed at Frank's jokes, and then he would hit the streets. Manhattan it most certainly was not, or Baltimore even, or Manchester, but it wasn't bad. It was better than nothing. It was a better start to the weekend than waking up beside Mrs Gilbey and having to discuss with her what to have for dinner that night – meat or fish. It made no difference. Going up to the car wash made a change. He'd walk a couple of times round the block – that was his exercise for the week – and then he'd stop for a coffee, a proper coffee, not like the chicory widdle you get in town, and a nice Danish at a little place he knew, run by a guy called Christodoulous. Frank always called him Christy, and actually Christy's real name was Cormac, but Cormac'd given up explaining the ins and outs to people – Greek father, Irish mother – and Frank wouldn't have been interested anyway. Every customer had a different name for Cormac – in a city you can be an Everyman to every man, but in a town you're just little old you – and Frank was a big tipper, so he could have called Cormac anything he liked and Cormac wouldn't have minded.

In the car Frank was working his way through a word puzzler book and sucking on a lolly. He kept the lollies and the word puzzler books in the glove compartment, and he would not be unique in this habit, in our town. Here, word puzzler books and Chupa-Chup lollies perform the same function that, say, cannabis and cocaine do for wealthy and artistic people seeking enlightenment or social ease in cities like London or New York, or so we've heard. Frank found they helped take his mind off things. They helped him relax, but they also helped him think. He'd tried crosswords, but he found them too difficult. Crosswords are a much harder drug, really, like heroin, which doesn't make any sense to people who aren't addicted.* The lollies and the word puzzler books are just the job, though: they helped Frank to free his mind.

Frank was sucking on a problem and the problem was the Quality Hotel. What frustrated him was that people didn't realise that the Quality Hotel was basically his pension. Frank didn't do what other people did. He did not save money. He invested – and the value of investments can, of course, go down as well as up. At the moment they were a little down – actually, they were more than a little down – and Frank could have done with a cash injection, just to pep things up a bit, and the Quality Hotel, when demolished, was just the sort of thing that would give him the boost he needed. This was going to be a prime piece of real estate; 'Absolutely primo,' said Frank, out loud, to himself. He liked to practise his New Jersey mobster talk in the car, trying it out on himself before risking it with others.

'Look, buddy,' he was saying to himself, 'the great thing about the Quality Hotel is that the services are there already:

* And we do have a few people in town who are: Colin Rimmer, for example, can't begin the day without at least having a go at *The Times* and he likes to tackle the *Guardian* at the weekend, although a *Guardian* can be hard to find here: people have been known to cross the county line for a proper broadsheet at weekends. Only the *Sunday Times* is guaranteed.

you've got your drainage, your electrics, your gas, your access and a huge freaking car park out front.'

Frank already had offers coming in: luxury apartments with a leisure club, needless to say, and some high-street developers who wanted to acquire a presence. And Bob Savory, of course, who wanted his new flagship store, the first Speedy Bap!, to have a central site.

People were beginning to understand that the tide was turning against out-of-town retail parks, against the likes of Bloom's. Frank had been saying this for years and now people were coming round to his way of thinking. The redevelopment of the town centre was something that everyone would approve of – and if Frank played his cards right he would be responsible for the shift. He imagined a town centre arcade: Gilbey's, perhaps, they could call it, to match his roundabout on the ring road. Bringing people back into the centre to shop, providing an alternative to the shopping experience at Bloom's: that was Frank's aim and intention. And the Quality Hotel was the only thing that stood in the way – why people couldn't understand that he didn't know. It was short-sighted of them. Frank could see a bright future for the town centre. He could even imagine pedestrianisation. That was how things were going. Something a bit more Continental. He'd seen it on his city breaks with Mrs Gilbey: Amsterdam, Paris, Brussels. He'd even seen it in America -- places that sold themselves as places, as 'downtown experiences'. This was Frank's vision for our town and he wanted everyone to share it. He was like a prophet.

You see, Frank could get you to believe that black was white and white was black. Because it was Frank who had been responsible for the destruction of the town centre in the first place. It was Frank who'd cut the ribbon on the ring road. Frank who'd rubber-stamped Bloom's. Frank who'd taken a slice out of every development and so-called improvement around town over the past twenty years. But Frank had enough charm to make you forget what he wanted you to

222

forget and to remember things that you didn't even know you knew. This was quite a talent, the kind of talent you only really get with dictators, with artists and with very wealthy businessmen, and Frank was the closest thing we were ever going to get in our town to a Picasso, or a General Franco.*

People had underestimated Frank Gilbey all his life. His father had underestimated him, but then his father had underestimated himself as well and had ended up drinking his life away. Frank's father was one of life's losers and Frank hadn't spared a thought for him in thirty years. He still worshipped at the shrine of his mother, though, of course, every day, who'd taught him everything he knew. Frank was an only child. His was the typical CV of the overachiever.

He had not excelled at school. He wasn't interested in school learning. He didn't want to get a job as a postman, like his father, who was known around town as the 'Drunken Postman' (even today some of our more senior citizens still refer to Frank as 'the Son of the Drunken Postman', not a nickname that Frank relishes). He didn't want to become a civil servant either, which was just about the height of what his family could imagine for him, a job in the council offices, filing. Frank had

* We have had our artists, though, of one kind and another: the work of 'Diamond Annie', Annie Coker, for example, who was a quilt maker back in the 1920s and a demon on the treadle machine, is now much sought after, by people from the city and abroad, the kind of people who like to hang old quilts on their walls rather than put them on their beds, which many of us here find difficult to understand, especially since the colours in Annie's quilts have rather faded and the stuffing's falling out, and you can get a perfectly good duvet and nylon cover from N'Hance at Bloom's for less than £30; and Archie Hillock, of course, who attended the Royal College of Art in the early 1950s and who was briefly renowned as one of the 'Kitchen Sink' artists, most famous for his tiny thick-and-crusty painting of a turd in a toilet; and George McGuigan, our own home-grown Impressionist, who lived on Fitzroy Avenue and who was rumoured to have met Manet, and whose own bravura style of portrait painting, featuring much apparently slapdash pink and yellow brushwork, earned him the nickname of the 'Egg-and-Bacon Artist'.

his eyes set on bigger prizes. He'd started up his first business when he was seven years old. He'd discovered by accident that if you removed ball-bearings from a pair of roller skates you could make a very satisfying rattling noise. He loved that rattling noise and he figured that other people might love it too. So he offered to fix their skates for them. Noisy skates were suddenly what everyone wanted. Once he'd fixed everyone's skates in school and around town, he then mentioned to a couple of people that in fact the really cool thing was silent skates. And so, eventually, everyone paid him to put the ball-bearings back in their skates. He made enough money from that one job to buy himself a bike, a Raleigh, second-hand, and a transistor radio, new, a Decca, for his mother. That was sweet, for a boy from the Georgetown Road: having money in your pocket, being able to spend it. That was a good feeling.

The roller skates were Frank's first experience of a very important business lesson, and one which he had never forgotten: you create demand. You may not think you do. You may think you only control supply. You may think that demand simply exists. But it doesn't. You create it. You tell people they want something – a ring road, say, or a shopping mall, or luxury apartments – and they might never have thought they wanted it before, they might never have conceived in a million years that this thing might be a good thing to have, but suddenly they'll all want it and they'll pay you good money to get it.

According to this principle you could sell people any old rubbish.

And he had.*

By the time he was forty he had the big house, the cars, the

---

* In his time Frank has successfully sold people worthless properties, blighted land, timeshares, conservatories and insurance. But undoubtedly his best and biggest offer has been himself, gift-wrapped in Armani and presented to us as mayor and councillor and pillar of the community – an offer which, like the people of Troy, we did not refuse and have come bitterly to regret.

companies, the properties, the lovely wife and the darling child, and his monthly cash flow from investments alone exceeded his monthly expenses. That was another good feeling. That was better than sex, actually, the realisation that if necessary he never need work again. Although, of course, he did work again. Seven days a week, in fact. Frank worked like a dog and organised his life like a Mafia don. If you treated people right, Frank believed, they treated you right. If you saw them right, they'd see you right. Councillors, for example, who enjoyed their golf were always glad of a gift of golf balls, or clubs, from a friend. Councillors who enjoyed their food and drink were glad of a Fortnum & Mason hamper at Christmas, with a nice pot of gentleman's relish, or an invitation to one of Frank's legendary parties, or a barbecue, where whole pigs were spit-roasted and a jazz band was bussed in from the city, to add a touch of class. Councillors are of course supposed to declare any interests, but everyone in our town has interests in everything and in everybody – our town is one big happy family, according to Frank, and he couldn't help whom he knew, or the fact that he was a generous man. There are lots of ways to get things done among friends in a town like ours and Frank had done them all.

He had run into trouble, though, with the Quality Hotel and the trouble he had run into had been with the kind of mealy-mouthed, pen-pushing, do-gooding gainsayers who didn't enjoy jumbo grilled steaks and trad jazz and golf, the finer things in life. These people were *Guardian* readers, Frank suspected, and fans of Classic FM. Vegetarians too, probably, and homosexual. First they had denied Frank planning permission, but fortunately he knew the Development Control Officer and the Divisional Planning Officer, so that was sorted. Then he was refused building regulations approval, but he knew the Building Regulations Control Officer, so that was sorted too. But then there'd been this ridiculous final thing that had come up: the conservation area consent. That's what had held him up. That's what had given him all the trouble.

That was Mrs Donelly's doing, who was not a *Guardian* reader, actually. She only ever read the *Daily Mail*, or the *Impartial Recorder*, and she ate chops, and she slept with her husband, that was all the window on the world she needed, but she'd got the council to agree to make the town centre a conservation area, *our* town centre, where there is almost nothing worth preserving, because we destroyed it years ago. She must have been crazy, shutting the gate after the horse had bolted, or maybe there was method in her madness, Frank couldn't decide. He wondered, looking back, if she'd been working up to it for years and he just hadn't seen it coming. It was Mrs Donelly, after all, who'd been responsible for the Shopfront Improvements Scheme, when she was first elected to the council, which had prevented the big stores, or at least the many competing card, giftware and charity shops, from putting up bigger signs. That was her first move. And then there'd been the Town Centre Improvements Scheme, she'd got that going too, had co-opted all the remaining small businesses on to the committee. The scheme was run by Enda Tierney and Ivan Cuddy, two of the more useless members of the council in Frank's opinion, who'd used all the power they'd had vested in them to plant a couple of birch trees down at the bottom of High Street, an initiative that had taken exactly eighteen months to see through, and in the meantime the carcass of the town had remained prey to marauding teenagers and unscrupulous developers, people like Frank, who just kept on knocking the old stuff down and putting new stuff up, ignoring Enda and Ivan completely, and the people who were caught in the middle were the small businesses, the people the scheme was supposed to help, who kept on paying rates in order to sustain Main Street and High Street for long enough for the bigger firms to come in and put them out of business. Frank couldn't believe how stupid all these people were. He didn't get it at all, what they thought they were doing, and what they were actually doing. They seemed to have no idea. They had no vision. They were certainly no match for Big Frank Gilbey. In his day, when he was mayor, Frank had widened roads and pulled down historic buildings – whole areas – in the time it took Enda and Ivan to agree on where to put a few dog litter bins.

But now these same useless individuals were giving him terrible trouble over the Quality Hotel, the thing he most wanted, the thing he most needed. Him, Frank Gilbey, who more than anyone had helped shape the town over the past couple of decades. Frank had been responsible for drawing up the town's first local plan, years ago, before anyone else had even thought of it – detailing policies, mapping out proposals, determining which sites should be developed. *That* was Frank, that was his doing. It was Frank who had helped draft the plan and who had made sure it was open to interpretation, so that it favoured his own interests, naturally. It was Frank who'd got people to start thinking of the town not as a corporation but as a business. It was Frank who'd got the council to start referring to citizens as 'customers' buying the council's 'products' and he had, of course, made sure that many of those products were his own, his own properties, and his own property management companies, and his own property maintenance companies. You can't possibly do that, people had said at the time. Yes you can, Frank had said. You can't delegate civic responsibility to private companies and individuals, they'd said. Yes we can, Frank had said. And they did. And it had worked. And Frank had become very rich.

And this was all the thanks he got.

Frank had not done anything wrong. He had bought a lot of land around town, years ago, but that was simply because he'd had the foresight to do so. And as for his relationships with the council's planning officers, well, they really were his friends. He wasn't pretending. And his own involvement as a councillor, well, if he didn't get involved, who would?

Shouldn't we be encouraging participation in local democracy? Of course we should.

And as for Bloom's, well, yes, he had known there were plans afoot. After the ring road, it was logical. But anyone could have worked it out. Anyone with their eyes open and looking to the future. Frank had been to America enough times to be able to see the future: malls, vast car parks. Convenience, that's what people wanted. And it rains here approximately 270 days a year, for God's sake, so you'd have had to have been stupid not to see that malls were the way to go. And Frank wasn't stupid, so he had gone about systematically buying up the land outlying the ring road, even before the plans were announced. Most of the deals had been straightforward, but there had been one or two problems. Miss McCormack's father, the Scotsman, Dougal, had some land, for example, where he kept his piebald. Frank needed the land, but the land had been in the family a long time and Dougal didn't want to move his horse. Frank knew everyone had a price, but the price wasn't always money. So Frank got to know Dougal. He found out what his weaknesses were. Dougal's only weakness was the horse. If there was no horse, there'd be no problem. So the piebald ate lavender one day and died. Simple. The horse's dying broke Dougal's heart and he sold the land within a month, he just wanted shot of it. And he moved further up-country, away from our town and from us, the townspeople, and our ambassador, Frank Gilbey. That's the way the world worked. That's the way Frank Gilbey did business.

Frank was lovely and cosy in the car, sucking his lolly, thinking his profound thoughts, and he didn't notice his wife getting in – she was not someone he had ever really needed to attend to. He had enough other things to worry about without worrying about her. She looked after herself pretty much, under his supervision. That was the great thing about Mrs Gilbey – she was easy. She was straightforward. They had never argued, the pair of them, not really. They never had. He'd married her partly because he was aware there was no chance of her arguing with him. She wouldn't have said boo to a goose.

She coughed.

'Right,' he said, starting up the car and setting off for home. 'Well?'

'Well what?' she said.

She was not going to tell him. She never did. She was determined. She was not going to give him the satisfaction. He'd only laugh at it. She was not interested in his opinion anyway, or anyone else's. If you've never tried it, don't knock it. That was Mrs Gilbey's new mantra. *If you've never tried it, don't knock it*. That's what she said to herself these days when she saw the look on the faces of her friends and the wives of some of Frank's business colleagues when she told them about the line dancing. Like Frank, they all thought line dancing was common.

'Oh, really, have you ever tried it?' she'd ask them, as they held their little retroussé noses up in the air. Plastic surgery was the big thing these days with a lot of them, and what was that if not common, thought Mrs Gilbey. Trimming your nose and your neck fat, like you were the Sunday roast going to waste? Having someone siphon fat from your belly, or pump it into your thin little lips? Going out to lunch with her friends was starting to get like going to Madame Tussaud's: they were all beginning to look like models of themselves, like they'd been freshly poured out of moulds and dressed up in lookalike clothing.

Mrs Gilbey was not into remodelling. It was not her style. With Mrs Gilbey you got what you saw. Which was a lot. Mrs Gilbey knew exactly who she was and how much of her there was, thank you very much, and she did not intend messing around with her essentials, or reducing the size of the portions. She was the same now as she'd ever been, although every Thursday night at seven she did go to the

'Dance Ranch', which is actually the badminton courts at the Leisure Centre, which during the day and at night hosts the full range of what a good local council leisure services facility should be able to offer, including Step Aerobics, Boxercise, Pilates, Spinning, several martial arts, and Seventies Disco Tums and Bums. And badminton, of course. And every Thursday night the badminton court announced itself as 'The Place for Foot Tappin', Heel Stompin', Clean Livin' Honky Tonk Fun', a claim that is entirely correct, as far as Mrs Gilbey is concerned, even though the place may still look like the badminton courts to you and me. In our town it helps if you can use a little imagination.

Frank had tried, of course, during his time as a councillor and his tenure as mayor, to get all the council's leisure services contracted out: he'd have happily seen the Leisure Centre taken over by a private company. He had tried, in fact, to get the council to make overtures to the Works, the private gym up on the ring road, to see if they might be interested in taking the place over, but he'd failed. People here in town seem to like fat, unattractive women behind the till, and graffiti on the walls, and wet floors in the changing rooms. Frank suspected that anyone who used the Leisure Centre was a socialist, and frankly they deserved verrucas and athlete's foot.

Mrs Gilbey was not a socialist, as far as she knew, but she had always liked country and western music, which was also suspect in Frank's opinion: it was but a short step from country-and-western to folk music, Frank believed, and folk music opened the floodgates to all sorts of silliness. You get one man strumming on a guitar, and before you know it you've got a whole load of people growing beards and burning their bras and going down to Yasgur's farm to demand equal pay for the disabled and single mothers. Mrs Gilbey was not keen on folk, but she had always liked Patsy Cline, ever since she was little, when her father had been a train driver, taking trains up to the city and back, and he used to do this country and western yodelling thing when he was driving the trains, and Mrs Gilbey used to travel up and down with him sometimes, at weekends, and she would sit and listen to him, and to the sound of the trains, and they'd eat hot pies and apples. And that's about as close to a communist childhood as we come in this town. At home her father liked to listen to Hank Williams and he also played the ukulele, an instrument which seems to have fallen out of favour, here and elsewhere, but which at one time was the instrument of choice for the working man and woman in town.

A ukulele is cheap, it's portable and you can learn to pick out a tune in an afternoon. It's a bright, happy instrument, an instrument of innocent pleasures and of limited range. Bill Bell and his French wife Antonietta – whom he picked up and brought back after the Second World War, quite a souvenir, everyone agreed – used to duet on Sunday afternoons in the Palm Court at the Quality Hotel, Bill on tenor ukulele and Antonietta on soprano. They even made a record, *The Two Little Fleas*, and it was a pretty good record, one of the only records ever to have come out of our town.* Mrs Gilbey's father had learned a lot from that record. Mrs Gilbey's own

---

* See also p.149. *The Two Little Fleas* has long since been deleted, alas, but copies do occasionally crop up on on-line ukulele music and memorabilia auction sites: the last copy to have surfaced, on www.ukesandbanjeleles.com, sold for £800 within forty-eight hours, which is ironic because Bill and Antonietta had had to pay to have the record produced in the first place, and when their son Richard was clearing out the house a few years ago, after they'd died, he threw away about 500 unsold copies which had been kept in the loft, and he has been kicking himself ever since. Now he saves everything that might one day be worth something: hundreds of his children's drawings and paintings, in case they become artists, thousands of photographs of them in case they become famous, their shoes, their clothes, hours of home-video recordings. His wife Lena is threatening to divorce him unless he stops. 'Don't you understand?' he tells her. 'This is history in the making.' 'Well, it looks to me like a rubbish dump in the making,' says Lena, 'and I can't get into the cupboards to put away the laundry. So it's your choice: it's either me or it's your memorabilia.'

all-time favourite performers were probably Waylon Jennings and Willie Nelson – they were classics, obviously, and they reminded her of her dad, but she also liked some of these younger women who'd come up over the past few years. Mary Chapin Carpenter she liked, and Shelby Lynne. Frank called them Chafin' Carper and Slippery Finn. Frank thought it was all very funny. Frank thought country music was a joke.

This was because Frank was not interested in emotions. And he did not like sentimentality. He did not agree with it. Emotions and sentimentality were pretty much one and the same thing to Frank; he could not distinguish between the two, like it's sometimes difficult to tell, just by looking at the light, whether it's dawn or it's dusk. Mrs Gilbey remembered once, a couple of years ago, she'd wanted to talk to him about Lorraine, when things were going wrong with the bad Scotsman – a necessary, difficult conversation – and he'd just said, 'Let's try not to have an emotional talk about this, shall we?' And that had shut her up. She'd never spoken to him about it since.

It was difficult to explain what she liked about the line dancing exactly; it wasn't just the emotions. You could have emotions at home. What she liked was going out and getting dressed up for it. Sometimes it can be good to have emotions outside the home, although it's not a habit many of us here in town have acquired, street preachers, drunks and small children excepted. Mrs Gilbey liked the clothes, wearing her pre-faded jeans and her cherry-coloured waistcoat, and the stetson, and the lace-up boots. She liked tucking her thumbs into the top of her jeans. She liked doing the slides and the splits, the slappin' leather. There was a period, a couple of years back, when everyone was mad on Toby Keith's 'A Little Less Talk and a Lot More Action' – she loved that song – and they'd do the ski bumpus and there was something about that leaning to the right, and leaning to the left. It was very . . . freeing is what it was. When she tried to explain it to

Frank he just laughed. But – and she never said this to Frank, it was pointless talking to Frank about it – if you've never tried you'll never know.

Actually, what Mrs Gilbey really enjoyed about the line dancing was that you didn't need a partner. You weren't stuck with someone like Frank. When you were line dancing you could forget you wore a wedding ring.

When they were young and she and Frank were courting they used to go to the dances, to the Quality Hotel and Morelli's, and they used to dance rock'n'roll, but Mrs Gilbey had never been keen on it. She couldn't have identified what she didn't like about it then, but now, now that she was older and wiser and she knew herself a bit better, she thought she knew what it was. It was partly that before she'd started stepping out with Frank he'd been courting this other woman – her old friend Mary, Mrs Donelly – and they were great dancers, Frank and Mary, the pair of them, and Mrs Gilbey just hadn't been able to compete. She'd always been a little bit large around the hips, truth be told, and a bit heavy up top, so she was a bit self-conscious when she was dancing, and particularly with that style of dancing, the rock'n'roll-style dancing, where the man stood still, pretty much, and the woman was supposed to jiggle all around him. She didn't like that, the man giving the lead. Mrs Gilbey was not a feminist, but she always thought rock 'n'roll dancing was just a formalised version of what went on in the home – the woman doing all the work, the man thinking he was in charge. Which was fine, but it wasn't that . . . freeing for the woman. It was boy's music, basically, rock'n'roll. It certainly wasn't ukulele music.

But now with line dancing everybody was equal, and you didn't have to answer to your partner, or for your partner. It just made more sense to Mrs Gilbey: it was fun. Frank and Mrs Gilbey didn't dance together these days. The most they'd ever do together now would be a last waltz at a golf club dinner.

The line dancing was her lifeline, really; it was her breath of fresh air; it revived her at the end of a week; when she was tired it gave her strength. It had even helped with her diverticulitis, although she couldn't say how. She was addicted now: she'd started to watch Country Music Television on satellite, and she would practise, in the bedroom, with the curtains drawn, doing the Electric Slide, or the Tush Push. She also watched *Friends* in the afternoons sometimes, on cable. That was the other thing she liked. Frank liked everything about America, but he couldn't stand *Friends*: he said it was unrealistic and unbelievable, and yet then he watched all these films with Sylvester Stallone or whoever it was in them, films with lots of explosions and shooting and fights. At least *Friends* was funny – shooting people isn't funny, Mrs Gilbey didn't think. And Mrs Gilbey believed it could be quite revealing, *Friends*, actually: you could tell something about people if they preferred, say, Rachel to Monica, or Chandler to Joey. She liked Phoebe the best. Phoebe was her favourite. Frank would probably have liked Joey. If only, she thought, there were somewhere like Central Perk here in town. There was Scarpetti's, of course, which hardly counted. So the next best thing was the Dance Ranch. You could get a cup of coffee from the machines after the session, and sit in the soft-seating area and talk to some of the others, if it wasn't too busy with the fellas from the ju-jitsu drinking Lucozade.

She'd had to give up drinking tea and coffee, though, Mrs Gilbey. There was something about tea and coffee. If she had a cup of tea or coffee, she had to have a cigarette. Or vice versa; she wasn't sure which came first. She'd tried drinking more water every day, like they said in all the magazines, but she'd started to wonder if this was leaving her bloated. When she looked in the mirror these days she was amazed to see how puffy she was looking. It was horrible, looking at it. She wore turtlenecks, to hide her chicken-wattle neck. She wasn't ashamed of it – she most definitely was not going for plastic surgery – but she didn't want to flaunt it either.

Frank had been encouraging her to have plastic surgery, just to lift the skin around her neck and her tired eyes a little, but she didn't want to change the way she looked and she didn't want Frank to want to change the way she looked. She wanted to change *who* she was, not what she looked like, although she knew that her face had become long-suffering. She could see it herself. It broke her heart to see herself in the mirror sometimes, the state of her. Her blonde hair and her blue eyes had always been her salvation – they'd got her a long way. Now her hair was dyed and her eyes were dull, like a dying animal's. She remembered she'd left school without a certificate to her name and her teacher had said to her, 'You are not suitable for anything but polishing your nails,' and she'd gone to work for Sloan's, the old coal merchants ('Group 1, Group 2, Group 3, Slack, Phurnacite, Wonderco, Coalite, and Glovoids') on Commercial Street, in the office, and the coal dust had got under her nails – it got everywhere – and she thought that was it, she thought that was going to be her life. But that was where she met Frank. People used to come in to pay, which is how she'd met him, coming in to pay his mother's bill. And she'd scrubbed up, scraped the coal dust from under her nails, and they'd started going to the dances together. She was a couple of years younger than the other girls he'd been going with.

Good for nothing, the teacher had said. Well, Mrs Gilbey had been good for something: she'd got her man. And look at her now. She had everything: central heating, wall-to-wall carpets, a self-cleaning oven, beautiful nails. The house was perfect and spotless, although she did have a cleaner, of course, to help. Her own mother had had to do it all for herself, had had it all mapped out for her: Monday was washing; Tuesday ironing; Wednesday cleaning; Thursday was her night at the spiritualist church on Old Victoria Street; Friday was baking for the weekend. *And* she'd had a job at Carragher's Drapery Warehouse up on Moira Avenue as well. *And* Mrs Gilbey had never heard her mother complain, not even once.

Mrs Gilbey, on the other hand, had hardly any routine and she complained all the time. Shopping was her only routine. She hadn't worked for years. She could do whatever she wanted, whenever she wanted. She and Frank had so much money they didn't know what to do with it. Literally didn't know what to do with it. It was just like people said. They never had to worry about spending money. For years, she'd bought the very best of food and clothes, but even that wasn't enough. Frank had encouraged her to take up hobbies. She tried French classes for a while, but she was embarrassed by the accent: it was a young person's game, the learning of the languages, she thought. She'd encouraged Lorraine to take it up, but she hadn't stuck with it either. Then she did tapestry for a while, but everything she made went wrong somehow, and the stuff piled up in the corner of one of the spare bedrooms where no one ever stayed and it looked messy. She'd tried upholstery – she'd quite enjoyed upholstery, that wasn't as tricky as the tapestry. She'd upholstered everything in the house, from top to bottom, and then there was nothing left to upholster. So she'd started doing the neighbours', but there are only so many footstools you can re-cover, even in our town. Then she'd got into the collecting: pot-pourri vases, sauce and cream boats, scent bottles, cameos, treen, carriage clocks. Small stuff, stuff you could take home with you on the day, that you didn't need to have delivered. She used to go up to the auction houses in the city. She'd enjoyed that. The excitement. It felt as though she were somebody. But as soon as she acquired a piece the excitement left her and she wasn't interested any more. She stored the things away.

Frank didn't understand. He suggested to her that she start buying bigger stuff – furniture, or paintings. But she didn't really want to collect the tangible. She didn't want more things. She wanted to collect something else: experience was what she really wanted to collect, but even when she thought that to herself it sounded silly. Experience! This was her experience. This was it. Here and now, in our town, with Frank, and it was running out on her all the time, like in an egg timer, or rising up against her, like a flood. She felt like Kate Winslet in the film *Titanic*. Mrs Gilbey was working against the clock now. She still worked hard on her looks, had her hair done once a week, up at Noreen Fry's new place, Fry's, on Abbey Street, but keeping fit had been a problem until she discovered the line dancing. The line dancing had been her salvation. The line dancing was helping her hold back time. It was a kind of sandbagging.

Frank had dominated and controlled her life for years. She cooked the food that Frank enjoyed. She wore the clothes that Frank liked. He expected her to look good all the time, a certain way. He was always saying these days that she shouldn't wear skirts because of her legs. That's why she liked the line-dancing clothes – *she* decided about the line-dancing clothes. In all other areas, her own likes and dislikes had ceased to matter, if they ever did. Her own likes and dislikes had gradually come to resemble Frank's, so eventually she found it difficult to judge what she really liked and what she didn't, what she saw as a duty and a chore, and what was a pleasure. It was Frank's likes and dislikes that counted, that existed. Even her values: her values had become Frank's values. She loved money, although she never really spoke about money. She called money 'plastic'. She talked to her friends about 'burning plastic'. That's what she was doing, burning plastic. And it was killing her. She assumed that everyone felt the same, that everyone was choking from the stench of money, like the smell of burning fat, and not a smoke alarm in the house.

The car was too hot. Frank liked it hot.

She was looking forward to getting home and making herself some nice Philadelphia cheese-on-toast. And maybe a glass or two of Chardonnay. She'd left Frank his dinner out earlier – some pastrami, some wheaten bread and a salad. He'd have binned the salad.

They didn't eat out much, her and Frank. Frank liked his food quite plain. A lot of her mornings were spent deciding what she was going to cook for him in the evening and then, once she'd decided, she'd go out and buy what she needed. Unlike virtually everyone else in our town Mrs Gilbey still does her shopping every day. She hated Bloom's. She hated the mall: it was so tacky. There was nothing there she wanted to buy. She'd exhausted the mall. What she wanted was not available in Bloom's. Actually, what she wanted was not available in our town. Mrs Gilbey wanted glamour. She wanted sophistication. And she usually bought lamb loin chops and floury potatoes – that's as close as she could get.

She didn't really enjoy eating out anyway; it's not as if that would have made much difference. She didn't really like eating in front of other people. She didn't know why. She was over sixty now, and she'd never liked it, and she was hardly going to start liking it now, when every mouthful made her fat and her whole face wobbled with every bite. She thought it was disgusting, actually, the sight of old people eating. Watching Frank eating – it was horrible. She preferred eating at home, in private. At mealtimes Frank always liked to offer his insights and opinions about the state of the world and his business philosophy, and at least if they were at home she could put the TV on, and she wouldn't have to listen to him. A load of old nonsense he came out with and she'd heard it all before. 'You don't work for money,' he'd say, 'you make money work for you.' And, 'The rich acquire assets, the middle classes acquire liabilities.' 'The bigger the elephant, the bigger the balls' – Mrs Gilbey had no idea what that was supposed to mean. He was full of that sort of stuff. 'You might make a better hamburger,' he'd say, eating his steak while Mrs Gilbey watched the news, 'so why aren't you McDonald's?' She could never decide if he was really talking to her or not, whether he'd have kept on if she weren't there. A lot of it was just clichés and common sense that he liked to recite to himself, and he did these funny voices sometimes, these American gangster voices; it was awful. 'You can't make an omelette without breaking eggs.' 'Money is only an idea.' 'The greatest losses are those from missed opportunities.' 'It's a dog-eat-dog world', that was one of his absolute favourites, which applied to just about everything and she hated it when he said that, which was at least once a week. She probably hated that one the most. Because saying that made him a dog. And her a dog. And everybody else: just dogs eating dogs. She didn't like that at all. It made her feel quite sick.

She'd thought she might have had grandchildren by now, naturally, to take up her time, to take her mind off things, to spend some money on. But there was no sign in that department from Lorraine, and not much chance either, now that she'd lost the bad Scotsman. It was what all Mrs Gilbey's friends talked about, these days – their grandchildren and their plastic surgeons. It seemed to have come on so quickly: one minute they were all excited, talking about Elvis Presley and how to get a fella and stuffing tissues up their jumpers, and the next minute they were all tired out and talking about their children, and then their grandchildren, and a little nip here and a little tuck there, and who'd died, and how, and how sad it all was. It was strange: Mrs Gilbey never felt like she herself was getting old. It was more like she was observing someone very like her getting old, not her self as such, but her doppelgänger.

It was the same feeling she had when she was reading a book. When she read a book she always felt like she was hearing a story that sounded like her life, but wasn't quite, like something that might have happened to her, or which still might. Even with Stephen King she felt that.

That was her other great escape, actually – books and the library. Frank always said he'd buy her the books, rather than her having to go to the library, but she liked going to the library. She liked the displays and the cracked lino and the public notices, and she didn't really have much use for a book once she'd read it. She liked Margaret, one of the librarians, who'd keep things aside for her if she thought they might interest her. She had always been a very good borrower: she'd never had an overdue book in her life. She loved Catherine Cookson.* Reading those books was her education. She told it like it was, Catherine Cookson. She'd always have a good cry over a Catherine Cookson. Frank was very sniffy about the books, obviously. He wasn't a great reader.

When she was dancing and everyone was moving together, that was what it was like when she was reading a good book. She couldn't explain it: things just seemed to make sense. It was like that feeling, sometimes, of driving round the ring road at night, when all the cars seemed to move in formation together. Or sometimes, when she looked outside on Fitzroy Avenue and she saw people going about their business, almost as if it was synchronised. There was a serenity there that was absent the rest of the time.

Not that she really had any complaints about her life, or about Frank, which is what made it hard. What did she have to complain about? He'd been an excellent husband, really. And a good father to Lorraine. They'd wanted for nothing,

---

* Although if there was no Catherine Cookson in the library she'd settle for a Joan Jonker, a Nora Kay, or a Mary Larkin. Philomena, one of the librarians, who is studying part-time for an MA up in the city, and whose tastes run more to the Angela Carter and Jeanette Winterson and Orange Prize for Fiction end of the literary spectrum, tried to set up a women's reading group in the library a couple of years back, to encourage some of the older ladies to experiment a little more in their choice of reading. She started them off with Elizabeth Smart's *By Grand Central Station I Sat Down and Wept*, which was a surprising success – there are a lot of older ladies in our town, it seems, who can readily identify with a story of sado-masochistic sex, love and abjection – and there was a brief period when Sylvia Plaths and Kathy Ackers were being requested on inter-library loan almost every week, but people's enthusiasm soon faded and Catherine Cookson re-emerged triumphant.

either of them. He was very kind, very generous to everyone. But there was this other side to him, a side that other people didn't really see. The way he'd talk about his colleagues, or competitors – she'd never liked that. He'd swear and shout about them – the language that came out of his mouth, you'd be surprised. He used the 'f' word a lot at home, and the 'c' word, if he thought he could get away with it. And sometimes he used the two in combination. That upset her.

Frank was just like that, though. That's what he was like. He could get quite abusive. He didn't like her going to the line dancing – he got quite abusive about that. He didn't mind her going to the market, or out to lunch with Ita, or Marjorie, that was fine. But he didn't even like her going out to the library on late-night opening on a Thursday (until eight o'clock). She was never sure why: whether he was jealous, or possessive, or just afraid that one day she might slip away and never come back. He'd always been funny like that. He was very insecure, Frank Gilbey, when it came down to it. That's what people didn't realise. He took quite a bit of mothering, Frank. But Mrs Gilbey was over sixty now, and she was sick of mothering.

There was a month left before line dancing shut up shop for Christmas, and Big Donna had been saying about this big evening up at Maxine's on Christmas Eve. Maxine's is a famous pub and club out in the country, 'The Pub with a Club'. There were going to be line-dancing clubs going from all over. You had to sign up if you wanted to go.

Mrs Gilbey really wanted to go. But she knew Frank wouldn't approve. On Christmas Eve Frank would expect her to be at home baking and making things special for Christmas, for him and for her, and Lorraine. Their little family. That was what always came first.

She'd waited for everyone else to leave the badminton courts, and while Big Donna was packing up, Mrs Gilbey quickly checked the list of names to see who'd signed up.

Quite a few. Someone had taken the biro. She only had an eyebrow pencil in her handbag.

Frank always dropped her off outside at exactly 7.00 and he always picked her up at exactly 9.30. He parked on the double yellows outside: he didn't care. So she didn't have much time. She'd had to decide.

They were driving up the gravel drive, and Frank was parking and switching off the engine. 'Frost tonight,' he said.

And she'd taken the eyebrow pencil and written, in her tiny but legible hand, her name: Irene.

16
Speedy Bap!

On the beauty of franchising

It hasn't rained for almost a week, but the Quality Hotel, like a lot of the older buildings around town, still has its big rain stain, right down the middle, which makes it look like it has peed itself, like the front of an old man's trousers, but it makes no odds to Bob Savory. Every man, after a certain age, knows what it is to feel a little dribble and dampness after rains, and so it didn't worry Bob, the sight of a building looking a little leaky. Like a member of the family, like all of us, Bob had seen the Quality Hotel at its best and at its worst, trousers up and trousers down, in all our four seasons: Soaking, Wet, Damp and Almost Dry.

Bob was driving past nearly every day now, on his way to see his mother, in his BMW during the week and his Porsche at weekends, eyeing up that precious, damp little corner on Main Street and High Street, imagining what it was going to look like once the Quality Hotel had gone and the space was cleared, and the new development was finished, and the first Speedy Bap! was opened, nice and prominent, at the very front of the mixed retail and apartment development, the big flagship scheme that Frank Gilbey had promised him he was planning. Bob had become obsessed with the Quality Hotel and the space that it occupied.

More than anything he needed the Quality Hotel out of the way.

He wished Davey Quinn would get on with it.

He wished the hotel could just somehow pull up its trousers, make its apologies and leave.

The funny thing is, Bob isn't really that interested in property. He needed a high-street presence, of course, it was part of his game plan, but he knew that the future really lay in clicks not bricks – he'd read that in a management book and he could remember it because it rhymed. (All the best ideas in management books rhymed, in Bob's opinion. In all books, actually: *The Cat in the Hat*, for example, that was a good book, according to Bob. Bob couldn't see much point in books that didn't have catchphrases and rhymes. There was no way you were ever going to remember the principles of sound accounting or refinancing, let alone the adventures of Flopsy Bunny or whatever it was, unless it could be reduced to a rhyme or a phrase. It was all about brand recognition, as far as Bob was concerned. He'd heard from Billy Nibbs that some poems these days didn't rhyme, which made no sense to him at all: if it didn't rhyme, how did you know it was a poem?)*

Bob had had big posters and laminates made up of his favourite business and management rhymes and mantras in order to help motivate his staff, and he had them placed all round the Old-Fashioned Foods (Cooked the Traditional Way) factory and warehouse, including in the rest areas, the toilets and the locker room: 'Success Depends on Choice Not Chance' employees were told, as they flushed, or washed their hands,

---

* Robert McCrudden covers this question in some detail in Week 2, 'But Is It Poetry?' of Creative Writing (Poetry) I at the Institute, Tuesdays, 7.30–9. 'Yes, it probably is' seems to be the gist of the answer, judging by the submissions to the *Impartial Recorder*'s Poetry Corner and the work published in the Institute's creative writing booklet, *Tears of a Clown* (£2.99, available from reception).

'Motivate Don't Dominate' they were instructed in the canteen, as they ate their subsidised Sandwich Classics and Snack Foods for the Discerning Palet, 'The Objective Is Greater than the Subjective' announced a sign in Accounts where you went to collect your wages, and 'Zap the Gaps' said the swing door into the packing room.

Bob devoured management books – books by grinning businessmen about grinning businessmen for grinning businessmen, and he sucked out the wisdom from those big cheesy books like a cat in a hat at a bowl of Whiskas Supermeat, and he knew from reading the books that in the future his business was going to need more of an on-line presence. That was the marrow and the jelly, that was the guts of all those books, the liver, the kidneys and the heart. That was all the raw information he took from them. At the moment he has a pretty basic website put together by Carl and Calvin Mathers, who are the sons of Johnny 'The Boxer' Mathers, our one and only remaining greengrocer there on Main Street. Carl and Calvin run a little graphic and web design company from the front room of their shared terraced house on Scotch Street, which constitutes our town's very own Silicon Valley: most of the other houses on Scotch Street have cable and Mr Portek, at number 19, who is seventy and still working, is an amateur radio ham, and the Maguires, at the end terrace nearest the High Street, have six children, three bedrooms, two computers and a modem. Carl and Calvin also run a business selling corporate recognition products – keyrings, T-shirts, pens, mouse mats and mugs – and they used to have a stall in the market on Tuesdays, selling ladies' clothes. Everyone in town agrees that they're two young fellas with a bright future ahead of them and the boys both look up to Bob Savory, and Bob admires their entrepreneurial spirit, although in all honesty the website is not very good – everything they know Carl and Calvin have learnt from books on loan from the library. At the moment the site only gives information about the product lines and the history of the company and a contact address, and Bob knew that pretty soon Sandwich Classics and Speedy Bap! were going to need more than Carl and Calvin could offer: the sandwich of the future was going to need a much stronger virtual presence.

The good thing about sandwiches, of course, their advantage in the twenty-first-century food retail market place, is that they don't need to be hot, they're small, they allow for an infinite range of variations to suit consumer preferences and they're cheap to make. They're a capitalist's dream, in fact, sandwiches; they are the epitome of market populism. They're economic and they're democratic. The only problem with sandwiches is the delivery mechanism, getting them to customers when they want them, where they want them. Garages and corner shops are fine, but in the frictionless economy of the future, with everyone on the move and everyone connected, the sandwich presented something of a blockage. Also, some people still preferred to make their own.

Bob's answer to this problem – the essential stay-at-home stickiness of the sandwich – was franchising and on-line ordering. He already had the catering contracts for a lot of local businesses and organisations, receiving orders by e-mail and telephone, manufacturing it all off site, in bulk, and shipping it in. Gourmet sandwiches with no fuss, no bother, no need for expensive facilities and hardly any wastage: offices, factories, schools, every institution in the county had lapped it up. That was pretty simple and the obvious next stage in the game plan, Bob believed, was taking the product to the streets and setting up his own franchise.

The beauty of franchising was obvious to Bob, just like the music of Elton John and Sting, or the interior of a brand-new German car. It was self-evident. All you had to do was develop a successful business format – the System – which you then sold to other entrepreneurs, offering them some kind of training and support, and then you just sat back and watched the money start rolling in. You charged an initial franchise fee and then a continuing franchise fee, and suddenly it's goodbye to local success and hello world domination. Like most people in our town, Bob had a vision of the Golden Arches on the horizon, except his wasn't just a vision of the drive-in McDonald's on the ring road. No, Bob had seen the future, and the future looked like two slices of wafer-thin honey-cured ham with freshly chopped vine-ripened tomato and French mustard between two slices of granary. Bob's future was butter side up and slathered with mayo. Bob had the touch, he had the knack and he also had the vision.

The great thing about franchising, the greatest thing, in fact, as far as Bob was concerned, is that you develop the product not by using your own finances, but by using someone else's, the finances of the franchisee, so you're spreading risk. Also, franchising relies on just one thing to make it work: quality and consistency. That's two things, actually, but in Bob's mind they were one and there aren't many people around town these days who would be in a position to put Bob right on something like that. Actually, if Bob said salt was sugar there are a lot of people around town who would probably have agreed. But in fairness to him, Bob's point held: there probably is no such thing as quality without consistency. In order to achieve quality you have to maintain your standards of service, that was the key, according to Bob. He already had his basic business concept: Sandwich Classics (and Snack Foods for the Discerning Palet) in a shop, with on-line and text message ordering available. He was going to call the shop Speedy Bap!. Like Pizza Express, except without the pizza. He'd employed a consultant from London to come up with that.*

* See note, p.250.

All he needed now was to get his pilot retail operation up and running.

Which was where the Quality Hotel came in.

As soon as the hotel was out of the way and the pilot shop was open, all Bob needed to do was develop a franchise package, an operational manual, market the package, select his franchisee, develop the organisation and roll out across the country, and bingo! A Speedy Bap! in every mall, every school, every business, on-line and in every town centre redevelopment project, so that it became unavoidable and inevitable. Ray Kroc, roll over.

The one thing Bob could not afford at this stage was for anyone or anything to disrupt the System. The System was what he had worked for years towards establishing and he was pretty close to perfecting it, the whole thing, every aspect of the Speedy Bap! brand, from the exact weight of a spoonful of mayonnaise used in a BLT, to the optimum cosy-cum-industrial sandwich-buying environment, all light and spacious and airy but with no-nonsense straight-backed wooden chairs and tables, that he was planning for the first shop. This was definitely the beginning of the big time for Bob Savory, the saviour of the sandwich.

He already had a head start, of course; he'd built up a certain amount of brand loyalty locally. If you were to stop at a garage on the ring road to buy a sandwich, for example, or even further afield, anywhere in the county, in fact, and in quite a lot of places up in the city, you'd automatically look for one of those distinctive red-badged Sandwich Classics triangular packs as a guarantee of quality. The little Sandwich Classics red badge shows a cottage loaf in profile, and the label reads 'SANDWICH CLASSICS: QUALITY GUARANTEED' and it tells you what your sandwich is, in writing that suggests it might be Bob's own handwriting and Bob's own signature, but it isn't. The use of the handwriting is of course supposed to encourage the consumer to associate the product with all the qualities of the home-made and the natural, which is good, but unfortunately Bob's actual handwriting is a terrible mess – the uneven, crooked writing of a man with better things to do than to write labels for sandwiches – and his signature is the signature of someone who'd never worked at it much beyond adolescence, so you'd be more inclined to associate the product with poor schooling at primary level. Bob had drafted in Calvin and Carl Mathers to design the labels, and they had chosen a nice handwriting font, the Edwardian™, whose tranquil curves and brisk uprights suggested both doughiness and mature good taste. It was the same trick with the cottage loaf. Bob had never actually used a cottage loaf in production, but in marketing and retail it's the thought that counts.

Bob had deliberately avoided the words 'fresh' and 'freshness' on all his packaging and products, 'fresh' being a word used by Bob's biggest competitor, the 5F food company, who are based up in the city. The problem with freshness as a concept and 'fresh' as a word, Bob thought, and the mistake his competitor Foster's Family Fresh Fast Foods had made was that talk of freshness immediately suggested staleness. Also, for a sandwich to be fresh was really the very least you expected of it. It was like boasting of water that it's wet. Bob wanted to create greater expectations than that. The expectation in the Sandwich Classics brand was suggested by the word 'Classics', which Bob felt implied certain standards, a certain timelessness, a touch of the Elton John, perhaps, or Humphrey Bogart, or Jennifer Aniston. Bob believed that when you ate one of his salami, Swiss and coleslaw sandwiches you could imagine that you were on the set of *Friends*, or in the studio recording a version of 'Candle in the Wind' with the bigwigged one himself. The London consultant, Terry Carey of the Niche Naming and Product Placement Consultancy, had prepared a hundred-page report on the

Speedy Bap! brand, which had cost Bob £10,000. It was worth every penny.*

To Bob, this seemed obvious. He always worked hard to get the little details right, to create the right expectations. He obsessed about them and he couldn't understand it when other people didn't understand his obsessions. Like most successful people, Bob Savory secretly despised the unsuccessful. The reason he despised them was because Bob knew the secret of his success – and the secret of his success was simply that he worked harder than other people. That was it. Work – sheer hard dedicated work – was the thing that really mattered. If you worked harder than other people, Bob believed, you were bound in the end to succeed.†

Bob had realised this when he was training as a cook. He went into the kitchens a boy and he came out a man – that's

---

* The report, *Summary Conclusions: Sandwich Brand Recognition Indicators*, compiled by Terry Carey, who basically *is* the Niche Naming and Premier Product Placement Consultancy, used the Niche Naming and Premier Product Placement Consultancy copyrighted methodology, 'Seven Simple Messages', to come up with the name Speedy Bap!. As Terry explains in point 1.1 of her 115.10-point report, 'I call these messages simple because they are binary in form (your product is "x", it is not "y", the opposite of "x"). For total market penetration, the product name must send out no more than seven simple messages. This is the key to successful niche naming.' Terry studied English Literature at Strathclyde University before going into PR and marketing, and it shows. Bob had skimmed through most of the report and concentrated on the conclusion. '115.10 Summary Conclusion. The suggested name, Speedy Bap!, works because it embodies Seven Simple Messages of successful Niche Naming. Bap is female. Speedy is male. Bap belongs to the past. Speedy belongs to the future. Bap is rustic. Speedy is urban. And, finally, ! is not ?.' Bob had never been to university, so he took Terry's word for it. He just liked the name. He'd had a friend at school called Bap.
† Bob, alas, like most of us, has never attended any of Barry McClean's classes in 'Philosophy for Beginners' at the Institute (Wednesdays 7.30–9.00), and so was not familiar with the fate of Sisyphus, the king of Corinth who was condemned repeatedly to roll a huge stone up a hill, which then rolled down again as soon as it reached the summit. There's a moral here, in the story of Sisyphus, according to Barry, who lists Albert Camus's *Le Mythe de Sisyphe* as recommended reading in Week 7, 'Philosophy of Religion'.

what he told himself and the *Impartial Recorder*, if they asked, and it was true. Bob had gone into the kitchen thinking that hard work was completing his homework on time and without complaint, and doing a paper round. But once he'd started working in the kitchens he realised that hard work was something else entirely. Hard work was why his dad fell asleep in front of the telly at night, why his hands were calloused and his hair was grey. Hard work killed you. It took your life from you. But it also gave a life to you. It was a blessing and a curse. It was the thing that conferred meaning and in exchange for meaning it took everything.

It was difficult, obviously, always to convince his staff of this plain truth. Most people, in Bob's experience, are happy just to put in the hours and take the money and go home, and kid themselves that they're living. In fact, in Bob's experience, about 99 per cent of people are complete time wasters, perpetual paper boys on a road to nowhere, and they don't even know it because they're too busy browsing the tabloids, or too lazy to care. This was one of the main things Bob had learnt from working in business and employing people, and it was another of his mantras – 99 Per Cent of People are Time Wasters – but he could hardly put that up as a poster around the factory, so he just worked on that assumption. Everyone was a time waster in Bob's book until they proved themselves otherwise. Bob believed that before you could expect any recognition or reward from your employer you had to prove that you deserved it: that was a basic rule of life as far as Bob was concerned, and it was reflected in the pay structures in the Sandwich Classics and Old-Fashioned Foods (Cooked the Traditional Way) factory. Loyalty and hard work had to be demonstrated and, if they were, if you worked really hard, your pay packet grew heavier, eventually exceeding the minimum wage. Bob could not tolerate time wasters, whingers and scroungers. He'd employed someone once who'd started at the end of a shift on a Friday morning and he'd sacked them by the afternoon, because they'd said to him, when he asked how they were getting on, 'Well, at least tomorrow's the weekend.' They were joking, but Bob hated that sort of attitude.

Food, Bob believed, was special and it deserved respect. It was not something to be scoffed at. People thought about food all the time, they devoted a lot of serious thinking time to what they were going to eat, and when and how, and Bob figured that if you could work out what people thought about food, you were close to understanding the secret of existence, or at least the secret of business. People thought about sex and money a lot as well, obviously, but for Bob food implied sex and money, and power. Food had given him all three things in abundance and he hadn't sought them: they'd come to him unbidden. Which is why he loved food – the implications of food are what he enjoyed, as well as the stuff itself. Food, for Bob, was magical. It was sacred.

And, naturally, he was one of the high priests. Bob decided how things got done. When he couldn't instruct his disciples any longer by word of mouth – when he was too busy in meetings, or travelling – he did it by written rules and precepts. There were laminated instruction cards everywhere in the factory and at the Plough and the Stars, from the Sandwich Classics No. 1 'Lay Out the Bread' card, right the way through to the Club Sandwich No. 75 'Garnish the Chicken Breast with $\frac{1}{2}$ Flat Teaspoon of Chiffonaded Parsley' card. If you were making Savory's sandwiches, you made it the way Bob Savory would have made it himself. Or you went elsewhere. At the Plough and the Stars the same principles applied. The food was not exactly haute cuisine, but as Menu Consultant Bob offered people what they wanted: and they wanted buffalo wings, nachos and steaks well done. The details had to be correct. The chips were Bob's chips, for example, and no one else's: there was a way to do it. Bob's way.*

* See *Speedy Bap!*, chapter 1, 'Bob's Way'.

This was maybe why Bob found his mother's illness so difficult to cope with. Illness is not a part of any system. It cannot be controlled with laminated instruction cards.

The only goal you could set yourself, if you were ill, according to Bob, was to get better. That was the goal: that was the only purpose of illness, in Bob's book. But Bob's mother wasn't going to get better. She wasn't going to die just yet either, so there was going to be no fulfilment either way and Bob was used to fulfilment. He wasn't accustomed to sitting around. He didn't want to wait and see. His mother had taught him that, the virtue of setting goals, and having aims and achieving them, and now she was sick and he couldn't believe it, he couldn't believe her attitude. It was as if she'd given up – she, who'd always taught him to work hard and persevere. She seemed to be perfectly content in her illness.

Bob could hardly look her in the eye any more, and because he couldn't look her in the eye he could hardly look himself in the eye. He'd even started shaving using an electric razor, so he could avoid using the mirror.

He'd always been punctilious in his personal appearance, but recently he'd found himself slipping – socks and pants unironed – and he knew he was somehow going to have to cut himself off from his mother. She was dragging him down. Her performance was affecting his own. The trouble is, you can't sack your parents when they fail to perform – although people in our town, obviously, try their best to do so. The sheltered housing, the old people's homes, these are big growth areas around here, and eventually Bob decided that it was time for his mum to go in among the others and join them. It was a difficult decision.

He went to look the place over – Mellow Mists they call it. It's up on the ring road, purpose-built, opposite Bloom's, and the sign outside says, 'We Specialise in Alzheimer's, Dementia and Wandering Problems', hardly a boast, one would have thought. The building is totally secure, and Bob had to be buzzed in from room to room and corridor to corridor. He arrived at a mealtime and there were people like his mother biting plastic knives and forks, and yelling because they couldn't serve the food themselves, or cook it, and there were big grown men sitting in restraint chairs and other people wearing waist pouches where they had finger food that they were nibbling on, while others were folding towels or cutting out pictures from catalogues.

It was appalling.

But the staff seemed friendly and efficient, and Bob's mother was definitely deteriorating. When she'd started getting ill it was just short-term memory loss and he could cope with that quite easily. But then she started with the Parkinson's as well and he'd had to get the nurses in. And then she became confused and now she was angry as well. The doctor called it 'increased agitation'. Bob called it going bonkers. She sometimes wore her pants on her head. She spat on the floor. She picked up imaginary objects and she'd say sometimes, when he brought her a snack at night when they were watching TV together, 'I have to go home. My son's coming home from school. I have to be there.' He couldn't cope with that. Other times she flirted with him, or she shouted at him – his mother, who had never shouted at him in his life. It was Bob's father who had always been the shouter, his father, normally a quiet and placid man but who would occasionally explode with rage, inexplicable, huge parental rage, and although he never hit or struck Bob, as far as he could remember, Bob felt there was always the threat, the possibility of being struck, and that was enough. That was terrifying to a child.

Bob remembered that feeling now, of fear and confusion and shame, and he remembered how he had struggled to cut himself off from his own fears and emotions. He'd succeeded, of course, like he succeeded in everything. When his father had died he hadn't grieved at all; he'd been able to protect himself from his emotions. And now, when his mother swore at him or shouted at him, Bob realised he was going to have to withdraw himself again, slowly but carefully disentangling himself, cutting himself off from her. Bob liked to think of himself as self-reliant but he had always secretly looked towards his mother for reassurance and approval, and now she couldn't give it to him any more. She was as good as dead to him. She was gone.

He made sure she had the best room in the whole place, away from the ring road, overlooking a small pond out back, surrounded by shrubs and roses. He'd point out the roses to her and sometimes, if he arrived at mealtimes, he'd help feed her. Getting her to eat was becoming a problem – just to get her to open her mouth sometimes you had to put your fingers under her jaw and press up; one of the carers had showed Bob how to do it. To get her lips to open, you had to use your thumb and finger, and squeeze her lips together. To get her to swallow you had to stroke her throat. He didn't like having to do that. It disgusted him. It was like feeding a helpless animal.

After he'd fed her he would set off home to his big empty house, and on the way he'd buy a bottle of vodka and a pack of cigarettes, even though he was virtually a teetotaller and a non-smoker, and then he would sit in his big kitchen by himself and drink and smoke and cry, and when he was done, he'd get on with his work. His mother's illness had made him vulnerable and he didn't like being vulnerable. He had always strived towards feelings of invulnerability. Which was why he was beginning to get fed up with the Quality Hotel: the Quality Hotel was making him feel vulnerable. He was going to have to take matters into his own hands.

17

Condolences

A dreadful chapter of much melancholy and confusion

He'd never liked October, Mr Donelly. It was a dog's breakfast of a month: rain and wind one minute, warm and settled
weather the next. You never knew where you were with
October. And now here he was, still receiving condolence cards,
weeks after – that was typical October. The postman, Jerome
Hegarty, did at least do Mr Donelly the courtesy of delivering
to him first, as if the cards were exam results. Mr Donelly had
known Jerome's father, John Joe; he had worked with him at
the printworks years ago and it was kind of Jerome to take
the time and trouble.* Mr Donelly was feeling pathetically

---

* But then that's the kind of person he is: Jerome is a gentle giant and an
absolute dear, according to the many older ladies on his round, for whom
and with whom he always has a kind word. He is a born-again Christian,
Jerome, and he works as a postman because it means he can share with his
wife Marion the considerable burdens of home schooling their five children,
maintaining their tumbledown house and half-acre smallholding just off the
ring road, and fixing up their perpetually leaky VW combi-van. Jerome and
Marion are not hippies, but they take the Sermon on the Mount at face
value, which amounts to pretty much the same thing, although without the
need for tie-dye or the Grateful Dead. (Jerome, for example, favours corduroy
and the music of Keith Green; Marion wears no make-up or adornment;
and their children are not much good at queuing or putting up their hands
but they are very good at reading; Daniel, their youngest, who is only four,

256

grateful at the moment, actually, which was not like him. He was all mixed up: it was October. He couldn't believe how many condolence cards they were getting. It seemed a lot of people had only just heard, people they'd known all their lives. People right here in town. People who had missed the funeral and who thought they'd just drop a note instead, like cancelling the milk when you go away on holiday.

Times had changed. He remembered himself when he was young, if someone died in town, you knew about it pretty soon, if not immediately, because of course you knew pretty much everyone in town, and you'd notice if they weren't around, and even if you didn't know them, if they were just someone's cousin, say, you'd still be happy to line the street with everyone else when the time came to give them a good send-off, and the men would take off their caps, and the children would be expected to bow their heads, and everyone would stand in silence. No one these days took off their caps, but then no one these days wore caps. It was baseball caps, if anything, and Mr Donelly doubted very much whether people took off their baseball caps as a hearse went by, he certainly hadn't noticed them doing so. These days even old men, who should have known better, and who should have been wearing proper caps, might see a hearse approaching from a distance and not even pause to nod.

Shopkeepers actually used to step outside their shops, in the old days, when a funeral cortège was going past. They'd shut up shop, even if it was only for a few minutes. Of course, now all the shops have moved to Bloom's and it was mostly charity shops on High Street and Main Street, so no one did that any more. No one cared. No one knew you anyway. Your passing away meant nothing these days to the community at large. Death was no longer a public event, unless it was a royal or a celebrity doing the dying, and then there was a ridiculous

can recite large parts of Doctor Seuss unaided and several poems by Robert Frost, and Genesis chapter 1, in the Good News translation of the Bible.)

fuss about it, people making up for all their silence and embarrassment surrounding the subject the rest of the time. Death, Mr Donelly felt, had been rather diminished in dignity and stature recently. Death somehow no longer had the clout it used to. It was like everything else that wasn't actually on the telly – it was no longer very important. It had become an amateurish, family affair, something you were expected to deal with all by yourself, and to clear up the mess after you. It was exactly the same with weddings. They'd been to the wedding of one of Mrs Donelly's nieces a couple of years back and the minister, who'd been wearing a lounge suit and tie, had actually announced from the pulpit – had actually said this – 'Please do not throw confetti either inside or outside the church. I'm sure you can appreciate,' he said, 'it's very difficult for us to pick up all the pieces.' Well, no, Mr Donelly couldn't appreciate it. He thought that's what churches were for: to pick up all the pieces. But you could no longer expect other people to join in your celebration, or your mourning these days, not even the church. It was down to yourself. If you wanted to throw confetti, well, fine, but you were expected to do it in the privacy of your own home. These days, you have to smoke in the garden, wear a helmet when you're riding a push-bike and cry alone. That's modern life for you.

The children had all made it back for the funeral. The youngest, Mark, he'd come straight over, right away, from America, as soon as Mr Donelly had picked up the phone and told him. Mr Donelly had rung him before breakfast and, before he knew it, there he was, Mark, standing in the kitchen, larger than life, eating a cheese-and-pickle sandwich before the clock struck midnight, giving Mr Donelly a hug. It was unbelievable, really. He'd got the hugging from America. Molly, his wife, had stayed behind to look after the children: they didn't want them upset. Mark said that Molly had told the children that Nana had gone to be with the angels. What Molly didn't say was that when she told them they'd said, 'Who's Nana?'

Mark had been a big help with the arrangements. His job with the hypodermic needle incinerator manufacturer had been the making of him. He was a man now, Mr Donelly realised. He was in management and he seemed able to deal with all life's little difficulties: that's what managers did, of course. They sorted things out: they brought people in and they laid people off, and it didn't really matter if it was dealing with personnel problems with a junior employee in tele-sales or accounts, or your own poor dead mother, it was just the same. Mr Donelly had never been a manager himself, so he didn't really understand how it all worked, or how you went about it, but he had to admit he was impressed. He could remember when Mark wouldn't say boo to a goose, and yet here he was, making arrangements on the phone, speaking to the funeral director, Sid Rodgers, who'd always done everyone in the family, and the solicitor, Martin Phillips, 'tying up the loose ends' as he put it. Someone had to. Jackie, Mr and Mrs Donelly's daughter, the nurse, she was there from London, but she was too upset to be of much use, and her and Michael just kept setting each other off, just the same as they had when they were children, tormenting each other with their sorrows. They'd always been the emotional ones. Tim had made it back too, but he was keeping his own counsel. Mark had managed to track him down in Thailand, Mr Donelly had no idea how, and he was too tired to ask.* He doubted he could even find Thailand on a map – he'd certainly have had to have a few goes – let alone find his son there. It was

* Mr Donelly is pre texting and e-mail, and is not even that keen on the phone. Nor does he send postcards, or write letters. There is a strict limit, therefore, to his understanding of how modern communication works. He gets all the information he needs from the *Impartial Recorder* and gets to have his own say in the Castle Arms, and pretty much everything else is waffle, according to Mr Donelly. He might benefit from the new Senior Citizen 'Pop-In Introduction to IT' at the library, or even perhaps one of the many part-time Media Studies courses at the Institute, except he's not a great one for classes.

Tim who was most like Mr Donelly himself – the eldest, the quiet one, the drifter, fond of dogs, of alcohol and strong opinions. Mr Donelly had never really got on very well with Tim. But still, it was nice to have him around.

So there they were, all in the house together again, for the first time in years, getting through toilet roll and tea bags like there was no tomorrow. They'd finished a large jar of Branston pickle that would usually have lasted Mr and Mrs Donelly six months or more, and there was not a dry tea towel to be had in the house, and they were all thinking the same, and they were all confused by the same thought: that this was rather nice, actually, to be all together again, and it was a shame they couldn't have got together for some other reason, because there was something missing now that spoiled the whole event, and just for a moment or two you couldn't quite work out what it was, but then you remembered.

She wasn't there.

They were without Mrs Donelly for the first time in their lives, and without her there was nothing and no one to hold it all together, and no amount of tea and sandwiches could put it right. This wasn't indigestion and it wasn't Christmas after all.

It'd been her, really, right from when the children were young, who'd made things OK, who'd made the whole thing work. Maybe that's where Mark had got it from, his managerial skills, just from observing his mother. Mr Donelly had no idea how it had worked, their lives: he'd just lived it. It was Mrs Donelly who always made sure there were enough toilet rolls and tea bags in the house, and sandwich spread for the lunches, clean nappies and clothes, big piles of them on the stairs, he remembered, and presents for the birthdays. The parents' evenings, the exams, the doctor's appointments: Mr Donelly had no idea how all these things had happened. He'd never even really noticed them, to be honest. He just took it all for granted. He used to get up before the children were awake, and put on the clothes Mrs Donelly had bought and washed and ironed and put away, and eat his toast, brush his teeth with the toothbrush and the toothpaste she'd bought, and go to work, and eat the sandwiches she'd made him, come back home again and eat the tea, read the books to the children that she'd chosen from the library. At weekends he did his bit, of course, put in a few hours with the wee ones, but he still found time to go to the pub and he still went to the football. All his needs were taken care of.

He wasn't entirely sure what he was going to do now.

The first night they were all together, before the funeral, was OK. There were a lot of tears but Mr Donelly found to his surprise that he didn't mind the tears. He was used to his children crying. He could still remember them crying when they were little. In fact, looking back, there were a lot of years, probably ten in all, the children spaced out the way they were, when the house had never been quiet, when there had always been the sound of a crying child: someone was hurt, someone was awake in the night, someone was sad. He could deal with that: reassurance, admonishment, a warm drink, a good night's sleep.

It was after the funeral that things had started to go wrong. Mr Donelly's head was reeling and his children were expecting him to have serious conversations with them, conversations about the future, and about them and about himself, that he found much more difficult. This was more like when they were teenagers, and he'd never known what to say to them when they were teenagers. He'd left all that to Mrs Donelly.

So he was glad when the time came for Mark to fly back to the States and for Jackie to return to London. Mark had always been Mrs Donelly's favourite, her baby. There was a bond between them, the youngest son and the mother – that was just the way it was. She was devastated when he'd moved to America, although she never told him how upset she was: she'd always said he had to live his own life, wherever he chose, and the trouble is, sometimes children take what you say at face value, they believe what you say, and Mark chose to live his own life far away from her, across an ocean, which was only an eight-hour flight away, he always said, but an eight-hour flight represented a leap of faith and more than a month's income to Mr and Mrs Donelly, and they were lucky if they saw him and the grandchildren once every couple of years. And the funny thing was, now his mother was gone, here was Mark trying to persuade Mr Donelly to come back to the States with him – he could come and live with them, he said. They had plenty of room. They had a guest room with a nice en suite and it'd be great for him to be around to see the grandchildren grow up.

Well, if Mr Donelly knew one thing for certain it was this: he was not going to be moving to the United States of America. He'd have had to leave the dog behind for starters, because Mark's wife Molly didn't like dogs. She was allergic. Mr Donelly had never met anyone who was allergic to dogs before – he supposed it was an American thing, she was also wheat-intolerant – but the dog was a good excuse and Mr Donelly was happy to use the dog as his excuse. Mark got quite upset about that. The bloody dog means more to him than his grandchildren, he told Molly on the phone. But that wasn't true. The dog was just a dog, even though he was The Dog With The Kindliest Expression. Mr Donelly just wanted to be left in peace, to stay on in town, but he couldn't think of a simple way of explaining that, and he didn't really see why he should have to explain it, since it seemed obvious and so simple, so the dog became his explanation. The dog represented his life here, in a way, and if Mark couldn't see that, well, fine, he was better off in America anyway, where he had his own life to manage – hypodermic needle incinerators didn't sell themselves, after all – and Mr Donelly had his own life to get on with. Mr Donelly still had a lot of the friends he'd known since school, and there was always the Castle Arms.

It felt rather like becoming a child again, actually, Mrs Donelly's dying, like the beginning of the school holidays, but he could hardly have explained this to his children. He knew his friends in the Castle Arms would have understood, and the dog. He was staying.

Brona and Michael had been arguing. Brona had gone and had her tan topped up for the funeral, and Michael didn't agree with that. Brona had said, 'Just because your mother's died doesn't mean I have to go around wearing sackcloth and ashes.' It did not, agreed Michael. On the contrary. But Brona had gone and bought a £300 black suit up in the city and she'd also bought the children new outfits – two little black dresses for Emma and Amber, with matching Alice bands and black patent shoes. Michael thought that was going a bit too far. He didn't like the fact that Brona had turned the death of his mother into an excuse for more shopping.

Jackie, meanwhile, was angry that she hadn't been told about her mother's illness – she was a nurse, after all. Actually, all the children were angry about that. Why hadn't Mr Donelly told them she was ill? He had difficulty explaining. He felt it was none of their business. But they obviously felt it was their business: Mrs Donelly was their mother. But she was a lot of other things too. She was his wife for starters, and she was his wife before she was their mother, and if the two of them had decided between themselves that they weren't going to tell anyone about her illness, well, it was up to them, as man and wife. It was their decision. Of course, Mr Donelly didn't say this to his children.

Of all the children it was Tim who seemed to be taking things hardest. Mrs Donelly's death had come at a bad time for Tim. It had cut short his trip of a lifetime, which Mr Donelly had hoped might have given him some kind of a clue as to where he wanted to be, and with whom, and what he wanted to do with his life. By the time he was Tim's age Mr Donelly was the father of four children, a man of responsibilities. Tim, on the other hand, before he went away, had spent most of his time listening to music alone in his room and going out with girls with multiple piercings, and had worked five days a week at McDonald's and weekends at Oscar's, the video shop, and had spent three years saving up to go away because he couldn't really think of anything else to do, and so he did rather begrudge his mother's death bringing him back home, and partly out of spite he'd got straight back into a routine of going out with his mates, drinking till the early morning and sleeping in till midday. He'd been secretly hoping that his trip away might have helped him to get his head together and he was disappointed that it hadn't. He was still the same old Tim in Thailand, it turned out, which was a shame. He'd quite fancied becoming Leonardo DiCaprio.

Anyway, Mr Donelly was sitting up in bed, by himself, waiting for the post, waiting for further condolences, thinking about his children. Or, actually, he wasn't thinking about them, because he never really thought about them. He counted them, rather, and wondered at them and was grateful for them: much as a man might enjoy his own butterfly collection, or his stamps, or his pet Pomeranians. Mr Donelly could not easily describe thoughts and emotions to himself, and had never really attempted to do so: thoughts and emotions that you couldn't or chose not to describe to yourself you couldn't feel; that was his theory, and it worked. Sadness, loss, doubt, depression – these were things that had never much troubled Mr Donelly. His refusal to give in to himself, his self-discipline, had helped see him through four children, and the usual ups and downs of a lifetime.

But as he lay there, holding on for as long as he could before the urge to go to the toilet became overwhelming, he found himself full of feelings and he didn't know what to do with them. He didn't have anyone any more to tell him what to do with them, or to annoy and distract him, to help him chase them away.

He pulled back the blankets and the sheet a little and looked at the space where Mrs Donelly had once lain. It was Mrs Donelly who'd always taken care of things in the bedroom department: as far as he could remember he'd never turned the mattress, had hardly ever made the bed, and after the necessary excitements of their first few years together he had rarely initiated sexual relations. He thought probably that Mrs Donelly had gone off it. He looked now at the imprinted outline of his wife's body, her empty trough, and he thought: it might be useful for keeping the paper in at night and his glasses. The bedside table was too small – a glass of water and a lamp, that was all there was room for, and he hated putting things on the floor. He thought – and he was amazed at thinking it, but there you are – he thought, well, there's always a silver lining.

He needed a wee.

He went downstairs and made the tea. Within just a few days, he'd found, he was able to remember to put out only one cup. He'd given up on leaf tea too, had gone straight on to tea bags. Mrs Donelly had opinions about tea bags. But tea bags were more efficient according to Mr Donelly. You could get at least three cups out of one bag. He was going to be making quite a lot of savings on his living expenses, actually. A lightbulb had gone in the hall yesterday and he'd put in a 60 watt rather than a 100, something he had been wanting to do for almost forty years. About a watt a year. To be in charge of the household after all that time – it was a strange feeling, like a retired captain put back in charge of his ship. It was power and he didn't quite know what to do with it. He felt a little rusty.

He got dressed and went out back into the garden, into the cold and the dark, eating the other half of the Cornish pastie he hadn't finished for his lunch yesterday, and he had another wee by the single silver birch which was supposed to shield them from their neighbours and which didn't. It was only 6 a.m. and there was no one to tell him not to. Tim was the only child left in the house now, the others had all gone back to their lives.

As he licked the Cornish pastie crumbs from his fingers Mr Donelly stared up at the back of the house, at the boarded-up window. He was going to have to try to get that fixed. He needed to get himself organised.

The funeral had taken it out of all of them. Mrs Donelly had stated in her will that she wanted open casket. Sid Rodgers had advised against it, but Mr Donelly wanted her wishes complied with and they'd had her laid out on the dining-room table, a fine, mahogany-effect table that Mrs Donelly had bought on credit from the big warehouse showroom, Jackson's Economic Furnishings, 'Strong, Substantial and Elegant Furniture and Furnishing Requisites at Exceptionally Low Prices', which used to be up on Moira Avenue. It had nearly bankrupted them at the time, that table – if you added up all the monthly payments you could have bought an actual mahogany table, or even an antique. Mr Donelly had polished it once a week ever since – his only household tasks being polishing, winding the clock and setting the fire – so you could almost see your face in the shine. They'd had to have the extending leaves fully out to accommodate the casket, but they had nowhere to put all the chairs, so it looked as if they were about to sit down to Christmas dinner.

Mrs Donelly had a look on her face when she was in the casket – it was difficult to say what it was. Not bemusement, exactly, nor perplexity, not amusement – it was a face of curious repose, as though she had recently been to the toilet. There was a smell, actually. It was a smell that reminded Mr Donelly of his own mother.

Mark had handled the oration very well. He was good at that sort of thing, what with living in America. He spoke a kind of middle management, which made it sound as though he were recommending some line of stock that was being discontinued. It was a nice talk, though.

And the burial itself was as burials are: so strange, so dramatic, that it managed your emotions for you. You hardly had to think about it.

Afterwards, Mickey had driven Mr Donelly back to the house for the wake and when he went to open the door Mr Donelly realised that he had no key.

Mrs Donelly had always looked after the keys – she looked after keys and cash and the bills. It was the way they worked things: he did the garden, the DIY, brought home the money. She did pretty much everything else. It was a workable arrangement: they had good clean gutters and the woodwork round the windows was freshly painted, and he didn't have to check the compound interest on their savings account at the building society, but now the system had broken down.

Mr Donelly checked all around to see if he'd left any windows open. He had not. He looked in the front room, where until that morning Mrs Donelly had been, but now she was gone, with the house keys, probably, and he suddenly realised that's what she was smiling about.

There was only one thing for it: he'd have to smash a window to get in.

Mr Donelly didn't want the embarrassment of all the mourners seeing the smashed window, so it would have to be a back bedroom window, where no one would see it unless they were out in the garden for a smoke.

Mickey had gone off to start ferrying everyone back, so Mr Donelly didn't have long. He was going to have to climb up himself. He didn't want to trouble anyone else with it.

Mr Donelly hadn't climbed up a building in a long time: fifty years probably, since he'd climbed on the roof of the Assumption with his friend Big Dessie, and they were beaten for it by a priest who came in specially once a day to beat bad children – strange job, when you thought about it, the priesthood.

Using a combination of windowsill, coal bunker, fence and

the next door neighbour's flat-roof extension, he managed to reach the first-floor windowsill, but he'd forgotten that he'd need to smash the window so he had to climb down again, take off his shoe and then climb back up. It took just a couple of knocks. He was glad they'd only double-glazed the front. This was easy and it was quite good fun – it wasn't something Mr Donelly would have wanted to take up professionally, but he could see how someone might begin to enjoy it. He reached in for the latch, opened up the window and climbed in.

The house looked different somehow. Coming in at a window changed everything: it was a bit like those aerial photos you sometimes see of people's houses. There was a company that did them. They took the photos and then came round selling them door-to-door. Dessie had bought one of his house: it didn't look like Dessie's house at all. It looked like an open prison.

Mr Donelly went downstairs into the kitchen to find the front-door key, but it wasn't hanging with the others. Then he checked the jar in the front room, where the many sausage rolls and quiches and tarts that Mrs Donelly had pre-prepared and frozen were now sitting ready, gathered in and fully defrosted from the many freezers of friends, on the mahogany-effect table, in place of the coffin.* But no keys there either.

She did sometimes have the keys in her purse, though, which she kept in the bedside drawer, so Mr Donelly went back upstairs to try.

Mrs Donelly's bedside drawer had remained a mystery to Mr Donelly for years. Privacy had been very important to

---

*See p.200. There was a nice lattice-work apple pie, however, conspicuous by its absence, which had been in Mrs Donelly's friend Pat's freezer, and which Pat and her husband Henry had eaten by mistake one night some months previously. Pat had tried to make up for it by substituting an apple pie of her own, but she never really had the hand for pastry and you could tell, even from a distance, that it was not one of Mrs Donelly's.

them, largely because they did not have that much to be private about, or much space to be private in. His shed, for example, was sacrosanct and Mrs Donelly was in charge of all the cupboards. So he was a bit nervous about going into the bedside drawer. He was worried what he might find in there.

He was certainly surprised to find a boxed set of black silk underwear.*

But he was even more surprised to find a birth certificate for Mrs Donelly's eldest son.

The boy's name was Colin.

* From Frank Gilbey's 'Romance' range – camisole, knickers and bra, a set – available from all Gilbey's ladies' lingerie shops and by mail order (catalogue available, £3.50). See p.39.

18

The Bridal Salon

*In which Lorraine overcomes her difficulties and goes
to the Garden Centre, and Davey Quinn goes with her*

The wind was battling at the door, howling through the metal
grilles over the windows like a little cold wet dog trying to
get in and nip you around the ankles and leap up at you. It
was annoying, like a little cold wet dog is annoying. Mr
Donelly had a little cold wet dog once, a Jack Russell, which
he had nicknamed Windy, as it happens, but that was for
another reason. It was annoying, then, the wind, but it wasn't
terrible by any means. There were no trees down. No one
was going to fall over in the street – and this had happened,
on several occasions, on Main Street, in big winds. Flushed
with excitement, coming from the market on their way to
Tom Hines for a chop, or a floury bap at the Brown and
Yellow Cake Shop, some of our old-age pensioners get up a
little too much steam, lean a little too far into the headwind
and before they know it they're down, and they're out, and
they're making the long journey round the ring road and up
to the city to the hospital, with their sprained wrist and their
blue plastic carrier bags full of cabbages and onions, and the
chops and the baps have to wait until next week, if they can
remember. That wasn't going to happen today: you might
have ended up with a lot of crisp packets and paper litter in

your backyard and your washing twisted round your line, but you weren't going to lose any roof tiles or chip your teeth. It was just gusty and annoying and unsettled, and no warmth to be had anywhere. It was big boots weather, woolly hat and fingerless gloves weather, and Davey Quinn had his big boots on, and his woolly hat, and his fingerless gloves, and jeans, fresh socks, a T-shirt, a pullover, a pair of bib and braces, and one of his many quilted shirts. He could have done with a smoke and a sausage in a buttered roll with a strong cup of tea from Deidre and Siobhan in the Brown and Yellow Cake Shop, but he was in the lock-up doing a stock check. It sounded like the wind was checking up on him.

The shelves all around him were filled with industrial quantities of paint and he went along slowly with the stock check book, checking things off: standard primers, undercoats, eggshell, gloss, emulsion, metal finish, sundries, wood preservers, stains, varnishes, wallpaper paste. Tick, tick, tick. An Aladdin's cave of every kind of covering and finish. There was probably enough here to redo the whole town – you couldn't have painted it red, but you could definitely have done it magnolia.

His brothers were gone already. They were out in the van. They were working on a couple of the big contracts – the new Collegiate School up on the ring road and some new apartment complex on North Street, where the old telephone exchange used to be. They're calling the new apartments the Tel-Ex – strictly speaking, of course, it should be the Ex-Tel-Ex, but that sounds more like a young person's drug, or a laxative, and the Tel-Ex was a good month's worth of work to Davey Quinn and Sons, so they weren't complaining, even if it was a daft name for a building. This is not New York and sometimes people need reminding: it's easy to get carried away here, like anywhere else. People watch a few too many episodes of *Friends* on the telly and suddenly they're into Mr Hemon in Scarpetti's, asking for flavoured decaff cappuccinos and blueberry muffins. But change here comes slowly and we're not there yet, and progress means more than being able to get a feather-cut hairdo, or the occasional availability of exotic fruit and veg.*

They had divided up, over the years, the Quinn brothers who'd gone into the business, and each one had found his niche and his forte. Danny was the man for the paper hanging, and the cutting-in. He was the closest thing to Davey Senior, a perfectionist. Gerry was the best for the coverage – he was a demon with the roller. He was the workhorse. He shifted and moved stuff, and he was also the one who sorted out problems and negotiated. He was big. You didn't argue with Gerry. He was also good outside and in tricky staircase areas. Craig was the creative one. He handled all the decorative finishes.

Davey didn't have a niche, or a role, which suited him fine. It had never been his ambition to play a part within the family

---

* There is still some debate here in town about the exact date of the appearance of our first avocado, an event which is generally considered to have marked the beginning of the end for our local turnip growers, a once prosperous group many of whom now run B&Bs or grow oilseed rape or live in Spain, or all three. No one in their right minds, not even here, is ever going to give up the sweet rich buttery flesh of a ripe Hass for the nostalgic pleasures of a plain boiled turnip. Some people date the beginning of our love affair with the avocado to the summer of 1974, when Johnny 'The Boxer' Mathers was forced to change his supplier to one of the big national companies, after his previous supplier, J. J. Farrelly, had been forced out of business by the first big supermarkets opening up in the city, who began importing fruit and vegetables from countries which remained a mere rumour to J. J., whose root vegetables simply could not compete with year-round sugarsnap peas and crispy iceberg lettuces. Certainly, prawn cocktails served on a bed of iceberg lettuce in the hollowed-out halves of avocado were a popular staple in the Quality Hotel Grill Room by the mid-1970s. The avocado and the Black Forest Gâteau, relative newcomers, have since become firmly rooted locally and have thrived and survived where garlic mushrooms with melted Brie, say, or warm Mediterranean goat's cheese tartlets have withered on the vine. Aubergines also never caught on – just too weird – and fresh herbs apart from parsley remain a rumour.

business and he had never tried to fit in. If Davey took after anyone in the family it was probably his mother, Mrs Quinn, who remained an outsider, the only woman among many men, and she was a distant, thin, dreamy kind of a person, with frazzled hair, good at playing games and smoking, and imagining. It was she, after all, who had agreed to marry Davey Senior, the seventh son, which must have taken quite a leap of faith, when you think about it, and a willingness to perform in the great Quinn family drama, taking on the responsibility for fulfilling the dream, for providing seven sons for a seventh son.

In those days, though, it didn't seem like that big a challenge. Seven children was not uncommon for families in our town, whichever church they attended and even among those who did not. Even atheists used to have big families in those days. Mr Galt, for example, who was a teacher at Central and who was famous around town as a bearded, duffel-coat-wearing, bicycle-riding socialist who refused to sing hymns in the school assembly and who was a member of CND, had five children of his own with his wife, Mrs Galt, who was the town's part-time registrar of births, deaths and marriages, and who therefore knew just about everyone, and they'd adopted two more children, a brother and a sister, two babies, Peter and Laura, whom Mr Galt always described as being 'of mixed race parentage' but whom older people in town always referred to as 'the wee darkies'. Peter, wisely, has long gone and is a policeman, apparently, in London, which probably has his bearded father turning, duffel-coated, in his grave, but Laura has stayed put and is a veterinary nurse at Becky Badger's Animal Centre and Pet Surgery on Windsor Avenue, and she looks after the woman she calls mother, Mrs Galt, who hasn't got long left, probably, who's in her eighties and who's soon going to complete her own trio of town hall certificates. It'll be down to someone else now, of course, to sign her off: Alex King, the son of Ernie King, who used to run the music shop on High Street, is the registrar these days, his impressive name and signature, a big florid A. King, which Alex has practised for years to the point of perfection, lending a certain glamour and dignity to what are otherwise always rather dull and disappointing proceedings. There's really nothing worse than arriving for one of the most important days of your life only to be greeted with a damp handshake from a fat man with a goatee in a sagging polyester suit attempting to look pleased to see you. Alex is no Angel Gabriel: in our town, with our dentists, it's hard to pull off a very convincing beatific smile and, frankly, if this was the kind of greeting you could expect in heaven a lot of people would have chosen right there and then to give the other place a try.

Mrs Quinn herself was of course from a good Catholic family of eight, four sisters and four brothers, perfectly balanced. But seven boys – she had wondered how she'd cope with that, if she succeeded. She'd worried most about the Quinn succession with her second son, with Gerry – he'd set the trend, really, and had made all the rest possible, like the second line of a poem, or the difficult second album, which is supposed either to confirm your early promise and set the rhythm, or to prove the doubters correct and to begin the long decline. Gerry was a triumph, though, a boy, and Mrs Quinn hadn't worried again about completing the set, getting all seven, staying in the groove, until it came to the last one, the seventh, to Davey himself, and then she had prayed and prayed, and tried to do everything exactly the same as she had for her previous pregnancies. She just couldn't have coped with six sons and a daughter: that would have looked like carelessness. With Davey she could not afford to slip up, or to skip a beat: Davey had to be a boy.

Davey Senior had also looked forward to the birth of his seventh son all those years ago, but he hadn't been that worried about it. He felt it was not his responsibility. All he'd had to do was what he always did, which wasn't really that difficult. When Davey was actually born, though, when the little fella was actually there in the flesh, the all-important number seven, and all the newspapers and the TV cameras started arriving, that was special. That had confirmed it for Davey Senior, his sense of destiny. He felt he had fulfilled what his father and mother had wanted him to achieve and now he could relax a little, now it was up to his son. For the first few years Mr and Mrs Quinn had watched Davey closely for any signs of supernaturalness. They didn't really know what to expect and Davey failed all their expectations. He walked late, he talked late and at school he was just OK. He seemed entirely without any of the powers one might have hoped for from the seventh son of a seventh son. He couldn't even charm a wart.

And Davey knew it. He knew from an early age that he was special, marked out, and yet somehow not quite special enough. Old men in the street would press money into his hands and pat him on the head, and they would look deep into his eyes, as if there might be some wisdom contained within there that they might be able to fish out – like the salmon of knowledge, swimming around in there, in the pools of his eyes, in the depths of his very being, waiting to be seen and comprehended and grasped. And old women, old women would want to hold him and kiss him, as if some of his good luck might rub off on to them as easily as their lipstick rubbed off on to him. And with all the patting and holding, Davey had grown big and fat and shy, and failed to flourish, and he vowed at an early age that he was going to leave our town and he was not going to have any children of his own. The seventh son of the seventh son had had enough.

As a teenager he'd tried to joke about it and to laugh it off, but all the time he'd been angry, boiling up all bitter inside, cooking up dark thoughts and fantasies at every mention of this irrelevance, this annoyance that was his life, this life that had been imposed upon him. He was waiting for the moment to make someone suffer for it, make someone regret having made him what he was, to let fly and spit it all out, to get it off his chest. And finally, when he was seventeen, the opportunity had arisen.

They'd been to a boxing match, him, Bob Savory and Billy Nibbs. None of them had ever been to a boxing match before. Billy had got the tickets from his dad, Hugh, the butcher, who'd got them from his friend the greengrocer, Johnny 'The Boxer' Mathers, who owed Hugh a favour. Their shops, the butcher's and the grocer's, used to be opposite on the High Street, up the top, near Dot McLaughlin's Happy Feet Dancing School, and Johnny had always supplied Hugh with parsley, and Hugh had kept Johnny in sausages, and on a warm day, if business was slow, they'd stand outside their shops and shout across the road and talk about football, and boxing, and Johnny would talk about the great featherweights he'd fought, and Hugh would compare the heavyweights. And this was in our lifetimes, remember, in our town: shopkeepers, with actual shops, in actual aprons, in the actual centre of town, talking to each other across a road which these days you'd be lucky to get across in the slack hours between 3 a.m. and 7 in the morning, some time after the final conclusive vomitings outside the club, Paradise Lost, and before the first of the council's electric street sweepers arriving to scoop up the polystyrene burger boxes, the beer bottles and yesterday's papers.

Davey and Bob and Billy had driven up to the city in Billy's dad's van, the meat van, with its cheery picture on the side of a bearded butcher, a plucked chicken in one hand and a cleaver about to enter into the head of a grinning pig in the other, and Davey had brought his cassette recorder and they were listening to loud music and they were singing along, in a way that teenage boys rarely do, because they're usually too self-conscious, and they'd parked up, and got a feed of drink into them, and then they made it to the big hall where all the men and women were screaming, and there was this fantastic chaos of tiny figures far away, grappling with each other, and they felt an excitement they could barely understand or contain. These were boys, really, who had hardly known a woman in any intimate sense, who had never been to war, who were young and strong and who wanted to be big, but who knew no excitements other than drinking beer and hanging around in the car park opposite the Quality Hotel. And after the boxing they came out into the street throwing punches at each other, and then in the pub they couldn't get served. There were too many people in, and Davey was signalling to the barman, his hand up, and he made eye contact, but the barman ignored him and he turned instead to serve someone to the left of Davey, a man with a shaven head, not much older than Davey himself, and about a foot shorter, and he'd turned, the shaven-headed one, as he put in his order, and he smirked.

And that was all it was, a smirk, nothing else. That was the thing that had finally driven Davey Quinn away from our town and which had taken him twenty years to get over. Smirks, sneers, mumbles, those little laughs behind the hand: these are things that can destroy a man.* Of course, this wasn't just any smirk, this smirk, this was the smirk that Davey Quinn had been seeing all his life, it was Life's Smirk, if you like, the very quintessence of smirk, the same smirk that he'd imagined seeing smeared on the faces of all those cameramen and photographers when he was born, taking pictures, as if he mattered, knowing that he was just a little kid, who knew nothing about myths and superstitions and

* The phrase 'What are you looking at?' is one that is often uttered here in town, both inside and outside clubs and pubs on a Friday and Saturday and Sunday night, and it is a phrase which is usually caused and prompted merely by a glance, and one which often leads straight to hospital – proving a direct causal link between a look and loss of blood.

who hadn't asked to be born. It was the smirk of the old people on the streets, and his teachers, and his friends, and his family, who all knew that he was nothing special, that he was just a wee boy born into a big family with a lot to live up to, and no way of knowing how. It was a smirk that let Davey Quinn know who he was and what he was: a travesty of himself.

Davey had gone berserk. Once he'd got him outside he was punching the shaven-headed man hard in the face, fists clenched, with a left hook and a right hook, swinging just like a boxer, using his height to his advantage, except it hurt more than Davey had imagined from seeing it in the ring, but suddenly the man's legs were going and then he was down, and then Bob Savory and Billy Nibbs were pulling him off, before he could do any more damage. Davey suddenly felt heavy and as light as a feather, and he could feel his heart beating, and he looked at his bleeding hands and he wished he'd been wearing boxing gloves. He had never been in a fight in his life. He'd only ever fought with his brothers and with his dad. He hadn't meant to do any harm to the fella. He'd just lost his temper. That was all.

And then there were all these other people outside the pub, and someone had phoned for the police, and Bob and Billy and Davey were running away down streets they didn't know, until finally they found Billy's dad's van, the meat van, and they hid Davey in the back, amidst the stench of all the meat, and Billy drove so fast back to town in silence they might have been driving to catch a funeral: it felt like they were in the presence of death.

They might as well have been. When he got home Davey packed his grip and he went first thing in the morning, without even leaving a note or saying goodbye to anyone, and he was so terrified, and so relieved, and he felt so blank, that he never came back for twenty years. Billy and Bob kept an eye out for news in the *Impartial Recorder*, and Bob rang the hospital, pretending he was a friend, and it turned out that the shaven-headed man was OK. Broken teeth. Broken nose. Stitches in his head. It was nothing serious. Nobody died.

Not that it would have made any difference to Davey Quinn. The outcome for Davey Quinn was assured: he knew he would have killed the man if he'd had the chance. He would have kept at him until there was nothing left. And that was the sad truth about Davey, which he'd discovered that night, aged seventeen. He had realised what he really was: a nasty, no-good shrivelled-up specimen of humanity. Just like everyone else, like he'd always known he was. Nothing special. He was the seventh son of a seventh son. And it meant nothing.

Once Davey had done the deed, once he'd let himself down, he found he could begin to face up to himself. He didn't have to impersonate himself any more, or pretend to be what he couldn't be and couldn't understand. As the seventh son of the seventh son he'd always struggled and tried not to stand out. If his brothers were behaving he behaved. If they misbehaved he misbehaved. He was, his teachers at school had said, easily led. He allowed other people to set the trend, to determine the tone, and he'd just copied, because he'd had no idea how to be himself. But now, defeated, and far away from our town, he was able to make himself up, however he wanted to be, to put himself together as a new person. He was doing his own thing. And he did – gloriously, for years, all over the globe, in all sorts of jobs and in all sorts of places – but in the end, of course, he knew he'd have to come back and try to be himself back home. Also, in the end it had meant coming back because he'd got a beating in a pub in London, when he'd started singing 'Danny Boy' after a football match on the big screen, and some blokes in England tops had taken exception and had set upon him, and the next thing he knew he had a ruptured kidney and he was pissing blood, and he was in hospital, and it was time to come home. He'd served his time. He was free to start over.

But as soon as he came back he'd been caught. He'd been suckered back into the family business and had started to lose his way. After the disaster with the stripping he could feel his brothers start smirking at him again. And his grandfather, speaking to him through the writing on the wall. Everyone wanting to catch up on where he'd been and what he'd done, and what he was going to do next, and everyone with an opinion. Davey Quinn Senior only allowed him to work on new properties on the estates round the ring road and he wasn't allowed to strip – stripping was definitely off the menu. Painting and papering, and fresh walls only. Doing the stock-take he realised that this was his life, this was going to be his life: calculating paint amounts, applying coats. He was the seventh son again and he was a nobody.

So by the time he shut the lock-up on that wind dog of a morning he'd decided.

There was no place for him here. He wasn't going to be hanging around.

He had no real friends here any more. Billy Nibbs had his head so far into his books that he was unreachable. And as for Bob Savory . . . Bob had become a parody of a business-man, who thought he could blackmail Davey and get him to do whatever he wanted. Which, of course, he couldn't.

Although. He had given Davey a way out, if he wanted it. Davey really didn't care about the Quality Hotel, or why Bob and Frank Gilbey wanted it out of the way. It meant nothing to him.

So he'd decided to do the job for Bob. He'd decided he was going to take the money and run.

And this time he would not be coming back.

But first he had to go and price a job for his dad.

It was Lorraine. She'd decided to redecorate. She needed a change. She wanted carpets instead of the laminate floors. She wanted new curtains. It was time she treated herself to a new duvet cover. It was time she washed away all memories of the Scotsman. She'd had a tartan biscuit tin, but that was away already.

Her brief marriage to the Scotsman, whose name had not been mentioned since he'd gone, had been the embarrassment that Lorraine had been waiting for all her life. The Scotsman was an alcoholic when he met her, but he never drank in company, or in the house, so Lorraine had never really noticed: he ate a lot of mints and he wore an expensive aftershave, so he always smelt nice; in fact, it was one of the things she liked about him. She'd never much liked the smell of men she'd been with before – smoke and beer and urine. The Scotsman smelt fresh in comparison. Compared with most of the men in our town the Scotsman was ambrosial. Her dad, Frank, had liked him a lot.

When they married, the Scotsman had taken to drinking secretly in the car, or in the garden shed, where he would stare out at a patch of grassed-over builder's rubble that he knew he was never going to plant as a garden. He used a mouthwash, actually, as well as the mints and the cologne – Lorraine never knew. And when he gargled, he swallowed. He got a buzz off the alcohol.

The crunch had come one night in November. They'd been married for three months and Lorraine was determined they should plant a garden before Christmas. In her mind she needed something to show for the first few months of marriage. The Scotsman had made it clear that he wasn't ready for them to start a family.

Lorraine loved her gardening magazines and books, and watching the television make-over programmes. Theirs was a new house on the biggest, most prestigious estate built outside the ring road, Woodsides. The houses there are all pretty high spec, despite the usual cost cuttings and obligatory subcontracted shoddy workmanship – they're all maple kitchens with under-heated Italian tiled floors and hotel-style bathrooms with slightly dribbly taps and wonky fittings.* Double garages come as standard. All the houses are sold now, but the main contractor's big blue van is rarely off site, replacing warped doors or cracked tiles, rewiring, reroofing and even, in some cases, reboring the drains. 'If You Live in WOODSIDES,' according to the estate agents and developers' exclusive, full-colour, typographically insistent promotional information packs, 'You Expect the Best' but to be honest, if you do Expect the Best, you'd do better not to Live There: most of our town's new-builds are a sure sign that Standards Are Slipping. A house built here in, say, 1995 has aged a whole lot quicker than a house built here in 1905, halogen spots or no halogen spots. Lorraine liked the house, though. She liked the double-length combined living and dining room, which was large enough to accommodate two white leather sofas and an eight-seater dining table which she'd covered with white damask. The sofas had been a gift from Frank and Irene to the young marrieds, and ever since the wedding Lorraine had been itching to get friends round to admire the sofas and the stainless steel and all their shared good taste, but somehow they hadn't got round to doing much entertaining. The Scotsman said he wanted them to get settled in a bit first, so Lorraine spent her evenings fussing over fabric books and catalogues. The four bedrooms would give them plenty of room for the children when they arrived, as they inevitably would, as surely as the fashion for curtain fabrics swung from swags to blinds and back again.

They'd bought the house off-plan, so they'd been able to

* Second phase, if you're interested, soon on release. 'Three Stunning New Designs of Detached Homes in this Prestigious Development: the Beech, the Hawthorn and the Oak. From Three to Five Bedrooms. All Designed to Suit Stylish Everyday Family Living! (Choice of kitchen doors and worktops as standard. Finishes to include moulded skirting and architraves, uPVC double glazing, quality facing brick and painted smooth render to exterior.) Prices start from £225,000.'

choose a lot of their own fittings and there was, to all intents and purposes, nothing to be done to the place when they moved in. It was an instant home. Thus, the garden had become Lorraine's obsession.

Frank had offered to pay for his own gardener – Little Mickey Matchett, who used to work for the council parks department, when there was a council parks department – to come and sort it out, but Lorraine wanted the garden to be the outward and visible sign of the inward and invisible grace of a married relationship, and she believed that her planting designs should be carried out by a dedicated husband, attending garden centres and nurseries with her on a Saturday, and happily planting and tending all day Sunday. In fact, the Scotsman spent Saturdays watching sport and Sundays recovering from a hangover and preparing for another week's drinking.

So Lorraine had gone to work on the garden herself. She'd had delivered enough bedding plants to maintain every roundabout on the ring road and beyond, and it was a Saturday when a trailer load of farmyard manure had been deposited on the front drive that finally did it for the Scotsman.

He'd arrived home from the golf club in his BMW saloon, about halfway through the day's drinking timetable, post gin and tonics and beer, and pre wine and spirits, and he saw the manure piled in the drive. He saw Lorraine inside the house, a pair of Marigolds on, gazing anxiously at the clock, and suddenly he saw his life flash before him: the mulch of years to come, the plants, the children, the pets, the elderly parents requiring care, and he suddenly turned the car round, and headed for the ring road and out on to the motorway. He retuned from Classic FM to Radio 1 and he never looked back.

Lorraine couldn't understand what had happened. He'd written after a few months – no return address – to apologise and said it was the drink. 'Don't blame yourself,' he wrote, but it was too late, Lorraine had already blamed herself. She'd tormented herself going over every little detail, looking for signs, and suddenly she saw the signs everywhere. Looking at the Scotsman now, in her mind's eye, all day and every day, more than she'd ever even noticed him when he was around, she saw what she'd never noticed before: behind the sweet accent, beneath the sweet breath and the smart-casual clothing, she saw a selfish, lying, lazy, pathetic, hypocritical brute. And looking at herself she recognised what she'd always known and what she'd now had confirmed: she was a naïve, gullible, weak, needy, timid, ugly, fat, desperate thirty-something who'd probably have fallen for the first serial killer to take an interest in her.

Everything they'd done together, she realised, was a sham. Every moment they'd shared was a waste. Their vows were meaningless. Each kiss was a mocking insult. He was laughing at her when they made love, sniggering at everything she said. She could still see him sometimes in the mirrors, mocking her: how could anyone love that?! Huh? How could anyone respect that? All those fabrics and soft furnishings. The sofas. She told herself she should have seen it coming, that anyone else would have guessed it, or would have done something to sort it out. Anyone else, even an idiot, the most stupid person in the world, could have worked out that the Scotsman would prove to be a bad bet. She saw it all now, in full focus.

A few weeks before he'd disappeared, for example, they'd attended his work's Hallowe'en party together, which had been arranged by his new PA, Angie, who was unmarried and who had arrived at the party dressed as a Renaissance sorceress, a costume which involved her having her blonde hair dyed black, and wearing a bustier, black leather boots and a free-flowing see-through chiffon skirt. The Scotsman had gone as Count Dracula, wearing a tuxedo, with a set of false teeth. Lorraine had gone as the Bride of Frankenstein. She'd worn her wedding dress – which she adored – and attached a plastic novelty knife dripping plastic blood. She'd thought it was funny at the time – a kind of a joke, and a good way to get some further use out of the dress. Now she realised it was a premonition. The Scotsman had spent all evening by the cocktails, chatting to Angie. Lorraine had assumed it was about work, but then she lost sight of them both for about half an hour and when she saw them again she'd noticed that the Scotsman was without his false teeth and the Renaissance sorceress had let her hair down. At the time she thought nothing of it. But now . . . It was terrible, the thought of it, her sheer stupidity. It tormented her. Anyone else, anyone except her, would have noticed.

The manure stood out front of the house for months, in humiliation. In the end, Frank had insisted that Little Mickey Matchett go round to clear it away and start work on the garden, but Lorraine had lost interest. She had always had a difficult relationship with her own body, but she now abandoned herself fully to bulimia and the music of solo female artistes. She'd got sick. The garden remained unplanted.

And then Frank had set her up in the Bridal and Tan Shop.

It was the shop that had saved Lorraine. It was the shop that had brought her back from the brink: the thought of all those dresses, and the lovely accessories, and the tanning bed, the responsibility of making other people's dreams a reality. She'd had to suspend trading a few times, because she just couldn't cope, but the beauty of it all kept bringing her back. 'A wide range of dresses to suit all tastes' read her advertisement in the *Impartial Recorder*. 'Whether you're looking for the cutting-edge modern styles or the traditional, we can provide you with everything for your perfect day.' As well as the clothes and the tanning she did a full bridal package: the wedding music, the wedding favours, musicians, the rings, the flowers, the hair and the make-up. If you wanted her to, Lorraine could arrange just about everything for you, and she'd be there on the day to see you through, from the moment you woke up in the morning to the minute you slipped away to your secret honeymoon location, or at least the hotel room upstairs. She loved all that.

But it was the clothes that she really cared about. She loved the clothes more than anything. Just the smell of the clothes – when there was no one in the shop she'd sometimes take deep breaths, breathing it all in, burying her face in the ivory chiffon and the antique lace, and the tulle skirts. The shoes as well, of course, she loved the shoes. All the shoes she sold were special shoes. She'd never have wanted to work in a regular shoe shop, like Irvine's, or Orr's, having to sell trainers and other awful things. She only sold slingbacks, and kitten heels, and ivory silk satin stilettos with T-bars. Princess shoes.

The shop has done well, surprisingly. Over the past couple of years there's hardly been a wedding in town that Lorraine hasn't played some small part in. The blue garters she sells by the bucket-load. In our town, Lorraine Gilbey *is* weddings. She *is* the Bridal Salon and Tan Shop. It's taken a while, but after the bad Scotsman she has managed to reinvent herself.

And now, finally, she's ready to tackle the house and the garden.

When they'd first moved in they'd had the house decorated almost entirely white. That was the Scotsman's idea. He'd wanted white walls and he didn't want anything on the white walls. He wanted it blank: he even refused to let Lorraine put up her photos in her favourite silver frames. Which was another warning sign, really, when you thought about it. When he went, he left Lorraine with nothing but white walls and all her photos still packed in a box, and genital warts. That'd hurt.

She'd been through the books and chosen her colours. She loved going through fabric books and the paint brochures – she was very much a colour person, actually, despite all the time she spent in the shop amidst white. She has deep mahogany skin, Lorraine, and french-polished nails, which look like tiny ivory handles on a large dresser. Her teeth have been whitened, and her hair is expertly highlighted and straightened. But her clothes – her clothes really were radiant – they were what set it all off. She'd had her colours done years ago in a Colour Me Beautiful™ session with her old school friend Kim Collins, who is a colour analysis consultant up in the city and who's doing very well with it, not just with individuals but with corporate accounts, and some men even, these days, and once Kim had done her colours Lorraine had never again strayed outside her colour palette. Lorraine is Light Spring, which means she looks best in pink, teal, salmon and periwinkle, and her best neutrals are gold and camel, and she knows a thing or two when it comes to matching separates and pulling together a co-ordinating outfit from a messy wardrobe. And now, she had decided, she was going to apply these principles to the house, and to her life.

When Davey arrived to price up the job he managed to dissuade her from paint effects. No rag-rolling, scumbling, or stencilling: very outdated, he said. He was quite firm about that. He was scared she'd make him do it, so he insisted it was the wrong thing to do. She'd agreed with him on that, but she refused his suggestion of magnolia for the walls. The Quinns kept a lot of magnolia in the lock-up and they called it different things to different people – 'Ivory White' was always very popular, and 'Lime White', 'Off-White', 'Old White', 'Pale White', 'Sand', 'Sugar Barley', 'Frosted Apricot', 'Almond Cream'. 'Nomad Trail', that was a good one. They just made them up. Davey was doing his bit to get it shifted. But it was pink and periwinkle for Lorraine, or nothing at all.

Davey got the job. Lorraine liked him, she liked the look of him, although he was not at all the kind of man she would normally go for. He was too tall, for starters, and he had large ears – but large ears, Lorraine believed, were a sign of intelligence. She'd read that in a magazine once. She wasn't sure about the ponytail, but she liked the look of his bib and braces and his quilted shirt, and the fact that he smelt of damp tobacco. Also, he has that shy, lopsided grin that's always been a big hit, right from when he was a child, the only winningly seventh-sonish thing about him. He reminded Lorraine of a big friendly dog.

Davey, on the other hand, had hardly noticed what Lorraine looked like, even though she'd made quite an effort to get her look exactly right for meeting and greeting the prospective painters and decorators. He had other things on his mind – getting out of town, mostly. It was nothing too much, actually, the look she'd gone for, she hadn't gone too far – a little bit of lipstick, a slight teasing of the hair, the little bubblegum pink cardigan, an old pair of jeans and her old tan cowboy boots. And she didn't bother to put in her contacts, she'd kept her little square black glasses on instead. It was a perfect Colour Me Beautiful™ look, a look that said, *Yes, workman, I am a woman, but be warned, do not try to take advantage of me, for I am also pretty tough, as is reflected, subtly but clearly, in the power colours of my colour palette, so don't think for a moment you can overcharge me and mess me about, because if you do I will quite happily throw you out on your ear*. It was a look that a Hollywood producer would have called feisty.

Lorraine had spent years perfecting her looks – the Bridal Salon and Tan Studio was really just an extension of her own interests and obsessions, and this is true in our town generally. Tom Irvine, of Irvine's Footwear, for example, he really is interested in shoes, he's not pretending. He notices them on other people, still, after all these years, and he still can't stand holes and scuffs and scratches – they make no sense to him. Tom himself would always have plumped for a nice pair of brogues, given the choice, and he had his doubts about slip-ons and suede. Similarly, at Priscilla's Ladies Separates and Luxury Hairstyling it would have been impossible for

Priscilla to conceive of a woman who wouldn't have wanted her hair set nicely for the weekend and in just the way that Priscilla set it. At King's Music, Ernie King's and his son Charlie's interest in music had always bordered on the obsessional: Ernie could have named you a Benny Goodman solo just from the sound of the maestro drawing breath, and his son could do the same for just about every guitar lick from the opening bars of 'Stairway to Heaven' to the closing notes of the legendary bootleg of Rainbow live at the Budokan. The butchers in our town all enjoyed their meat, from head to tail, and the grocers all loved vegetables, even turnips and the bitter little local apples. You had to. You had no choice. Your business was your life.

At Bloom's, on the other hand, up at the shopping mall, business has been successfully divorced from life, from obsession and from passion. Desire has been set free from its object, and has become a goal in itself, a realm of fantasy and constant stimulation, a place of ever tinkling fountains and frothing cappuccino carts. You could spend your whole life working in a shop up at Bloom's and never have any idea exactly what it was you were selling, or why. Indeed, that seemed to be pretty much the case with most people working in the shops at Bloom's. Of course, this new free-floating world of goods and services has its advantages. It means you're not tethered to your job. It means you can live a rich, fulfilling life, while ostensibly working eight long hours a day in ladies' clothes, or giftware. Little Steffie Hutchinson, for example, works on the meat counter in the supermarket and she's a vegetarian (although she does eat fish), and she works a split shift so that she's always home to pick up her children from school. Johnny Portek, son of the town's only Pole, is pigeon-chested and has a peanut allergy, but he's still able to work in the in-store bakery and to travel the length and breadth of the county at weekends, playing with his mod tribute band, the Kasuals. He's the rhythm guitarist. You don't owe all your allegiance to your job any more. And it doesn't owe it to you. Everybody's satisfied all the time and nobody knows what they want.

Davey got stuck into the decorating job at Lorraine's and had been at it about a week, with Lorraine shutting up the Bridal Salon and Tan Shop at lunchtimes and coming home to make him a sandwich and a cup of tea, and to talk to him about her day and ask him about his. When Davey told Lorraine his stories about all the different places he'd been to and everything he'd done, it seemed to her that he had lived the life she'd always dreamed of, a life of wandering and drifting, far away from responsibilities and away from this town. She imagined all the different colours in all the different stories and all the different scenes – the big red splash of tulips in Holland, the profound winters of Berlin and the soft summer tones of the south of France.

The basic problem with our town, actually, is its colour. It's grey. Grey is the dominant colour all year round and it's not a palette of grey – it's not a range of fancy greys that you might see in one of Lorraine's paint brochures. It's just pure grey-grey, plus a kind of wet-grey when it rains. So our town is really the wrong place for someone who likes colour and Lorraine did like colour. Lorraine even likes colourful drinks and colourful foods. She would always take a glass of rosé over a glass of Chardonnay, for example, because the colour seems to her much more expressive, of what she does not know, but of something, she is sure. Rosé is within her colour palette and she just enjoys bringing a little colour into her life whenever she can.

That's why she loved working in the shop. The clothes were white, but it was all about colour, really. She loved advising women in the Bridal Salon, helping to put a little bit of colour and sparkle into their lives. She knew exactly what women wanted for their wedding day, or at least what they want in our town, which is usually something sexy, flouncy, something with a little bit of a heel, and something white. She did offer other colours apart from the white, but they were never popular. And the heels – well, she could always persuade people into heels, even women wearing Doc Martens.

'I couldn't possibly walk in those,' they'd say.

'You're not supposed to be able to walk in them,' Lorraine would say and, pausing for a moment, she'd add, 'They're not for walking in.' Then she'd pause again, for a longer moment, and lower her voice, almost imperceptibly. 'They're for lying down in.'

And that'd be a sale.

Lorraine had always talked quietly, so you had to lean in a little to hear her, and she spoke a language of extreme diffidence, combined with an extreme, unexpected sauciness, which always worked with her customers, and it had worked also with the Scotsman, who had met her at a Rotary Club Christmas dinner at the Plough and the Stars and who had fallen for her when she was calling out the raffle, when she'd made a glazed ham, a box of Milk Tray and a bottle of supermarket champagne sound like telephone sex. Her voice worked with most people.

But it didn't with Davey Quinn. Davey was used to working with women in all sorts of circumstances all over the world, women who had never had their colours done and who did not rely on sweet-talking in order to get their way. He'd worked with an Aussie spark in Berlin, for example, Margot she was called, and she was something: a tattoo on the inside of her upper lip, smoked roll-ups, and drank like a fish, worked harder than most of the men. There'd been androgynous fruit pickers from Uzbekistan, and Germans who used to finish a ten-hour day on the sites and go and lift weights for laughs. He'd worked for women bosses who pinched men's arses and made sexist comments, women in hard hats and women who looked like they cut their own hair, women who were like fellas, most of them, and they did not behave in the way women here in town behaved, so Davey had grown accustomed over the years to treating women as equals, which is still something of a novelty here – it was only a few years ago, after all, that women started wearing slacks to church. Mrs Donelly had been a pioneer in this area: she gave up skirts on Sundays in 1977, the year of the Queen's Jubilee and the Sex Pistols at number one in the charts, although it was not clear which of these two events, if either, had influenced her decision. But even though they now wore the trousers, women here on the whole still shopped, cleaned, and had the job that paid for the children's clothes and the holidays, even if that job was as a head teacher or an independent financial adviser. That was the way it had always been and that was the way it would continue. A woman was expected to be either a daughter or a wife, without very much room for variation in between.

With Davey, though, Lorraine behaved more as though they were friends, which is uncommon for men and women in town over the age of thirty, and so she didn't bother much with the voice, or with the exercising of her feminine charms. Lorraine had been an only child and Davey was the seventh son of a seventh son, but the effect was pretty much the same; neither of them had ever really had an intimate; they had been expected to rely upon themselves and to work things out for themselves. So they enjoyed being friends and pretty soon they had little jokes going together. Lorraine started leaving Davey funny notes if she wasn't going to make it back for lunch. They cheered each other up. They made each other laugh.

Davey was certainly not like any man Lorraine had ever known before. She tended to measure men against her father, Frank, whom Davey was most unlike. He wasn't nearly as competitive, or as aggressive. Frank would have wiped the floor with him. Lorraine's first memory of her father was of him mowing the lawn and he even mowed the lawn as though he were in a race: he didn't pause at either end, just swung it straight round and came haring back the same way. This was before he'd entered his vicuna overcoat phase, before they had a gardener. He was racing against himself, even then. He had been an absent but dominating presence in her childhood, a figure who had always embarrassed her and scared her, and she'd always thought that's what men did. When he was angry he would shout so loud that it made her mother cry and when they went out to eat, as they increasingly did as he started making money on his property deals, he would always have to make a scene. One of his favourite phrases was 'Let's make an occasion of it' and Lorraine hated him for always making an occasion of it. He was always wanting to make things happen, to let people know who he was. They used to go to the Quality Hotel, in the old days, to what was called the Grill Room and he would order a steak, but it had to be done right – always rare – and it was never quite rare enough and he'd send it back, and they'd have to cook him another. He would probably have preferred to eat the steak raw, actually, with his bare hands. Her mother, meanwhile, would always order a salad, and Lorraine could never understand that, as a child, but she felt she should order a salad also – to show solidarity. So she did. But it always left her hungry. So when she got home she'd raid the fridge, to fill herself up. And then she'd feel disgusted with herself, so she'd make herself sick. That was the effect men had on you, in Lorraine's experience. They made you behave in ways that made you feel quite nauseous and unhappy.

But not Davey. With Davey she would happily sit and eat a cheese-and-pickle sandwich, and talk about his travels and the meaning of life. She did not mention the Scotsman, but she did speak of seeking out new horizons, and needing to get her head together, and getting out of town. All the years he'd spent away Davey had really only talked to people under the influence and at night, in foreign countries, so it was shocking to be talking to someone about the meaning of life over a cup of tea, in our town, during the day. He liked it. As Davey got to know her, he became convinced that he had led a wonderful, colourful life, that he was not someone who had simply run away from his responsibilities as the seventh son of a seventh son. He was an adventurer. He was, to Lorraine, the person he had always known himself to be in his own head.

He worked hard on the job. He made sure he touched up any spots and drops and drips. He tidied up after himself every evening. He ventilated the rooms properly. He made no mistakes and he made the job last. And when at last he'd finished, Lorraine asked him if he knew anything about gardening. A bit, he said, not much.

Well, would he do her a favour, she asked. Would he like to join her in a trip to the garden centre, just to pick up some plants?

He would, he said.

The best and biggest garden centre around here is without doubt Gardenlands, out on the Old Green Road. Mr and Mrs Crolly, of course, run a little place they call the Shrubbery, at the back of their house, up on the edge of the industrial estate, but it's really only for aficionados and lovers of hedging. They don't sell Christmas decorations, for example, or whimsies, and they don't do tray bakes, or provide a soft-play area for children. Gardenlands, on the other hand, is out beyond the ring road, where there's enough room to begin to stretch out and provide not just plants and shrubs, but more of a garden centre experience.*

* 'From Perennials to Annuals, and Pots to Pot-Pourri, Let Your Imagination Run Away with You at Gardenlands, the One-Stop Gardening Shop. Be Inspired by Our Stunning Displays of Plants. Relax at Threshers, Our Award-Winning Café and Events and Banqueting Suite. Enjoy Our Amazing Range of Garden and Home Products, Including Chimeneas, Barbecues, Indonesian Teak Garden and Conservatory Furniture, Taylor's Stone Statuettes™, Bandff Sheds and Quality Giftware. At Gardenlands, the One-Stop Gardening Shop, Something for All the Family.'

It was a beautiful sunny day when Lorraine and Davey arrived and they spent a long time wandering around, bending over and sniffing at herbs together, and kneeling down to look at tiny little alpine plants, squeezing down aisles of pots and planters, and after they'd had a cup of coffee and a slice of apple strudel in the garden centre café, Threshers, and Davey had got hold of a large trolley for Lorraine, and they were pushing it along together, he slipped his hand gently over hers – it was somewhere between the cotoneaster, Lorraine remembered, and the broad-leafed Indian bean trees.

And it was only three o'clock when they got back to the house and unloaded, but they agreed they could plant up tomorrow.

So it wasn't until the next day, when Lorraine went to write Davey a cheque for the job and he glanced over it, just to make sure everything was in order, that he noticed her signature.

Lorraine's marriage to the Scotsman had lasted so short a time that she had never even had the chance to change the chequebooks, so it still bore her maiden name: Lorraine Gilbey. Frank's daughter.

The man for whom Davey Quinn was about to burn down the Quality Hotel.

19

Country Gospel

*In which Bobbie Dylan practises intercostal diaphrag-
matic breathing and Francie McGinn loses his nerve*

The rain was playing timpani on the roof of the People's
Fellowship, and a snare, and high hats, and cymbals – it was
kind of free-form, overspilling every bar and filling up all the
spaces. There is no musical notation for rain, as far as I am
aware, but if there is, we could do with someone explaining
it to us here in town, if it wasn't too complicated, so we could
begin to distinguish one day's rainfall from another, like
Eskimos and their snow. The weather here is our only form
of syncopation.

Bobbie Dylan was rehearsing the Worship Band up at the
front of the church, before the altar. Actually, she wasn't
rehearsing the Worship Band so much as begging them to
play, bullying them into playing, chastising them, cheering
them on, coaxing them, teasing them, willing them into some
kind of shape, some semblance of musical sense. In Bobbie's
mind what she had before her was a bunch of flabby new
recruits, a bunch of teenagers who'd decided to join the army
and were having trouble getting through the basic training.
They lacked discipline, of course, that went without saying,
but they also lacked the basic skills, or the muscles, so it was
almost impossible to get them to do what she wanted. If it

had been up to this lot to blow their horns and bring down the walls of Jericho, the Canaanites would probably have still been living there today, getting up to all sorts of unnatural practices, and Joshua would be remembered as just another obscure servant of Moses, and the Promised Land would have remained just that.

Bobbie had most trouble with Gary, the drummer, inevitably. A Christian drummer is a contradiction in terms. Drummers are pagans, in their heart of hearts: there's something about beating skins with sticks that brings out the infidel in a man, or a woman. To be a good drummer you have to understand the downbeat as well as the upbeat; you've got to be able to see the other side; you've got to be able to think differently from other people; you have to be able to hold steady, but you also have to be able to *swing*. Gary had plenty of swing – or as he liked to put it, taunting the rest of the band, and quoting one of his favourite James Brown tunes, he had 'More Bounce to the Ounce'. He also had a lot of issues that he needed to lay before the Lord: like, basically, he was an arrogant little shit. He was into Frank Zappa, and jazz, while the rest of the band were more into the Christian equivalent of 1970s Pacific coast rock.

Apart from Gary's kit, which was Yamaha, and green, the Band's gear wasn't much good. It was ancient amps and dodgy cables, and microphones as big as your head, and poor old Bobbie was used to working with professionals, or at least semi-professionals, certainly people who had to fill in a tax return and who knew how to fiddle their expenses and get a good, clean, dry sound when they needed to, so it really was a strain to her, having to cope with all this cheap, rattling second-hand gear, on top of everything else. The Worship Band were just a bunch of amateurs, when it came down to it, in every sense.

She kept thinking to herself, what am I doing this for? Why am I bothering? Don't I have better things to do with my time than prepare a bunch of no-hopers for a Christmas Eve concert that is going to be a disaster, very probably? And when she thought those thoughts, which was often, Bobbie liked to put on some music – a little Mahalia Jackson, maybe, or some Ella Fitzgerald, or M People – and she would remind herself of why she was doing what she was doing. It was for the glory of the Lord, naturally. She did her best not to try to understand or analyse the other reasons why she chose to perform in case she didn't like what she saw. That's what she'd told the *Impartial Recorder* one time, when they'd interviewed her, and they'd published a photograph of her on stage at Maxine's, 'The Pub with the Club', which is out in the country, between here and the city. Joe Finnegan had taken the photo, but he'd put in some time at the bar first, so it was not the best photograph of Bobbie that's ever been taken – he'd cut off the top of her head, and caught her leaning forward on the microphone stand, with her mouth wide open, like she was about to be sick, or spew out frogs or something. She was interviewed by Tudor Cassady, who was never really known for his sympathies, and in the interview he quoted her as saying, 'I don't know why I sing. Sometimes I wonder myself. Sometimes I don't know if it's a gift from God, or from the Devil.'* She was joking, of course, and she was tired after performing a full set of country gospel classics to an unappreciative audience of non-Christians who were hoping for something more like the Blues Brothers, but local newspapers can't really tolerate late-night irony in interviewees, so the article was titled 'Devil Woman?'. Bobbie had turned down requests for interviews with the *Impartial Recorder* ever since.

All Bobbie could say for sure was that she had wanted to perform for as long as she could remember. When she was nine years old, apparently, she had announced her intention

* See the *Impartial Recorder*, 13 May 2001.

298

to become a singer/songwriter/actor/performer, a kind of entertainment all-rounder, like Olivia Newton-John. Bobbie's mother, Ivy, had always been happy to encourage her daughter in her ambitions, although it was difficult to know exactly how to encourage someone in the singer/songwriter/actor/ performer/all-round entertainer direction, particularly in our town, where it's difficult to see how to make the leap between here and Olivia Newton-John. It certainly takes more than high heels and tight leather trousers. Everybody in town of course knows someone who's sung in a pub band at one time, or a show band, but Ivy wasn't that keen to get her little girl started on a circuit of singing songs about love and death in pubs and clubs in front of men in quilted shirts drinking beer, so she signed her up for elocution lessons instead.

She'd tried her at Dot McLaughlin's Happy Feet dance school, which had seemed like the logical first step, but Bobbie didn't like the ballet, she thought it was boring, and unfortunately we had nothing like a stage school in our town in those days, although we do now, of course, now that just about everyone's ambition is to get on the telly, and now that Colette Bradley runs the Studio in the Good Templar Hall on Wednesdays after school (six- to eleven-year-olds), and Saturday afternoons (eleven- to sixteen-year-olds). Colette doesn't so much teach a Method as encourage the children to express themselves and to use drama as a way of exploring new ideas and cultures, which is no bad thing in our town, where new ideas and cultures are pretty thin on the ground: her strictly goyische version of *Fiddler on the Roof*, for example, was something to behold. She'd had to call in Mr Wiseman, one of our town's only proud possessors of a yarmulke and a set of McGinn speciality kosher sinks to help with details like prayer shawls and the pronunciation of the word *shabbes*, and he was thanked in the programme notes as the 'Jewish consultant', which pleased him and would have pleased his mother, because it made him sound like a doctor.

He runs the industrial and contract cleaning firm, CleenEezy, actually, up on the industrial estate, which is a good business, but hardly what his mother would have wanted.

This year Colette is tackling *Othello*.

But back in the old days, before anyone had even heard of *Bugsy Malone* and *Fame*, or seen reality TV, it was elocution lessons only, and Eileen, Miss McCormack, was *the* elocution teacher in our town. Her sister, Elspeth, the other Miss McCormack, was of course the English teacher at Central, but Eileen was generally considered to be the artistic one, although the only way you could distinguish between the two from a distance was that Eileen always wore a brooch of a Celtic design, a silver brooch with enamel inlays and a thistle-like ornament at the end of the pin. She also sometimes wore a shawl and what looked like ballerina pumps, as though any moment she was about to throw off her shawl and break into a jig. Everyone loved Eileen. Her front room was equipped with a piano, the obligatory aspidistra and more books than is normal in our town. It was said that she knew the whole of Shakespeare by heart and could speak French like a French person. Bobbie used to have to stand by the piano and recite poems and sing, unaccompanied, and she entered festivals, where she won prizes for recital, for creative storytelling, and for sight-reading, and she learnt how to breathe using the intercostal diaphragmatic method, not something that a lot of teenage girls here know how to do. Miss McCormack taught her other useful stuff too: how to shout without getting a sore throat, how to whisper 'ah', how to smile a real smile without feeling happy, and how to clear her mind while lying on her back with her knees pointing to the ceiling and her feet flat on the floor. All these things had come in handy later in life.

If she ever did try to explain to herself why she enjoyed performing so much, Bobbie would describe it as a simple desire and an ability and a willingness to entertain others, to bring pleasure to them and frankly, in our town, there are not that many people who are prepared to do that.* It's a risk, making people happy, and we are generally averse to risk taking here: fluctuations in the stock market, for example, have never worried us too much, because hardly anyone has stocks and shares; there's still quite a lot of money kept in tin boxes under beds, or in building society current accounts, which amounts to pretty much the same thing. Risk is not something we admire.

We have had, of course, our professional risk takers and entertainers over the years – Wee Willie Gibson, the 'Laughing Dwarf', for example, was from here originally, and he really pushed the boat out and made it on to the bill of a Royal

* Bobbie may have inherited her inclination and ability, in fact, from her father, Ken, who rose from humble washer-upper to become maître d' at the Quality Hotel Grill Room at the height of its fame and popularity, when people would come from miles around to enjoy its prawn cocktails with sauce Marie Rose and its scampi tails, and its medallions of pork, and Black Forest Gâteau, and to admire Ken's skills in showing-to-table and elaborate napkin folding. He was a showman, in his way, Ken, and even though he's in his late sixties now he still does some silver service at weekends, for weddings and banquets at the out-of-town banqueting and conference centre, Riversides (which is not actually beside a river, but which is close), instructing young people in the forgotten arts of place setting and tray carrying, ashtray clearing and the proper use of service cloths. Bobbie's first memory of her father is of him putting on his tailcoat and white waistcoat, his wing collar and his black bow tie, ready for work. He used to scrub his hands every morning at the kitchen sink with a pumice stone and bleach, to remove nicotine stains, and apply brilliantine to his hair: 'I must not disappoint my audience,' he would say. When his audience eventually moved on, to thick-crust pizza and chicken tikka masala, and the Grill Room closed, Ken was sacked, after thirty years' service, and was reduced to serving behind the bar in the Castle Arms. He received no redundancy payment, but he took with him from the Grill Room a full set of silver cutlery, including fruit knives and forks and a lobster pick, some finger bowls and a solid-silver salver which he'd handled for over twenty-five years. As a child, Bobbie thought everyone measured the space between plates at table and ate with asparagus tongs and French mustard spoons. She can still fold a mean lotus blossom napkin, and a good neat bishop's mitre.

301

Variety Performance back in the late 1950s, but Willie was really only funny because he was short. He didn't have much of a routine as such. He performed a double act with a woman called Millie Strecker, who was over six feet tall, and most of the act consisted of some clumsy physical theatre and double entendres. Wee Willie was four foot eleven tall, exactly one inch too big to count as a dwarf, medically, and he retired from the stage when he and Millie divorced: without Millie there really was no Willie. People in town said he never got over having failed in auditions for a role as a Munchkin in *The Wizard of Oz* back in the late Thirties: that extra inch had done for him and he'd walked with a stoop ever since.

We have the usual amateur magicians as well, of course, in town, some of them even members of the Magic Circle, and children's entertainers, karaoke enthusiasts, folk singers, Big Tom Tyrone – who if not a country music legend is certainly a persistent rumour – and Barry McSweeney, who's a twenty-stone window cleaner but who also does a nice Meatloaf tribute, 'A Slice of the Loaf', and who has featured on national TV a couple of times, wearing his wig and sitting on a motorbike, holding his ladder.* But it's Suzie Ferguson who's probably our all-time most famous showbiz export, the

* Since writing, alas, Barry has died, from stomach cancer. He was only forty-two. See the *Impartial Recorder*, 12 June 2003. There was some controversy when the Reverend Griffiths at St Martin's, the parish church, refused to allow 'Bat Out of Hell' to be played at the funeral service. 'Celine Dion is one thing,' he is reported as saying, 'but this is quite another.' Barry's family and the Reverend eventually arrived at a compromise, however, having haggled over 'I'd Do Anything for Love (But I Won't Do That)' and 'Heaven Can Wait', settling upon 'Dead Ringer for Love' as the most appropriate send-off for the big fella. Barry's mother, June, made a huge meatloaf for the wake, in a giant-size turkey roasting tin, an old family recipe which consists in large part of tomato ketchup and bacon bits, and which Barry had always loved, and the talk at the wake was, of course, all about whether Barry had got into Meat Loaf because of the meatloaf or vice versa, and opinions differed, but either way 'we did him proud', according to Barry's heartbroken father, George, and he was right. It was a good send-off.

lady who got out and took the most risks. Suzie was born plain Susan on the Georgetown Road here, but she had elocution lessons with Miss McCormack and got out of town and into drama college, and ended up touring in rep and doing some stand-up, and then moving to California and landing herself with a big cocaine habit and a small part in *Joanie Loves Chachi*, a spin-off series from the TV programme *Happy Days*, which was pretty popular back in the 1970s. Suzie lives alone now, with her dogs, in Borehamwood, and is not generally considered to have been a good example to the young aspiring actors and actresses of our town. Only Miss McCormack – who is retired and who has abandoned herself to the pleasures of daytime television – still remembers Suzie fondly. She still keeps a signed photo on top of the piano which says, 'To Eileen, Who taught me everything I know, With Love, Suzie'. If a family here gets stuck with a show-off or a joker then the name of Suzie Ferguson is often spoken in warning and alternative career plans are made. Bobbie is, in fact, one of the few locals who has weathered the warnings and comparisons and stayed put, ignoring the knockers and singing her little heart out for us, although, frankly, when she's rehearsing the Worship Band she really does wonder why she ever bothered.

She didn't just do it for other people's amusement, that was for sure, or she'd have given up long ago. It was God who remained Bobbie's prime target audience – and He was a permanent audience, obviously, a bit like having broadband, or your radio tuned permanently to the BBC World Service. The good thing about God as an audience, Bobbie found, apart from the fact that He was always attentive, was that He was also open-minded, pleasant and prepared to accept whatever she brought before Him. God, in fact, in her mind, was not unlike Eileen McCormack, right down to the brooch and the ballerina pumps: she imagined God as having excellent three-tone resonance and no glottal stopping. Bobbie was a Bible-believing Christian but she'd never really had any use for Jesus in her work as a singer/songwriter/actor/performer, because she suspected he might be a critical and fidgety audience, who'd attempt to upstage her and who probably spoke with a whiney voice.

There were eight of them in the Worship Band, including Bobbie – two guitars, bass, drums, keyboards, a horn section comprising a single trumpet and a percussionist/tambourine player who doubled up as a backing singer. Their ages ranged from fifteen to seventy and the best musician, apart from Gary on drums, was probably the youngest, the guitarist, Phil, who was still at school and who played lead. The other guitarist is Nick, who is somewhere in his thirties and stuck on rhythm. Chick, in his fifties, plays bass without distinction but with his eyes closed and Brian is the eldest band member, aged seventy, the trumpeter and a trad jazz fan. Johnny, a recovering addict – though from what no one is sure, although he looks like he's tried most things – shakes with the tambourine and sings with gusto. And finally keyboards was Samantha, a witchy-looking woman in her early twenties who is a legal secretary and who needed a make-over, and Bobbie would have been happy to oblige, but she sensed some hostility there – Bobbie had come in and taken over as queen bee, after all, and Samantha didn't seem to like it. Samantha was used to being the special lady among all the drones, and once Bobbie had muscled in, Samantha had started to skip rehearsals. Bobbie would gladly have sacked her, but Francie wouldn't allow it. Bobbie had her eye on a fella in the congregation called Adam as Samantha's replacement – he was a primary schoolteacher with long fingers – and she figured it probably wouldn't be long before she got her way. Which would mean that it would be Bobbie plus an all-male backing band, which is what she was used to and what she was most comfortable with. Bobbie had always preferred the company of men to the company of women – that's just the way she was and she made no apologies for it. She had lived with her mother, Ivy, for years after her parents had divorced, until finally she'd managed to save up and buy her own little flat on Kilmore Avenue, with its velux windows which gave a view of the People's Park, if you stood on a stool, and she felt she knew enough about women. Women did not greatly interest her. Men interested her more.

The Band, then, was a challenge. They were rehearsing now three or four times a week in the hall at the People's Fellowship, for about two hours per session, and they always began with a time of prayer, and after their various intercessions and invocations they'd kick in with 'Green Onions', just to get them loosened up and in the mood, with Bobbie herself subbing on keyboards if Samantha didn't show. They were working on the basis of an hour-long set for the Christmas Eve concert. They'd be performing a number of Bobbie's own songs – 'Lord, Rein Me In', 'I Am Yours', 'It's Risin'', and 'True Surrender' – but she knew that what was really going to draw in the kids was the covers with the alternative Christian lyrics. They were working hard on them. Their version of Katrina and the Waves' 'Walkin' on Sunshine' – 'Let the Son Shine' – was a show stopper, if only they could get the instrumental breaks right. Brian, the horn section, didn't like being told what to do: he had a problem with women in authority. He thought it was unscriptural. Bobbie would point him towards Lydia, and Sapphira, and Tabitha, in the Book of Acts, and Brian would bring up the stuff in Corinthians and 1 Timothy about silence and submissiveness, and then Bobbie would suggest they discuss it outside rehearsals, and would ask him to please concentrate on the music please, thank you, Brian.

But Bobbie had to admit it, her mind wasn't entirely on the music either. There were problems at home with Francie – problems of a personal nature.

*   *   *

Francie had never had any problems before in that department – quite the contrary. Francie's views about sex had largely been formed during his Catholic upbringing, when he was taught that man was diseased by lust, so as a teenager he had, of course, been consumed with feelings of guilt and self-loathing. But in becoming a charismatic evangelical Bible-believing Christian – what the sign at the front of the People's Fellowship called 'Pentecostal, Evangelical, Trinitarian' – he believed he had escaped for ever such legalism and strictures, and had entered into a personal relationship with Christ, and had embraced a theology which emphasised the goodness of God's creation and the freedom of the human will. Unfortunately, Francie had exercised his human will to enter into a relationship with a woman who was not his wife, and pretty soon feelings he had last known in his teens were returning in droves to torment him, and these feelings wore Roman collars and held rosaries.* It was enough for him to wake up and see Roberta's leather trousers on the chair at the end of the bed for him to lose confidence in his heretical ministry and to crawl back under the sheets, and to the Holy Roman Church. Francie was not feeling good about himself.

He was getting these terrible stomach cramps and cease-less rumblings, like someone was playing tom-toms in his belly, and he was on the toilet half the day, and his wee was bright yellow, and it was either because he was drinking too much black coffee or it was God's judgement, or maybe both, he couldn't decide. Francie had always believed that when a

---

* And they were saying to him the catechism he had learnt at school:

Q: Say the sixth commandment.
A: Thou shalt not commit adultery.
Q: What is forbidden by the sixth commandment?
A: All unchaste freedom with another's wife or husband.
Q: What else is forbidden by the sixth commandment?
A: All immodest looks, words, or actions, and everything that is contrary to chastity.

man and woman were joined together in holy matrimony they became one flesh, and that this joining was indissoluble. But he had broken that bond. He had committed a sin. And 500 years of Reformation theology seemed to have gone straight out of his mind.

He couldn't deny that he'd had a good time with Bobbie – that it had been, in one of Bobbie's favourite phrases, 'life-affirming'. She had helped turn the church around. There was no doubt about that. She'd been an inspiration, in many ways: they'd done a lot of good things together. They'd gone up to the city, once, and eaten sushi in a Japanese restaurant – that was something. He'd only ever had Chinese takeaways before, from Wong's. He liked the sushi so much Bobbie sometimes brought some home from a supermarket up in the city, an unbelievable extravagance for a minister of a church in our town: priests and pastors here are supposed to be able to subsist pretty much on an unvarying diet of tea and biscuits, plus an evening meal of lentil soup, maybe with a ham shank thrown in, if you're a Catholic. Francie had also enjoyed seeing the director's cut of *Blade Runner*, several times. It was Bobbie's favourite film. During the course of his ministry Francie had missed out on years of films: the last time he'd seen a film Tom Hanks wasn't even invented, and Leonardo DiCaprio was still in short trousers. He couldn't believe how old Robert De Niro was looking these days. Bobbie brought home videos for the weekends, and sometimes, on a Saturday night, when he should have been working on his sermon for the next day, she would drag him into the front room and they'd sit and watch a romantic comedy, and one thing would lead to another, and the next day he wouldn't perhaps go into Thessalonians quite as thoroughly as he had intended. They'd also been to a hotel together. Midweek, though: Francie had said no to a Saturday night. A Saturday night had seemed wrong, for a minister of the gospel. It was a hotel with a swimming pool. He would *never* have done that with Cherith.

With Cherith they only ever went on caravan holidays, once a year, with other members of the congregation. He had allowed Bobbie to become his chaperone into this whole other world and it had turned out that she had led him somewhere he should never have been: a dead-end street. He had even allowed her to persuade him to remove the sign from outside the church that said, 'The People's Fellowship – Pentecostal, Evangelical, Trinitarian', and replace it with a sign that said, 'The People's Fellowship – the Happy Church'. He couldn't believe he'd agreed to that.

He couldn't imagine, either, the example he was setting to his daughter Bethany.* Whenever he got to see her – and Cherith had granted him very generous visiting rights – she always just said she was fine, and she was really enjoying living with Cherith and Sammy, which made Francie feel about *this* big.† Francie always tried to quiz her – very, very gently and very carefully – to see how she was doing at school and he'd ask her about her friends, and she'd be cool about that too and say fine, everyone was fine, no problems, Dad, fine, fine, fine. But he *knew* she wasn't doing fine. He'd seen her around town hanging out with skaters and smoking. He had no idea what she was smoking and he didn't want to know. He saw her once giving a boy a kiss – in public, at the car park in front of the Quality Hotel. It was extraordinary. It was like Sodom and Gomorrah down there, with these young people skating along walls and jumping over little ramps, and trampling on the flower beds, and Francie had abandoned his daughter to this, but he was in no position to do anything about it: he was a man living in the proverbial glass house.

---

* It was certainly not the example he'd imagined. He was mindful of the Psalmist – 'That our daughters may be as cornerstones, polished after the similitude of a palace' (Psalms 144:12). He was never sure what that meant exactly, but he was conscious that Bethany was not shaping up as a cornerstone and he couldn't help thinking that it was his fault.
† Where *this* is small.

He was no better than them. He didn't have a leg to stand on. He might as well have been wearing hooded tops and flared trousers himself, and chains, and spray-painting his tag all over town. He might as well be performing flip tricks on a skateboard in the car park in front of the Quality Hotel.

Cherith he saw around town occasionally and he hardly recognised her. She looked slimmer, and fitter, and more confident than she ever had when she was married to him, and the Oasis was going from strength to strength. He'd even considered himself joining a class in Slim Yoga, but he was worried he might bump into Sammy – he had nothing against Sammy as such, but he couldn't get over the feeling that Sammy was married to his wife. In fact, Sammy *was* married to his wife. People never tell you this about divorce, but when you get divorced it feels like other people are living your life, like they have become you and you have become them: it's impossible to imagine other kinds of domestic arrangement. So, in his imagination, Francie had been replaced by Sammy. And Bobbie had replaced Cherith. It was as if they'd swapped. It was confusing.

He turned to Scripture as a comfort in his confusion. Never theologically sophisticated, he relied upon God's inspiration to lead him to the right passage, and thus he took the Bible in his hand, opened it up and stuck his finger in, and in his torment he found himself reading from the book of Isaiah: 'But we are all as an unclean thing, and all our righteousnesses are as filthy rags; and we all do fade as a leaf; and our iniquities, like the wind, have taken us away.' Francie was not so deranged, though, that he couldn't figure out that this was probably a fluke, so he tried again, to see if God might like to rethink on the issue. And his finger found this: 'Make not provision for the flesh, to fulfil the lusts thereof' (Romans 13:14). This was not what he wanted to hear either. He'd never felt that comfortable with St Paul, though, so he decided to give God the best of three and he flicked back through the

New Testament, thinking he might find something a bit more cheering in the gospels. And he got this: 'And if thy right eye offend thee, pluck it out, and cast it from thee; for it is profitable for thee that one of thy members should perish, and not that thy whole body should be cast into hell.'

If that wasn't a sign he didn't know what was.

20

Cigars

*A celebration which proves that there is no
goodness without malice*

It was below freezing, nothing like as bad as the winter of
1962, of course, which people still talk about here, a winter
when they say you couldn't have gone outside for fear of
blinking and your eyeballs freezing over, a winter when the
headlines from the *Impartial Recorder* told pretty much the
whole story: 'THE BIG CHILL', announced the paper one week,
and then 'THE BIG FREEZE' the next and, finally, 'THE BIG THAW'.
Back then, when the thaw eventually turned to flooding, the
sewers collapsed at the top of Main Street and there was a tide
of unspeakable waste – about fifty years' worth of town centre
dregs and spoilings – that swept down towards the Quality
Hotel and took half the new tarmac road surface with it. The
Impartial Recorder – whose own basement composing room
and presses were under 3 feet of filth and water, and which
only made it to the news-stands due to the valiant efforts of
Ron English, who had served at Verdun in the First World War
and who had sandbagged around his precious old Linotype
machine – ran a one-word headline: 'DELUGE!'* The last time

---

* Ron died in 1990, one of our last veterans of the Great War. He was from
London originally, a proper cockney, but he married a local girl, and he was

311

the paper had resorted to an exclamation mark was on VE Day, and since 1962 we've had only four more: President Kennedy, men on the moon, Princess Diana and the big winds in 1989.

It's nothing like as bad as that now, nothing like exclamation mark weather, but it's certainly cold enough to make you catch your breath – it's more like comma kind of weather, you might say, or maybe a semicolon. You could feel the cold from the top of your balding head right through to the bottom of your thin-soled shoes as soon as you stepped outside the door, and you could tell that people all across town were making a mental note to ask for a hat-and-glove set this year from Santa, and to go up and see John 'The Leatherman' Brown, who has relocated from his old premises on the windy exposed corner of Commercial Street and Main Street, to the twenty-four-hour warmth of Bloom's, but who has retained his same sense of humour, the same mechanical cobbling gnome and the same sign in his window: 'Time Wounds All Heels'. And he still doesn't accept cheques or credit cards.

We like to drive everywhere here in town, obviously, if we can, from home to school to work, to Bloom's and back again, to avoid walking, even in summer, but in this weather you tend to see even fewer people out on the streets than usual. Sales of de-icer and thermal socks and Bisto and Bird's custard powder were brisk, and in Scarpetti's, Mr Hemon was dismayed to see only his regulars. It was not weather for passing trade or for popping out for a cup of tea, chips, peas

---

typical of his generation, a modest, practical, gentle man who in old age – from fifty – sported a thick white moustache, who wore a waistcoat with a fob watch and suits on Sunday, who kept an allotment and rode a bicycle with no gears in all weathers to the market on Wednesdays and who called black people 'darkies', who despised 'homosexualists' and who, having had the privilege of travelling abroad to fight for king and country, knew for a fact that this is the best of all possible worlds and ours the best of all possible towns: we won't, as they say, see his like again.

and Irish stew (£2) or a curry sauce baked potato with cheese. It was weather to stay at home, to put on your slippers and to eat cook-from-frozen supermarket pies, sweet or savoury, or preferably both.

But Christmas was coming and at Christmas you can learn to love the cold a little, you can learn to reach out and linger with it for a moment, to appreciate that festive chill as you stride to the bus stop or to the car with your kettle, allowing your shiver merely to increase the anticipation of your first warming glass of wine at your office party, or your seasonal Advocaat with lemonade and a glacé cherry, or that extra £20 in the pay packet. Christmas was coming, thank goodness, and the sun had been shining all day, high in a cold blue sky, and there had been a slow and steady build-up of heat and excitement in the glass-fronted offices of the *Impartial Recorder*. Looking out from the freezing, broken windows of the Quality Hotel, if you were a pigeon, say, or a big fat chilly rat up from the sewers, looking out across the car park deserted by even the most hardy of skaters towards the red neon lights of the *Impartial Recorder*, you'd have been feeling pretty jealous of what we humans sometimes get to enjoy, even in the depths of winter. In the offices of the *Impartial Recorder* the egg-nog, the champagne and the cocktail sausages were flowing, and anyone or anything, a pigeon even, or a rat, from a distance, could have sensed that strange human glow, that exaggerated, cartoonish extra-physical presence of people with something to celebrate. It was difficult even for Colin Rimmer not to feel excited.

Like most of us, Colin preferred to hide his emotions, if at all possible. He was impassive – not a word we use often here, but if we did, we would use it as a term of praise. Impervious is good also, obviously, and imperturbable is a state to aspire to. Before Colin, the editor of the *Impartial Recorder* had been a man called Ivan, Ivan Nolan, who had a Russian name and a Mediterranean temperament, but who

313

came from Magherafelt. Ivan was the classic hysterical style of editor, one of the rant-and-tirade brigade, who'd had a brief career on the night desk on a tabloid in London and who was someone as likely to embrace you when you'd found a good story as to shout at you when you hadn't. Ivan was a man of the moment, and it showed, both in his life and in his death. Basically, Ivan lived the life of a feral animal – he had the intelligence of a fox and the instincts of a polecat, and all the appetites of a grizzly bear – and he died of a heart attack, while drinking champagne out on his yacht, a ridiculous luxury he could hardly afford and could barely sail, while married to his third wife, who was twenty-two years younger than him and a former model.

'Where did it all go wrong?' people asked at his funeral.

Colin isn't like that. Colin is going to die of cancer, probably, slowly, alone and with grim determination. Colin was not Ivan. Colin valued consistency and he'd always tried to be measured: tough but fair, that was his motto. To be honest, Colin believed that you couldn't afford to have emotions in his line of work. He believed you had to choose very carefully what to get upset and excited about, even though we don't actually have that much to get upset and excited about here in town and frankly the chance would be a fine thing. Nonetheless, as the editor of a journal of record, Colin felt that he could not allow himself to get carried away even with our little dramas, our little local triumphs and tragedies. He believed you had to keep things in perspective, even here, a place of infinite receding perspectives. There were only so many times, it seemed to Colin, that you could write the words 'The driver of the vehicle, who has not been named, died when the car struck the tree', or 'The couple, who were engaged to be married, were both killed instantly when the car they were travelling in crossed the central reservation', only so many times you could write those words before your emotions learnt to take the back seat and wear a seat belt.

In twenty years of reporting for local newspapers Colin had had to cover every kind of fatal car crash, house fire and miserable scene of crime and suspected suicide, and you simply could not afford to get caught up in all that. 'Local family struck by tragedy', these were words that Colin had written many, many times, but you always had to handle them carefully: they had a way of creeping up your arm and into your mind, killing off a little part of you, a part which Colin tried to keep alive by listening to the music of U2, buying box-set videos of classic TV comedy series and working on his magnum opus. There were also sentences, of course, which began 'He grew the 10-foot sunflower in a bag of tomato feed', or 'The congregation presented him with an inscribed crystal vase', or 'Five-times local pie-eating champion', and these words and phrases killed off other parts of the self, parts which Colin did his best to keep alive by reading hard-boiled American crime fiction, watching thrillers and smoking cigars at every opportunity. To be an editor, particularly the editor of the *Impartial Recorder*, is to learn to maintain oneself between contraries. To be fully human here, we believe, is to learn how to keep a straight face: smiles are frowned upon and frowns are for the short-sighted.

Tonight, though, was a night to let it all hang out, a night for enthusiasm and emotions, and big grins. Tonight it was a cigar for yourself and for all your friends.

Unfortunately, Colin does not believe in friends. In a small town like ours, where there is only so much love and hatred to go round, some of your friends will eventually inevitably become your ex-friends and some of them will become your enemies. Colin did not wish to run this risk. He was divorced already, after all, and so his ex-friends included his children, his erstwhile in-laws and everyone who had forked out for wedding presents. Friendship, in Colin's opinion, like marriage, marble cheese domes and non-stick frying pans, was overrated. He didn't really have time for friends, unless those friendships were carefully cultivated, in which case they became contacts rather than friends, part of the network, part of Colin's local landscape of stories and sources. Colin felt happier dealing with employees, people whom he could rely upon, because they were being paid money to perform a task.

It was cigars for your employees, then, tonight.

A cigar for Billy Nibbs, his top undercover reporter. And for good old Tudor Cassady, who handled Arts and Features. For Gilbert, on Sports. For the whole team, for the reporters, the subs, the production staff. For Mervyn, Minnie, Rosie, Terry, Elaine, Joan, Patricia, Archie and for Lena, Regina and Philomena, the weird sisters, as Colin called them, the three newsroom managers, who kept the whole place going and who got through a packet of biscuits each per day, bourbons for Lena, custard creams for Regina and Rich Tea for Philomena, who's on a diet. Colin paid for the biscuits out of his own pocket; it was important to keep the ladies sweet. A cigar and a biscuit even for Justin Grieve, with his novelty cuff links and his £30 haircuts, who was the advertising manager and a thorn in Colin's side. A cigar, certainly, for the office cleaner, Mrs Portek, who had given up smoking, with her husband, using the patches, two years ago, and who had a mouthful of gold teeth. She said she'd keep the cigar for her son, Johnny, who was back in Poland at the moment, looking for a wife. Local girls lacked a little something, according to Mrs Portek. Class, perhaps. Or warmth.

Mrs Portek called Colin the King Pig, because his office was a mess. It was like a pigsty, according to Mrs Portek, although in fact it was more like a hamster cage or a cat litter tray. Colin lived among newspapers much as a pet hamster lives among them. They were everywhere, the papers, little scraps torn out and tucked into box files with no names or sorted into vast yellowing piles. Colin read all the dailies and the Sundays, and he also subscribed to *Time* magazine, *Hello!*, the *New Yorker* and *The Economist*, and he occasionally bought men's magazines, purely for research. He had two computers, two TVs and two radios in the office, which were on all the time. At home he had broadband, satellite, and a TV and radio in every room, and he'd had to install an alarm – someone had tried to get in one night, whether to get hold of some of his many consumer durables or for some other purpose it wasn't entirely clear. The police had suggested that Colin might like to review his personal security measures: he was the editor of a paper, after all, which meant some people were going to take exception to what he printed, even if it was only inaccurate cinema listings or grammatical errors, and Colin had indeed received calls in the night sometimes, telling him that they were coming to get him, but they never did.

Colin knew that there were some strange people out there, people who were obsessed with split infinitives, for example, and who clearly had too much time on their hands, but he didn't think they were mad enough or bored enough actually to come and kill him, so he wasn't too concerned. Even the threatening letters he'd been receiving had turned out to be from Spencer Bradley, who was upset about losing his bat watch column. Colin had decided not to press charges. But there were a few others, more serious, who might have been keen to get at him: there was a garage owner, Roger Manon, for example, who'd been exposed by the *Impartial Recorder* and taken to court over his Health and Safety record. One night Roger had arrived down at Colin's house with a big knife and a claw hammer, and had proceeded to ring on Colin's front door and show him what he intended to do to Colin the next time he gave him any trouble, by slashing the tyres on his car, smashing the windscreen and breaking off the wing mirrors. Unfortunately for Roger, it wasn't actually Colin's car; it was his next door neighbour's, Brendan's, and you don't mess with Brendan. Brendan drives a lorry for T. P. McArdle, and T. P. is one of Roger's best clients at the garage, so mad

Roger Manon had gladly agreed to pay for the damage and then some on top, and so his little plan of intimidation hadn't worked, although for a while afterwards Colin did get dog shit through the letter box. Even Roger couldn't miss with dog shit.

Colin loved it, though. It was a sign he was doing something right. It made him feel like someone important. That's what kept him going, to be honest.

So, it was cigars tonight, for everyone, for Spencer Bradley and Roger Manon even, in their absence and their madness, for the whole bloody lot of them. A cigar for everyone who had ever read the *Impartial Recorder*, or appeared in its big beautiful pages. Which is pretty much all of us.*

* It's a rare individual who doesn't feature in a cutting somewhere, but there are some, a few, people who live lives even quieter than the average here, which is already of course quite a way below the national average, and which may even compare with the average excitements in the lives of hermits, say, or anchorites, or prisoners in solitary confinement, or vegetarians in primitive tribal societies. There is Clarence Kemp, for example, who lives alone on Prospect Road, near the crematorium, and who has never married, who was an only child and who is retired now, but who worked all his life as a cleaner at the council offices. Clarence drinks only Bovril and eats only ready-meals – years ago we would probably have called Clarence simple, but these days you might say he has special needs. You'd think that Clarence would hardly have any story to tell, but he has a big collection of beer mats, and he knows a lot about Tamla Motown, and when he was fifteen years old his father hit him so hard that he broke Clarence's jaw, and Clarence had to have it wired up for two months, and he couldn't clean his teeth, and when the dentist, P. W. Grieve, took the brace off and took a look in Clarence's mouth, he decided it would be just as easy to whip out all Clarence's teeth rather than try to repair the damage, making Clarence the youngest possessor of a set of false teeth in town, and possibly in the county, quite an achievement, in a place as fond of sweets as we are. This is a true story and clearly of some human interest, but even the *Impartial Recorder* would have had trouble knowing exactly what to do with it, a story which is neither exactly happy nor exactly sad, and which just goes to show that there's a surfeit out there, more stories than we can ever know what to do with, and even a paper is only just scratching the surface. The cuttings are not a summary. The cuttings are only the beginning.

Colin had always loved the idea of working for a paper. Not necessarily the *Impartial Recorder*, of course – he thought maybe it would be something more like the *Washington Post*, or the *Boston Globe*, or the *Sunday Times*. He'd always loved everything about newspapers. When he was growing up, his parents, Fee and Philip, used to spend most of a Sunday reading the papers, drinking sherry, eating roast beef, taking walks and attending evening service at St Martin's, the parish church, and so newspapers were for ever associated in Colin's mind with all the forces of good in the world. His heroes when he was growing up were the *Sunday Times* Insight team, and Woodward and Bernstein, but of course no one on his staff had even heard of Woodward and Bernstein, and the *Sunday Times* is now merely an advertisement for expensive ladies' underwear and London restaurants. Everyone on the staff these days just wanted to write hilarious columns about their boyfriends and their crazy lives, just like in the *Sunday Times*. No one these days seemed to remember what a paper was really for. A paper is supposed to ask the six essential questions: What? When? Who? Where? How? Why? In that order. Although, actually, to be honest, with the *Impartial Recorder* it was usually just the one essential question, plus a query and a satisfied sigh. Who? Really? Well, well, well.

Everything had changed on the papers within Colin's lifetime. Colin was old enough to remember galleys, and men in pork-pie hats in pubs, and boys running around with corrected proofs, and cigarette ends piling up in clamshell ashtrays next to typewriters and waste-paper bins full to overflowing. It wasn't like that now. It was all done on screen now, and e-mail, and press releases, and he seemed to spend half his time in meetings with Justin, talking about advertising features and how much they could wring out of the DIY superstore or Bob Savory if they granted them a full-colour eight-page insert. All the fun had gone out of it. But a night like tonight made it all seem worthwhile.

Cigars for everyone!

Colin's success as an editor and his prodigious work rate he ascribed to his constitution, to alcohol, to Scarpetti's fried breakfasts with grated Parmesan cheese, to high-tar cigarettes and to prescription drugs. He'd been taking Prozac for about five years now, ever since his wife had left him. You weren't supposed to be on it for that long, but Doctor Armstrong at the Health Centre didn't seem too bothered about it, so neither was Colin. He simply kept on with the repeat prescription and there was never a problem. The great thing about the Prozac, Colin had found, was that it smoothed you out. It left you feeling a little less on edge, more satisfied, like you'd already had a couple of glasses of wine, and maybe a gin and tonic a half-hour or so before that, and a small ramekin of hand-cooked crisps, or some Bombay mix. With the Prozac Colin found it easier to take difficult decisions. For example, the decision he had just made: he knew that if he went to press with what he had on Frank Gilbey there'd be trouble. But the Prozac had helped him to understand that he really had no choice. The Prozac offered him the reassurance he needed.

Colin had said to himself, 'I don't know about this. This story is going to be controversial.'

And the Prozac had said, 'Whatever.'

This was going to be Colin Rimmer's ticket out of here. This was what was finally going to release him from his dependence, his addiction to this town. He had solved a bona fide mystery and now he could leave. He had earned his passage. He was away. Colin had always kept a cycling machine in his office, because he'd read that Harold Evans used to keep a machine in his office, and Harold Evans was another hero. Colin's cycling machine was planted right in front of the window, amidst the piles of papers, overlooking the car park and the Quality Hotel, and he liked to cycle for twenty miles every morning while watching the breakfast news, and sometimes while he cycled and watched TV he imagined himself cycling up and out of the window and up and up and over the car park, over the top of the Quality Hotel, like the boys in *ET*, which was his all-time favourite film, and over the ocean to the offices of the *New Yorker*, where he would park his bicycle outside, and go upstairs and sit down at his manual typewriter and bang out a Talk of the Town.*

Recently, while he'd been cycling, though, Colin had not been thinking about *ET* or the *New Yorker*. He had been thinking about Frank Gilbey. There had been plenty of times the *Impartial Recorder* could have gone for Frank, but they hadn't; Colin had held off, or his hand had been stayed. There was the mysterious slurry run-off, for example, a few years ago, on the fields around Bloom's, which had ruined many farmers' land, and which had allowed for the mall development not only to go ahead but to expand far beyond its original intended limits: Frank was behind it, Colin was sure, but he'd been unable to get enough proof. Then there was the problem with the supply of shoddy materials being used in the building of Bloom's: large parts of the roof had to be replaced within six months of the mall having opened, at huge expense; the main roofing contractor had subcontracted to a

* And it's not completely unfeasible: we do feature in the *New Yorker*, after all, or we have done in the past, just the once, admittedly, but that's better than nothing, courtesy of the tap-dancing McLaughlin twins, who got a mention in a 'Notes and Comments' in August 1943, the great E. B. White comparing the McLaughlins' 'bouncy little dance' in the Broadway musical *Hold on to Your Hats* with the frantic mating rituals of the natural world. Two of our local boys, two of *us*, exciting a lovely little bit of thistledown prose from a master of the form with their soft-shoe shuffle; that certainly put us on the map. The cutting still survives, framed in gilt, on the wall of Dot McLaughlin's Happy Feet Tap and Ballet School, and 'That's what can happen, if you practise,' Dot tells her pupils, tapping the frame: she means it as an encouragement, but a lot of her pupils look at the fading yellow scrap and regard it as a warning. 'That's it?' they think. 'That's as good as it gets?' Well, yes, it is.

subcontractor who had subcontracted to one of Frank's development companies, but the complicated paperchase had been too much for Colin to handle on his own. And then, of course, there was the general, unexceptional, unremarked awarding of council contracts to companies either owned by or connected to Frank: Colin knew what went on, everyone knew what went on, but that was just the way things were around here and if that's the way things were, that's the way they stayed. There was nothing you could do about it. Colin had other fish to fry. He couldn't get too excited about it. He remained, as it were, impassive. But in late November, Frank Gilbey had given Colin the excuse he needed and the determination to become implacable.

Colin could just about cope with running sycophantic interviews with councillors: that was part of the job. He could just about cope with the paper's ridiculous new red masthead, which made it look like an amateur tabloid, but which he agreed was a necessary updating, and he'd managed the big change from the old Linotype machines to computers and photocomposition, which, in his opinion, made the paper look like a cheap photocopied newsletter, and which took away all the romance involved in going to press. He could just about cope with Justin's continual demands for increases in advertising space, which paid for the paper, after all, and the occasional use of press releases as news, which Colin justified to himself as being due to a lack of staffing. He could even cope with the ghastly syndicated pictures of so-called celebrities, which had begun to creep into the pages, and the slow steady drip of disinformation from the council's press officer, who now handled all enquiries regarding local council business. The police were the same: you couldn't get to talk to anyone any more up at the station or in the pubs. It all went through the press office. That was understandable, that was OK. What Colin could not cope with, though, was the distortion of facts. Colin may not have been a Woodward or a Bernstein, he may have failed in all his early ambitions, but he liked to think that his paper stuck to the facts. Facts, Colin believed, were the life and blood of a paper, the spirit and the soul, and they were sacred. Facts could not be bought and sold, and to suggest that they could was sacrilege. So as far as Colin was concerned, Frank Gilbey had committed the sin against the Holy Spirit.

In early November, Frank had asked Colin to run a story suggesting that Bloom's would be reporting a pre-Christmas surge in profits and that they were predicting their best Christmas yet.

But Colin knew *for a fact* that this was not the case.

Colin knew that consumer spending was down. He had enough contacts at Bloom's himself to do his own digging. John 'The Leatherman' Brown had been a friend of Colin's parents – he was into light opera and listened all day to Classic FM – and he kept Colin informed of what was happening up there at the mall. There were rumours, according to John, that some of the bigger stores, which were owned by multi-nationals, were going to be issuing profits warnings.

Frank had suggested to Colin, over lunch in the Plough and the Stars, that the story had to be run 'for the sake of the town', and that was it, that was too much for Colin. *For the sake of the town!* Frank Gilbey was not interested in our town. Frank Gilbey had destroyed the town. Frank was responsible for the three things that had ruined the way we were, the way Colin remembered things: the ring road, Bloom's and the luxury apartments. These three things had destroyed the little micro-communities that had made up the town, communities that you'd have hardly known existed, but which made the town what it was, the little communities where people had grown up, where Colin grew up, and Davey Quinn, and Francie McGinn, and Bob Savory, and Cherith, and Sammy, and Bobbie Dylan, all of us, places with no names but with their own little small row of shops, and a patch of waste ground or a scrap of park where you could play football and smoke, and fight wars, places where twenty-four-hour garages had now replaced the shops, and where the waste ground now housed exciting developments of luxury loft-style apartments, with electric gates and high fencing all round. Colin knew that this was progress, but he wasn't so foolish as to think it was a good thing. The town had been destroyed and Frank Gilbey was largely responsible, so when Frank stuffed a big artery-clogging slice of Banoffee pie into his big fat greedy mouth and uttered that phrase, 'for the sake of the town', Colin's heart was hardened against him.

Over coffee – which he took black, no sugar, with characteristic fortitude – Colin decided to return to the chase. He had a paper to run and his resources were limited, but he had someone now he could trust, who would do his bidding and do his digging for him, and that someone was Billy Nibbs.

Billy had loved being a part of the paper. He loved being among people who regarded writing as a natural, normal experience, and an activity for which it was possible to get paid. To get paid, for writing: that was just incredible for Billy. For Billy, writing had always been a troubled and troubling enterprise, something you did in private and in secrecy, and which offered no prospect of paying its own way. To Billy Nibbs working at the *Impartial Recorder* was therefore like attending a banquet at the court of an all-powerful king – it was both delicious and corrupting. In his first few weeks at the paper he'd been invited out a couple of times by the legendary Tudor Cassady, the Arts and Features editor, a man almost as wide as he is tall, who lives up to his name by resembling in all but crown and furs the late Henry VIII and who writes the 'Forks and Corks' column, and who has done so for over thirty years, and whose little chin-bearded face peers out from a photograph at the top of the page, for all the world as if he were about to issue the command, 'Off with Their Heads!'

Billy couldn't believe he was actually being paid to eat out. Tudor also gave him a few books from the stash on his desk. They were first novels, mostly, but still. They were free – free books! He was even sent to see a play for free. It felt like he'd died and gone to heaven. Billy had had no idea that this sort of thing went on, in our town.

It was when he wrote his first review that Billy finally felt he had crossed over. He was no longer a creator but a destroyer and he realised that there was no going back. He was no longer a poet. He had become a journalist. The play he went to see was in the town's playhouse – and yes, we do have one, although it remains a well-kept secret, Dreams, a tiny theatre on McAuley Street, which is in the premises of the old Home for the Industrious Blind, and which exists largely because of the fund-raising efforts of Colin Rimmer's parents, Fee and Philip, who believed that what our town really needed back in the dark days of the 1970s was somewhere people could go to see Alan Ayckbourn plays and hear Gilbert and Sullivan. In fact, Dreams is used mostly for theatre in education projects, where children are taught about the evils of drugs and under-age sex by out-of-work actors from the city who stand outside after their performances, smoking, signing autographs and struggling with their sexuality.

Billy knew people in the play he was sent to review, which was a modern dress version of *The Duchess of Malfi* – he'd actually been to school with the Duchess herself, who was played by Laura Buckle in a black wig and a 1920s cocktail dress. He sat up all night after the performance, eating biscuits and drinking cans of Red Bull, and writing what amounted to a complete demolition, a total destruction of what he'd just seen: if he could have pulled down the scenery and the proscenium arch as well he probably would have done. He spent a lot of his time trying to find synonyms for 'pathetic' and 'risible' in *Roget's Thesaurus*, and consulting Colin Rimmer's in-house style book, which now took pride of place on his desk at the end of his bed, replacing his once prized rhyming dictionary. When he handed in the piece the next day, Colin himself had seen to it, ripping through it with a red pen and interrogating Billy over every phrase and sentence – 'What do we mean here?' he would ask and Billy would try to explain, and Colin would say, 'No, I think what we mean here is this' and then he'd rewrite the passage, minus adjectives and clauses. When the piece was published later that week Billy bought two copies of the paper – one for everyday use and one to keep – and when he read the review he did feel a little guilty about what he'd written, particularly his criticism of the Duchess, whom he described as having a face like a mouldy potato and a voice like toasted ham and cheese, which was supposed to be a joke, but then he bumped into Laura Buckle when he was in Tom Hines's one day buying his bacon, and he tried a sheepish smile, but she looked right through him and he realised that that was that. It was too late. There was no going back. The die was cast.

Billy gave in, then, to the impulse to criticise everything and everybody. There was hardly a meal or a play or a book or a film that came his way that was not in some way deficient and which Billy did not take great pleasure in picking apart, for his own education and amusement, and for the education and amusement of others. Unknown to him, he had passed the test: Colin had wanted to see if he had what it took. And he did. Billy had proved to have that rare combination of utter cynicism and unbounded enthusiasm which was required by the good jobbing journalist. Years of working at the dump had already confirmed Billy in his belief that people are basically dirty, smelly, waste-producing animals, whose remains and discards are good merely as food for vermin, wild dogs and seagulls, with the rest fit only to be burned or buried in a hole, and his reading of the work of the great modernist writers had convinced him of the same. He therefore had the makings of a truly great local journalist:

326

he was a bitter man with huge dreams who was capable of infinite disappointment.

So he was more than prepared when Colin had set him on to Frank Gilbey.

'Imagine you're writing a review,' Colin had said. 'Except this time it's a review of someone's life.'

Billy had no idea what he was looking for, but he knew where to start and he spent weeks in the *Impartial Recorder*'s old basement composing room, which had become the de facto library and archive, trawling through back issues of damp and crumbly bound volumes. He took notes and he set up interviews.

But the breakthrough, when it came, like every lucky break, was not from some insight gained through research, but from a tip-off from a man in a pub. Billy had been in the Castle Arms, talking to his old friend Noel Savage, who is a landscape gardener. When he was still working up at the dump Billy used to allow Noel to offload straight from his trailer without using the weighbridge: tradesmen were supposed to pay a small fee for dumping, according to the size of the load, but Billy turned a blind eye for friends and people who were polite. Noel happened to mention to Billy that he was working on Frank Gilbey's garden, thinning out some of the trees, sorting out a couple of the borders, and Billy had asked Noel, offhand and unthinkingly, if he'd seen the famous horse trough and the drinking fountain that had gone missing, all those years ago, and which people always claimed had ended up at Frank's. Noel laughed and said he couldn't remember seeing them, but he said that Billy could accompany him to the garden if he wanted to, to check for himself.

Billy checked back first in the basement for old photos of the trough and the fountain, and he found some archive pictures from the 1950s, when the town still looked complete and still made sense, untouched by the spoiling hand of developers. It wasn't until 1984, after the completion of the road-widening scheme at the junction of High Street and Main Street that anyone noticed that the trough and the water fountain had gone missing, and before anyone could protest they had been replaced with concrete bollards and a couple of trees in circular tree grates, and a bronze so-called piece of sculpture which looked like a man with half his head melted, all supplied by a firm owned by Frank Gilbey.

Billy dressed in his old boots and boiler suit to accompany Noel to the garden. It was a nice garden. Gardens in our town tend not to contain many mature trees, or flowers – they're more trouble than they're worth. We're more of an evergreen shrubby kind of a town, with the average plot not in excess of about 12 foot by 8. Frank's garden, in comparison, was something more like the forest of Arden, or the grounds at the palace at Versailles. Frank lives in a big bluff red-brick mansion, the biggest and the bluffest in town, right up at the far end of Fitzroy Avenue, where the town used to become country, and where it now becomes the ring road. Noel pointed out to Billy some of the plants trained up against the house: a wisteria, and a *magnolia lennei*, he said, and a palm, a *trachycarpus fortunei*. Billy wrote these words down in his notebook and asked Noel to spell them for him, in case they came in useful, 'for colour', Billy had said and Noel had nodded, impressed. Noel had only known Billy as the man at the dump, and Billy only knew Noel as a gardener; he had no idea that a gardener might know some Latin, and Noel had no idea that Billy might want to write. It is customary here in town to underestimate other people – this is how small towns work. If you want a slap on the back for just being who you are, well, you're welcome to live in the city, where there are plenty of people who'll tell you how great you are. In a city, people talk each other up, that's the deal: everybody's great and everything is wonderful. In a town, we prefer to talk things down. If you think you're special, or you want people to think you're a genius, don't get to know your neighbours.

Spreading out in front of the flagged terrace at the back of the house there was a huge lawn, surrounded by mixed borders, and again Noel pointed out various shrubs and herbaceous plants. 'Nicely done,' he said, indicating to Billy how the shrubs broke up the line of vision, and created the impression of depth and space.

Billy agreed and he was pleased for Noel, that he was obviously an artist too, but he still couldn't see what he was looking for. Then, at the end of the lawn they passed through into a rose garden, with some old-fashioned shrub roses on trellis-work, and they came upon some pathways leading to different areas – an enormous old greenhouse at the end of one path, a small pool surrounded by hostas and shaded by tall trees down another. Variegated poplars, Billy wrote in his notebook, prompted by Noel. Mature oak. Eucalyptus.

'What about down here?' Billy asked eventually, pointing down another gravel pathway. Noel had never been down there, and so they crunched their way past a long winding hedge and there, in the very farthest corner of the garden, hidden from the view of the house and from the Old Green Road running along outside, was a patio area, set with tables, and a large stone horse trough and a marble drinking fountain.

Billy had his scoop. He'd brought a camera with him. He took the photos.

Cigars all round.

As soon as he got the photos, Colin had made an appointment to go and see Sir George Sanderson, the proprietor.

Colin did not like Sir George, but he had to admire him, because Sanderson was old enough and rich enough not to care what people thought about him or his opinions, and actually his opinions happened to be pretty much Colin's own: like Colin, Sir George was counter-intuitive, except he was counter-intuitive by breeding rather than by choice. He simply knew that what most people thought was right was often wrong, that hunting was a good, for example, and that nuclear power was absolutely fine and not something to get all fussed-up about. He didn't need to work out his opinions, like his wife had to. He had inherited them, along with the estate.

When Colin arrived he found Sir George and Lesley Sanderson in the library, hoovering. They no longer kept a staff and they did pretty much everything themselves. Colin knew they'd lost a lot of money a few years back, when the dotcom bubble burst, having invested heavily in their gay son's on-line dating business, but this was something that was not talked about.*

'Rimmer!' said Sir George. 'Good of you to come. Well?' Sir George did not waste his words. You didn't get to where Sir George is on pleasantries and chat.

'I have a story that I want to run, but it might be a bit controversial,' said Colin, who wasn't a great one for the small talk himself.

'Controversial! Good! That's what the place needs. A good shaking up. Nothing to do with me I trust?'

'No. But it does concern Frank Gilbey.'

Sir George had known Frank Gilbey for many years and he'd done a lot of business with him – who hadn't? – so there was a bond of loyalty there. Then again, Frank was a horrid

---

* Alex, their son, was a merchant banker who'd attended Barneville House and Emmanuel College, Cambridge, and who had a Harvard MBA and who'd lived for some years in New York and who thought he was pretty smart, actually, all things considered, and who moved to London to ride the crest of the dotcom wave, back in 1999, and who'd persuaded his parents and some venture capitalists to plough vast amounts of money into his can't-fail on-line dating business, and who was bankrupt within a year. He's bounced back, though, of course – you can't keep the likes of Alex down. He's in Moscow now, working for Coutts, and he owns his own dacha and at weekends he drinks vodka until he can't see and he entertains young Russians in his private banya, beating them with twigs. Life's not so bad, for Alex – he lives a life not dissimilar to his ancestors – but, alas, relations with his parents have irretrievably broken down.

little man, who'd ogled Lesley at one of those dreadful Rotary Club dinners a few years ago, and he dressed like an American gangster. Sir George glanced at Lesley, who raised her eyebrows non-committally – she'd never liked Frank, for obvious reasons. He was common.

'Is it business?' asked Sir George.

'No,' said Colin. 'It's personal.'

'Well, I can't see any problem then.'

Colin started to open his mouth to tell Sir George the details.

'No!' said Sir George. 'No need to know.' If he didn't know he could always deny it. 'Run it past the lawyers, though, won't you?'

End of conversation.

End of Frank Gilbey.

The story was going in tomorrow.

And there was still champagne to be drunk tonight.

21

Christmas Eve

A concluding cyclorama

The snow, when it came, started as a flurry, hardly enough to worry even the most anxious of bookmakers – in our case here the Cuddys, Hugh and Eamonn, twins, two men in grey suits who look like greyhounds but who enjoy all the human vices, or at least all those available to the middle-aged man of means here in town. They like to smoke whatever they can lay their hands on and to drink to excess at home and at length in public bars, and to use just a touch of gel on their thinning hair and a dab too much cologne in the mornings. They like to do these things, to commit these small-town sins, almost as much as they like to gamble. The Cuddys are men for whom a day has almost never gone by without them placing, accepting, collecting or paying out on a bet. They were racing snails at the age of three, they ran a poker school pretty much full-time at St Gall's, worked as tick-tack men down south in their teens, and once they'd reached their twenties they'd travelled the length and breadth of the country and been back and forth to America, surviving only on bar bets and working their system in clubs and casinos. They'd been barred from more places than the average punter could even dream of visiting, and they only retired from full-time gambling when Eamonn broke both his hips when he was thrown down some concrete stairs by bouncers acting on the instructions of the management at a casino in Reno. These days you can tell the difference between the twins quite easily. Eamonn's the one who walks with the sticks and Hugh is starting to get a little heavy – his wife, Patti, is American, from Toledo, Ohio. Hugh met her in an all-you-can-eat seafood restaurant in Chicago, where she served him big bowls of chowder and half a dozen plates of lobster and langoustine, and she's a great cook, renowned for her generous hand with the butter and spices, and in the evenings, after dinner and before bed, she and Hugh play poker, which makes her pretty much the perfect partner according to Hugh, and according to Eamonn also, who just wishes that Patti had a sister.

People say that alcoholics should never run pubs and that gamblers should never run a bookie's, but who else would bother? Here in town, as elsewhere, you don't so much choose a profession as it chooses you: here we are lived by our lives rather than the other way around.

The Cuddys have to pay out for a white Christmas only if flakes are actually falling on Christmas Day, so a chilly wind and some sleet on Christmas Eve are nothing for them to worry about. Even snow on the ground on Christmas Day, deep and crisp and even, doesn't count – it actually has to be coming down on the day itself and the chances of that, as the Cuddys could tell you, are pretty slim – so they were comfortable in the Castle Arms, the pair of them, as was their wont on Christmas Eve, their frowns and stoops as yet unsoothed and undiminished by drink and tobacco, smoothing their hair, straightening their ties, preparing themselves for some serious end-of-season drinking and reflecting on another good year.

We like to gamble here in town as much as anyone else, although we probably gamble smaller sums of money and with a lot less expertise – Wonderland, the big new Bingo hall up at Bloom's is the closest thing we have to a casino – and the brothers Cuddy have done well out of us. It's horses for most of us, of course, but we have also been known to throw away our money on football and dogs, and every other kind of game, race, fight, or pointless endeavour that humans can possibly have a punt on. The Cuddys had opened a book on the Third World War a while back, and there was even some money coming in from that. Not at Christmas, though: people tend to lose interest in wars around Christmas. They have their families to think about.

The flurries had started around eight, just as Margaret was pulling Hugh his first pint and Eamonn was tucking into the first of his double whiskeys, which he drank several of daily, medicinally, for the sake of his hips. They were drinking the proceeds from the annual White Christmas bets – people never seemed to learn. When the pint had settled, Hugh raised his glass and proposed a toast to the ghost of Charles Dickens. They have a lot to thank Dickens for, the Cuddys: the idea of snow in particular.

Mr Donelly – a Dickensian figure if ever we had one, a man despairing of decency and who might well have suited a frock coat and beard, had he been born a couple of hundred years earlier, which frankly he wished he had – was himself setting out for the pub that selfsame evening, at around the same time, at the beginning of the flurry, stone-cold sober but completely befuddled, with his dog, Rusty, who like all good dogs is a thoroughly Dickensian dog, generous in every way, limited only in intelligence, and shabby-genteel in the style of a cross-breed and the lower middle classes. Recently the dog has not been well. She's incontinent, and Mr Donelly wondered also if she was going senile – she hadn't been behaving the best. There'd been lots of rages and barking, and her coat was turning grey. Mr Donelly was already having to give her anti-inflammatory drugs for her arthritis, and the poor thing had been bitten by another dog a few months back and her left ear had been stitched back on, a bit wonky, by

Becky Badger in her Animal Centre and Pet Surgery. It broke Mr Donelly's heart these days to see the dog shuffling along in front of him and himself shuffling along behind. He'd nearly skipped the walk tonight, but he didn't want to be in an empty house on Christmas Eve.

Once his wife had been decently buried and his children had returned to their former lives, briefly interrupted, Mr Donelly found himself alone with his dog and living the life of an indigent gentleman. He would wake early in the morning and dress straight away, in clothes he had left folded on the end of the bed, clothes which he had to admit he no longer changed every day. He'd always felt that fresh, clean clothes were an extravagance, like embossed toilet tissue, and he felt he had now been proved right. Constant washing, of the self, of one's clothes and of the house, was a kind of conspiracy, according to Mr Donelly, like so much else in modern life. Mr Donelly believed that democracy was a chimera; he believed that if voting changed anything they would have abolished it; that the European Union was an unmitigated evil; that modern washing powder rotted clothes; that cleaning products were a waste of money; and that for most chores and grooming purposes you'd be better off using some bicarbonate of soda mixed with a little vinegar. If the worst came to the worst, a bit of borax did for most things. He had never been able to convince Mrs Donelly of these obvious truths, but he hadn't bought a single bottle of bleach now since she'd died and the toilet looked just fine, and he could easily stretch his clothes for a week, if not more, and no one ever noticed, or at least no one commented. And Europe was a mess and the country was going to the dogs. So.

He'd quickly established a new routine. Routine was everything when you were living alone. He would get up, put on his stinky clothes, use the rimey toilet, and go and walk the dog, and buy a newspaper from Eva in Wine's, and then go into Scarpetti's, where he would drink boiled tea and eat cold toast and occasionally have the fry, although the Parmesan cheese was not to his taste early in the morning or indeed at any other time of day, and he stuck to brown sauce. He sometimes sat with Billy Nibbs if he was in – he'd known Billy's father, Hugh, and like every other decent dog owner in town he was sad when Hugh had died, the death of our last real and jolly butcher, with the consequent loss of a ready supply of free scraps and bones. Tom Hines, the remaining so-called and miserable butcher, charges for bones, which is outrageous, clearly, and a sure sign of a civilisation, or at least a small town in decline. So Rusty was back on the Pedigree Chum. She seemed not to mind. It was Mr Donelly who minded. Feeding the dog from the butcher's had always appealed to Mr Donelly's great sense of the tragedy of life, life as a series of bloody scraps and bones thrown down into the sawdust from the butcher's block. But you get no real sense of pathos from a can, and the sight of a two-kilo bag of multicoloured doggy biscuits just about summed up what the world had come to for Mr Donelly.

After his cup of tea and his toast in Scarpetti's, Mr Donelly would take a stroll home and potter around in the garden or in the house until lunchtime, which was any time between about 10.30 in the morning and 3 in the afternoon. Sometimes he skipped lunch, in fact, and went straight from breakfast to a kind of high tea around 4, plus a late-night supper, or an early-morning breakfast and an early lunch and a full dinner later on, but sometimes breakfast, lunch, tea, dinner and supper all just seemed to segue from one into another, to merge into one vast unregulated day-long snack. He was surviving like a dog on scraps, in fact, eating when he wanted to, whatever he wanted to. He was eating a lot of frozen potato waffles at the moment, actually, having worked his way through everything else that was in the cupboards and the freezer, and he couldn't understand why everyone didn't eat them, they were so easy: you just pop them in the toaster and they're done, and you can have anything you like on them. He liked a fried egg himself, or a couple of tinned sardines – he could eat that any time of the day or night. It was a movable feast.*

In the afternoon he sometimes watched TV: the TV was great company, he'd found. Mrs Donelly had always been a great one for the quiz programmes and the soaps, and Mr Donelly had never really bothered with them, he'd always stuck to sport and documentaries and films. But actually some of the quiz programmes on in the afternoons were quite good, he was surprised. You got a sense from some of them that the presenters actually knew you, which was nice. He was even coming round to the soaps. You could get quite involved in the stories after a while. In fact, Mr Donelly had ended up watching nearly all of Mrs Donelly's programmes, as if he had somehow inherited them from her. Maybe this is what people mean when they say that an individual lives on through the lives of others. All good things must come to an end, but TV goes on and on, and now, with videos and satellite and cable, your love for *Fawlty Towers*, say, or the early episodes of *Countdown* need never die.

Mr Donelly was also spending more and more time up at Bloom's. He probably spent at least two days a week up there, and he would pop in first to see people he knew when he was working in the delivery warehouse, and then he'd go to one of the coffee shops – to Café Kilimanjaro, which does a nice caramel square, made properly, the old-fashioned way with condensed milk, or to Bradley's, which is designed more for the young people, with big sofas and video screens but

---

* Biscuits, also, were a godsend. Eaten with cheese, Mr Donelly found that three digestives provided him with a perfectly satisfactory lunch, with perhaps a custard cream or a bourbon to follow. He'd never been keen on pasta, and he now also avoided potatoes and rice – the only complex carbohydrate he could still be bothered with was bread. He bought a small white lodger twice a week from the Brown and Yellow Cake Shop. He found he could no longer stomach heavy bread.

which does free coffee refills, an innovation Mr Donelly would have liked to see copied across town. He'd mentioned it to Mr Hemon in Scarpetti's, but Mr Hemon had just laughed.

'Why not?' Mr Donelly had asked.

'Coffee costs money,' replied Mr Hemon, before plating up another fry.

There was no answer to that and it got Mr Donelly to wondering how Bradley's could afford to do it. It was probably because, while Mr Hemon charged 40p for a cup of coffee, Bradley's charged £1.50. To get his money's worth from Bradley's Mr Donelly had therefore started drinking up to five cups of coffee at a sitting, which was no mean feat for a man of his age and with his bladder. You got to watch a lot of MTV on five cups of coffee; five cups of coffee represents an awful lot of flesh and jiggling around.

If he was spending the day up at Bloom's, after his coffee and his tray bake and the toilet Mr Donelly would wander around the shops, in a kind of caffeine-and-sugar-and-MTV daze, refreshed and tingling, not buying anything, just looking at all the nice bright clothes in Gap, and the shiny new glasses in Specsavers. Lovely stuff, all of it. He particularly liked a shop called Fine Things, which sold the full range of fine things, including Lilliput Lane, and the Harmony, Kingdom and Sherratt ranges of whimsies and figurines, Royal Doulton, Tyrone Crystal, Swarovski, and a whole lot of other sorts of china and glassware. He could spend hours browsing, which was strange because he'd never have done anything like it before with Mrs Donelly. He used to leave all the shopping to her – he took no interest in or responsibility for things like shopping. To his knowledge he'd never even bought anyone a birthday or Christmas present, not even Mrs Donelly herself. He just used to give her the money and she'd spend it in the January sales, usually buying herself a new nightie: Mr Donelly had never known a woman like it with the nighties. A new one every year, at least, by his calculation, while he'd been running the same two pairs of pyjamas in tandem since the early 1970s. He'd miss the new nighties, though. He looked at them in Marks, trying to guess which Mrs Donelly would have chosen – she was quite daring, actually, right into her sixties. She'd probably have gone for the one with the puffy sleeves and the plunging neckline.

He wished he'd known about browsing round the shops, that it was so relaxing. When he'd worked in the warehouse at Bloom's it was just like working in a warehouse anywhere, and he'd hardly ever set foot in the mall, but now he'd really come to appreciate the atmosphere and the environment – warm and welcoming, without being too stuffy. He'd turned off all the radiators in the house because he didn't agree with central heating, so it was nice to go somewhere where there was a bit of heat and no draughts, a nice, safe, controlled, constant environment, where the unpredictable had been all but eliminated. Uniform temperature. Uniform light. Men in uniforms at the door. Mr Donelly had used to think it was like a morgue, Bloom's, like you see on the telly in detective programmes about serial killers and psychopaths, and it was, a bit: the temperature, the humidity, the cleanliness. No windows. No street noise or dirt. He used to think it was all artificial and he didn't like it. But now it suited him and he didn't think it was like a morgue at all any more. It was the opposite, in fact: Bloom's seemed to him full of all of the possibilities of life. Youth, warmth, companionship. It was absolutely true, the slogan: 'Every Day a Good Day, Regardless of the Weather'. He had to leave the dog outside, but that was OK. Bloom's was clearly no place for an incontinent Dickensian mongrel like Rusty. The only dogs you ever saw in Bloom's were guidedogs for the blind, stately Labradors, dogs which looked like they only ever ate from Marks & Spencer's.

While he was wandering round Bloom's, Mr Donelly was busy working through the stages of grief, although he didn't know it. His children knew it, of course. Mark had e-mailed

Jackie and Tim with a link to a website that explained the processes of grieving. Mr Donelly had missed out on the website, obviously – he didn't even have a mobile phone, let alone a computer. He didn't even really agree with the cordless phone, which Mrs Donelly had bought to replace their perfectly good trimphone with an excellent long curly flex. You knew where you were with a phone with a cord: cordless phones were a menace, according to Mr Donelly. Mrs Donelly never used to put it back on its stand – one time she left it in the pocket of her cardigan and it went in the wash. It was lucky it was only woollens.

The website had been quite a help for the children. According to the site, in any period of grieving there is first the stage of denial, which lasts a few weeks. This is when you keep trying to live the life you lived before. In Mr Donelly's case this stage was apparent in his attempt to keep eating the same food he had always eaten, trying to re-create the meals Mrs Donelly used to cook. Unfortunately, he had no idea how to make a cottage pie, or how to do that thing she did with lamb cutlets and potatoes in the casserole, and after a few weeks there didn't seem to be much point in trying, or putting out a place setting, or coming up with a different pudding for every night of the week, so he'd started eating his microwaveable ready-meals sitting on the sofa, watching TV.

This represented the end of the stage of denial, after which, according to the website, comes the stage of shock and disbelief, which is when you find yourself sitting on your sofa watching *Countdown*, eating a Pot Noodle at four o'clock in the afternoon, completely alone, and you suddenly realise that your old life has vanished, has gone for ever and will never return. This is when you realise that you are not on holiday, that this thing, this sense of devastation and loss is permanent. This is when you cry.

Which is bad enough, but then comes guilt and disorientation. Mr Donelly's frequent visits to Bloom's and his eating of frozen potato waffles might safely be said to have marked this stage in his grieving – every time he bit into the salty-sweet mush that was a toasted potato waffle, and every time he sat drinking his quart of coffee staring up at the video screen showing MTV and the wriggling teenagers, and all the people rushing about from supermarket to discount designer clothing outlet, he was reinforcing his complete and utter inability to understand who he was, where he was and what the hell he was doing.

His son Mark had sent him a pack, from America, called *The Book of Death*, which was a kind of a scrapbook bound in imitation red vellum, where you were supposed to paste in your favourite photos of your dearly departed and make a note of special memories. It was a new thing, Mr Donelly supposed. The booklet that came with it said that *The Book of Death* would help the grieving individual to achieve something called 'closure'. Mr Donelly wasn't exactly sure what 'closure' meant. All he knew was that he didn't have it. He was open all hours at the moment, frankly, Mr Donelly, like the petrol stations on the ring road and like Bloom's itself – his emotions were open to all comers and to all traffic, and seemed to be illuminated by those same sodium lights that gave the town at night its horrible flat yellowish tinge. He was sick from his twenty-four-hour grieving.

What was really strange, though, and what was horrid was that he couldn't seem to get Mrs Donelly clear in his mind at all any more, and what he could remember came to him only in sudden vivid bursts, huge arousals of memory, which seemed to loom up within him several times a day and sometimes at night, flooding him with emotion, leaving him shaken and exhausted. Washing his socks, for example, one day, loading them into the washing machine out in the garage at 7 in the morning, he remembered their old twin tub, and he suddenly saw Mrs Donelly standing there, in his memory, with a big pair of wooden tongs in her hand, and he just started blubbing like a baby, right there, about to put on a cool wash with some bicarbonate of soda instead of washing powder, unable to control himself. It was terrible. It was Mrs Donelly, but she was kind of mixed up with memories of his own mother as well. It was confusing.

Another time he went to brush his teeth and the brush felt damp when he picked it up, and he remembered arguing with Mrs Donelly about her using his toothbrush once, and that set him off again, unable to control himself, wiping snot and tears on his pyjamas, and he had to watch TV and drink whiskey for hours afterwards to steady himself.

They'd had the conversation, of course, him and Mrs Donelly, about what it was going to be like and how he was going to cope.

'What am I going to do without you?' he'd said.

'You'll be fine,' she'd said, 'everything'll be fine,' which is pretty much what she'd said to every difficulty and crisis over the years, and she'd been right, of course, and when she said it he just took it for granted that it was true.

But there was no one there to tell him now, he had to tell himself, and unfortunately it wasn't true any longer: everything was not going to be fine. Everything was not going to be all right.

He was thinking about her now, walking the dog through the sleet. He was wondering what to put on the headstone. How to remember her. How not to remember her.

The flurry was getting heavier. He was walking down Main Street.

Over there, where the old gas holder used to be, it had been waste ground for years, before it had been turned into the Pay and Display car park, and he could remember picking primroses there on the waste ground, on Good Friday, him and Mrs Donelly and the children, and it felt like yesterday, and he could still see Jackie falling over and hear her crying, and she must have been what, two years old?

342

And over there he could remember standing outside what was once the Co-op and is now a building society, swapping fag cards with his friend Joe Mahon, who was dead twenty years now, who was crushed in an accident up at the quarry. Mr Donelly had swapped him a Jack Hobbs for a Larwood.

And here, right here, right outside the Kentucky Fried Chicken, he could remember the rat he saw once when he was coming home from the Castle Arms one night, only recently – what, ten, fifteen years ago? It was as big as a dog, that rat. You could have put a leash round its neck and led it around town and had children riding on its back.

And over there, running down Commercial Street towards Main Street, there used to be a little stream they called the Lea where he used to catch minnows and chubbies as a child. The stream had long since disappeared. God only knew where it had gone – underground.

And here, here he could remember once when he'd been cycling home from work, long before they had a car, he was fined five shillings for riding his bike without lights. That was right here.

He had no idea where it had all gone, all of that, the things he'd known.

And now all these things he hadn't known.

He was keeping the birth certificate in his wallet.

He had no idea what to do with that kind of knowledge.

Nothing, probably – that's what we tend to do with knowledge here in town, if we possibly can.

Mr Donelly concentrated on making it to the pub. He noted that the traffic signals controlling the traffic exiting Commercial Street at the junction with Main Street had been altered: the timings had been changed. He always noticed such things out on his walks.

Which is why, this evening, he noticed the Quality Hotel.

*   *   *

So did Francie and Cherith, who were parked in the car park in front of the hotel. They were talking. Or, at least, Francie was talking and Cherith was listening, carefully and without excitement or resentment, to what he had to say. It was extraordinary, actually, she found it quite amazing, the mild-ness she felt these days towards Francie – a man who had once been her own husband. The man for whom she had once cooked and cleaned and kept house. The man she had prayed with twice a day, the man for whom and with whom she had given her life to Jesus, stepping into Eternity with him, and the man she now recognised as being an averagely weak-minded and merely typically feeble individual.

He had a better haircut, though, she had to admit. But then so did she. They had both lost a lot in their divorce – each other specifically, obviously – but they had also gained something. Francie had gained a sex life, for example, and a new lease of life as a minister, and he wondered sometimes if these two things were connected, which worried him. And Cherith had gained the business and Sammy.

Francie was talking now to Cherith about God, and about forgiveness, and about King David, which is pretty much what Cherith had expected him to talk about. She had been married to him, after all, for over ten years, so she knew pretty much what he was going to say at any particular moment and in any circumstance. There were people in town – Francie clearly among them – who would have said that Francie and Cherith were destined to get back together. But Cherith did not believe in destiny. There was no way they could possibly have got back together, not really. Francie had not only been her husband, he had been her best friend, and he had cheated her. He had let her down. And besides, now she had Sammy.

As they sat talking in the front of Cherith's car, a Mercedes, a car which Cherith didn't know she needed until she got it and which she could not now imagine living without, she thought about all the things she and Francie had had together

– a second-hand Toyota Corolla and a house up on the Longfields Estate, and she thought, well, all things considered, I quite like what I have now. Sammy was going through a bit of a rough patch, admittedly, but they'd get through that together.

Francie, meanwhile, was thinking entirely other things. He was convinced he was winning the argument. Strange how even here in our town, a place where we all went to the same schools, where we all wear the same kind of clothes, pretty much, give or take the occasional item of eccentric holiday headgear or party high heels, and where we watch the same television programmes, and eat the same kind of food at the same kind of time, and read the same papers, even here it's possible for two people occupying the same space and time and the same brand of jeans and trainers to misunderstand each other completely and utterly. It does not bode well for the future of humankind – if we can't read each other right around here, then where? We talk and nobody listens, and what we care about others despise: every day here we disprove the ideals of human communication.

Francie knew that he could no longer sustain his relationship with Bobbie Dylan. She was destroying his ministry. He could no longer pray effectively, he was no longer seriously studying the Scriptures, and he was ashamed at some of the antics they'd got up to, in public and in private. He bitterly regretted dressing up in a gorilla suit, for example, for a children's service about original sin, substituting a banana for Eve's traditional apple – that was a mistake. Some of the younger children were so scared they became hysterical and wet themselves, and little Curtis Robinson had led the five- and six-year-olds in an act of collective assault, knocking Francie to the ground, pulling off his gorilla mask and engaging with him in hand-to-hand fighting in a pool of urine and banana mush. Persuading the congregation to take part in a sponsored head shave for Traidcraft, that was a mistake too: they looked like a bunch of Hare Krishnas, and people assumed they were all undergoing chemotherapy. The latest scheme Bobbie had dreamed up, which he had agreed to, unbelievably, was to preach a sermon called 'Freedom from Bondage?', which was really a straight gospel message, but which had been advertised on posters around town and in the *Impartial Recorder* with a blurred photograph featuring a woman in what was quite clearly a black leather jumpsuit (Bobbie had bought the suit from Sensations). There was something wrong with that, Francie knew. Even when he'd argued with Bobbie about it, and she had compromised by allowing him to soften up a bit and preach a sermon the following week called 'Will My Bunny Go to Heaven?', illustrated with a poster featuring the rabbit Thumper from the Disney film *Bambi*, he knew that things had gone too far. He'd lost his balance.

And the only way Francie knew how to regain his balance was to get back with Cherith.

'Well,' he began, in Cherith's Mercedes, preparing for his final appeal to her, based largely on a reading of 1 Corinthians 10 and St Paul's account of his thorn in the flesh.

'Look,' said Cherith, pointing up towards the Quality Hotel.

Mrs Gilbey saw it too, on her way out of town.

By five o'clock that Christmas Eve Mrs Gilbey had completed everything that was expected of her as a wife and homemaker at this special time of year. She had been shopping for weeks, laying things down and laying them in: boxes of amaretti biscuits and macadamia nuts and special crackers, all the festive and exotic things that Frank had come to expect. Smoked salmon he liked at Christmas, and a nice ham done with cloves and demerara. Port and Stilton.

She had followed, as usual, the instructions in *Delia Smith's Christmas* – a book which, like her old *Good Housekeeping* recipe cards and her copy of the Reader's Digest *What to Do in an Emergency*, had helped keep her and the household going in times of trouble. Mrs Gilbey loved her Catherine Cooksons, but if it had been a toss-up between Delia and Catherine, Delia would have won hands down. In the end, alas, experience will teach you everything you can ever read about in a novel, but no amount of experience will ever reveal to you the secrets of how to make Stollen: you have to be told; a thing like that doesn't happen just by accident.*

With Delia's help she had her turkey and her vegetables all prepared, the trifle made, and the chestnut stuffing and cranberry sauce ready and waiting, enough food for a banquet in the court of a king, although there would, in fact, only be the three of them this Christmas, as there had been for many years, since both her and Frank's parents had died, and Frank had fallen out with everyone else in the family. Mrs Gilbey, Frank and Lorraine, that was their family. Mrs Gilbey threw away a lot of food every year, which made her feel ashamed. She hated having leftovers.

Scraping the remains of sausagemeat stuffing and chestnuts from under her fingernails, Mrs Gilbey slipped upstairs and prepared herself. Tonight she had decided to wear her new chisel-toed lace-up white leather ankle boots with the tapestry side panels. They were a bit young-looking on her, but they really were quite something and it was Christmas, after all. She was also going with her imitation suede skirt, which she kept for special occasions, with the tasselled fringe and the diamanté trim on the seams. And she was teaming that up with her sparkly red, white and blue round-neck sleeveless top: her arms weren't as bad as her neck. It was quite an outfit, if she said so herself. She'd had her hair done that morning, in Fry's, by Noreen Fry herself – who has lovely teeth, Mrs Gilbey noticed, for the first time. She'd had her

---

* See *Delia Smith's Christmas*, pp.20–1.

hair cut and blow-dried, just the usual, but with a touch more colour, for the festive season.

Tonight, on Christmas Eve, Frank would be going round town with the Rotary Club, dispensing his largesse, and he wouldn't be home till midnight at the earliest, so he wouldn't even notice that she hadn't been there.

After carefully laying out Delia on the granite work surface ready for the morning, she took a taxi to the Leisure Centre, where she saw her fellow dancers already on the coach and Big Donna standing up front, resplendent in sparkly red stetson and white leather chaps. She smiled a big smile when she saw Mrs Gilbey climbing on board. 'Hello, pet,' she said. 'We'd almost given up on you. I'm so glad you could make it.'

And the whole coach clapped.

Mrs Gilbey blushed to the roots of her Christmasy hair and as the coach set off she found herself seated next to a man wearing a plaid shirt, blue jeans and a fringed suede jacket. He was a pleasant enough sort of a fellow. He said his name was Spencer Bradley. He used to write a column for the *Impartial Recorder*, he said. She might have heard of him?

'No,' said Mrs Gilbey, she didn't think so.

'The bat watch column?' he said.

'Oh,' said Mrs Gilbey, 'the bat watch column.'

He worked at the Spick and Span car wash up on the ring road these days, he said – did she know it? Yes, she knew it, although Frank refused to take any of their cars there. Spencer Bradley said that his real love was still for animals, even though he no longer wrote the bat watch column. He kept a smallholding just outside town, where he raised chickens and a few sheep. It wasn't a bad life, he said. 'But enough about me. Tell me about yourself.'

'Well,' Mrs Gilbey began, as the coach made its way up Bridge Street, past Macey's the chemists, and Tommy Tucker's chipper, up towards the ring road, 'I'm not a terribly interesting person actually.'

'Come on,' said Spencer. 'You look like a pretty interesting person to me.'

That's actually what he said, word for word, and Mrs Gilbey simply could not believe it. *My God, my God, my God!* she thought, as Phoebe might say in *Friends*. Was this a compliment? Mrs Gilbey had almost forgotten what it was like, a man paying you a compliment. It was quite nice, actually, if rather shocking and a little OTT – a bit like a bird displaying its plumage in one of those nature programmes, or Delia's recipe for the Christmas goose stuffed with prunes.

'No, really,' she said, looking out at the big new purple call centre and Kwik-Fit, and becoming conscious of fingering her hair, 'there's not much to tell.'

Oh. My. *God*!

'Come on,' said Spencer, reaching into the bag beneath his feet, 'I've told you all about myself. Maybe this'll help loosen your tongue a bit.' And he produced a miniature bottle of brandy and a couple of plastic cups. 'Happy Christmas,' he said, pouring large measures and handing a cup to Mrs Gilbey. 'Cheers!'

'Cheers!' she said, accepting. This could be fun.

'Look,' said Big Donna, pointing back towards town, as they pulled up on to the ring road, heading for the motorway.

Frank had seen it too.

He'd been feeling pretty uncomfortable all night in his Santa suit, what with one thing and another, and now he was flaming red with itches. He'd acquired the suit some years ago, when he was maybe a stone or two lighter, and Mrs Gilbey had patched it since, adding a large piece of what had once been the red velvet curtains from the dining room into the crotch and sewing a large 'V' into the waistband, but at the end of the day nylon is nylon, and it was stretched tight across his belly and up under his armpits, and it was giving him hell, and his beard kept falling off, and he was freezing cold. Frank was not feeling very festive.

The sleigh he rode on every year was in fact two large pieces of sleigh-shaped plywood tied on to a trailer on loan from T. P. McArdle, and hitched to the back of Martin Phillips's Range Rover, which had a large red nose tied to its bonnet, Rudolph-style, and strange to say people actually paid for the privilege of having Frank Gilbey trussed up as Santa sat on the back of the trailer to come and visit their home and wave to their children on Christmas Eve, but then all the proceeds do go to charity and we are generous givers to charity here, although we prefer charities we can relate to: the Cancer Research Campaign, for example, is very popular, and Help the Aged. Oxfam is slightly suspect – all those ethnic items in the shop.

Frank was wondering if perhaps he wasn't getting a little old for this game and whether it was time to hand on the reins, and the boots, and the beard to a younger, slimmer man. They were still only about halfway through their rounds this evening and Frank had had enough. He was at a low ebb, which was unlike him: Frank's tides are nearly always high. The piece in the *Impartial Recorder* accusing him of having stolen council property – or 'our national treasures', as the article had put it – had undoubtedly damaged his reputation. All he could do was hope it'd all be forgotten by the New Year. He'd weather the storm. Publishing a story like that just before Christmas was a pretty foolish move – people's stomachs are bigger than their memories – and he was currently taking legal advice from Martin Phillips on the best way to win redress from the paper. What Frank really wanted was the head of the editor, but tonight he just wanted to get to his glass of malt at the golf club and then home. Mrs Gilbey would have all the Christmas stuff prepared. She usually left him out a little something on Christmas Eve – a mince pie and a glass of milk, as if he really were Santa. He'd sleep in the spare room, so as not to wake her.

350

And as they drove down the High Street he could see the Quality Hotel in the distance.

Bobbie Dylan saw it too. She was just introducing the Band to the audience during 'Green Onions'. It was difficult to sanctify a number like that, because it didn't have any lyrics – and Bobbie didn't believe that any melody in and of itself, any melody alone, could be either sacred or profane – but Brian had perfected this nice little thing on his trumpet where he kind of quoted 'Amazing Grace', which was enough to raise 'Green Onions' to something approaching sacred status, and it looked like 'The People's Fellowship Annual Big Night Out, Featuring Bobbie Dylan and the Band, the Wise Men, the Virgin and the Little Baby J' was going to be a success.

Bobbie had been up at the microphone all night, doing her intercostal diaphragmatic breathing and singing her heart out. They had a pretty good crowd in and this was what it was all about: praising the Lord in the only way she knew how. Giving back a little of what she'd received: love, mostly, or something, she was never quite sure what.

No sign of Francie, though, in the audience: he'd said he was going to have to do some pastoral visiting. He seemed tired and anxious at the moment, and Bobbie wondered sometimes if he was really up to it. She'd put together a few notes for sermons herself, actually, some ideas, and she was wondering if perhaps God was leading her to extend her ministry in that direction. Maybe Francie could keep the morning service and she could take care of the evenings: that was an idea. She was thinking something a bit more casual, maybe a cappuccino cart by the entrance, so the congregation could purchase refreshments on their way in, coffee and chocolate-chip cookies, and maybe a few sofas instead of stackable chairs. She'd have to pray it over with Francie.

She'd nearly finished introducing the Band when she saw it out of the window.

'Ladies and gentlemen,' she was saying, 'I want you to put your hands together for probably the best bass player this side of Memphis, and certainly this side of the ring road: Mr Chick Stevens.' Cue crowd. And then she went on, 'And of course last but not least, behind him, and behind us all, keeping us all together, on drums . . . Jesus Christ!'

At this the audience, as one, looked up at Gary behind his drum kit.

Gary really is no one's idea of the Second Coming, unless you happen to believe that Jesus has put on a little weight since the last time around and has taken to wearing Nirvana sweatshirts and sweatbands, and is balding; Phil probably comes closer to most people's idea of the Messiah, minus the beard, but he was playing guitar rather than drums. So it was only when the audience looked to where Bobbie was pointing, behind them, out of the window, that everybody saw it.

Billy Nibbs was pointing also. He'd been putting the finishing touches to a review – a devastating critique, if he said so himself – of the town's pantomime, *Open, Sesame!*, which had just premièred at Dreams, with an all-ages cast, and which was a combination of Aladdin, Ali Baba and the Forty Thieves, Sinbad the Sailor and *Sesame Street*. In his review Billy laid the blame for the worldwide decline in pantomime standards fairly and squarely at the door of the writers and producer and director and cast of the show, although he did admit that there was a problem with the form generally, which he blamed upon the rise of the novel, and he also took the opportunity to discuss at some length the question of predestination and free will, and whether Scheherazade was the first postmodern narrator, and the debt of the West to Arabic modes of storytelling, and he quoted Aristotle, F. R. Leavis and Jacques Derrida, not names that appeared often in the pages of the *Impartial Recorder* and which Colin Rimmer would soon be pulling out.

*   *   *

Colin could have done with a holiday. He would be driving up to the city tomorrow, Christmas Day, to drop off his presents to his daughters, who would be staying with his ex-wife and her omni-competent new husband, Stephen, who would only offer him the coolest of welcomes and a glass of chilled festive orange juice, because Colin was driving, and who preferred it if the children made all their presents, and then it'd be back to the house for a bottle of brandy by himself and a Christmas Dinner ready-meal from Marks. He might try to put in some work on the magnum opus, which he'd neglected recently. Lisa would be laughing on the other side of her face when he had the novel published and was working as a columnist on a London paper.

In the meantime he was stuck at the *Impartial Recorder* and he'd had quite a struggle with the lawyers, clearing the Frank Gilbey story, but he'd managed to push it through in the end, the week before Christmas, where they'd usually have had something soft as a lead, and Colin had splashed the headline 'FOUND: HIDDEN TREASURES'. It was not quite as hard-hitting a headline as he would have liked, but the lawyers had insisted. He'd been intending something more along the lines of 'THIEF!' or 'SHAME!' or 'LIAR!' or even the headline he had always wanted to run but had never quite found the opportunity to use, the headline that every editor dreams of and believes in his heart of hearts his every word approximates: 'THE TRUTH'. In order to illustrate the story Colin had sent Joe Finnegan to get a photograph of Frank looking shifty, which shouldn't have been too difficult, since Frank is pretty much the personification of shifty, but Joe knew Frank from way back, when Joe was still in the picture-framing business and Frank had put quite a bit of business his way, providing frames and prints for various show homes and apartment developments around town, so Frank had actually looked quite poised and confident in Joe's photograph – benevolent almost, and ever so slightly contrite, with his head a bit bowed and wearing a nice dark suit. In comparison, Billy's photograph of the trough and the fountain, which Colin ran alongside Joe's flattering portrait, perhaps lacked a little definition, but you could certainly tell that the objects photographed were the trough and the fountain that used to be down at the bottom of Main Street and which had disappeared, but it wasn't entirely clear from the blur exactly where they were, or why, so the overall effect was less immediately impressive than it could have been.

The story had certainly put on sales, though – a lot of newsagents were reporting no returns, which was something that hadn't happened for a long time, not since one of the teachers at Barneville House was sent to prison recently for doing things he said he didn't do at the school back in the 1970s.*

For all the initial impact, it looked like Frank was going to try to brazen it out. A man like Frank didn't go down without a fight, but he would go down, Colin was sure of that: this might not have been the end, or the beginning of the end, but it was certainly the end of the beginning. Or the beginning of the beginning of the end. Or something like that. He really did need a holiday.

Once he'd brought Frank down, Colin was going to move on. Next year was going to be his year, he was sure of it. He was going to finish his book and put his life in order. Sort himself out a bit. He was even thinking of going in search of his birth parents.

It was Billy who called Colin over. Colin thought it would be just another plea for a semicolon. It was not.

As Colin stared out of the window, he was already composing the headline in his mind.

Bob Savory saw it at the same time and was making his own swift mental calculations.

* See the *Impartial Recorder*, 22 October 2001.

Bob's mother was doing absolutely fine in the home, if a person who needed help to dress, eat and go to the toilet could ever be said to be doing fine, which in our town they could, actually, because if nothing else we are taught from a young age not to grumble and to be happy with what little we've got, so frankly if you're still breathing you're doing fine here, even if you're on a ventilator, and it looked as though Bob's mother might be fine in the home for some time to come. She wasn't going anywhere. She was not about to drop off her perch.

Bob, on the other hand, had started going to all sorts of places. He had flown the nest.

Now that he didn't have his mother at home to worry about, Bob sometimes found himself in the evenings with nothing to do and no one to do it with. He hated watching the TV alone. Even TV with his mum was to be preferred to watching TV alone. Having his mum there talking to it or at it or just staring mesmerised at the screen made you realise just how bad TV was, and what it was for, and who it was aimed at: TV is aimed at people with a serious brain dysfunction. If you realise that it's easier to understand it – you can appreciate it better. He was also beginning to tire of the waitresses at the restaurant – he just couldn't manage the necessary chat any more – and so he found he had a little spare time now, for the first time in years, and he had started visiting clubs, in search of companionship and something else which he couldn't quite put his finger on. He'd been to quite a few places up in the city, but tonight, because it was Christmas Eve and he didn't want to drive, and because this was going to be his first Christmas without his mother at home, and because he needed a drink, Bob decided he would stay in town and visit Paradise Lost.

He'd been in there for only half an hour or so, admiring the thirty-foot zinc bar and the mirrors, and the fake tropical vegetation and palm trees, and the snakes coiling around columns everywhere, their fibreglass bodies cool to the touch and glistening under the lights.* He'd got talking to the barman, Peter, who was from Australia, a backpacker who'd made it all the way over from the other side of the world and had somehow ended up here. He'd wanted to experience real life, he told Bob – he was from Melbourne – and so he had avoided all the usual glamorous destinations and chosen here as a stopping-off point, a kind of archetypal nowhere, he said. It's hardly flattering to have your town described as a nowhere, but even a nowhere's a somewhere to nobodies like us and, anyway, most of us here are impervious or just plain dumb enough to take criticism as a compliment. He'd enjoyed real life here so much, in fact, Peter the Australian, that as soon as he'd earned enough money he was getting the hell out and moving on to New York. This was a lot more information

*Paradise Lost is the creation, or the miscreation, or the brainchild, shall we say, of a forty-two-year-old blonde interior design consultant who calls herself Kitty these days, but whom we all know as plain brunette Katherine Crone, who is originally from here, but who now lives far away, and who works for the big pub-and-club-and-restaurant conglomerate Donovan's, who own, lease, or otherwise control and manage most of what used to be our town's little privately owned and personally run pubs and bars. Kitty travels hither and thither, sprinkling her fantastical designs like fairy dust over dry and dusty drinking holes and crippled old discos, transforming them into absurd, hyper-real palaces of delight. She specialises, according to her pale-pink business card, in 'Creating and Sourcing Innovative Themes', and Paradise Lost is certainly a theme, if not entirely innovative. It is more lush, more exotic, more simply picturesque than anywhere else in town, perhaps with the exception of Bloom's, and possibly the Leisure Centre when the line dancing is on, and it boasts more nature, frankly, and has more healthy-looking fronds per square inch than even the People's Park, which looks brown and dirty and broken in comparison, naked and denuded, particularly in winter, which lasts here from around about 1 September until Easter. Paradise Lost looks like a Polynesian jungle all year round: a Polynesian jungle, that is, with the added benefit of tequila slammers, a chill-out room, and a state-of-the-art PA and sound system. Bob had considered getting Kitty in to design the first of his franchise Speedy Bap!, but he was really looking for something a little simpler, a little less like Babylon and a little bit more Seattle. He was thinking *Frasier*.

than you'd usually get out of a barman here in town – even if you've known him since childhood, which many of us do, but it made no difference, because barmen and women here are obliged to take a binding vow of silence and surliness at the age of eighteen – and Bob had to admire the young man's ease and confidence and eagerness, and his obvious bartending abilities. He had mixed an excellent rum and Coke, which had become Bob's drink of choice while out clubbing, a return to adolescent enthusiasms, before the beer and then wine and then the whiskey had got a hold of him.

The club was half empty. It was still early.

Bob had found in the music and in the crowds at the clubs exactly the distraction that he needed and desired; the perfect alternative and replacement, in fact, for a mother with Alzheimer's. When he wasn't working these days Bob was either thinking about work or visiting his mother in the home and that was it, that was his life: work, mother, work, mother. There was nothing else, except the gym and investing his money, which wasn't as easy as it looked, when you considered the recent worldwide downturn in stocks and shares. What with trying to get the franchise together on the sandwich place, Bob's plate was pretty full. But when he went to clubs and he was assaulted by the music and the people and the atmosphere, and the drugs, admittedly, he found that he forgot all about his everyday concerns and considerations, and became conscious of other ideas and desires forming within himself: ideas and desires he could not articulate; and did not want to; and which had nothing to do with his mother, or sandwiches, or money; ideas and desires which had never really occurred to him before.

With his mum in the home Bob had begun to realise, had begun to work out what he really valued in life, what mattered to him, what he enjoyed, and these things were, in decreasing order of importance, Beauty, Luxury and Brilliance, none of them, obviously, readily available in our town, where stocks are low, and he had started wondering if he might need to take a break from here and from work, and visit somewhere like San Francisco, or Melbourne even, to get a little top-up. Somewhere different, for a sabbatical. Somewhere where Beauty, Luxury and Brilliance grow on trees, and are waiting to be picked and plucked by passers-by. Maybe when his mother had died – there was no use denying it, he'd had the thought, ashamed though he was to admit it.

He loved dancing in the clubs – that was his holiday in the meantime – or even just watching people dance, people who were generally about twenty years younger than him, which did not perturb him. On the contrary, he enjoyed their youth on their behalf. He admired the fact that youth did not require discipline to acquire beauty – that it did not know even that it was in possession of beauty. To the young, beauty is simply a given, a gift, something they are born with which eventually is taken from them and which they are never able to get back. Bob had been working hard on his abs recently at the gym, and he'd started to see results, but it took so much work, just to burn off those few extra pounds, that sometimes he wondered if it was really worth it. For the young people in the clubs there was no such work involved: their abs just were; they existed, like them. The club was for Bob in some ways the fulfilment of the gym, but it was also its opposite: in the gym you were working and attending to yourself and your own business. But in the clubs you were there to be devoted to some other thing, some other feeling, or piece of music, and you became unconscious of your own existence and became part of a bigger, living, breathing organism. It was like when he was young, just him and his mum, eating sandwiches, staring out of the window, watching the world go by, that delicious feeling of things simply being right without your even having to try.

Yet he also found at the clubs that he was overcome some-times with unaccountable feelings of pain and longing, feelings which made him uncomfortable and angry with himself.

He was feeling angry tonight, actually, for some reason, drinking his rum and Coke, watching a young man dancing – there were only about half a dozen people on the dance floor and all the rest of them were women, so the man stood out. He stood out also because he was taller and he looked impudent. His head was held more erect, and he had close-cropped hair and wore an earring, and was dressed in a tracksuit top and stonewashed jeans, an utterly unremarkable-looking young man who danced in an ungainly, rollicking fashion, our own local variation on the style of the times, his knees slightly bent, throwing his arms and hands up into the air, his face entirely blank, and yet he seemed, in a way that Bob could not fully articulate, he seemed to be utterly complete, and in and of himself, to be perfectly self-contained and yet to have lost himself successfully in the music. He had something that Bob didn't have and which Bob wanted very badly, Bob thought, and he almost said out loud, 'I want you.'

Bob found this thought unnerving, understandably for a man who as far as he was previously aware was around about 150 per cent heterosexual, yet it was a thought that merged quickly into a feeling and the feeling quickly overcame him, and he was seized suddenly with the need to get outside, to get a breath of fresh air and to regain his composure – if he could get outside he'd be fine and he'd forget all about this.

And it was when he stepped outside the club, into the dark and cold, that he too saw the Quality Hotel.

Paul, of course, had been the first person to see it. He was actually in the Quality Hotel. He was there.

He'd had everything ready and everything arranged. Scunty, his friend from the Institute, who was working in the Big Banana, the record shop up on High Street, had done him some great flyers, showing the hotel looking like a Gothic castle, with a huge, all-seeing, blood-red eye in the centre, and he'd also got someone he knew on a pirate radio station up in the city to put out the word. They'd got into the hotel the night before, the two of them, their baseball caps pulled low, through the old entrance into the Italian garden on Tarry Lane, and they'd shifted a lot of debris. It was a creepy kind of a place at night, there was no denying it, although both Paul and Scunty did their best to pretend otherwise.

'It's like Scooby-Doo,' said Scunty, who was the kind of man who collects old *Marvel* comics and who still lives with his parents. His bark was worse than his bite, Scunty. Even his tattoos were quite sweet, when you got up close – snakes, mostly, and flames, but he also had a little Scottie dog on his shoulder, in memory of his gran's dog Floofy, who'd wandered on to the ring road years ago, when it was first built, obviously thinking it was still fields. But no one need know about that tonight: Scunty was security for the evening.

There was a lot of scurrying inside the Quality Hotel, the sound of rats on the remains of parquet, and there were these curious winds and draughts, and it was impossible to see much because of the dark. It looked a lot better from the outside, actually, than inside, the Quality Hotel, but that would be true in town generally.

Scunty had managed to borrow a van, and they'd gone and picked up all the gear: some bass-bins, and a smoke machine, and some UV lights from a place up in the city, and the candyfloss machine and the hot-dog stall, and the Slush Puppie maker, and they'd got a hold of a few milk crates for people to sit on, and Paul had set up his turntables in what More O'Ferral had intended to be the chapel, but which had ended up as the library and then the dining room, and finally the place where you could get a Knickerbocker Glory on a Sunday.

'It's gonna be totally crazy,' Paul had kept saying to Scunty in encouragement and in the closest thing to a kind of black American patois that he could manage, as they lugged the gear into the deserted building and across the moonlit lobby into the chapel. 'It's gonna be wicked.'

Paul had had to scale down his original and rather more wicked plans. He hadn't had time to pull everything together. He'd had to take a job – he couldn't turn it down, or he'd have lost all his benefits. He'd had an interview and before he knew it, there he was, working, actually working, for a firm who had a franchise to operate coin-operated children's rides in shopping malls and in leisure centres and in hospitals and in indoor soft-play areas. He had to start out at Bloom's early in the morning, at 6 a.m., before anyone else was there, cleaning the rides and collecting the money, and he was paid the minimum wage and he had to wear a black polo shirt with WILLOUGHBY RIDES embroidered in white over the breast, and he felt like a Roman slave, branded with his master's name. By the afternoon the malls were all like cattle markets, but early in the morning he didn't mind, early in the morning a place like Bloom's felt more like an amphitheatre or a cathedral: the hush, the vast floor spaces. It felt like an arena, somewhere where something might happen, and where Paul was a part of it. He was supplied with rags, and Marigolds, and antiseptic surface cleaners, and baby wipes, and he'd added an old toothbrush of his own, to help him get into those difficult-to-reach corners: Hank's Hot Dog Van was an absolute bugger.

It wasn't a bad job, really, and it was the rides that had given him the idea: some kind of Christmas Eve fairground or circus in the Quality Hotel. That was his big idea. An event. A space. Rides and entertainment. But once he'd made a few calls he realised that a fairground wasn't practical: the rides were too expensive. Far too much. Even for a juggler you were looking at £100 cash in hand, money up front. He was amazed – he thought street performers were all hippies who'd have been glad of a swig from a bottle of cider and the chance to pass round the hat. But everyone these days, it seems, is a professional. He'd even rung a local children's magician, 'Laughing' Norman Needy, and Norman had asked him about insurance, for goodness' sake.* So Paul had to scale down. He did some basic cash projections and business plans on the back of the Willoughby Rides brochures. Tickets for the evening would cost, say, £10, and he reckoned he could attract up to 500 people, and once they were inside they were his. He'd get a Slush Puppie machine – that only cost £50 for the night's hire, and then he could charge £2 per drink. Candyfloss as well, similar. If his calculations were correct, he reckoned he'd be able to take about £20,000 in one evening, what with all the other merchandising opportunities: helium balloons, sparkly wands. And the drugs, of course. Scunty knew a couple of people and Paul thought he could guarantee exclusive rights to them.

He'd had it all worked out. This was going to be the start of something big. Tonight was just the beginning, the beginning of a new kind of scene in our town, something really intense, something with that kind of vibe and that kind of feeling you get off the music when it's really working.

But the only feeling he'd had so far tonight was of panic. He was down about £2000 so far – all the gear had taken a

---

* Norman had learnt the hard way. He'd been booked a few years ago to do a children's party up in the city – the parents were lawyers, which should have been a warning. Norman had double booked by accident and had to cancel the engagement at the last minute, and the parents had sued him for breach of contract. It had ruined him. He'd had a nice little semi outside the ring road, and had been working for years in show business, and working on his garden: he had his own koi pond, and grew lovely geraniums and strawberries in the summer, lovely happy fruits and flowers. He was living in a caravan now, out on Womack's caravan park on the Old Green Road, with just a couple of plastic planters for a garden, and he'd thought about giving it all up, especially after he'd had the heart attack, but then he thought, well, if he was going to be dead soon, which he was, he might as well keep going. Norman believed in magic. But he wasn't daft. These days he also believed in insurance.

huge chunk of the budget, and on top of that there'd been all the money he'd had to agree to pay Scunty's friend Ricky for taking care of the drugs. Any money he'd had to pay up front he'd taken out of Joanne's building society account: it was the money they were saving up for a deposit on a house. He was planning to pay her back, of course, as soon as he had all the money in later. He hadn't told her about it. He wanted to surprise her. She wouldn't have understood.

They were expecting most people to turn up around midnight. By then it'd be packed. You wouldn't be able to move. Ricky said he'd be coming in at about 10 with the drugs. Loads of people from the Institute were coming after pub chucking-out time. Wally Lee, even, who was playing a gig himself up at Maxine's, some line-dancing thing, said he'd be in later.

'It's gonna be totally crazy,' Paul told Scunty again, as he lined up his records. 'It's gonna be massive.'

A couple of people had turned up at 8, but they were local grungy teenagers just, and they handed over their money, wandered around the ground floor of the hotel, and then sat down on the milk crates in the old chapel, rolled something up and started smoking it. The teenagers were Bethany, in fact, Francie and Cherith's daughter, and her boyfriend, Kirk, who is several years older and who owns a car.

Bethany is not like Kirk's other girlfriends – as a minister's daughter she has all the appeal of forbidden fruit, the guileless, trusting nature of the truly meek and mild, and she is reckless enough to try anything. It's a winning combination and Kirk is completely obsessed with her. Bethany, meanwhile, remains obsessed with CO_2 emissions, the hole in the ozone layer, CFCs, acid rain and the prospect of nuclear war: she's into what Kirk calls globiality. Kirk couldn't get into it himself. What Kirk and Bethany have in common is the same musical taste, beginning with Nu-Metal and Marilyn Manson, and going right back to Nirvana and further back even to the

Doors. Music is what had brought them together in the first place and why they were here – the promise of something so loud that it would take them out of themselves and out of our small town. They were discussing where to buy drugs and whether amyl nitrate was any good or not. Kirk claimed it was excellent, although he'd never had any and wasn't quite sure what it was. He assumed it was something you got in a chemist's.

After smoking what they believed to be a joint of the highest quality THC dope and which was, in fact, tobacco sprinkled with Tesco's Mixed Herbs, but which seemed to have had the required head-spinning effect, Bethany tossed the butt away and embraced Kirk in what she hoped was a passable imitation of a vampish manner and kissed him, using her tongue in the way her last boyfriend, Danny, had taught her. The technique certainly seemed to work with Kirk, although all the herbs made it taste a bit like kissing an omelette, and she had to take a break after a few minutes to catch her breath and to pick a few strands of rosemary from her teeth.

Paul saw them kissing at the same moment he saw the flames, and right away he knew it was time to get out.

It began along one of the chapel's remaining panelled walls, a wall crusted thick with a century's dirt and varnish but which still held an engraved metal tablet listing the names of all those from our town who had died in the Great War, names familiar to all of us still today, the Cuddys and the Cannings and the Grieves and the Hawkinses and the McCruddens: the great unfallen. It was a slow starter, the fire, appropriately enough, but then it suddenly found its feet and leapt up into the hidden cavities and voids behind the panelling, and spread upwards and outwards, round the walls and up and out into the dining room and the arcade and the bedrooms upstairs, leaping, jumping and breaking through all the enclosures of the Quality Hotel, through every wall and vaulting every obstacle, the flames and hot gases catching on to the natural air currents and moving out and across the plastic fibre carpets, through the stud walls, along the suspended ceiling tiles and rushing through the ventilation and lift shafts. The twentieth century was destroyed within minutes. The rest of the building took longer.

People die in a fire for one of two reasons: either they burn to death quickly or they're slowly asphyxiated, and Paul did not intend to die either way. He had assembled all of this, all the gear, all the people soon to be arriving. He had made something happen. Or at least something which was about to happen. But now he was going to have to close down before he'd even properly begun. It was a disappointment, but he had no choice.

He did two things.

He shouted 'Fire!' and then he ran. Scunty and Bethany and Kirk followed him out into the Italian garden, where, like the rest of the town, they stood and watched.

The last person to see it was Sammy.

It was just a small flame, which had danced along the top of the roof of the Quality Hotel, until it reached the adjoining building, the building which housed the Oasis, where Sammy was inside.

He was in the spa pool, as usual – the Oasis was shut down for Christmas, but he was there, in the pool just the same, and in his mind he was with little Josh. In his mind Josh was about fourteen tonight, which was a good age, because it meant he still enjoyed Christmas but he was also good to talk to, and so the two of them talked about how the past year had gone, and Josh was delighted with the presents Sammy had bought him.

At first Sammy thought he was smelling in his imagination, which he'd done before – he'd smelt Josh many, many times, reminders of the evening when his little boy had died, when he'd let him down – but then the smoke began to fill his lungs, and it felt like acid, and the more he tried to breathe, the more he found himself choking, and he'd try to take a breath and then another breath, but it felt like someone pouring burning liquid into the back of his throat. He retched and tried to take a deeper breath, which was worse, and finally to escape the fire he went down under the water.

Davey Quinn missed it all. He didn't see a thing. He didn't look back. He never took his eyes off the road.

Davey wasn't going to lose the momentum of this journey. It had taken a long time to build up to it. There was no way he was stopping now. This could be the start of bigger and better things. As he passed the golf club, the outskirts, with their stone sleeping lions, he gave a sigh of relief.

He was leaving town, with Lorraine.

He threw the bus up on to the motorway. He'd earned his PCV licence years ago when he was living in London, and now a job had come up, driving a tour bus round Europe – he'd found it on the Internet – and he'd jumped at it.

They were getting away. First stop London, then Paris, Rome, down to Spain and back again. They'd be gone for eight months of the year, staying in a different hotel every night. It sounded absolutely perfect. He'd heard of people who'd gone as far away as Turkey.

It was funny, leaving. Everything looked exactly the same: the same rolling hills, the same patches of fields and houses, the same roundabouts, the motorway. It was all just as he remembered it. Nothing had changed. Only the weather.

'Wow,' said Lorraine, pointing, excited. 'Snow!'

'Huh,' said Davey.

Index of Key Words, Phrases and Concepts

The index is intended for the curious, the wary and the professionally lazy. It is perhaps less interesting than the Preface and probably less informative than the Acknowledgements. Its one great advantage is that it may be used as a substitute for reading the book itself – no bad thing. Skimming and skipping are two of the great pleasures of reading, although the fastidious may, of course, disagree; they may also take courtesy for a gimmick.

The entries are by no means exhaustive. Some words – 'I', for example – have been deemed too insignificant for inclusion, while some concepts – let us say 'love' – have been regarded as too large. As a guide the index will therefore prove insufficient. But as an evocation it is my hope that it proves adequate.

of brand new German cars are
all examples of, according to
Bob Savory, 246
– *see also entries under* luxury *and*
brilliance
beer,
– Czech, 127
– other (including Guinness), 57,
76, 91, 103, 163
Being,
– and Doing, compared and
contrasted, 77
bells!,
– Hell's, 206
betrayal,
– myriad depressing examples of,
83, 109–110, 133–134, 135n.,
147, 283–285, 330–331
Bible, the
– and the Body Shop, 182
– confused with God, 72–73
– How Not to Read, For All It's
Worth, 309–310
– more effective than a hot milky
drink, 181
– watching romantic comedies on
video instead of studying, 307
bicycle polo, 57
big-headedness, 196–197, 199
birth, 3, 5
– Davey Quinn's, a disappointment
even to himself, 4
biscuits, 29, 37, 90, 195, 210, 307,
316, 325
– are a godsend, 337
blame, 104–105, 152, 253, 284
blasphemy, 32, 188
blind, the
– leading the blind, example of, 71,
90–91, 188
boat,
– push the, out, 61, 64, 198, 301
bondage,
– freedom from, 346
– is hoarse, 216
bones,
– a bag of, 89

– let's make no, about it, 331
– sticks and stones may break my,
279
– unavailability of from local
butchers, 336
books, 28, 52, 65, 108, 150,
165n., 346–347
– as the long alternative route to
friendship, 154
– borrowing, 239–240
– business, 143, 244, 245
– self-help, 107, 209
– the best, are usually rhyming, 244
– *see also entries under* autodidacts
and writers
boot,
– put the, in, 110, 331
born,
– again, no good time to be, 75
– to the manor, 152–153, 165
bowels,
– in the, of the Lord, 306
boxing, 90, 100, 276–277
boys,
– will be boys, 193–194, 277–278
brain,
– not apparently in use, 25, 146
– *see also entries under* idiocy *and*
lechery
breakfast, 91–92
– dog's, 256
– fried, 57, 193, 336
– *see also entries under* eating *and*
food
breast,
– making a clean, of it, 345
breathing,
– Benny Goodman's, the sound of,
289
– intercostal diaphragmatic method
of, 300, 351
bribery, 147
bric-a-brac, 48–49, 236, 367–388
brides,
– to-be, 290–291
brilliance,
– currently unavailable, 357

kitchens,
– empty, 48
– kosher, 78, 86
– middle-class, 122
– standard of, in private rented
    accommodation, 93
– unutterably depressing, 122
knitting, 2
– see also entries under woolly hat
knives, 22–23
knowledge,
– carnal, 181
– is strength, 114
– scientific, 113
– what to do with, 343
Korea,
– Bobbie Dylan is big in, 75

language,
– foreign, (French), 236, 300
– foreign, (Italian), 3n., 39–40
– prison-house of, 39, 71, 123n.
lechery, 82, 83
liberality, 82, 83
library,
– you should really support your
    local, 239–240
life,
– friends, is boring, 210
– 'is hard', unhelpful statement of
    obvious truth that, 98
– secrets of a long and happy, 116
– 'this is the', 138
literary,
– failure, feels like a kicking, 111
literature,
– like Guinness, is good for you, 64
loathing, 153
– self-, 29, 95, 112, 211, 284, 306
local, 19
logic, 78
– diabolical, 227–228
London, 10
– availability of funny spaghetti,
    truffle oils, and novelty cheeses
    in, 29
– Hell is a city much like, 5, 7

– Mrs Gilbey cannot see the point
    of, frankly, 138
– teenage ambitions to visit, in
    order to visit Soho, 22
loss,
– of luggage, 7–8
luxury, 37
– in short supply, 357
– see also entries under beauty,
    biscuits and brilliance

magnificence,
– examples of, 2, 38, 83, 112,
    169
make-up, 76, 193
– see also entries under face
malevolence, 227–228
mal-talent,
– example of, 94
manure, 283, 285
marriage, 36–37, 77, 89–90,
    180–181, 213–214, 267, 315
– and paranoia, 95
– and Reformation theology, 307
martini, 116
– dry, best in the world, 65
massive
– desire to be, 95–96, 108
meaninglessness,
– and transitoriness of human life,
    2, 102
meatloaf/ Meat Loaf, 302n.
Mediterranean,
– the weather is, almost, 115
– goat's cheese tartlets, warm,
    272n.
memory, 7–8, 97, 173–174, 266,
    341, 343
men,
– all sorts and conditions of, 35,
    135–137, 182–183
– and women, are not the same,
    177, 211
– ruined, 22
– smell of, the, 58, 281, 288
menu,
– suggested, for a week, 124

status, 19, 38, 42, 108
storm,
– the gathering, 54, 69, 114,
   242
success, 19, 39, 108, 117, 120,
   138, 235
– cast-iron guaranteed secrets of,
   250–251
suicide, 4, 197n.
Sunday,
– lunch, 29, 90–91, 319
sunflowers,
– Van Gogh's, evidence of the
   unendingness of art, 111–112
sunshine, 55, 70, 115, 180, 207
sushi,
– and Christian guilt, 307
sweets, 87–88, 149
– *see also entries under* butter-balls
System, The, 248

tan,
– the St. Tropez, 40
tea, 91, 116, 149, 153, 265
– and wine, 124–125
teacher,
– 'career', euphemism for, 134
– English, 63–64
– leather-jacket wearing, ready-
   rubbed rolling, 66
– Music, 135n.
teenagers, 261
teeth, 21
– Monica Hawkins's father's, true
   story about, 46n.
– Clarence Kemp's, true story
   about, 318n.
television,
– is a huge comfort, 28
– Morecambe and Wise on, 36
– programmes, inheriting other
   people's, 337
– stool, the, 122
– wide screen, 127
temptation,
– and the smell of barbecued
   meats, 83

– is Christmas in Tenerife, 194
texting, 31, 74
– a guide to Christian, 32n.
themes,
– disowning of, xi
– residual evidence of, 1ff
time,
– and money 120–121, 251
– 'Wounds All Heels', 312
'Too much pudding will choke the
   dog', 169n.
tragic, the, 103, 314–315
travellers,
– and the pool of Narcissus, 139
– are tourists in other people's
   reality, 356
– change climates, not conditions,
   264
True Christian Manliness,
– the Boy's Brigade and, 141
truth,
– is very probably non-existent,
   162–163
Twain, Shania,
– video, as an aid to communi-
   cating effectively to the church's
   young people, 83
twilight,
– the coming of a universal, 15–18,
   29, 54, 100–101, 107

ukuleles, 231
underwear, 39, 269
unhappiness,
– irreducible, 29, 82, 154, 238,
   255
upholstery,
– as a business, 118
– limits of, as a hobby, 236
urine, 5, 207, 306

Van Gogh, Vincent, 112
– *see also entries under* sunflowers
velocity,
– maintaining, importance of, 13,
   18, 54
violence, 63, 105, 278

Acknowledgements

For previous acknowledgements see *The Truth about Babies* (Granta Books, 2002), pp. 335–7. These stand. In addition I would like to thank the following. (The previous terms and conditions apply: some of them are dead; most of them are strangers; the famous are not friends; none of them bears any responsibility.) I am particularly grateful to *The Enthusiast*.

The Alabama 3, Janet and Allen Ahlberg, Mulk Raj Anand, Gerry Anderson, Aharon Appelfeld, Robert Alter, Diane Arbus, Louis Armstrong, Matthew Arnold, Roger Ascham, Clement Attlee, Erich Auerbach, Edward L. Ayers Jr, Ronnie Barker, Mel Bartholomew, Susan Wise Bauer, the Be Good Tanyas, Simon Russell Beale, Richard Beckinsale, Derek Bell, Hilaire Belloc, Arnold Bennett, Irving Berlin, Rodney Bewes, Lexy Bloom, Dirk Bogarde, Paul F. Boller Jr, George Borrow, Louise Bourgeois, David Bowman, Myrtle Brown, Sir Thomas Browne, Kurt Brungardt, Gavin Bryars, Robert Burton, Aldo Buzzi, Café Brazilia, Abraham Cahan, Sandra Calder, Stephen Calder, Calexico, Betsy Cameron, David Cannadine, Frank Capra, Joe Carey, Anthony Caro, Harry Carpenter, Humphrey Carpenter, David Carradine, Jim Carrey, Alison Carson, Charlie Carson, Ciaran Carson, the Carter Family, Nick Cave, CBBC Scotland, Paul Celan, Anton Chekhov, G. K. Chesterton, Nick Clarke, George Clooney, J. M. Coetzee, Nik Cohn, Eddie Condon and his Band, Caroline Cooper, Mr and Mrs Cooper, Mrs Conville, Henry Cooper, Brendan Cormican, Ben Cove,

Miles Coverdale, Jim Crace, Mr and Mrs Cromie, David Dabydeen, Nick Davies, Sara Davies, Les Dawson, Peter Day, Richard Deacon, Daniel Defoe, Iris DeMent, Govindas Vishnoodas Desani, John Dewey, Hugo Duncan, Dave Eggers, Barbara Ehrenreich, Ralph Ellison, Lucy Ellmann, D. J. Enright, *The Enthusiast*, Bill Evans, Gil Evans, Lee Evans, John Evelyn, Robert Faggen, Frantz Fanon, Ronald Firbank, Carol Fitzsimmons, Richard Flanagan, John Florio, Northrop Frye, Janice Galloway, Ray Galton and Alan Simpson, Dr Gaston, Malcom Gladwell, Philip Glass, Brian Glover, Nikolai Gogol, Ray Gosling, Antonio Gramsci, Mark Gray, Anna Greene, Davey Greene, Jane Greene, Jenny Greene, Sophie Greene, Jane Greenwood, Alec Guinness, the Tyrone Guthrie Centre, Reg Gutteridge, Christine Hall, Terry Hall, Sophie Harrison, Alethea Hayter, Hannah Henderson, Werner Herzog, Christopher Hitchens, Peter Hitchens, Eric Hobsbawm, David Hockney, Courtney Hodell, Min Hogg, A. M. Homes, Rachel Hooper, Irving Howe, Susan Howe, Victor Hugo, T. E. Hulme, Julian Humphries, Tilly Hunt, Kenneth T. Jackson, Kevin Jackson, C. L. R. James, Sid James, Skip James, Tove Jansson, Richard Jefferies, Justine Jordan, John B. Keane, Alice Kessler-Harris, Khaled, the Sir James Kilfedder Memorial Trust, Roy Kinnear, Victor Klemperer, Ivan Klíma, Eric Korn, Karl Kraus, Kronos Quartet, Andrey Kurkov, Jean de La Fontaine, John Lahr, Le Corbusier, Kim Lenaghan, Daniel Libeskind, the staff of the Linenhall Library, Belfast, Professor Longhair, Edna Longley, Michael Longley, Robin Lustig, George McAuley, Peter McDonald, Robert MacFarlane, Rev. F. W. McGee, Liam McIlvanney, Cherrie McIlwaine, McKeown's, James MacMillan, Dr McNutt, Ian McTear, Bernard Malamud, Neeraj Malhotra, Sir Thomas Malory, David Mamet, Greil Marcus, Marcel Mauss, Vladimir Mayakovsky, Jonathan Meades, Arthur Mee, Johnny Mercer, Billy Miskimmin, Trevor Miskimmin, Eugenio Montale, Eric Morecambe, William Morris, Grandma Moses, Frank Muir, Randy Newman, Michael Newton, Red Nichols,

Lorine Niedecker, Catherine O'Dolan, Charles Olson, Peter Owen, Camille Paglia, Tom Paulin, Nicholas Pearson, Itzhak Perlman, Harold Pinter, Sadie Plant, Cole Porter, Robert Potts, Francis Poulenc, Philip Pullman, Gordon Ramsey, the Redskins, Dan Rhodes, Charlie Rich, Jonathon Richman, Richard Rorty, Jonathan Rose, Leonard Rossiter, Julian Rothenstein, Josiah Royce, John Ruskin, Mark Russell, Edward W. Said, Will Salmon, Sampson's Cycles, Robert Sandall, Ted Sansom, Gerald Scarfe, András Schiff, Ben Schott, Kurt Schwitters, David Sedaris, Richard Sennett, Doctor Seuss, John Seymour, Shakira, Verity Sharp, Carol Shields, Sho'Nuff Records, Roger Scruton, Aura Sibisan, Mike Skinner, Christopher Smart, Smylie's Sectional Buildings, Sharon Smith, Stevie Smith, Muggsy Spanier, the Specials, Johnny Speight, Francis Spufford, Graham Swift, Jonathan Swift, Jeremy Taylor, Tesco.com (Knocknagoney), Edward Thomas, Irene Thomas, Rosie Thomas, Rosie Thornton, Peter Townend, Louise Tucker, William Tyndale, Ralph Vaughan Williams, Geza Vermes, Gina Vitelli, David Wardle, Steve Wasserman, Evelyn Waugh, Tim Westwood, David Wheatley, E. B. White, Hugh Fearnley Whittingstall, David Widgery, Norman Wisdom, Ernie Wise, P. G. Wodehouse, Stevie Wonder, Ilsa Yardley, Rafi Zabor, Israel Zangwill, Slavoj Žižek.

P.S.

Ideas,
interviews
& features ...

Q & A

What objects do you always carry with you?
With me I always carry spare spectacles, too much change, credit card, debit card, library ticket, library books, my Homebase discount card, receipts, satellite phone, multi-band shortwave radio, two-litre water bottle, water purification tablets, Maglite, waterproof matches, whistle, gill net, candles, large metallic foil bag, Leatherman multi-purpose tool, plasters, antihistamine, sterile dressings and gauze, Vaseline, suturing needles, anti-diarrhoea pills, tetracycline, a hexamine block, a chequered handle picnic knife, an extra-expanding calf-skin gusset purse, some choice-blended China tea in willow pattern enamelled tins, a solid ivory fitted Russian leather dressing case with tortoiseshell comb and toilet requisites, a razor, strop, corkscrew, pencils (H, HB, B, 2B), correspondence cards, mounting solution, prayer book, Bible, Irish linen handkerchiefs, knee shawl, sleeping socks, leather gauntlets, Scotch yarn home-knit jersey, night shirt, Malacca cane, a door wedge, thimble, tape measure, bodkin, sewing needles, one card each of black and white thread, pearl shirt buttons, linen buttons, safety pins, galvanized iron padlocks, repeater alarm clock, 18-carat gold full hunter, eyelet punch, picture cord, piano wire, tack lifter, table vice, firefly grinder, files for fretwork, skinning knives, skull cap, folding opera hat, life belt, combination knife, fork and spoon set, steering compass, anemometer, rain gauge, portable sketching easel, leather carriage cushion, brushes for water-colour painting, unbleached handmade drawing paper, two bottle travelling ink-stand,

fountain pen with 14-carat gold nib, moleskin notebooks, silver hand blotter, ivory paper knife, mortar and pestle, household lubricant, chicken broth, primus travelling stove, folding stretcher bedstead with spring wire mattress, rabbit's foot, amulets, small *memento mori* figurines, smoking equipment, wood bound steel cabin trunk, Banbury cakes, potted meats, half a cooked ham, a tin of mixed biscuits, and some boiled sweets. I don't get out much.

What is your greatest fear?
James Thurber has a little story, 'A Box to Hide In', in which a fearful man seeks refuge from the world in the haven of a box. The only trouble is, he can't find a box big enough. What is it Larkin says? 'Life is first boredom, then fear.' I couldn't possibly say what is my greatest fear. I'm kind of hoping things will all work out OK. I do know I wouldn't want to be a chicken in a bag of cats.

Which living person do you most admire?
I try not to, on the whole, although of course one can't help but admire all enemies of despair and ignorance, of enslavement, intolerance, torture, poverty, and injustice. But then just about everyone is admirable in some way, aren't they? Even the promoters of despair and ignorance, even the total wasters, and the intolerant, and the people in television, the liars and the panderers, the professional heavy-hitters, writers even, and literary critics: the whole heap. To admire is not a virtue, and eventually everyone lets you down. T.S. Eliot lectured on poetry to 13,000 ▶

> ❝I couldn't possibly say what is my greatest fear. I do know I wouldn't want to be a chicken in a bag of cats. ❞

Q & A *(continued)*

◄ people in a Milwaukee football stadium, and he had that thing about Jews and rats, and he married his secretary. Samuel Beckett wrote his one-act play *Ohio Impromptu* for a conference held in his honour, 'Samuel Beckett: Humanistic Perspectives', held at Ohio State University, 7–9 May 1981. Pope John Paul played Wembley in the summer of 1982: he also did a rap on *Abbà Pater*. It's best not to look up. Or down. 'All our righteousnesses are as filthy rags; and we all do fade as a leaf.' (Isaiah 64:6.)

What is your idea of perfect happiness?
That's a poser. I'm not even going to try and answer that one, for obvious reasons; but let me use Milton as my excuse. In *Paradise Lost*, in Pandaemonium, after Satan's 'great consult' with his fallen angels, some of the angels amuse themselves 'with feats of arms', others sing 'with notes angelical', some go exploring the four infernal rivers, and yet others, perhaps the most pathetic, sit apart,

> and reasoned high
> Of providence, foreknowledge, will and
>   fate,
> Fixed fate, free will, foreknowledge
>   absolute,
> And found no end, in wandering mazes
>   lost.
> Of good and evil much they argued then,
> Of happiness and final misery,
> Passion and apathy, and glory and shame,
> Vain wisdom all, and false philosophy.

Thinking about happiness can make even the fallen angels pious, so I'll spare you my own glory and shame. Suffice it to say that I believe happiness to be a ubiquitous feeling most often encountered in love, in the religious and sexual emotions, in retrospect, in passing, possibly during sleep, and in the contemplation of, say – as I think Samuel Beckett may once have put it – a neatly folded ham sandwich.

Where do you go for inspiration?
The *OED*, *Roget's Thesaurus*, *The Enthusiast* (www.theenthusiast.co.uk), Norfolk, Peckham, Auden, butter, milk, God, geniality, the garden, the park, the market, the seafront, the sea, the swimming pool, the bathroom, hospital, church, the *New Yorker*, the *County Down Spectator (and Ulster Standard)*, the ball in your court, the cheese counter at Spice (on Market Street, Bangor), the gardens and tea rooms at Mount Stewart, BBC Radio 1, BBC Radio 2, BBC Radio 3, BBC Radio 4, BBC Radio Ulster, American National Public Radio, the salt of the earth, the opera, Old Town Clothing, McGrory's Hotel, Sho'Nuff Records, the Bible, Whitstable, swings and roundabouts, Romania, Arthur Mee's *Children's Encyclopaedia*, life's rich tapestry, Amazon.co.uk, the X that marks the spot, Bangor Public Library (80 Hamilton Road, Bangor, Co. Down, BT20 4LH; Hours: Mon, Tue, Wed, Fri, 10am–8pm; Sat, 10am–1pm, 2–5pm).

Why were you interested in writing about small towns?
A small circle is as infinite as a large circle. ▶

> ❝ Suffice it to say that I believe happiness to be a ubiquitous feeling most often encountered in love and in the contemplation of a neatly folded ham sandwich. ❞

LIFE AT A GLANCE

BORN
....
I was born in a little town
called Brentwood, which is
in the county of Essex, in
England. How unjust the
world is to Essex.

EDUCATED
....
I attended primary and
secondary schools in
Essex, and the ancient
universities of Oxford and
Cambridge – which are
OK, for people who like
that sort of thing.

BACKGROUND
....
These days I live in
Northern Ireland and
people from England
often ask, 'What's it like
living in Northern
Ireland?' and there are
unpleasing aspects,
obviously, but there are
disadvantages to living
anywhere, and Northern
Ireland has its
allurements: there's the
Giant's Causeway, for
example, and a lot of good
agricultural shows, a fine

Q & A *(continued)*

◄ **Right. Could you say any more?**
Erm . . . No. Not really. Sorry.

Why not?
Oh, dear, I don't know. I'm really not very
good at this sort of thing.

What sort of thing?
This.

What?
This . . . book chat.

Book chat?
Yes. It gives me a headache. It always sounds
so silly, frankly. It's like when people appear
on chat shows on the radio or the television,
or at literary festivals or readings in provincial
town halls, to talk about their film or their
book or their new solo album – and I just
think, oh no, please, don't, please, stop, you've
really gone and spoilt it now, you're making
my toes curl, stop, please, *please*, I used to
think you were so great, and now it turns out
you're an absolute wally. I mean, really, do you
think Herman Melville would have had
anything interesting to say about whales on
Parkinson?

I don't know . . .
Well, anyway, believe me, I really don't have
anything interesting to say about small towns.
Anything I do have to say about small towns is
never going to be as interesting as anything
you could learn about small towns from
reading, say, George Eliot or Chekhov or
Sherwood Anderson's *Winesburg, Ohio* or

Harry Kemelman's *Rabbi David Small* books or reading the local paper.

I see. So what was the point of ...
Writing the book in the first place?

Exactly.
Writing's not just about explaining. It's not just about giving information.

So you're just not into explaining?
Well, it depends on what's being explained, obviously: how to cook perfect roast potatoes, for example, that's fine. That's important knowledge to impart. Or the history of the Ottoman Empire. Or phenomenology. That sort of stuff. That's one sort of explanation. But explaining why you write or explaining the meaning of your book in public is just ...

Just?
It's like trying to explain one's marriage or one's children – it's a recipe for disaster. It can only lead to doubt, and regret and self-recrimination. 'You said ...', 'No, I didn't ...', 'Yes you did ...', 'But what I meant was ...'. The attempt at clarification inevitably becomes a blurring and you're on a hiding to nothing: you start explaining your books and it comes out as drivel, but if you don't make the effort, well, it seems ungenerous. Also, if you keep asking yourself how and why you're doing what you're doing, you don't do it – it's like driving round the M25, or the North Circular, if you thought about it for too long, you'd just get a bus. ▶

LIFE AT A GLANCE
(continued)

tradition of home baking, Tayto cheese and onion crisps, the Fermanagh lakelands, the Mourne Mountains, the Linen Hall library, the Ulster Museum, the No Alibis bookshop on Botanic Avenue in Belfast, the North Antrim coast. And there are frequent flights to Stanstead in Essex.

Q & A (continued)

◄ **Other people manage to do it.**
What, drive round the North Circular?

No. Explain their work.
Yes. I know.

Coleridge.
Yes. Precisely. Henry James.

Nabokov.
Exactly. Dave Eggers. But they're different – at least three of them are geniuses. Me, personally, I just find it embarrassing to talk about my books.

Really?
Yes. Even to say that, 'my books', that makes me squirm. It makes me feel uncomfortable, like I'm running a slight temperature and am about to do something I know I shouldn't really be doing and don't know how to do: like kissing a woman who is not my wife, say, or operating some kind of heavy machinery, or sitting a Maths exam; it makes me apprehensive. Talking about 'my books', it makes me want to check over my shoulder for my younger self, a younger, slimmer, hairier self who I know would be seething and sniggering at my arrogance and pretension, or maybe just standing there ashen-faced, mortified, struck dumb, ashamed by this big galoot up front who's assuming that anybody cares about what he has to say about some book he's written; I mean, really, get back to me when you've got your *Paradise Lost*, and then we'll talk. When I think of all those years when I'd have given an arm and a leg to be

❝ I mean, really, do you think Herman Melville would have had anything interesting to say about whales on Parkinson? **❞**

8

able to say that I'd written actual books – whole books! – and then to have them actually published, by actual publishers, and to see them on the shelves in actual bookshops, and then to have the gall to talk about my writing them, as if the writing and the publishing of them were something that just had to happen, the fulfilment of manifest destiny, as natural and as inevitable as for some other people it is natural and inevitable to have to get up in the morning and go to work at the post office, or to go fitting tyres and clutches or cleaning out septic tanks. Honestly. It's just too much. Whenever I hear anybody, including myself, talking about their books, I find my inner Essex teenager rising up within me, my censor and my guide, saying, 'Who cares?' It's a shame really. You dream and you work and you stay up late at night and you read the *Writers' and Artists' Yearbook* for years and years and then one day, by sheer luck and determination you finally have your book and your agent and your publisher, all your ducks lined up in a row, and somehow all you feel is shame and embarrassment, and there's your chuckling younger self breathing down your neck and taking you by the elbow and pointing out the rows upon rows of newly published books in Waterstone's, and all the 3 for 2 offers, and all the little signs and stickers and displays of recommendation and approval and bestsellability, and your book's not there, it's just disappeared almost as soon as it came into existence. So it's a funny old life. Sometimes it seems like you just can't win. ▶

‘ If you keep asking yourself how and why you're doing what you're doing, you don't do it – it's like driving round the M25, if you thought about it for too long, you'd just get a bus. ’

Q & A *(continued)*

◄ **Don't you think a lot of other writers feel the same?**

I don't know. I try to avoid writers as much as possible: terrible manners, and the language, honestly, you'd be surprised. But I guess a lot of people do feel the same: I mean, life offers everybody plenty of opportunity for embarrassment and disappointment, doesn't it. I don't think I'd be alone in feeling a little shy of the world. If anything, writers seem to me to be pretty brazen, on the whole, and more than willing to bang on about their own personal philosophy, and what life has taught them, and their great debt to the great writers of the past who mean so much to them, and blah, blah, blah, like some man at a party boring you to death with his pet theories. Not that I blame them. I mean, look at the kind of interviews you read with writers and artists in newspapers and magazines: all those clever people with something clever to say and a clever way of saying it, and nice clothes to say it in. It's not their fault they're not embarrassed: they have nothing to be embarrassed about.

Are you embarrassed?

Hm. What? At this moment? No. Why? Am I dribbling?

Well ...

Sorry. Now?

No.

OK. So, no, I'm not embarrassed. But I think embarrassment probably has a lot to do with the way I write like I do. It's not that I think

6Whenever I hear anybody, including myself, talking about their books, I find my inner Essex teenager rising up within me, saying, "Who cares?" 9

embarrassment is a necessary qualification for becoming a writer – not like, say, raging narcissism, which is pretty much an essential. It's just that I'm not the sort of person who takes my shirt off in the summer. I'm the sort of person who's quiet on trains, and in the crowd. I keep myself to myself, and even then I'm easily embarrassed, even in my own company. I have a beard for goodness sake. Maybe that's the reason I write, in fact ...

Because you have a beard?
No. Because I need to write about things that other people are unembarrassed to talk about. Maybe that's it. That could be one explanation of what I'm doing.

Well, thank you. We got there in the end.
We did? ∎

❝ I have a beard for goodness sake. Maybe that's the reason I write. ❞

Favourite Books/Authors

Oh, I don't know. Just off the top of my head:

The Epic of Gilgamesh
The Egyptian Book of the Dead
The Bible
The Mahabharata
The Bhagavad-Gita
Homer, *The Iliad*, *The Odyssey*
Aeschylus, *The Oresteia*
Sophocles, *Oedipus the King, Antigone,*
    Philoctetes
Euripides, *The Bacchae*
Aristophanes, *The Birds*, *The Frogs*
Thucydides, *The History of the Peloponnesian*
    War
Aesop, *Fables*
Ovid, *The Metamorphoses*
Martial, *Epigrams*
Saint Augustine, *The Confessions*
Beowulf
Dante, *The Divine Comedy*
Giovanni Boccaccio, *The Decameron*
Miguel de Cervantes, *Don Quixote*
Geoffrey Chaucer, *The Canterbury Tales*
Sir Thomas Malory, *Le Morte D'Arthur*
Sir Thomas More, *Utopia*
Edmund Spenser, *The Faerie Queene*
William Shakespeare
John Donne, *Sermons*
Francis Bacon, *Essays*
Robert Burton, *The Anatomy of*
    Melancholy
Thomas Hobbes, *Leviathan*
John Webster, *The Duchess of Malfi*
Thomas Middleton and William Rowley, *The*
    Changeling

John Bunyan, *The Pilgrim's Progress*
John Milton, *Paradise Lost*
Jonathan Swift, *Gulliver's Travels*
Samuel Johnson
Daniel Defoe, *Robinson Crusoe*
Henry Fielding, *The History of Tom Jones, a Foundling*
Laurence Sterne, *The Life and Opinions of Tristram Shandy, Gentleman*
Michel de Montaigne, *Essays*
François Rabelais, *Gargantua, Pantagruel*
Jean-Jacques Rousseau, *The Confessions*
Erasmus, *In Praise of Folly*
Johann Wolfgang von Goethe, *Faust, Pts I & II, Dichtung und Wahrheit*
Victor Hugo, *Les Misérables*
Stendhal, *The Charterhouse of Parma*
Gustave Flaubert, *Madame Bovary*
Henrik Ibsen
Jane Austen, *Pride and Prejudice, Emma, Mansfield Park*
William Hazlitt, *Essays*
Charles Dickens, *Great Expectations, Bleak House, Hard Times*
John Ruskin, *Unto this Last*
Anthony Trollope, *The Chronicles of Barsetshire*
George Eliot, *The Mill on the Floss, Daniel Deronda, Middlemarch*
Robert Louis Stevenson, *Treasure Island*
Friedrich Nietzsche, *The Birth of Tragedy, Beyond Good and Evil*
Nikolai Gogol, *The Complete Tales, Dead Souls*
Ivan Turgenev, *Fathers and Sons*
Fyodor Dostoevsky, *Crime and Punishment, The Idiot* ▶

Favourite Books/Authors *(continued)*

◄ Leo Tolstoy, *War and Peace*
Anton Chekhov
Ralph Waldo Emerson, *Essays*, *The Conduct of Life*
Henry James, *The Portrait of a Lady*, *The Ambassadors*
William James, *The Varieties of Religious Experience*
Italo Svevo, *The Confessions of Zeno*
Fernando Pessoa, *The Book of Disquiet*
Marcel Proust, *Remembrance of Things Past*
Albert Camus, *The Stranger*
Tristan Tzara, *Seven Dada Manifestos and Lampisteries*
Thomas Hardy, *Tess of the D'Urbervilles*, *Jude the Obscure*
Rudyard Kipling
Max Beerbohm, *Zuleika Dobson*
Joseph Conrad, *Lord Jim*, *The Secret Agent*
Ronald Firbank
Ford Madox Ford, *The Good Soldier*
D.H. Lawrence, *Sons and Lovers*, *The Rainbow*, *Women in Love*
Virginia Woolf, *Mrs Dalloway*, *To the Lighthouse*, *The Waves*
James Joyce, *Ulysses*
Samuel Beckett, *Murphy*, *Watt*, *Waiting for Godot*, *Krapp's Last Tape*
Henry Green, *Loving*
Evelyn Waugh, *A Handful of Dust*
Iris Murdoch, *The Black Prince*, *Bruno's Dream*
Graham Greene, *Brighton Rock*, *The Heart of the Matter*
Aldous Huxley, *Brave New World*
William Golding, *Pincher Martin*
Mervyn Peake, *The Gormenghast Trilogy*
George Orwell, *1984*

Bertolt Brecht, *Poems*
Franz Kafka, *Stories, The Trial, The Castle*
Thomas Mann, *The Magic Mountain, Death in Venice*
Robert Musil, *The Man Without Qualities*
Walter Benjamin, *Illuminations*
Joseph Roth, *The Legend of the Holy Drinker*
Mikhail Bulgakov, *The Master and Margarita*
Boris Pasternak, *Doctor Zhivago*
Aleksandr Solzhenitsyn, *One Day in the Life of Ivan Denisovich*
Knut Hamsun, *Hunger*
Bohumil Hrabal, *I Served the King of England, Too Loud a Solitude*
Isaac Bashevis Singer, *Collected Stories*
Malcolm Lowry, *Under the Volcano*
William Faulkner, *As I Lay Dying, The Sound and the Fury*
John Cheever, *Stories*

I also like some living authors. But really, who cares. What I've read doesn't matter. Reading's not sufficient, any more than writing is sufficient. I had a teacher who used to say, 'Don't tell me what you've read. Tell me what you've understood.' I also recall Graham Greene writing honestly of his reading: 'Of course, I should be interested to hear that a new novel by Mr E.M. Forster was going to appear this spring, but I could never compare that mild expectation of civilized pleasure with the missed heartbeat, the appalled glee I felt when I found on a library shelf a novel by Rider Haggard, Percy Westerman, Captain Brereton or Stanley Weyman which I had not read before.' I wish Richmal Crompton had written another. ∎

> ❛I had a teacher who used to say, "Don't tell me what you've read. Tell me what you've understood."❜

A Critical Eye

IF YOU CAN'T JUDGE a book by its cover, the reviews on its cover can, it seems, help. Writing in the *Observer*, Geraldine Bedell confessed, 'I knew I was going to love this novel when I read the back jacket reviews of Sansom's previous book, *The Truth About Babies*.' (A round of Speedy Bap! Brie, Bacon and Avocado wraps to the design team for that one.) 'I laughed,' she claimed, 'more times than I can remember over a novel in years . . . In a world swamped by Hollywood products and other multinational offerings, *Ring Road*,' she went on, 'reminded me why novels are such a relief, so endlessly, incorrigibly surprising.' Michael Moorcock in the *Guardian* struck a similarly wistful note: 'few books published these days,' he mused, 'can fairly be described as charming and fewer still are the product of so generous an intelligence'. *Ring Road*, he said, was like 'a distant Sally Army brass band on a warm Sunday evening . . . mellow, intelligent and very funny, a perfect anecdote for melancholy'. Describing it as 'a wonderfully comic novel', the *Daily Mail*'s reviewer praised the author for his 'acute sense of the absurd'. Sam Thompson in the *TLS*, meanwhile, found 'something fearless in the gaze Sansom turns on banality'. For Thompson, the novel, 'in the end', achieved the 'surprisingly gripping feat of coming to terms with what ordinary life is like'. Ordinary life may be portrayed in all its ignominious glory but, as Francis King remarked in the *Spectator*, 'here is no ordinary talent'. Sansom, he concluded, is 'a writer with a viewpoint and voice very much his own'. ■

Sandwich Spread
by Travis Elborough

Sandwich A piece of meat between two
slices of bread; so called from the Earl
of Sandwich (the noted 'Jemmy
Twitcher'), who passed whole days in
gambling, bidding the waiter bring him
for refreshment a piece of meat between
two pieces of bread, which he ate without
stopping from play. This contrivance was
not first hit upon by the earl in the reign
of George III, as the Romans were
very fond of 'sandwiches', called by
them *offula*.

The Dictionary of Phrase and Fable
by E. Cobham Brewer (from the new
and enlarged edition of 1894)

YOU'VE PROBABLY NEVER HEARD of Bill
Currie. I'll admit, among the pantheon of
culinary innovators, the people who can be
said literally to have changed the tastes of this
nation – the Contance Sprys, Fanny
Craddocks, Elizabeth Davids, Galloping
Gourmets, Robert Carriers, Madhur Jaffreys,
Delias, Jamies, Nigels and Nigellas – Currie is
a figure of marginal interest. But chances are
that if you took a British Rail train during the
1970s and found yourself moseying up to the
buffet car, a crackle of manmade fibres,
stomach rumbling, that morning's bowl of
Golden Nuggets a dim and distant memory,
and selected (probably against your better
judgement) a forlorn-looking cheese and
pickle sarnie (nothing fancy, you understand:
white sliced bread, mild rubbery cheddar,
cloying brown glue that yielded the
occasional crunch) then you sampled a ▶

Sandwich Spread *(continued)*

◄ sandwich made to Bill Currie's exacting standards. Standards as exacting as our very own Bob Savory's, although obviously wafer-thin turkey and chicken tikka pieces in a yogurt dressing lay an oil crisis and a recession or two away.

Concerned about the beleaguered reputation of the British Rail butty, it was Bill, in his capacity as Director of Catering, who in November 1971 issued guidelines to help staff prepare and serve perfect sandwiches.[1] From then on, if you were making a sandwich for British Rail, you made it the Bill Currie way. (What Bill and his team liked to call 'the best on the track' way.) A sardine and tomato sandwich, for instance, wasn't fit for consumption unless it contained 2/3oz of sardine and a 1/3oz of tomato. These ratios were also demanded of the luncheon meat and cress combo – 2/3oz meat, naturally. (Whatever your opinion of luncheon meat, 2/3oz of cress really is inedible. You'd be picking the stuff out of your teeth for weeks afterwards for a start.) But with a frankfurter bap, a full oz of sausage was required – evidently Bill was canny enough to understand that in the wake of the Mexico 1970 World Cup and decimalization, generous portions, configured in imperial measurements, would be needed to lure hungry British passengers towards such dangerously Mitteleuropean fayre.

If Bill was fastidious about the proportions of the sandwich fillings, his instructions for

> 6 From November 1971, if you were making a sandwich for British Rail, you made it the Bill Currie way. 9

[1] British Rail catering did not escape the beady eye of Elizabeth David. In a chapter on Toast in *English Bread and Yeast Cookery* (1977), David berates BR for charging 12 pence a slice for toast when a 12-slice white loaf at that time cost a mere 15p.

their construction were no less exacting. Knowing which side of the bread to butter (the side onto which the filling was placed is normally the preferred option, though Breville toasting machines did, of course, undermine this orthodoxy for a short while) is one thing. Knowing how much butter, and precisely where to spread it to ensure a flavoursome and yet visually appealing sandwich, is quite another matter entirely. And Bill, perceiving a dearth in the latter, commanded his staff to spread two-thirds of the butter, and then place at least a third of the filling, in the centre of the bread. When the sandwich was cut, diagonally corner-to-corner (like putting the milk in first when preparing tea, only plebs slice horizontally), and displayed hypotenuse outward on the counter, the filling and butter – plump and weeping from the middle – created a mouth-watering aspect. That was the theory, anyhow.

Just as Swift's Lilliput and Blefuscu warred over which end of an egg should be eaten first (big end vs. little end), distribution of butter and fillings (piled in the middle or, *pace* Bill, spread evenly across the bread) splits opinion. The American food writer M.F.K. Fisher (of whom W.H. Auden once claimed, 'I do not know of anyone in the United States who writes better prose') probably would not have enjoyed one of Bill's comestibles. Fisher comes down firmly on the side of an even spread. 'The filling', she writes in *With Bold Knife and Fork* (1968), 'should be of good quality, and should be spread or laid right to the sides of the foundation, and even spill over a little if feasible, rather than lie lumpishly in the middle.' Decorum prevents ▶

Sandwich Spread *(continued)*

◄ her from divulging the recipe in full but the sketch she offers for her family's favourite ham and mustard Railroad Sandwich (American diners, it's worth remembering, began life as railway dining cars) includes a secret ingredient (not very secret since it appears in the book) that even in the free-and-easy, kids' climbing-frames on concrete bases, municipal drinking fountains 1970s Bill would have rejected outright on health and safety grounds. The sandwich must be sat on for *at least* twenty minutes. British Rail passengers were no doubt at leisure, and certainly provided with ample opportunities, to experiment along these lines themselves while travelling or simply awaiting their connections. And who knows how many commuters, inadvertently creating this delicacy as they wrestled with four down (Flourished with craving for bacon {6}), arose from their seats, swore, peeled a squashed BR double-round from the seat of their trousers and cast them into the bin before ever savouring the unique mix of wool pinstripe, compressed ham, mustard, butter and Mother's Pride.

How Fisher herself fell upon the idea is anyone's guess. Her wartime cookbook, *How to Cook a Wolf,* includes a prune roast. Cowardice has, so far, prevented me from trying it but I, for one, am not sure I'd be that pleased about letting anyone rustle up a batch of Railroads for high tea knowing that prune roast had earlier featured as the *plat du jour*. Serendipity and mobility are the abiding leitmotifs in sandwich history. Without the carelessness, and/or drunkenness, of a Nile-dweller who mixed ale instead of water into a dough mixture in around 3000 BC we wouldn't have leavened bread; brewing and bread making developed symbiotically; the commonest Egyptian ale, *haq*, was produced by soaking partially baked red barley loaves in water for a day or so until they fermented (a sound historical reason why the patrons of the Castle Arms might find Margaret's plain cheese and ham sandwiches hit the spot with a pint).

In Exodus 12, Yahweh, unimpressed by these new-fangled breadstuffs, potent symbols of Egyptian decadence and Israelite oppression, tells Moses and Aaron to get the tribe to feast upon roasted lamb with unleavened bread and bitter herbs, once the whole shenanigan of daubing lintels with said lamb's blood is finished with. And after the Avenging Angel had had its way with the Egyptian firstborns, the Israelites, fleeing in haste, began their journey to the Promised Land with unleavened bread, remembered at *Pesach* in the *Sedar* and with the banishing of *chametz* from the home. The precise rules for the *Pesach* observances were given to Moses during the Israelites' second year in the wilderness of Sina'i. Yahweh was not, however, quite as exacting as possibly he could have been, as, perhaps, in the same position we can conceive Bill or Bob would have been. At Numbers 9:11, Moses is told that the *Pesach* offering should be eaten 'with matzah and bitter herbs'; in Hebrew this is written as '*al matzot u'marorim*' but '*al*' literally means 'on top of '. Faced with this textual ambiguity, the great Rabbi Hillel proposed that the meat and bitter herbs be stacked on top of the matzah in what became ▶

Sandwich Spread *(continued)*

◄ known as the *korech*. The open-topped
sandwich was then officially born to
commemorate a swift departure after years of
enforced confinement; a couple of thousand
years later, passengers on British Rail could
only munch into their luncheon meat and
cress sandwiches and yearn for such a speedy
deliverance. ■

Have You Read?

The Truth About Babies: From A–Z
Taking Cyril Connolly's 'pram in the hall' for
a spin round the block, Sansom offers a series
of meditations on every aspect of babies –
from bathing, boredom, breastfeeding and
buggies to weaning, weight, words and work.
The result is a profound, philosophical and
frequently very funny Dictionary of Infants.

'Packed full of wry, poignant observations on
all aspects of babydom . . . One to enjoy with a
nightcap' *New Baby*

'A true and beautiful book . . . Every new
parent should have a copy for their journey
through that first year' *Guardian*

'Funny and touching and true' *Evening
Standard*

If You Loved This,
You'll Like ...

The Scheme for Full Employment
Magnus Mills
Crushed by the wheels of indolence and infighting, a utopian work scheme involving a fleet of white vans hits the buffers in a spellbinding novel that puts the K into Fred Kite.

Mondo Desperado: Stories
Patrick McCabe
Welcome to Barntrosna! As writer in residence Phildy Hackball reveals, this seemingly charming little Irish town has witnessed some mighty strange goings-on – go-go dancing swingers, exploding novice priests, lesbian nurses and Kung Fu superstars. Oh yes, all life is here, sister.

The Life and Opinions of Tristram Shandy
Laurence Sterne
The shaggiest dog of all shaggy dog tales, Sterne's masterpiece is the blueprint of every digressive, playful and textually adventurous novel since. See Robert McCrudden's Creative Writing course (Lecture 7: '*The Novel – Making Things Up for Pleasure and Profit*') at the institute.

The Third Policeman
Flann O'Brien
Murder, a mad scientist and the story of an unrequited love affair between a man and his bicycle. O'Brien's absurdist satire about a village police force is a masterpiece.

Three Men in a Boat
Jerome K. Jerome
Three clerks ('to say nothing of the dog') go
on a jaunt up the River Thames in Jerome's
whimsical but still wonderful comic classic.

A Heartbreaking Work of Staggering Genius
Dave Eggers
Eggers's gambolling memoir about losing
both his parents and raising his younger
brother really does live up to its title.

Sweet Desserts
Lucy Ellmann
Surely, any novel with an index which actually
has an entry for the index (Index, 143–5)
deserves a place in your life and on your
bookshelf? Tuna sandwiches feature to boot.

Find Out More

http://www.theenthusiast.co.uk
Two of Billy Nibbs's poems graced *The Enthusiast*'s debut issue. Need we say more? I think not.

www.mcsweeneys.net
In the worldwide web, where ever more convenient shopping has usurped *Content, the Old King*, Dave Eggers's McSweeney's Internet Tendencies is an online institution worth clinging onto.

www.sandwich.org.uk
Home of the British Sandwich Association.

http://ukulele.org
Sadly, copies of Bill and Antoinetta Bell's masterwork *The Two Little Fleas* are rarer than hen's teeth these days. Visit this site, though, to discover more about this mellifluous stringed instrument and, perhaps, download a copy of *The Fleabag Songbook*.

BOOKSHOP

Now you can buy any of these great paperbacks from Harper Perennial at 10% off recommended retail price. FREE postage and packing in the UK.

How Mumbo-Jumbo Conquered the World
Francis Wheen (ISBN: 0-00-714097-5)   £7.99

Home Land
Sam Lipsyte (ISBN: 0-00-717037-8)   £7.99

Popular Music
Mikael Niemi (ISBN: 0-00-714551-9)   £7.99

The Scheme for Full Employment
Magnus Mills (ISBN: 0-00-715132-2)   £7.99

Topics About Which I Know Nothing
Patrick Ness (ISBN: 0-00-713944-6)   £7.99

The Third Policeman
Flann O'Brien (ISBN: 0-586-08749-4)   £6.99

Total cost _____

10% discount _____

Final total _____

To purchase by Visa/Mastercard/Switch simply call **08707 871724** or fax on **08707 871725**

To pay by cheque, send a copy of this form with a cheque made payable to 'HarperCollins Publishers' to: Mail Order Dept (Ref: B0B4), HarperCollins Publishers, Westerhill Road, Bishopbriggs, G64 2QT, making sure to include your full name, postal address and phone number.

From time to time HarperCollins may wish to use your personal data to send you details of other HarperCollins publications and offers. If you wish to receive information on other HarperCollins publications and offers please tick this box ☐

Do not send cash or currency. Prices correct at time of press. Prices and availability are subject to change without notice. Delivery overseas and to Ireland incurs a £2 per book postage and packing charge.